ANAL

*General Editor: Nic...*

*Further titles are in preparation*

# Jane Austen:
# The Novels

NICHOLAS MARSH

St. Martin's Press
New York

JANE AUSTEN

St. Martin's Press, Scholarly and Reference Division,
175 Fifth Avenue, New York, N.Y. 10010

First published in the United States of America in 1998

This book is printed on paper suitable for recycling and
made from fully managed and sustained forest sources.

Printed in Great Britain

ISBN 0–312–21370–0 clothbound
ISBN 0–312–21371–9 paperback

Library of Congress Cataloging-in-Publication Data
Marsh, Nicholas.
Jane Austen : the novels / Nicholas Marsh.
p.   cm.  — (Analysing texts)
Includes bibliographical references and index.
ISBN 0–312–21370–0. — ISBN 0–312–21371–9 (pbk.)
1. Austen, Jane, 1775–1817—Criticism and interpretation.
2. Women and literature—England—History—19th century.   3. Austen,
Jane, 1775–1817—Outlines, syllabi, etc.   I. Title.   II. Series.
PR4037.M33  1998
823'.7—dc21                                           97–50415
                                                          CIP

For Disraeli

# Contents

# General Editor's Preface

This series is dedicated to one clear belief: that we can all enjoy, understand and analyse literature for ourselves, provided we know how to do it. How can we build on close understanding of a short passage, and develop our insight into the whole work? What features do we expect to find in a text? Why do we study style in so much detail? In demystifying the study of literature, these are only some of the questions the *Analysing Texts* series addresses and answers.

The books in this series will not do all the work for you, but will provide you with the tools, and show you how to use them. Here, you will find samples of close, detailed analysis, with an explanation of the analytical techniques utilised. At the end of each chapter there are useful suggestions for further work you can do to practise, develop and hone the skills demonstrated and build confidence in your own analytical ability.

An author's individuality shows in the way they write: every work they produce bears the hallmark of that writer's personal 'style'. In the main part of each book we concentrate therefore on analysing the particular flavour and concerns of one author's work, and explain the features of their writing in connection with major themes. In Part 2 there are chapters about the author's life and work, assessing their contribution to developments in literature; and a sample of critics' views are summarised and discussed in comparison with each other. Some suggestions for further reading provide a bridge towards further critical research.

*Analysing Texts* is designed to stimulate and encourage your critical and analytic faculty, to develop your personal insight into the author's work and individual style, and to provide you with the skills and techniques to enjoy at first hand the excitement of discovering the richness of the text.

NICHOLAS MARSH

# A Note on Editions

References to *Pride and Prejudice*, *Mansfield Park* and *Emma* are page references to the Penguin Classic editions of 1996. References to *Persuasion* are page references to the 1985 Penguin Classics edition which includes C. E. Austen-Leigh's *Memoir* of his aunt. Where the full title of the novel would be clumsy, the abbreviations *PP* for *Pride and Prejudice* and *MP* for *Mansfield Park* have been used. Where it is obvious from the context which novel is being quoted, the page number appears on its own.

# PART 1

# ANALYSING JANE AUSTEN'S NOVELS

# 1

# Language and Texture

Many critics enthuse about Jane Austen's 'style'. They say that she wrote superb English, and that her style is 'perfect', 'marvellous' and 'wonderful'. I agree with them, but for students of literature this is only a beginning. We want to understand how she achieves her effects, and define what those effects are. In other words, we want to appreciate how her style works, in precise detail.

It is important for us to recognise just how rich these texts are, at the start. Jane Austen's novels are written in a way which packs every sentence with competing meanings and implications. So, in this chapter, we take very short extracts from each of the four novels, and focus on the structure and texture of the language she uses as closely as possible. Jane Austen's writing is so consistently rich in meaning that it would not matter very much if we chose our first extracts at random, but the extracts analysed in this chapter are all narrative, without dialogue; and in three cases come from the opening chapter of the novel in question. This helps us to focus on the texture of her writing as closely as possible.

We begin with part of Chapter 22 of *Pride and Prejudice*. Mr Collins proposed to Elizabeth Bennet, and she rejected him. A few days later, he proposes to Elizabeth's friend, Charlotte Lucas:

> The Bennets were engaged to dine with the Lucases, and again during the chief of the day was Miss Lucas so kind as to

listen to Mr Collins. Elizabeth took an opportunity of thanking her. 'It keeps him in good humour,' said she, 'and I am more obliged to you than I can express.' Charlotte assured her friend of her satisfaction in being useful, and that it amply repaid her for the little sacrifice of her time. This was very amiable, but Charlotte's kindness extended farther than Elizabeth had any conception of; – its object was nothing else than to secure her from any return of Mr Collins's addresses, by engaging them towards herself. Such was Miss Lucas's scheme; and appearances were so favourable, that when they parted at night, she would have felt amost sure of success if he had not been to leave Hertfordshire so very soon. But here she did injustice to the fire and independence of his character, for it led him to escape out of Longbourn House the next morning with admirable slyness, and hasten to Lucas Lodge to throw himself at her feet. He was anxious to avoid the notice of his cousins, from a conviction that if they saw him depart, they could not fail to conjecture his design, and he was not willing to have the attempt known till its success could be known likewise; for though feeling almost secure, and with reason, for Charlotte had been tolerably encouraging, he was comparatively diffident since the adventure of Wednesday. His reception, however, was of the most flattering kind. Miss Lucas perceived him from an upper window as he walked towards the house, and instantly set out to meet him accidentally in the lane. But little had she dared to hope that so much love and eloquence awaited her there.

In as short a time as Mr Collins's long speeches would allow, everything was settled between them to the satisfaction of both; and as they entered the house he earnestly entreated her to name the day that was to make him the happiest of men; and though such a solicitation must be waived for the present, the lady felt no inclination to trifle with his happiness. The stupidity with which he was favoured by nature must guard his courtship from any charm that could make a woman wish for its continuance; and Miss Lucas, who accepted him solely from the pure and disinterested desire of an establishment, cared not how soon that establishment were gained.

*(Pride and Prejudice*, pp. 102–3)

Look at the passage as a whole. What stands out? There are certain words that cause us to smile as we read. For example, 'kind' and 'amiable' describe Charlotte; while 'fire', 'independence', 'diffident' and 'eloquence' are comic descriptions of Mr Collins. Charlotte sets out to meet him 'accidentally'. We do not find it difficult to understand the ironic meanings of these words. For example, 'accidentally' does not mean *by accident*, it means *deliberately, but with an artificial appearance of chance*. 'Deliberately' means the opposite of 'accidentally', so this word is sarcastic. We can use the same method to analyse each of these words. For example, the normal meaning of 'fire' in a character is passionate impulsiveness, but our previous knowledge of Mr Collins tells us that this is absurd (we remember Elizabeth overcome with laughter at the thought of him 'being run away with by his feelings' [p. 89]). The implied meaning must be something else: it highlights the lack of 'fire' in Mr Collins and provokes us to think about his eager-ness to find a wife – any wife – and the fear which motivates his sly 'escape' from Longbourn.

So far, we have picked out amusing words, and compared their literal meaning with the reality of the characters and story. If we look at the passage more closely, however, we see that each of these words is set within an immediate linguis-tic context. Notice, for example, that 'accidentally' contrasts with the other adverb 'instantly' and the deliberate phrase 'set out to', intensifying our amusement. The sarcasm of 'accidentally', then, is further set off by contrast with its immediate surroundings. 'Fire' stands in a wider linguistic context. There are contrasting terms for Mr Collins's feelings in the passage, such as 'anxious', 'almost secure' and 'comparatively diffident', but they are more than thirty words distant.

The first thing we noticed, then, was that a few words stand out because they amuse us. Now we understand why they made us laugh: they highlight the difference between pretentiousness and a cynical truth which we understand.

On the other hand, analysing their immediate context shows that amusing words do not stand alone: they are set within language which highlights their irony ('accidentally') or provokes more complex cynical thought about the character ('fire'). What else surrounds and 'sets off' these words?

We will take the example of 'diffident'. We noticed this because it is a travesty of the truth to call Mr Collins 'diffident'. There is no trace of diffidence in him, and the very idea of a shy Mr Collins makes us laugh in the way Elizabeth laughed at the thought of him losing control of his feelings. Now look at the context. First, he is said to be 'comparatively diffident'. Since he had no diffidence at all, the qualifying word 'comparatively' is meaningless. It means, 'he is more shy than when he was not shy'. Now look at the other two pairs of words, in the sentence leading up to this. 'Almost secure' has the same slightly absurd quality: 'almost' does not belong with an absolute like 'secure'; and 'tolerably encouraging' is an understatement, since we know that Charlotte has blatantly encouraged Mr Collins. In fact, the word 'diffident' comes to us within a context which repeatedly juxtaposes softening, qualifying words against bald, cynical truth. Mr Collins feels secure, because Charlotte has brashly 'set her cap at him', but he is self-conscious ('comparatively diffident') because – to his own surprise – Elizabeth said 'no' to him two days ago. 'Almost', 'tolerably' and 'comparatively' have a dual effect. First, they add a gloss of civilisation to the coarse vulgarity of the two characters' actions; but at the same time, they suggest lack of meaning or absurdity, as if the well-bred forms which give us words like 'tolerably' can barely conceal the gross insincerity and self-interest of Charlotte's and Mr Collins's engagement.

There is tension, then, between the characters' actions and motives on the one hand, and the more or less ironic use of qualifying language on the other. In other words, there is a smooth surface in ironic contrast to the stupidity and self-interest of the characters. Jane Austen constantly plays upon this tension by modulating the phrases and words she chooses, so that the gap between polite surface and coarse underlying reality, narrows and broadens continuously as we read. For example, 'almost secure' is only slightly ironic: it is close to the truth about Mr Collins. When Austen describes his 'fire' and 'independence', on the other hand, the gap with reality is very wide – it is ridiculous to apply these terms to him.

This effect constantly amuses and excites us as we read. However, sometimes the language and the truth are so far apart that they are directly opposite. We have already noticed that Charlotte deliberately meeting her lover becomes 'accidentally'. In the final sentence of our extract opposition appears again, in three distinct stages.

First, Mr Collins's stupidity 'must guard his courtship from' any charm. This is writing in opposites, in the sense that a 'guard' usually protects the good from the bad, but in this case protects 'stupidity' against 'charm'. Second, Charlotte accepts him from a 'pure' materialist motive. Our morality normally describes idealistic and romantic motives as 'pure' and materialism as grubby or 'impure'; but it is possible to understand her motive as 'pure' materialism, in the sense that there was *no* romance or ideal added to it. Finally, however, Jane Austen cheekily uses the word 'disinterested' (without self-interest, or unselfish) for Charlotte's motive. This does create a complete opposition between language and truth. It can be paraphrased as 'unselfish greed'.

What has happened is that Jane Austen has progressively turned truth upside-down. She has created a precise antithesis ('disinterested' materialism). Notice how carefully the sentence prepares us for this, so we are smoothly led to the point where language is the opposite of truth. This care given to the preparation and context of each effect helps create the impression of polished perfection we gain from Jane Austen's writing. There seems to be a harmony and ease between all the parts. Yet, we have noticed that our author can express the most outrageous cynicism under the guise of the harmonious texture of her style.

We have gained an insight into the way Jane Austen's writing works, then, from this first study. There are two further features to notice briefly, before we look at how she handles the narrative. First, Jane Austen often provides several words for the same thing. The reader is thus given a choice and encouraged to think about the ironic differences between different terms. We already noticed 'secure' and 'diffident' as alternative views of Mr Collins's confidence, both of which are ironic when compared with the self-satisfied character we know. Another instance is the word 'eloquence' at the end of the first paragraph, and 'long speeches' at the start of the second, describing the way Mr Collins talks. It will be helpful to look for pairs or groups of terms for characters or what is happening, when analysing Jane Austen: this helps us to define the range of possible ironic interpretations the text suggests.

Second, the tone of Jane Austen's language varies. For example, in this extract Charlotte rushes out to meet Mr Collins, hoping to provoke a proposal of marriage. Jane Austen comments: 'Little had she dared to hope that so much love and eloquence awaited her there.' The inverted construction 'Little had she dared' is archaic and imitates the mannered style of a gushy romantic novelist. This contrasts with the plain calculation of her chances in which Charlotte weighs a 'favourable' appearance against the shortness of time because Mr Collins is due to leave 'so very soon'; and her unemotional materialism in the final sentence, which says that she 'cared not' for anything about courtship except the chance of an 'establishment'. Jane Austen seems to be satirising romantic style in this sentence, then. The satirical effect is enhanced by 'fire', 'independence', 'love', 'eloquence', 'earnestly entreated' and 'the happiest of men', all of which belong to the diction of a passionate lover, the pretence Mr Collins adopts because he thinks it is the done thing. A satire of hypocritical romantic behaviour is present throughout the passage, created by this contrast between dictions.

The passage seems to adopt a straightforward narrative form. The first sentence tells us that the Bennets dined with the Lucases, and Charlotte listened to Mr Collins. The author seems to take a simple storytelling stance; but perhaps – like the polite texture of her language – this may also prove deceptive when more closely examined. Notice that the one significant event – the proposal itself – is not narrated. It happens in between the two paragraphs of our extract. The final sentence of the first paragraph anticipates the event; and the next sentence is retrospective, declaring that 'everything was settled between them'. Between these two sentences is 'as short a time as Mr Collins's long speeches would allow' – the time of the actual proposal. When we notice a manipulation of the narrative like this, it is worth asking ourselves why it occurs. The two paragraphs we are studying reveal the insincerity of both characters; so it is reasonable to suggest that Jane Austen skips the event itself to further emphasise what a meaningless charade it is. By omitting the dialogue, she effectively tells us: 'I don't want to bore you with all their dishonest declarations of love – let's get on with the nasty truth behind it.'

One other noticeable feature of Jane Austen's narrative method is brought home to us as we read: the fact that characters do not understand each other seems to be brought to our attention repeatedly. To analyse this effect further, we can make a series of brief statements about what characters know or do not know, thus:

1. Elizabeth thinks Charlotte is being kind (sentences 1–3)
2. Ambiguous: Charlotte is being kind or self-interested (sentence 4)
3. Charlotte wants to marry Mr Collins (sentences 5 and 6)
4. Mr Collins is eager to marry but uncertain about Charlotte's views (sentences 7, 8, 9 and 10)
5. Charlotte is uncertain about Mr Collins's views (sentence 11)

6.   They discover each other's views and reach an under-
     standing (sentence 12)
7.   Charlotte thinks Mr Collins is stupid (sentence 13)

These statements can be reduced, to highlight Jane
Austen's insistent presentation of misunderstandings:
*Elizabeth does not understand Charlotte, Charlotte does
not understand Mr Collins, Mr Collins does not understand Charlotte, Charlotte does not understand Mr
Collins, Charlotte and Mr Collins understand one another,
Mr Collins does not understand Charlotte.* Reading the
rest of Chapter 22 we find that the narrative highlights
similar dramatic ironies between Mr Collins and Mr
Bennet, and finally returns to Charlotte and Elizabeth. We
could say that the whole chapter is an excursion, a round
trip of misunderstanding and partial understanding
between characters. It begins with Elizabeth's thought that
Charlotte is 'kind', and ends with Elizabeth convinced that
Charlotte is 'disgracing herself' and as 'sunk in her esteem'
(p. 105). In other words, Elizabeth completely changes her
mind during the chapter. The narrative is organised into a
succession of revelations, in situations where the characters' thoughts are hidden from each other but revealed to
the reader. This produces a sensation of continuously
penetrating to deeper levels of truth, as we read; yet at the
same time, we are aware that there is an infinite possibility
of further revelations, always ahead of us. Such close-
packed density of meaning is characteristic of Jane Austen's
writing: no fewer than six revelations occur in the two
paragraphs of this extract.

*        *        *

The features we have noticed in our first extract will be
found repeatedly in Jane Austen's novels: we have already
made useful progress by analysing her style. Here is the
opening of *Emma*, our second extract:

Emma Woodhouse, handsome, clever, and rich, with a comfortable home and happy disposition, seemed to unite some of the best blessings of existence; and had lived nearly twenty-one years in the world with very little to distress or vex her.

She was the youngest of the two daughters of a most affectionate, indulgent father, and had, in consequence of her sister's marriage, been mistress of his house from a very early period. Her mother had died too long ago for her to have more than an indistinct remembrance of her caresses, and her place had been supplied by an excellent woman as governess, who had fallen little short of a mother in affection.

Sixteen years had Miss Taylor been in Mr Woodhouse's family, less as a governess than a friend, very fond of both daughters, but particularly of Emma. Between *them* it was more the intimacy of sisters. Even before Miss Taylor had ceased to hold the nominal office of governess, the mildness of her temper had hardly allowed her to impose any restraint; and the shadow of authority being now long passed away, they had been living together as friend and friend very mutually attached, and Emma doing just what she liked; highly esteeming Miss Taylor's judgment, but directed chiefly by her own.

The real evils indeed of Emma's situation were the power of having rather too much her own way, and a disposition to think a little too well of herself; these were the disadvantages which threatened alloy to her many enjoyments. The danger, however, was at present so unperceived, that they did not by any means rank as misfortunes with her.

Sorrow came – a gentle sorrow – but not at all in the shape of any disagreeable consciousness – Miss Taylor married. It was Miss Taylor's loss which first brought grief. It was on the wedding-day of this beloved friend that Emma first sat in mournful thought of any continuance. The wedding over and the bride-people gone, her father and herself were left to dine together, with no prospect of a third to cheer a long evening. Her father composed himself to sleep after dinner, as usual, and she had then only to sit and think of what she had lost.

*(Emma, p. 7)*

We can begin by trying the approach developed in our analysis from *Pride and Prejudice*. In these opening paragraphs of *Emma*, there are fewer noticeable words. Where we quickly identified several ironic or sarcastic words in the first extract, the first four paragraphs of this narrative contain some remarkable phrases, but no outstanding individual words. Phrases which attract our attention include 'the best blessings of existence', 'the intimacy of sisters', 'the shadow of authority', and possibly 'the disadvantages which threatened alloy'. In the fifth paragraph some single words reach the reader's ear with comparable effect: notice 'loss', 'grief' and 'lost'.

Let us begin with a word – as we did before – and build upon what we find. 'Grief' is used to describe Emma's feeling when Miss Taylor marries. This is an overstatement: the next paragraph assures us that Miss Taylor's marriage is a happy event, not a sad one; that she and her husband will live only half a mile away; and the rest of the novel attests that the friends see each other virtually every day. So, the word 'grief', normally used in a case of bereavement, overstates Emma's situation. A quick glance at our other examples confirms that they are all overstatements: 'loss' and 'lost' are too absolute to describe the friends' separation, since they will still meet every day; and the phrases we picked out from the first four paragraphs are all rather too dramatic to apply to what happened. Notice, for example, that Miss Taylor had a 'mildness of ... temper' which made her a very lenient governess even when Emma was small. So 'the shadow of authority' is far too dramatic a phrase to describe her influence. In fact, all of our examples seem to have this same quality: they overstate and over-dramatise Emma's situation.

This element of the novel's style has been introduced gradually: the first phrase is hardly questionable, and the second only contains the gentlest of hints – that Emma may not have been intimate with her elder sister. The third, 'the shadow of authority', introduces the effect we discussed in the first extract, for the first time: here, the author gives an exaggerated phrase for a reality she has already told us is less lurid. We know that Mr Collins's character does not contain any 'fire' because we know Mr Collins. In the same way, we know that Miss Taylor never had strong authority, because Jane Austen has just told us so. 'Grief', 'loss' and 'lost' further develop the gap between a reality the author conveys to us, and an over-dramatic description of Emma's state.

Clearly, our method works again: select outstanding words and phrases, and compare them with the reality you know from other parts of the narrative. Now let us add to our scrutiny of the style by looking at sentence structure. Look at the first two paragraphs, which consist of three sentences.

All three are in the same form: they are double sentences, the second half introduced by the simple conjunction 'and'. This structure gives an effect of balance and orderliness. Emma was rich and happy, we are told, *and* (unsurprisingly) had lived without distress. Her father loved her and her sister married, *and* she ruled the house. Her mother died, *and* she had an excellent governess. These sentences convey a simple outlook on life, in which every event has a solution or a beneficial consequence which is stated in the second half of the sentence. Even Mrs Woodhouse's death is an event with an immediate positive outcome.

When we come to the third paragraph, however, the longer double sentence (the one beginning 'Even before Miss Taylor ceased ...') is more complex. We can summarise it as 'Miss Taylor never restrained Emma, *and* when she was no longer a governess, Emma did what she liked.' The 'and' in this sentence seems different, as if the author is tricking us, because we realise that the two halves of the sentence (before and after Miss Taylor stopped being officially employed as a 'governess') actually paint the same picture. In both halves of the sentence, Emma has her own way.

The double-sentence structure does not return until the final sentence of the extract; but when it does, it comes as an ironic parody of the simplicity with which the novel started: 'Her father composed himself to sleep after dinner, as usual, *and* she had then only to sit and think of what she had lost' (my italics). Clearly, Emma's state has changed between the good fortune of the first sentence and the mournful contemplation narrated here. Jane Austen seems to have echoed the sentence structure, parodying the structure she previously used, in order to highlight both the difference of Emma's mood, and at the same time, ironically, to highlight the underlying simplicity of her outlook, whether Emma is happy or sad. After all, dwelling on her exaggerated grief will not help Emma; and there are better things to do in life than to indulge self-pity.

We have noticed, then, that Jane Austen uses the same type of sentence five times; and the last two examples are deceptively ironic, parodies of the first three. These two satirical versions of the opening sentence modify our view of the world. The one about Miss Taylor's lack of authority questions the simple structure of *cause, effect* or *event, consequence* which was established in the first two paragraphs. In this sentence, suddenly, there is no change, and no real event takes place (i.e. it makes no difference whether Miss Taylor is called 'governess' or friend). The final sentence apes the same structure to point out that happy or sad outlooks make little difference: a simplistic view of life is still a simplistic view of life. Self-satisfaction is just as limited as self-pity.

Does Jane Austen play with sentence structures elsewhere in the passage? In the fifth paragraph we read the following two sentences:

> It was Miss Taylor's loss which first brought grief. It was on the wedding-day of this beloved friend that Emma first sat in mournful thought of any continuance.

Here, the first sentence is a short and abrupt statement using the plain, strong terms 'loss' and 'grief'. Notice how these become elaborated in the next sentence, which is identical in structure. 'loss' becomes 'the wedding-day of this beloved friend'; 'grief' becomes 'mournful thought of any continuance'. Amusingly, 'loss' turns into an elaborated, flowery turn of phrase, but 'grief' becomes much less violent as a half-sarcastic description of a sad mood. The effect is that the two bald statements of emotion are both undermined; and Emma's romanticised but insubstantial way of thinking and feeling is revealed in the process. We can expect to find such repeated and parodied sentence structures frequently in Jane Austen's writing.

Several of the other features we analysed in the first extract are also apparent in *Emma*. First, this passage also has many qualifying and moderating words, from the first cautious verb 'seemed', to 'chiefly' and 'rather' which mask Emma's power and self-will, and including phrases which constantly polish the rougher edges of Austen's narrative, such as 'fallen little short of' and 'a little too well'. So, the tension between a smooth linguistic surface, and unpalatable cynicism of content, occurs here as in *Pride and Prejudice*. Second, we again find alternative words which stimulate us to think ironically about the truth behind them. For example, Emma has three advantages which appear as a list: she is 'handsome, clever, and rich'. We cannot avoid laughing, because these three sit so ill together. Then, she has had very little to 'distress or vex' her. Again we wonder: a person in 'distress' has a real cause of grief, but a trivial irritation may 'vex'. These alternative words convey the shallowness of Emma's outlook at the start of the story. To her, vexation is the same as distress; and being rich (an external accident) is listed with being clever (an inherent quality of character). Later, we will wonder whether this equation is a comment on Emma or on her society. Finally, notice that Jane Austen again manipulates the narrative by omitting the main event. Miss Taylor's marriage is not narrated, and we pass on to the evening after that event with the wedding itself in the past: 'The wedding over and the bride-people gone...'

Now we can turn to the opening of *Mansfield Park*, the third extract for analysis in this chapter:

> About thirty years ago, Miss Maria Ward, of Huntingdon, with only seven thousand pounds, had the good luck to captivate Sir Thomas Bertram, of Mansfield Park, in the county of Northampton, and to be thereby raised to the rank of a baronet's lady, with all the comforts and consequences of an handsome house and large income. All Huntingdon exclaimed on the greatness of the match, and her uncle, the lawyer, himself, allowed her to be at least three thousand pounds short of any equitable claim to it. She had two sisters to be benefited by her elevation; and such of their acquaintance as thought Miss Ward and Miss Frances quite as handsome as Miss Maria, did not scruple to predict their marrying with almost equal advantage. But there certainly are not so many men of large fortune in the world as there are pretty women to deserve them. Miss Ward, at the end of half a dozen years, found herself obliged to be attached to the Rev Mr Norris, a friend of her brother-in-law, with scarcely any private fortune, and Miss Frances fared yet worse. Miss Ward's match, indeed, when it came to the point, was not contemptible, Sir Thomas being happily able to give his friend an income in the living of Mansfield; and Mr and Mrs Norris began their career of conjugal felicity with very little less than a thousand a year. But Miss Frances married, in the common phrase, to disoblige her family, and by fixing on a Lieutenant of Marines, without education, fortune, or connexions, did it very thoroughly. She could hardly have made a more untoward choice. Sir Thomas Bertram had interest, which, from principle as well as pride, from a general wish of doing right, and a desire of seeing all that were connected with him in situations of respectability, he would have been glad to exert for the advantage of Lady Bertram's sister; but her husband's profession was such as no interest could reach; and before he had time to devise any other method of assisting them, an absolute breach between the sisters had taken place. It was the natural result of the conduct of each party, and such as a very imprudent marriage almost

always produces. To save herself from useless remonstrance, Mrs Price never wrote to her family on the subject till actually married. Lady Bertram, who was a woman of very tranquil feelings, and a temper remarkably easy and indolent, would have contented herself with merely giving up her sister, and thinking no more of the matter: but Mrs Norris had a spirit of activity, which could not be satisfied till she had written a long and angry letter to Fanny, to point out the folly of her conduct, and threaten her with all its possible ill consequences. Mrs Price in her turn was injured and angry; and an answer which comprehended each sister in its bitterness, and bestowed such very disrespectful reflections on the pride of Sir Thomas, as Mrs Norris could not possibly keep to herself, put an end to all intercourse between them for a considerable period.

(*Mansfield Park*, pp. 5–6)

We can begin by recognising some of the features found in our first two extracts. First, there are words which give an elaborate or smooth impression of an extreme or rough event. For example, Jane Austen prepares us for something outspoken with 'in the common phrase'; but the description of Miss Frances's marriage, which follows, is 'to *disoblige* her family' rather than the expected, stronger, 'to *spite*'. In the next sentence we expect that she could 'hardly have made a *worse* choice' but the author uses a reinforced negative again, 'untoward', softening the blow. This passage also offers us a choice between alternative terms. Notice that Lady Bertram is 'tranquil', 'remarkably easy' and 'remarkably ... indolent' in temper. These terms all describe her passivity, but they allow us to choose how we judge her. We may approve of her being 'tranquil', and be surprised that she is so 'easy'; but we condemn people who are 'indolent'.

Second, there are elaborate phrases similar to those we found in *Emma*. Here, Maria Ward's sisters would be 'benefited by her elevation' and marry 'with almost equal advantage'. Mr and Mrs Norris begin a 'career of conjugal felicity' and Sir Thomas Bertram wants his relations to be in 'situations of respectability'. Descriptions of character are also blandly glossed in this way. Sir Thomas's 'general wish of doing right' is a vague but positive quality; while Mrs Norris's 'spirit of activity' does not seem pernicious in itself. Again, we find that the amusement and meaning of these phrases grow when they are considered in context. For example, the Norrises' 'conjugal felicity' sounds exemplary – but we just read that Mrs Norris 'found herself obliged' to love the Reverend. So the word 'career' takes on two overtones: first, it suggests the comic idea of rushing into, or grabbing a marriage; and second, it reminds us that marriage was a woman's livelihood, her 'career' in the sense that it was her life's work. Again, Sir Thomas's benevolence is a 'general' wish. This provokes us to ask whether his wish did any actual good, and the context reveals that he was too slow. They quarreled 'before he had time' to do anything. This 'general' goodness quickly becomes a hallmark of Sir Thomas's character. He has good intentions which turn awry throughout the novel. Finally, we come to Mrs Norris's 'spirit of activity'. There is nothing wrong with a 'spirit of activity' in itself, particularly in contrast to Maria's 'indolent' temper. However, the sting in this phrase is thoroughly exploited in the context and marks just how obnoxious we will find Mrs Norris to be. She is a slave to her 'spirit' because she 'could not be satisfied till' she had written a rude letter; and she 'could not possibly keep to herself' the angry reply that letter elicited. Mrs Norris's 'spirit of activity', such a gentle phrase, quickly reveals itself to be something else: a malevolent compulsion to meddle and interfere.

Finally, the sentences repay analysis again. Look at the opening sentence, which is typical of Jane Austen's narrative. As in *Emma*, this structure treats us to a simple and organised view of events: there is a wedding and its consequence. We are given the names and addresses of both parties, then the conjunction *and* before the subject ('Miss Maria Ward') is raised to 'baronet's lady', 'comforts' and 'consequences'. The sentence has a positive flow from 'Miss Maria Ward' to 'large income', and the *cause:effect* structure is strong. A sentence from later in the extract, however, shows a similar structure but much more complicated content. The sentence beginning 'Miss Ward's match' leads happily towards 'conjugal felicity' and 'very little less than a thousand a year'. However, the subject of the sentence has shifted twice, from Miss Ward to Sir Thomas, and from there to 'Mr and Mrs Norris'. The similarity of the two sentences seems to highlight Sir Thomas's intervention, and underline a truth: life's formula is not always as simple as 'single girl plus marriage equals wealth'. This time it is 'single girl plus match equals nothing, but with match plus rich brother-in-law it may equal comfort'.

These features are similar to those found in previous extracts. Reading *Mansfield Park* seems slightly different from the other novels, however. What is this difference? The answer is, a subtle change in the author's stance. It shows itself in the manner Jane Austen adopts when expressing her own opinion. Look at the difference in value, for example, between Jane Austen's opinion in *Emma*, and this one from the present extract:

> It was the natural result of the conduct of each party, and such as a very imprudent marriage almost always produces.

Here, Jane Austen makes a generalisation: *imprudent marriages almost always lead to a breach with the family*. This seems to be a reliable opinion, not undercut by irony. In the case of an imprudent marriage, the author seems to say, it is likely that both parties will conduct themselves badly and quarrel. The author, then, makes a generalised statement about people's behaviour. She implies that there are pre-determined patterns of behaviour which *will* happen, and that individuals can effect little change in the long run.

In *Emma*, Jane Austen appears to voice a similar generalisation. The 'best blessings of existence' are to be 'handsome, clever, and rich, with a comfortable home and happy disposition'. However, when we examine the wording and context in *Emma*, we find that the author's statement is heavily undercut by irony. First, Emma merely 'seemed' to unite these blessings – which implies that the truth is different. Second, these are only 'some of' the best blessings – implying that there might be such a long list of them that each 'blessing' becomes insignificant. Finally, the statement is self-evidently absurd because the list of 'blessings' is made up of qualities of character, chance, and material possessions, in no order, with no discrimination between them. In short, this is clearly not Jane Austen's own view: it is a view adopted for the sake of ironic amusement, and to satirise a society which entertains such muddled ideas.

Now we return to *Mansfield Park*, where we find the author making judgments about the world in a way which suggests that they may be her own opinion. Jane Austen writes that '... there certainly are not so many men of large fortune in the world as there are pretty women to deserve them'. Despite the acid phrase 'pretty women' (remember that the character concerned is Mrs Norris), this is another believable general statement from the author. So, in *Mansfield Park*, Jane Austen expresses her ideas directly to the reader with much less irony than we found in our previous two extracts. This in turn conveys an impression that the world can be predicted and is pre-determined. In other words, the author presents a more **determinist** outlook in this novel. As we read and study *Mansfield Park*, we may be surprised at how consistent this philosophy becomes: think of the number of scenes which lead to a predictable or obvious outcome. For example, we know in advance that the discussion of Mary Crawford between Fanny and Edmund, at the beginning of Chapter 7, will lead to Edmund persuading himself to excuse Mary's faults. Jane Austen soon underlines the inevitability of Edmund's attraction towards Mary:

> A young woman, pretty, lively, with a harp as elegant as herself; and both placed near a window, cut down to the

> ground, and opening on a little lawn, surrounded by shrubs in
> the rich foliage of summer, was enough to catch any man's heart.
> (*Mansfield Park*, p. 55)

Jane Austen's mockery of sentimental conventions is funny, on a first reading. However, this differs from similar sallies in her other novels because it is sarcastic and not ironic in style. Remember the satire of sentimental behaviour in our Pride and Prejudice extract above. Then, the joke arose out of the difference between what was described and what we knew to be the reality. In other words, the humour arose from irony. So, Mr Collins's 'love and eloquence' was absurd: he was neither in love nor eloquent. Charlotte's 'accidental' meeting with him was not 'accidental'; and so on. Here, on the other hand, there is no such joke. Miss Crawford and her harp *are* elegant; the garden *is* pretty; and Edmund *does* fall for her. In addition, the author generalises from her characters so that we think of them less as individuals than as examples of a type. Here, Miss Crawford is 'a young woman', and Edmund is 'any man'. In *Mansfield Park*, then, the author adopts a different relationship with the reader. Her thoughts about life and society are directly visible to us, from time to time, and this is not the same as the elusive, ironic masks she wears in the other novels.

\*     \*     \*

Now let us turn to *Persuasion*. The novel begins with an account of the Elliot entry in the Baronetage. On the second page, Jane Austen describes Sir Walter Elliot's character:

> Vanity was the beginning and the end of Sir Walter Elliot's character; vanity of person and of situation. He had been remarkably handsome in his youth; and, at fifty-four, was still a very fine man. Few women could think more of their personal appearance than he did; nor could the valet of any new made lord be more delighted with the place he held in society. He considered the blessing of beauty as inferior only

to the blessing of a baronetcy; and the Sir Walter Elliot, who united these gifts, was the constant object of his warmest respect and devotion.

His good looks and his rank had one fair claim on his attachment; since to them he must have owed a wife of very superior character to any thing deserved by his own. Lady Elliot had been an excellent woman, sensible and amiable; whose judgment and conduct, if they might be pardoned the youthful infatuation which made her Lady Elliot, had never required indulgence afterwards. – She had humoured, or soft-ened, or concealed his failings, and promoted his real respectability for seventeen years; and though not the very happiest being in the world herself, had found enough in her duties, her friends, and her children, to attach her to life, and make it no matter of indifference to her when she was called on to quit them. – Three girls, the two eldest sixteen and four-teen, was an awful legacy for a mother to bequeath; an awful charge rather, to confide to the authority and guidance of a conceited, silly father. She had, however, one very intimate friend, a sensible, deserving woman, who had been brought, by strong attachment to herself, to settle close by her, in the village of Kellynch; and on her kindness and advice, Lady Elliot mainly relied for the best help and maintenance of the good principles and instruction which she had been anxiously giving her daughters.

(*Persuasion*, p. 36)

By now, we are familiar with many of the features of Jane Austen's writing found in this passage. Alternative words for us to choose from include, about Sir Walter, 'vanity', 'conceited' and 'silly'. Lady Elliot is described as 'excellent', which is then glossed as 'sensible' and 'amiable'. Her friend (Lady Russell) is, on the other hand, 'sensible' and 'deserv-ing'. As readers we pick our way among these epithets, comparing word to word and character to character, being provoked into doubting the values of words, and drawing fine distinctions between qualities. We remember that this technique gave us Mr Collins's 'diffident' and 'secure' in the extract from *Pride and Prejudice*, producing a broad comic effect; and drew our attention to the difference between 'distress' and 'vex' in *Emma*, provoking critical thought about her experience and outlook. In *Persuasion*, the two descriptions 'sensible and amiable' (Lady Elliot) and 'sensible and deserving' (Lady Russell) echo each other, highlighting our question. What is the difference between 'amiable' and 'deserving'? Why the more restrained approval for Lady Russell? Does this hint at a lack of personal charm, or lack of openness, in her character?

The writing is characteristic of Jane Austen, then. We now want to focus on sentence structures, in order to develop a more detailed sense of how these work. Look at the first paragraph, which consists of four sentences. Rereading them shows that they are all constructed along similar lines – they all divide into two sections. The first section of the first sentence is 'Vanity was the beginning and the end of Sir Walter Elliot's character', and the second section is 'vanity of person and of situation'. This sentence is in two balanced sections, and its structural symmetry is emphasised: both sections begin with the strong word, 'Vanity'; and both sections contain double phrases repetitively expressed, 'the beginning and the end', and 'of person and of situation'. Why? We can suggest that the obsessive tidiness of this sentence expresses the obsessional care Sir Walter gives to his appearance. Later in the paragraph the author explains that 'beauty' and a 'baronetcy' (notice the alliterative link) are all Sir Walter thinks necessary in the world. So, in his symmetrical and simple-minded way, he accords himself two forms of vain admiration: 'respect and devotion'. In fact, the whole paragraph is constructed to emphasise pairs, from 'beginning' and 'end' to 'respect' and 'devotion'; and an emphasis on pairs is built into the structure of each sentence.

Within this structure, Jane Austen places devastating satirical ideas. The most obvious is the comparison between Sir Walter and a valet (sentence 3), where the joke only dawns on us as we finish the sentence and recall the first section. More subtly, a suggestion of decay is introduced in sentence two by matching 'remarkably handsome' with the parallel phrase from the second half of the sentence, 'very fine man'. Jane Austen's choice of this final phrase seems perfect: it exactly conveys the tone of patronising pity used for a man who is past his prime, and the implication that this is how Sir Walter thinks of himself hints at his lack of shame and his stupidity, as well as the 'vanity' we already know.

When studying the extract from *Emma*, we found it useful to describe the relationship between two parts of a sentence. Here, we could say that in sentence 1, the second half **explains**; in sentence 2, it is a **consequence**; in sentence 3, it is parallel, or an alternative to the first half; and in sentence 4 it is a **consequence** again. Sentence 4 in particular expresses the closed system of Sir Walter Elliot's limited mind: the **consequence** is his monumental vanity, which is apparently utterly logical, deduced from the premise that beauty and a baronetcy are the most important things in the world. The author's ironic voice, on the other hand, is heard in the second halves of sentences 2 and 3, where the **consequence** expressed is found in nature – beauty fades – and the **parallel** gives the author an opportunity to introduce a contemptuous comparison.

Two-part sentence structure predominates in this extract. In the second paragraph, **consequence** is used to keep us in suspense about the true import of the sentence (sentence 1 – 'a wife of very superior character ... etc.' is kept to the end); and **parallel** structure offers the reader bland and outspoken alternatives (sentence 4, where the bland 'an awful legacy for a mother to bequeath' becomes much more specific, and critical of Sir Walter, as 'an awful charge rather, to confide to the authority and guidance of a conceited, silly father').

This extract, then, has shown again how closely we can analyse Jane Austen's style; and how the text repays detailed attention to Austen's choice of words and phrases, and the structure of her sentences.

## Conclusions

1. From looking at four extracts in this chapter, we have realised how rich Jane Austen's writing is. Humorous and ironic effects are constantly interwoven, created by the choice of words and phrases, the order of revelations to the reader, and the structure of passages and sentences. Readers are constantly provoked to laugh, question, compare elements of the text, and think for themselves. Additionally, the diction and attitude of the text rarely stand still. A single phrase in the language of one character, for example, can modify our perception of a whole sentence. So, we are constantly provoked into thinking both forward into the story's future, and backwards, to reassess what has already happened.

2. With the exception of the authorial interventions in *Mansfield Park*, we have found that there is always an interplay between an explicit and an implied judgment. Often, the irony operates on more than two levels: we can infer further ironic or mocking insights even beyond the immediate satire of the text. This happens in the case of *Emma*, for example, where the heroine's tendency to magnify her emotions is the target of satire. The author's sympathy for Emma's lack of experience and her narrow life, is a further ironic point of view which emerges gradually. Similarly, in *Pride and Prejudice*, we are encouraged to laugh at Charlotte's and Mr Collins's materialism; but our laughter is undercut later when Elizabeth half-truthfully remarks that the beauty of Pemberley caused her to fall in love with Darcy, or when Charlotte's stratagems for making her married life tolerable are revealed.

3. In Jane Austen's writing, the 'voice' of the narrative can alter with a single word, and often alters during a sentence. This further complicates points of view, and often traps the reader into judgments and reactions whose absurdity is then exposed.

## Methods of Analysis

1.  Look for the terms (words and phrases), which describe characters and their qualities or states of feeling. Build lists of alternatives: these reveal Jane Austen's concerns and her ironic method. We did this with Mr Collins's qualities (such as 'diffidence', 'secure', 'eloquence', 'fire', and 'independence') when studying the extract from *Pride and Prejudice*.

2.  Look at the words or phrases which stand out as amusing or shocking. Analyse their immediate context closely to discover how they gain their effect; then describe how the particular effect contributes to character revelation or themes in the novel. We approached the extract from *Emma* in this way. We began by noticing several over-dramatic phrases such as 'the shadow of authority' and overstated words, such as 'grief' and 'loss'. This helps us to appreciate how the style presents Emma's self-dramatising outlook.

3.  Analyse the structure of sentences. It is often helpful to divide Jane Austen's sentences into two parts, and ask about the relationship between them. Look in particular for sentences expressing **consequence**, **explanation**, or constructed as **parallel** or **alternative** expressions of the idea. In *Emma*, for example, we found that solutions were frequently the **consequence** of problems, revealing Emma's complacency; and in *Persuasion* we found a symmetrical **explanation** exactly expressing Sir Walter Elliot's narrow-minded conceit.

4.  The above approaches are practical ways in to analysing Jane Austen's style, and they will yield rich rewards. However, it is important to approach her style flexibly, and to be responsive to all her manipulations of language. For example, we found that a rhetorical construction 'little had she dared to hope' indicated satire of sentimental romance, in the passage from *Pride and Prejudice*.

## Suggested Work

It is useful to practise the close analysis of short passages. Apply the methods demonstrated in this chapter to another passage from one of the four works. Here are suggestions of extracts which would repay close analysis:

- From *Pride and Prejudice*, look at pp. 16–17, from 'His sisters were very anxious for his having an estate ...' and as far as '... but she smiled too much'. This describes the Bingleys and Darcy, and contains numerous alternative terms for their characteristics, as well as other noteworthy features.
- From *Emma*, analyse pp. 118–19, from 'Her tears fell abundantly ...' to '... without any danger of betraying sentiments or increasing them'. This passage occurs after Mr Elton's attempted proposal, and displays constant alterations in the 'voice' of the narrative.
- From *Mansfield Park*, look at the first four paragraphs of Chapter 22, which describe in double-edged sentences how Fanny's stock rises after her cousins' departure (pp. 171–2, as far as '... would be indubitable to her aunt Bertram').
- From *Persuasion*, try studying the description of Captain Benwick from p. 118, beginning from 'They were by no means tired of wondering ...' and going as far as '... sympathy and good-will excited towards Captain Benwick was very great'. Here, the portrait and its context, and Jane Austen's care in choosing words and manipulating the 'voice', repay close scrutiny.

# 2

# Characterisation

Jane Austen's novels are called 'novels of manners'. This means that the novelist observes and reports her characters' behaviour, and we understand them largely by analysing this. Jane Austen does also report characters' feelings, their thoughts and decisions; but the text is dominated by the formulated, conscious level of the mind: what characters think to themselves and how they reason their decisions, rather than the complex, self-contradictory impulses and sudden unexplained emotions we find in many modern novels.

In a novel of manners, then, we receive a detailed external account of people, and a rationalised account of their reactions and motives. On the other hand, Jane Austen's novels often convey major themes of self-deception and self-knowledge. It follows that the author's knowledge of her characters is far greater than their knowledge of themselves, that the characterisation has a 'psychological' dimension. Somehow, we understand that her characters have irrational impulses and suffer from mental and emotional conflicts.

In this chapter, our aim is to discover how the complex 'psychological' dimension of character is created within a novel of manners, so all four of the extracts we examine focus on the heroines. Before we turn to these detailed studies, however, we should take a more general look at Jane Austen's delineation of character.

## Characterisation in General

The main point is to read the text critically, observing nuances of language closely, as we did in Chapter 1. Here is the introductory description of Harriet Smith, from *Emma*:

> She was a very pretty girl, and her beauty happened to be of a sort which Emma particularly admired. She was short, plump and fair, with a fine bloom, blue eyes, light hair, regular features, and a look of great sweetness; and before the end of the evening, Emma was as much pleased with her manners as her person, and quite determined to continue the acquaintance.
>
> She was not struck by any thing remarkably clever in Miss Smith's conversation, but she found her altogether very engaging – not inconveniently shy, not unwilling to talk – and yet so far from pushing, shewing so proper and becoming a deference, seeming so pleasantly grateful for being admitted to Hartfield, and so artlessly impressed by the appearance of every thing in so superior a style to what she had been used to, that she must have good sense and deserve encouragement.
>
> (*Emma*, p. 21)

The first of these two paragraphs provides us with a clear picture of Harriet. The words are short and very simple indeed. She is 'short', 'plump', 'fair'; her eyes are 'blue', and she has 'light' hair and 'regular' features. Not only does this give a simple and vivid impression of Miss Smith, but also the language is simple enough to suit Harriet's mind. The second paragraph is in marked contrast. The constructions are elaborate and several of them are negative ('not struck by anything remarkably clever ... '; 'not ... shy'; 'not unwilling to talk'; 'far from pushing'). Suddenly, the vocabulary is sophisticated and allusive. These are Emma's words, so we understand that the narrative has adopted Emma's point of view: 'becoming', 'deference', 'pleasantly grateful', 'admitted', 'artlessly impressed', 'so superior a style'. This sudden contrast in language tells its own story. Emma lays a smoke-screen of complicated language over the simple truth of Harriet, so we naturally translate Emma's circumlocutions into short plain words, in order to penetrate nearer to the truth about Harriet. We have heard that she is 'short' and 'plump'; so when we read that there was 'not ... anything remarkably clever' in her talk, we think her 'vapid'; when we read 'not inconveniently shy, not unwilling to talk', we think she 'prattles'.

Later in the novel we are given samples of Harriet's conversation which confirm our suspicions (see her answer to the question whether Mr Martin reads, on p. 23, for example); and her development into a snob in her own right, selfish enough to use her apparent 'artlessness' to 'catch' a man infinitely superior to her in intellect, can be heard in her voice on pp. 336–8 (for example, 'I hope I know better now, than to care for Mr Martin').

Many of Jane Austen's characters are memorable for their style of speech: the long monologues of Harriet Smith, Mrs Elton, Miss Bates, Mr Collins, Mrs Bennet, Mrs Norris and Mary Musgrove are pure comic self-revelation. Each has a characteristic way of expressing their thoughts, usually conveyed in the structure of sentences, and their characters can often be clarified by tracing the way their thoughts succeed each other, the way they pass from one subject to the next.

However, it is also characteristic of the figures in these novels that they reveal as much about those around them as they do about themselves. Look, for example, at the arrival of Mr Collins's letter in Chapter 13 of *Pride and Prejudice*. The letter itself reveals Mr Collins to be pompous, patronising and sycophantic. Afterwards, however, there is a discussion in which Mr Bennet, Jane, Elizabeth and Mary give their opinions, one after another. Jane Austen then tells us the letter's effect on Lydia and Kitty, and on Mrs Bennet. Mr Collins's character, then, becomes an occasion for more subtle distinctions to be drawn between the Bennets' different preoccupations and perceptions.

Similarly, the plots provide regular social gatherings when the behaviour of each character can be observed and interpreted; and in most cases there is a post-mortem discussion of the social event between two or more people, which enables different interpretations to be expressed. The 'truth' about a character is thus constantly speculated about, guessed, analysed and deduced by others, and we are encouraged to sift all these views when reaching our own conclusions. For example, the dinner at the Coles' in Chapter 26 of *Emma* is full of private and public conversations speculating about others' behaviour. Who sent Miss Fairfax a pianoforte? This question is the subject of general speculation, then secret guesswork between Emma and Frank Churchill; next Mrs Weston and Emma speculate about a romance between Mr Knightley and Miss Fairfax, and Emma and Mr Knightley discuss the pianoforte. In Chapter 27, the following morning, Emma and Harriet discuss the previous evening's gathering.

Characterisation of secondary figures in these novels tends to contribute to our understanding of the more complex principal characters. This is true of the extract about Harriet Smith quoted above. When the voice changes to Emma's thoughts, we read that she noticed Harriet's silliness; but for some reason did not allow herself to think this judgment clearly. Instead, she uses a confused negative phrase in her own mind, avoiding the idea that Harriet is stupid (she 'was not struck by any thing remarkably clever'). After this, Emma constructs a weak rationalisation, that Harriet's deference proves her 'good sense'. Here we can follow the processes of Emma's mind as she suppresses the evidence of her own observation, then argues herself into an opposite opinion. A similar effect occurs in *Pride and Prejudice*, when Elizabeth meets Wickham. She initially objects to his story of Darcy's dishonesty, but is easily talked into believing him. Later, when Jane raises the same doubts, she replies that Wickham must be telling the truth because 'there was truth in his looks'. Here, as in *Emma*, we see that the heroine arrives at a judgment against her own sense and intelligence, suppressing her own perceptions. In both of these cases, the introduction of a new character reveals the process of self-deception in the heroine's mind.

## Self-deception and Self-knowledge

Now we return to this chapter's main inquiry: how is the psychological complexity of characters portrayed within these novels, where the accent is upon manners and conscious thought? The extracts we look at seem to raise further questions about the heroine's character and feelings, in each case, so close study should reveal how these questions are provoked. The first passage comes from Chapter 36 of *Pride and Prejudice*, when Elizabeth has just read Darcy's letter and is adjusting her opinions of both him and Wickham:

> If Elizabeth, when Mr Darcy gave her the letter, did not expect it to contain a renewal of his offers, she had formed no expectation at all of its contents. But such as they were, it may be well supposed how eagerly she went through them, and what a contrariety of emotion they excited. Her feelings as she read were scarcely to be defined. With amazement did she first understand that he believed any apology to be in his power; and steadfastly was she persuaded, that he could have no explanation to give, which a just sense of shame would not conceal. With a strong prejudice against everything he might say, she began his account of what had happened at Netherfield. She read with an eagerness which hardly left her power of comprehension, and from impatience of knowing what the next sentence might bring, was incapable of attending to the sense of the one before her eyes. His belief of her sister's insensibility she instantly resolved to be false; and his account of the real, the worst objections to the match, made her too angry to have any wish of doing him justice. He expressed no regret for what he had done which satisfied

her; his style was not penitent, but haughty. It was all pride and insolence.

But when this subject was succeeded by his account of Mr Wickham – when she read with somewhat clearer attention a relation of events which, if true, must overthrow every cherished opinion of his worth, and which bore so alarming an affinity to his own history of himself – her feelings were yet more acutely painful and more difficult of definition. Astonishment, apprehension, and even horror, oppressed her. She wished to discredit it entirely, repeatedly exclaiming, 'This must be false! This cannot be! This must be the grossest falsehood!' – and when she had gone through the whole letter, though scarcely knowing anything of the last page or two, put it hastily away, protesting that she would not regard it, that she would never look in it again.

In this perturbed state of mind, with thoughts that could rest on nothing, she walked on; but it would not do; in half a minute the letter was unfolded again, and collecting herself as well as she could, she again began the mortifying perusal of all that related to Wickham, and commanded herself so far as to examine the meaning of every sentence. The account of his connection with the Pemberley family was exactly what he had related himself; and the kindness of the late Mr Darcy, though she had not before known its extent, agreed equally well with his own words. So far each recital confirmed the other; but when she came to the will, the difference was great. What Wickham had said of the living was fresh in her memory, and as she recalled his very words, it was impossible not to feel that there was gross duplicity on one side or the other; and, for a few moments, she flattered herself that her wishes did not err. But when she read and re-read with the closest attention, the particulars immediately following of Wickham's resigning all pretensions to the living, of his receiving in lieu so considerable a sum as three thousand pounds, again was she forced to hesitate. She put down the letter, weighed every circumstance with what she meant to be impartiality – deliberated on the probability of each statement – but with little success. On both sides it was only assertion. Again she read on; but every line proved more clearly that the affair, which she had believed it impossible that any contrivance could so represent as to render Mr Darcy's conduct in it less than infamous, was capable of a turn which must make him entirely blameless throughout the whole.

(*Pride and Prejudice*, pp. 168–9)

In this extract, Elizabeth's prejudice against Mr Darcy, and in favour of Mr Wickham, succumbs to the more probable truth of Darcy's account, contained in his letter. Elizabeth is caught in a conflict between reason and prejudice, then. Her prejudice is in the ascendant when she attempts to close her mind to the letter's influence ('put it hastily away, protesting that she would not regard it, that she would never look in it again'). Her reasonableness is in the ascendant when she 'weighed every circumstance' and 'deliberated on the probability of each statement'.

Several features of the passage contribute to conveying this conflict and the violence of Elizabeth's struggles. Certain key words are repeated, for example: 'eagerly' and 'eagerness'; 'wish', 'wished' and 'wishes'. Powerful emotions are described: 'contrariety of emotion', 'amazement', 'impatience', 'angry', 'feelings ... acutely painful', 'Astonishment, apprehension, and even horror', 'mortifying'. The strength of Elizabeth's feelings is also conveyed by a repeated insistence on her inability to think clearly: 'hardly left her power of comprehension', 'incapable of attending to the sense', 'scarcely knowing anything of the last page or two', 'commanded herself ... to examine the meaning'. Jane Austen uses powerful language to portray the tumult of Elizabeth's mind.

The events of the passage add to its effect. She begins by reading the letter 'eagerly', but then 'put it hastily away'. In 'half a minute', however, she unfolds it and begins to read again. During this perusal she dwells on the part about the will, 'she read and re-read with the closest attention', then she 'put down the letter' and tried to think before 'Again she read on'. The passage could have been a static, passive scene: after all, Elizabeth is only confronted with written information, and could have read silently. But Jane Austen's treatment makes mental turmoil physically active as well. The repeated taking out and putting away of the letter, and Elizabeth's loud exclamations, are dramatic events.

Jane Austen's sentences are uncharacteristically wild in these three paragraphs. They vary in length from the shortest sentence of 6 words, to the longest multiple sentence of 63 words. Two other sentences are only 7 words long, and three others are almost 60 words. The longest sentence, the first of the final paragraph beginning 'In this perturbed state of mind ...' chronicles five actions: she 'walked on', the letter 'was unfolded', then 'collecting herself' she 'began ... perusal' and 'commanded herself'. Her 'perturbed state of mind' is expanded in a subordinate clause; and her effort to collect her thoughts is described twice. Additionally, there are long parentheses between dashes, showing sudden and interrupted thoughts in Elizabeth's agitated state of mind.

Finally, notice that we are again given alternative expressions of her opinion. Near the end of the first paragraph, she observes that 'He expressed no regret for what he had done which satisfied her.' This observation becomes stronger in the second statement, 'his style was not penitent, but haughty'. The third statement, however, is a sweeping, angry generalisation: 'It was all pride and insolence.' This progression from a reasoned observation about his lack of regret, to a furious denunciation of 'pride and insolence', charts the progress of Elizabeth's feelings as she reads on, becoming angrier and angrier.

So far, we have analysed features of the style which convey the tumultuous state of Elizabeth's emotions. This brings us a rich and detailed understanding of Jane Austen's technique in bringing her character alive; however, it tells us no more about Elizabeth than the simple facts we know from a first reading: there is a conflict between her better reason, and her prejudice. More probing questions about her character look for more complex understanding: how was her prejudice formed? Which of her desires supported it despite contrary evidence? What emotional force within Elizabeth fights so fiercely on the side of prejudice? Which emotions are attached to discovering Darcy's innocence?

These are questions Elizabeth herself could not satisfactorily answer, so we must be doubly careful. Remember that Elizabeth is a character in a novel, not a real person; she does not exist beyond the words Jane Austen has written in the text. It is therefore absurd to speculate about what Elizabeth 'may' or 'should' feel, as if she existed outside the book. It is our legitimate business, as literary critics, to ask these questions; but we may have to put up with no answers if there are none in the text.

First, then, let us look a little way ahead and see what answers the character herself gives to these questions. A few pages after our extract, Elizabeth is heartily ashamed of her long mistake about Darcy and Wickham. She identifies two faults in herself. She 'prided' herself on her 'discernment' and 'valued' herself on her 'abilities'; and she was 'pleased with the preference of one [Wickham]' and 'offended by the neglect of the other'. So, she was vain about her intelligence, and her vanity was alternately flattered and offended by the two men. Her 'folly' is 'vanity': this has been the cause of everything.

We can agree with Elizabeth's analysis. She is fond of her wit, and Jane's 'generous candour' does provoke Elizabeth to go to cynical extremes, compensating for her sister's excessive trust. We can also recognise how hurtful Darcy's original slight must have been, and remember the heady flattery of Wickham's attention ('Mr Wickham was the happy man towards whom almost every female eye was turned, and Elizabeth was the happy woman by whom he finally seated himself' [p. 66]). So this explanation carries some conviction: Elizabeth has been vain, and her vanity has contributed a great deal towards her prejudice.

On the other hand, Jane Austen regularly suggests that there is more: there are feelings and motives that Elizabeth does not penetrate in this shaming moment of self-discovery.

Look at the passage again. First, a 'renewal of his offers' is mentioned. Notice that Jane Austen places this suggestion in the most teasing of all constructions: *if she didn't expect it, she expected nothing else*. We may ask, did she or did she not expect him to propose again? If so, why? If not, why not? This question goes to the deepest level in Elizabeth's character, since she has, unwittingly, been enticing Darcy into her power. The author leaves the suggestion in the air, unanswered; but at the end of the novel Elizabeth clearly understands how she attracted him, asking Darcy 'did you admire me for my impertinence?' (*PP*, p. 306).

The second suggestive element is Jane Austen's determination not to define Elizabeth's feelings. This is not an omission – a lack of emotional description – it is a repeated presence in the narrative, either as a bald statement (Her feelings were 'scarcely to be defined', her feelings were 'more difficult of definition') or in the form of descriptions which convey the strength but not the kind of the emotion she felt ('a contrariety of emotion', 'eagerness', 'impatience', 'alarming', 'Astonishment, apprehension, and even horror', 'perturbed'). This contributes to creating the unknown area in Elizabeth's character: her emotional conflict is so powerful that she cannot understand or think about what she is reading. Notice, also, that some of the terms for her emotion are tantalisingly ambiguous. 'Apprehension', for example, suggests both fear (because her 'cherished opinion' is about to be overthrown) and sudden understanding – as if her feelings (but not her mind) sense the truth of Darcy's letter at once.

All of these elements in our extract tell us nothing definite. They are, however, suggestive that there is something more in Elizabeth's heart than she is aware of. In these circumstances, it is helpful to step back from the text and summarise the character's predicament in plain language. This may provide a pointer to the character's deeper motives. Here is a summary of Elizabeth's predicament at the start of Chapter 36.

*Elizabeth has had an account of Wickham's dealings with the Darcy family, from Wickham – a persuasive young man whom she likes – and she believes this account. She reads a letter from Darcy – a man she dislikes – which gives a different version of events. Elizabeth now believes Darcy.*

The first point to strike us is that Elizabeth's change of opinion is illogical. It seems that there must be some other reason for her to change her mind. Now we return to the extract, looking for a compelling reason which would account for her change of mind. She compares the two accounts of the will, but she can only conclude that 'there was gross duplicity on one side or the other'. When she has 'read and re-read' the crucial passage, she can only 'hesitate'. Finally she puts down the letter and thinks about every statement 'with what she meant to be impartiality', but even this effort is inconclusive. Finally, she can only think 'On both sides it was only assertion.' These details do not answer our question, they make it more urgent: even the closest examination gives no clue. Why does Elizabeth desert her 'favourite' Wickham, and believe the hated Darcy?

Jane Austen does not answer this question. However, on the next page Elizabeth's turnaround is complete. She considers looking for further proof by asking Colonel Fitzwilliam, but in a manner reminiscent of her belief in Wickham because there was 'truth in his looks', she dismisses the idea from 'the conviction' that Darcy would not suggest this if he did not know what the Colonel would say. The appearance of Wickham's character has now changed: 'How differently did everything now appear in which he was concerned!' (p. 170). Now, she perceives Wickham's inconsistencies and interprets his actions differently. Elizabeth happens to be right, but Jane Austen is still gently laughing at her. Now, she founds her right judgment on the same hearsay evidence and shaky interpretation of a deceptive reality as she used in building her original prejudice.

This extract, then, has revealed something different from the apparent conflict between prejudice and reason. Our analysis shows that Elizabeth is swayed by something else apart from reason, so there is something more in her heart than 'vanity' about her intelligence, and a desire for attention from men. Whatever this 'something' is, it is powerful enough to paralyse her understanding and logic, and she cannot define it. It must have contributed to her change of mind, so it must be a 'something' in favour of Darcy. The nearest it comes to appearing on the surface of this extract, is the phrase 'what she meant to be impartiality'. This tells us that, however hard she tries, Elizabeth is not impartial when she reads the letter for a second time. Since her next idea is that Darcy 'must' be 'entirely blameless', we can conclude that she is swayed by a strong emotion in favour of Darcy.

This is as far as we can go from the extract. However, turning forward to Elizabeth's introspection two pages later, we find further suggestive details. First, she approaches the idea that she was in love: 'Had I been in love, I could not have been more wretchedly blind', but immediately dismisses this in favour of 'vanity, not love'. Here, Jane Austen hints that a more powerful emotion than vanity was at work. Elizabeth almost realises this, then shies away from the discovery. Second, Elizabeth remembers events in the wrong order. 'Pleased with the preference of one' is remembered before 'offended by the neglect of the other'. We remember that she met Darcy before meeting Wickham. Noticing the enmity between the two men prejudiced her in favour of Wickham. It is revealing that Elizabeth reverses the two meetings in her memory. It is as if her mind is trying to diminish the importance of Darcy's influence on her, even now. A psychoanalytical interpretation would suggest that she suppresses the love she has felt for Darcy from the start, and this repressed love causes the 'mistake' in her memory. We cannot go that far; but we are able to notice that Jane Austen uses deliberate reticence and ambiguous suggestions, at this crucial point in Elizabeth's development, to suggest powerful feelings for Darcy. These feelings are clearly below the conscious level: Elizabeth cannot define them, and chooses to ascribe her own conduct to 'vanity', a self-analysis which only partly satisfies us.

We have been able to see deeper than the apparent level of Elizabeth's character, then. At a first reading, it seems that her emotions are all on Wickham's side. In other words, there seems to be a conflict between emotion and reason. Now we realise that the conflict is between emotion and emotion: part of her wishes to cling to her approval of Wickham, but there is also a powerful feeling which pushes her to find Darcy 'blameless'. Elizabeth is not yet aware of this feeling, but we have been able to interpret what could be called a 'subtext': features of the writing that hint at something more than the character knows. In this passage, we noticed the repeated failure to define her emotions, repeated insistence that her reason is overwhelmed, and some hints and ambiguities, supported by further hints in her own meditation about herself, two pages further on.

*          *          *

There is 'psychological' characterisation in Jane Austen's novels, then. This contributes a wry irony to the theme of prejudice (Elizabeth's emotions lead her to both error and truth) and adds depth to the author's constant exploitation of the deceptiveness of reality. This kind of characterisation has further implications for the novel's meaning, but before we discuss these, it will be helpful to look at a passage from *Emma*. Emma and Mr Knightley argue about the suitability of Harriet Smith and Robert Martin:

> 'Upon my word, Emma, to hear you abusing the reason you have, is almost enough to make me think so too. Better be without sense, than misapply it as you do.'
> 'To be sure!' cried she playfully. 'I know *that* is the feeling of you all. I know that such a girl as Harriet is exactly what every man delights in – what at once bewitches his senses and satisfies his judgment. Oh! Harriet may pick and choose. Were

you, yourself, ever to marry, she is the very woman for you. And is she, at seventeen, just entering into life, just beginning to be known, to be wondered at because she does not accept the first offer she receives? No – pray let her have time to look about her.'

'I have always thought it a very foolish intimacy,' said Mr Knightley presently, 'though I have kept my thoughts to myself; but I now perceive that it will be a very unfortunate one for Harriet. You will puff her up with such ideas of her own beauty, and of what she has a claim to, that, in a little while, nobody within her reach will be good enough for her. Vanity working on a weak head, produces every sort of mischief. Nothing so easy as for a young lady to raise her expectations too high. Miss Harriet Smith may not find offers of marriage flow in so fast, though she is a very pretty girl. Men of sense, whatever you may chuse to say, do not want silly wives. Men of family would not be very fond of connecting themselves with a girl of such obscurity – and most prudent men would be afraid of the inconvenience and disgrace they might be involved in, when the mystery of her parentage came to be revealed. Let her marry Robert Martin, and she is safe, respectable, and happy for ever; but if you encourage her to expect to marry greatly, and teach her to be satisfied with nothing less than a man of consequence and large fortune, she may be a parlour-boarder at Mrs Goddard's all the rest of her life – or, at least, (for Harriet Smith is a girl who will marry somebody or other,) till she grow desperate, and is glad to catch at the old writing master's son.'

'We think so very differently on this point, Mr Knightley, that there can be no use in canvassing it. We shall only be making each other more angry. But as to my *letting* her marry Robert Martin, it is impossible; she has refused him, and so decidedly, I think, as must prevent any second application. She must abide by the evil of having refused him, whatever it may be; and as to the refusal itself, I will not pretend to say that I might not influence her a little; but I assure you there was very little for me or for anybody to do. His appearance is so much against him, and his manner so bad, that if she ever were disposed to favour him, she is not now. I can imagine, that before she had seen anybody superior, she might tolerate him. He was the brother of her friends, and he took pains to please her; and altogether, having seen nobody better (that must have been his great assistant) she might not, while she was at Abbey-Mill, find him disagreeable. But the case is altered now. She knows now what gentlemen are; and nothing but a gentleman in education and manner has any chance with Harriet.'

'Nonsense, errant nonsense, as ever was talked!' cried Mr Knightley. – 'Robert Martin's manners have sense, sincerity, and good-humour to recommend them; and his mind has more true gentility than Harriet Smith could understand.'

Emma made no answer, and tried to look cheerfully unconcerned, but was really feeling uncomfortable, and wanting him very much to be gone. She did not repent what she had done; she still thought herself a better judge of such a point of female right and refinement than he could be; but yet she had a sort of habitual respect for his judgment in general, which made her dislike having it so loudly against her; and to have him sitting just opposite to her in angry state, was very disagreeable. Some minutes passed in this unpleasant silence, with only one attempt on Emma's side to talk of the weather, but he made no answer. He was thinking. The result of his thoughts appeared at last in these words.

'Robert Martin has no great loss – if he can but think so; and I hope it will not be long before he does. Your views for Harriet are best known to yourself; but as you make no secret of your love of match-making, it is fair to suppose that views, and plans, and projects you have; – and as a friend I shall just hint to you that if Elton is the man, I think it will be all labour in vain.'

Emma laughed and disclaimed. He continued:

'Depend upon it, Elton will not do. Elton is a very good sort of man, and a very respectable vicar of Highbury, but not at all likely to make an imprudent match. He knows the value of a good income as well as anybody. Elton may talk sentimentally, but he will act rationally. He is as well acquainted with his own claims, as you can be with Harriet's. He knows that he is a very handsome young man, and a great favourite wherever he goes; and from his general way of talking in unreserved moments, when there are only men present, I am convinced that he does not mean to throw himself away. I have heard him speak with great animation of a large family of young ladies that his sisters are intimate with, who have all twenty thousand pounds apiece.'

'I am very much obliged to you,' said Emma, laughing again. 'If I had set my heart on Mr Elton's marrying Harriet, it would have been very kind to open my eyes; but at present I only want to keep Harriet to myself. I have done with match-making, indeed. I could never hope to equal my own doings at Randalls. I shall leave off while I am well.'

'Good morning to you,' – said he, rising and walking off abruptly. He was very much vexed. He felt the disappointment of the young man, and was mortified to have been the means of promoting it, by the sanction he had given; and the part which he was persuaded Emma had taken in the affair was provoking him exceedingly.

Emma remained in a state of vexation too; but there was more indistinctness in the causes of her's, than in his. She did not always feel so absolutely satisfied with herself, so entirely convinced that her opinions were right and her adversary's wrong, as Mr Knightley. He walked off in more complete self-approbation than he left for her. She was not so materially cast down, however, but that a little time and the return of Harriet were very adequate restoratives. Harriet's staying away so long was beginning to make her uneasy. The possibility of the young man's coming to Mrs Goddard's that morning, and meeting with Harriet and pleading his own cause, gave alarming ideas. The dread of such a failure after all became the prominent uneasiness; and when Harriet appeared, and in very good spirits, and without having any such reason to give for her long absence, she felt a satisfaction which settled her with her own mind, and convinced her, that let Mr Knightley think or say what he would, she had done nothing which woman's friendship and woman's feelings would not justify.

(*Emma*, pp. 55–8)

At the start of this extract, Mr Knightley unequivocally states what the reader knows: that Emma misuses her intelligence, rationalising to justify her wrong actions. Mr Knightley's voice is characteristically pithy and concise: 'Better be without sense, than misapply it as you do.' Many of the details elaborate this central point. So, Knightley makes clear the potential damage to Harriet: 'Vanity working on a weak head, produces every sort of mischief.' Emma is willing to be dishonest in order to defend herself: 'I will not pretend to say that I might not influence her a little; but I assure you there was very little for me or for anybody to do' (distortion of the truth), 'I have done with match-making, indeed' (downright dishonesty), and 'Emma laughed and disclaimed' (concealment). It is clear that Mr Knightley urges all good and right reasons, while Emma opposes him with bad and wrong ones.

We could analyse this passage at length, then, merely to show that Mr Knightley tries his best to bring Emma to her senses; and that Emma persists, with some ingenuity, in justifying and denying her interference in Harriet's life, both to Mr Knightley and herself. We could also look at the patronisingly patriarchal tone Mr Knightley adopts, and analyse the passage from the point of view of gender warfare. However, our particular interest is in Emma's character, and we want to penetrate to a deeper level than merely her headstrong, self-opinionated wilfulness. We should therefore assume that we know *what* Emma is like, and focus our analysis on discovering *why* she is like that. In our analysis of Elizabeth Bennet, we were able to deduce that she felt 'something more' than she understood herself, because Jane Austen told us that these feelings 'were scarcely to be defined'. Is there anything similar in this extract, suggesting that Emma has feelings she cannot fathom? Yes: when Knightley leaves, Emma feels 'vexation', but the author tells us that 'there was more indistinctness in the causes of her's, than in his'. This 'indistinctness' surrounds Emma's 'vexation' with herself. This is clear because it is contrasted with Mr Knightley's 'more complete self-approbation'. So, we are justified in concluding that Emma feels dissatisfied, but does not understand why – does not understand the 'causes'.

The earlier description of Emma's feelings corroborates this view. She feels 'uncomfortable' and has a 'dislike' of the way she feels, which is 'very disagreeable' and gives rise to 'this unpleasant silence'. Emma's feelings are negative, then; but they are not connected with the apparent subject of the argument ('she still thought herself a better judge ... '), and her uneasiness is couched in vague terms: 'a *sort* of habitual respect for his judgment *in general*' [my italics].

Emma's situation stands a close comparison with Elizabeth's: in both cases the heroine has a conscious determination to uphold her opinion; but there is something else inside the heroine, described as a powerful sensation ('... apprehension, and even horror' [*Pride and Prejudice*]; '... uncomfortable ... disagreeable ... vexation' [*Emma*]) which resists clear definition ('scarcely to be defined' [*Pride and Prejudice*]; 'indistinctness' [*Emma*]), which pushes against her conscious effort and undermines her certainty. In both extracts, it is clear that this unconscious, emotional 'something' is within the heroine. It is not the truth of Darcy's letter or Knightley's sound reasoning – it is a powerful but vague emotional energy inside Elizabeth and Emma respectively. So, here again, we can confidently say that Jane Austen depicts repressed emotion. Now we want to find out the whys and hows of Emma's feelings: why they are repressed and how she copes with them.

When studying the extract from *Pride and Prejudice*, we found it useful to summarise the heroine's circumstances. We can try the same approach with *Emma*:

*Emma argues about Harriet with Mr Knightley. He tells her that most men are too sensible to marry only for good looks. She disagrees, saying that men desire pretty, tractable wives. They part in anger. She feels unhappy, but feels better when Harriet returns.*

This summary does not throw up such a clear question as was the case with *Pride and Prejudice*. Then, we had to ask 'why does Elizabeth change her mind?' since there was no good reason, on the surface, for her to do so. This time, there is a good reason for Emma to feel unhappy: she has had a bad-tempered argument with the man who is her closest family friend. On the other hand, the author says that the 'causes' of her unhappiness were 'indistinct'. Perhaps the most surprising point about what happens is the effect of Harriet's return: why does Emma feel so much better, just because Harriet returns in 'good spirits'?

Let us look more closely at the change in Emma's feelings. Her equanimity is restored, apparently, by 'a little time' and 'the return of Harriet'. During the 'little time' between parting from Mr Knightley and Harriet's arrival, the focus of Emma's feelings changes. When Mr Knightley left, her 'vexation' was focused within herself, was an absence of 'self-approbation' and was full of 'indistinctness'. Next, Harriet's absence began to 'make her uneasy'. Emma then imagines a possible meeting with Mr Martin and has 'alarming ideas'. The 'dread' of failure then takes the place of her unknown inner feelings, and becomes 'the prominent uneasiness'. Emma's feelings are now entirely focused on Harriet: she has replaced her worries about herself with worries about Harriet. Indeed, Emma goes so far as to suppress her inner vexation, making the external anxiety about Harriet 'the prominent uneasiness'. At the end of the paragraph, we can see how thoroughly Harriet has taken her own place in her mind: when the external anxiety is dispelled, Emma 'felt a satisfaction which settled her with her own mind'. This is re-stated on the next page: 'Harriet's cheerful look and manner established hers' (*Emma*, p. 58).

Two other features of this process deserve mention. First, Emma manufactures her feelings from nothing: there is no reason for her to be anxious about Harriet, and she builds up her worry to a high pitch by wilfully imagining a second proposal from Mr Martin (remember Emma's own comment that Harriet refused him 'so decidedly ... as must prevent any second application'). Why does Emma wilfully increase her anxiety? The obvious answer is, because this helps her to displace, or drown out, her unhappy inner feelings. Second, notice that Emma's worry reaches a ridiculously exaggerated pitch. She feels 'dread' of failure. This word – one of the strongest expressions of fear in the language – reminds us of 'grief' and 'loss', which we noticed in Chapter 1. Emma's tendency to over-dramatise her situation is used here to magnify her artificial feelings about Harriet. This time, however, the over-powerful word has extra overtones: it does not suit her worry about Harriet, but it aptly conveys the depth and strength of her unconscious feelings.

We know that Emma is 'using' Harriet. She is there to fill Emma's time, and this is clear from her first invitation to Hartfield, when Emma 'no longer dreaded' the evening (*Emma*, p. 21). This extract shows that Emma also uses Harriet emotionally. Interfering in Harriet's life helps Emma to push her own unhappiness out of her mind. The emotional energy which lurks unrecognised within Emma, is channelled into plans, hopes and fears on Harriet's behalf. So, a part of Emma which is denied to herself lives vicariously through Harriet. We can say that Emma is using Harriet to displace or deny part of herself.

Analysing this extract, then, has revealed a complex psychological situation within Emma. She is headstrong, wilful and wrong; we knew these faults already. Now, however, we sense the deep dissatisfaction and unhappiness in the heroine; and we understand the process by which she suppresses her negative feelings, and channels their energy into the vicarious experience of controlling Harriet. We do not have the space, in the present chapter, to develop this analysis fully; but the following brief discussion indicates the direction such development might take. Notice that much further analysis comes in the form of leading questions and their answers, and that a reader's general knowledge of the novel is sufficient to enable you to think and develop your conclusions in this way.

What does Emma use Harriet for? To marry a man. What kind of a man? A gentleman of position and some fortune. In other words, a man suitable for Emma, not a man suitable for Harriet (as Mr Knightley points out). It seems reasonable to suppose, then, that Emma is unable to face the issue of marriage herself and has to face it through Harriet, instead.

The next question is obvious: why is Emma unable to face the issue of marriage? Several possible answers spring to mind. First, the problem of her father: she cannot leave him, and he is grotesquely dependent on her. This is the reason she gives for not considering marriage. Second, one of the issues of marriage is a conflict between financial and romantic considerations. Emma is financially independent, so she does not need to marry and gives this as a further reason why she does not intend to. However, she does find romance and materialism difficult to reconcile, as shown in her ambiguous belief that Mr Elton will fall for Harriet's 'pretty' looks and tractable nature. The ambiguity is that Emma imagines 'passion', and uses a lot of romantic clichés in promoting the courtship; while Harriet's naive, pretty personality is a feminine stereotype which, according to Emma, will allow her to 'pick and choose'; so Emma's match-making is a kind of sexual commerce, where Harriet's 'femininity' is a commodity that will buy her a rich man. This only masquerades as romance.

The dilemmas facing women of Emma's class are a major theme of the novel (for example, see the crisis of Jane Fairfax's story: she must marry or, failing that, go into a life of degrading servitude as a governess). These themes will be discussed in greater detail in Chapter 5. For the present, we can notice that our analysis of Emma's deeper feelings has led us to consider her situation from this point of view: she feels unable to confront the issue of marriage. The extract we have been studying confirms that sexual politics are a constant and major issue in Emma's mind and heart.

The argument with Mr Knightley is carried on in explicit gender terms: Emma refers to 'you all' and 'every man'; Mr Knightley counters with 'men of sense', 'men of family' and 'prudent men'. He says that he has heard Mr Elton speak 'in unreserved moments, when there are only men present';

Emma counters by thinking herself 'a better judge of such a point of female right and refinement' than Knightley can be. Eventually this conflict between male and female expertise resolves itself into that between romance and materialism. Emma champions 'a strong passion' in conflict with 'all interested motives' and 'prudence', the male qualities Mr Knightley ascribes to Mr Elton. So, the conflicts within Emma and that between her and Mr Knightley are pointers to the major, unresolved ambiguities of the society in which they live. Our character analysis has led us to a central, all-pervading duality in the novel's world. On the one side stand 'men of sense' and 'prudence', weighing up each decision with a conservative predisposition towards cautious materialism. On the other side stand romance and the power of emotion to overthrow good sense. We will return to this and other similar central dualities in Jane Austen's writing, again and again.

Similar implications lie behind Elizabeth Bennet's experience. We can use our 'summary' approach again, looking at Elizabeth's situation in relation to issues of marriage:

*Elizabeth is a lively, intelligent girl whose only chance of a fulfilled life is through marriage. She is of a romantic disposition, as we know from her argument with Charlotte (Chapter 6). Her parents' imprudence leaves Elizabeth with a very small dowry, unlikely to buy a man of equivalent upbringing to her own. Elizabeth meets a handsome man. He is very rich, and his behaviour emphasises the gulf between his level and hers.*

This summary puts Elizabeth's situation at the start of the novel in very clear terms. It suggests a possible reason for the violence of her prejudice against Darcy. As far as she understands the issues of marriage, any feelings she may have for a man like Darcy are doomed to disappointment, so it is safer to suppress them from the start. Of course, the callous remark she overhears makes this easier. Notice that the forces of romance, and a rigid, stratified materialism, again collide within Jane Austen's heroine.

*          *          *

We now turn to *Mansfield Park*. Our extract comes from Chapter 46, when Fanny Price is in Portsmouth and has just heard the news of Henry Crawford's and Maria Rushworth's elopement:

> What would be the consequence? Whom would it not injure? Whose views might it not affect? Whose peace would it not cut up for ever? Miss Crawford, herself – Edmund; but it was dangerous, perhaps, to tread such ground. She confined herself, or tried to confine herself to the simple, indubitable family-misery which must envelope all, if it were indeed a matter of certified guilt and public exposure. The mother's sufferings, the father's – there, she paused. Julia's, Tom's, Edmund's – there, a yet longer pause. They were the two on whom it would fall most horribly. Sir Thomas's parental solicitude, and high sense of honour and decorum, Edmund's upright principles, unsuspicious temper, and genuine strength of feeling, made her think it scarcely possible for them to support life and reason under such disgrace; and it appeared to her, that as far as this world alone was concerned, the greatest blessing to every one of kindred with Mrs Rushworth would be instant annihilation.
>
> Nothing happened the next day, or the next, to weaken her terrors. Two posts came in, and brought no refutation, public or private. There was no second letter to explain away the first, from Miss Crawford; there was no intelligence from Mansfield, though it was now full time for her to hear again from her aunt. This was an evil omen. She had, indeed, scarcely the shadow of a hope to soothe her mind, and was reduced to so low and wan and trembling a condition as no mother – not unkind, except Mrs Price, could have overlooked, when the third day did bring the sickening knock, and a letter was again put into her hands. It bore the London postmark, and came from Edmund.

DEAR FANNY,

You know our present wretchedness. May God support you under *your* share! We have been here two days, but there is nothing to be done. They cannot be traced. You may not have heard of the last blow – Julia's elopement; she is gone to Scotland with Yates. She left London a few hours before we entered it. At any other time, this would have been felt dreadfully. Now it seems nothing, yet it is an heavy aggravation. My father is not overpowered. More cannot be hoped. He is still able to think and act; and I write, by his desire, to propose your returning home. He is anxious to get you there for my mother's sake. I shall be at Portsmouth the morning after you receive this, and hope to find you ready to set off for Mansfield. My father wishes you to invite Susan to go with you, for a few months. Settle it as you like; say what is proper; I am sure you will feel such an instance of his kindness at such a moment! Do justice to his meaning, however I may confuse it. You may imagine something of my present state. There is no end of the evil let loose upon us. You will see me early, by the mail. – Yours, &c.

Never had Fanny more wanted a cordial. Never had she felt such a one as this letter contained. To-morrow! to leave Portsmouth to-morrow! She was, she felt she was, in the greatest danger of being exquisitely happy, while so many were miserable. The evil which brought such good to her! She dreaded lest she should learn to be insensible of it. To be going so soon, sent for so kindly, sent for as a comfort, and with leave to take Susan, was altogether such a combination of blessings as set her heart in a glow, and for a time, seemed to distance every pain, and make her incapable of suitably sharing the distress even of those whose distress she thought of most. Julia's elopement could affect her comparatively but little; she was amazed and shocked; but it could not occupy her, could not dwell on her mind. She was obliged to call herself to think of it, and acknowledge it to be terrible and grievous, or it was escaping her, in the midst of all the agitating, pressing, joyful cares attending this summons to herself.

*(Mansfield Park*, pp. 364–6)

As is natural at this point in the story, the passage focuses on Fanny's feelings. These feelings are also natural in the circumstances: Fanny is shocked, and strongly impressed by the effect Maria's elopement will have upon the feelings of Sir Thomas and Edmund. We can again accept the surface of the narrative as being self-explanatory and believable. We are searching for more complex elements in Fanny's character, so we begin by looking for features of the style that stand out, which might betray a more complex situation.

First, there are repeated, similar, descriptions of Fanny's state. In *Pride and Prejudice*, the author repeatedly told us that Elizabeth's emotions could not be defined; so here, we are repeatedly told that Fanny has to struggle to control her thoughts, and does not succeed entirely. Fanny senses that some ideas are 'dangerous', so she 'confined herself, or tried to confine herself to …'. After reading the letter, she senses that she is again 'in the greatest danger of being exquisitely happy' so she was 'incapable of suitably sharing the distress' and she attempts to control herself: 'She was obliged to call herself to think of it' for otherwise 'it was escaping her'.

Fanny's situation is simpler to unravel than either Elizabeth's or Emma's because she is aware of the feelings she tries to control. Fanny knows that she loves Edmund, and hopes that this shocking elopement will separate him from Mary Crawford. This explains why, when she thinks of the consequences to Edmund, she stops herself, believing that it is 'dangerous, perhaps, to tread such ground'. Fanny has also always felt pleasure when she has been of use to the Bertram family, so the summons to Mansfield is a compliment which makes her happy. She also hates Portsmouth and misses the countryside. So, there is no mystery about her inner conflict. She has sudden selfish pleasures and hopes, and she is both frightened of indulging them without good cause (her hopes may be 'dangerous' or unfounded) and feels guilty because the Bertrams' catastrophe brings her pleasure.

Other features of this extract are noticeable but less easy to interpret. Look at the passage again: some words and phrases seem to stand out in the same way as 'grief' and 'loss' stand out on the first page of *Emma*. Fanny thinks that 'instant annihilation' should fall on the entire Bertram family. This seems an excessive reaction, even in the context of Fanny's strict principles and the mores of the time. It is prefaced by the phrase 'as far as this world alone was concerned', which seems too grandiose a scale of reflection both for the event and for Fanny's habitual timidity. The next paragraph refers to her 'terrors', and the postman's knock is 'sickening'. Jane Austen gently suggests that there is exaggeration in Fanny's state, by describing Mrs Price as the only mother 'not unkind' who could remain unaware of her daughter's collapse. The joke here may be aimed at Mrs Price's habit of ignoring Fanny; but it may also suggest that Fanny's 'low and wan and trembling' condition is more extreme in her own mind than it appears to anyone else.

We have noticed, then, that certain features of Fanny's reaction seem melodramatic, out of proportion; and this is not characteristic of her. Notice, for example, that Fanny thinks in absolute terms of 'instant annihilation'; while Edmund weighs the opposing powers of shock and resistance to it in his father, saying that he is 'not overpowered'. We are prompted to ask why Fanny's thoughts are so lurid, but there is no obvious answer. We have used the summary method in these circumstances, so here is a summary of Fanny's situation, and what happens in this extract.

*Fanny is shocked by news of the elopement. She becomes increasingly terrified during three days when there is no further news. Fanny receives a letter from Edmund, confirming that Maria and Henry have eloped. So has Julia. Things could not be worse. Fanny is summoned back to Mansfield. After receiving the letter, Fanny is extremely happy.*

This summary highlights the glaring lack of logic in Fanny's feelings. She was not sure whether the catastrophe was true, before reading Edmund's letter. The letter confirms bad news and adds further bad news. She is sure of the truth, after reading the letter, and becomes happy. If

Fanny hoped that it was a false rumour, or that Maria's disgrace could be covered up; and feared that it was 'indeed a matter of certified guilt and public exposure', then Edmund's letter would bring her final misery. Illogically, it has the opposite effect. This only makes sense if Fanny's hopes and fears are really the opposite way around: she fears that it might be a false rumour, and she longs for the shocking report to be confirmed. When Edmund's letter confirms it, Fanny is relieved of anxiety and becomes happy.

Other details support this reading of her feelings. First, the melodramatic phrases Fanny uses about the effect of the elopement stand out, because they are partly artificial: she thinks what she ought to feel, not what she does feel. Second, notice that she finds it hard to summon any feelings at all about Julia's elopement. Beneath her ritual concern for the Bertrams, she does not care about Julia at all: 'She was obliged to call herself to think of it, and acknowledge it to be terrible and grievous, or it was escaping her.'

Notice that we have not learned about secret feelings in Fanny, from studying this extract: she knows that she is in 'danger' of feeling too happy, and comments on 'the evil which brought such good to her!' so the revelation that she hopes the disaster proves true, is not a complete surprise. On the other hand, we appreciate the depth and realism of Jane Austen's characterisation more fully after close analysis. The unspoken touches of characterisation – what we can call the 'subtext' of the extract – reveal the sheer power of Fanny's selfish joy overwhelming her principles and guilty scruples, and making her moods blatantly irrational.

Again, understanding the heroine provokes insights into the themes of the novel as a whole. For example, a major theme of *Mansfield Park* is the fraught relationship between a conservative, cautious and principled world, represented by Sir Thomas, the house itself, Edmund and Fanny; and a new lively world of London, fashion, extravagance and lack of principle, represented by the Crawfords, Maria and Julia, and Tom before his accident. These two worlds attempt to join through Edmund and Mary, Henry and Fanny. In the end, the unprincipled characters misbehave badly, and the two worlds crack apart for good.

What is Fanny's fear, in this extract? She talks of 'terrors' and is reduced to 'so low and wan and trembling a condition' with no hope to 'soothe her mind'. Our analysis suggests that her overwhelming fear is that the unprincipled people may not have misbehaved after all. Fanny is most frightened of finding Henry Crawford capable of reforming, of being led to respect and eventually to marry him. She is overwhelmingly relieved when she knows that this can no longer happen. This is the relief that gives such force to Fanny's phrase 'certified guilt', since her terror has lasted as long as Crawford's guilt has remained concealed. The irony is bitter: it was Crawford's love that terrified Fanny. She always disapproved of him, but she was never frightened of his immorality.

*       *       *

Finally, we look at Anne Elliot's reaction to news of Captain Wentworth, some weeks after the accident at Lyme. Our extract comes from p. 130 of *Persuasion*:

> With regard to Captain Wentworth, though Anne hazarded no enquiries, there was voluntary communication sufficient. His spirits had been greatly recovering lately, as might be expected. As Louisa improved, he had improved; and he was now quite a different creature from what he had been the first week. He had not seen Louisa; and was so extremely fearful of any ill consequence to her from an interview, that he did not press for it at all; and, on the contrary, seemed to have a plan of going away for a week or ten days, till her head were stronger. He had talked of going down to Plymouth for a week, and wanted to persuade Captain Benwick to go with him; but, as Charles maintained to the last, Captain Benwick seemed much more disposed to ride over to Kellynch.

There can be no doubt that Lady Russell and Anne were both occasionally thinking of Captain Benwick, from this time. Lady Russell could not hear the door-bell without feeling that it might be his herald; nor could Anne return from any stroll of solitary indulgence in her father's grounds, or any visit of charity in the village, without wondering whether she might see him or hear of him. Captain Benwick came not, however. He was either less disposed for it than Charles had imagined, or he was too shy; and after giving him a week's indulgence, Lady Russell determined him to be unworthy of the interest which he had been beginning to excite.

*(Persuasion*, pp. 147–8)

There is little about Anne in this extract. The first paragraph summarises the news about Captain Wentworth; and the second paragraph focuses on Captain Benwick. The only part which centres upon Anne is the incidental picture given at the start of the second paragraph, of her 'returning from any stroll of solitary indulgence in her father's grounds, or any visit of charity in the village' and wondering about Captain Benwick.

However, this passage does reveal the gentle subtlety of Jane Austen's technique in conveying the movements of her heroine's mind. In order to appreciate this fully, look at the passage in context. First, what is the story of Captain Wentworth's feelings? At Lyme, Anne was looking beautiful, and Wentworth noticed the stranger's admiration. He gave Anne 'a momentary glance – a glance of brightness' (p. 125) which she compares to the way he used to look at her. After Louisa's accident, 'Captain Wentworth's eyes were also turned towards her [Anne]' (p. 131). Anne then witnesses an ambiguous sight, of him leaning over a table 'as if overpowered by the various feelings of his soul' (p. 132); overhears his praise of her; and receives his appeal to her to stay at Lyme, when he spoke 'with a glow; and yet a gentleness, which seemed almost restoring the past' before she blushed and he 'recollected himself' (p. 134). On the journey to Uppercross Captain Wentworth berates himself for acceding to Louisa's wish to jump again, calling her 'Dear, sweet Louisa!' Anne thinks of his preference for a headstrong rather than a pliant character: 'She thought it could scarcely escape him to feel, that a persuadable temper might sometimes be as much in favour of happiness, as a very resolute character' (p. 136). Finally, he consults Anne on the question of how best to break the news to the Musgroves, and 'the remembrance of the appeal remained a pleasure to her – as a proof of friendship, and of deference for her judgment, a great pleasure' (p. 136).

Let us put ourselves in the position of a first-time reader. These clues to Wentworth's emotions are ambiguous. He appreciates Anne's qualities more than he did, but he may still be attracted to Louisa; so the reader cannot interpret him. On the other hand, we observe the characters and the world largely through Anne's eyes as we read *Persuasion*. We do not know what Wentworth feels, but we do know that Anne speculates; and that the direction of her thoughts is towards him regaining a more reasonable estimate of female character, and reviving the love he used to feel for her. Twice, at Lyme, Anne was reminded of the way he once loved her.

Now we arrive at the present extract. We immediately enter Anne's point of view. The word 'hazarded' quickly establishes her constant eagerness and anxiety to hear about Captain Wentworth. This contrasts with the ease with which she previously 'enquired after Captain Benwick' (p. 127). Next, we read three sentences where the structure emphasises natural inevitability. He was feeling better 'as might be expected'; his recovery symmetrically matches Louisa's; he is 'quite a different creature' in a construction again neatly balanced between 'now' and 'the first week'. Then, in Mary's inconsequential manner (for it is clearly Mary's monologue the author reports), the connection between him and Louisa is suddenly broken, followed by a sentence of complex, modifying and qualifying structure. Reading this sentence, we sense some effort to justify the fact that he had not seen

Louisa (he was 'so extremely fearful' and 'did not press for it at all') and some surprise that he thinks of going away, expressed in the perplexed phrase 'seemed to have a plan'. In short, we attend to the news of Captain Wentworth in the same anxious, detailed way that Anne does; and the marked alteration in sentence structure emphasises the sudden contrast between what Mary expects (assuming that he loves Louisa) and what Mary cannot explain (that he does not see her, and plans to go away). Finally, we hear that Benwick will not accompany him.

The narrative, then, leads us to speculate about Wentworth's motives in the same way that Anne does, and the news is suggestive: he may no longer be attached to Louisa. Now let us examine the role of Captain Benwick in this scene, again considering the context as if we were first-time readers.

Anne meets Benwick at Lyme. He is apparently grief-stricken. They do not expect to see him in the evening, but 'he ventured among them again'; Anne finds that 'though shy, he did not seem reserved' but that he had 'feelings glad to burst their usual restraints'. When they walk on the Cobb, 'Anne found Captain Benwick getting near her', and later, 'Anne found Captain Benwick again drawing near her' (these quotations are drawn from pp. 121–9). The portrait of this mourning officer is gently satirical: he is not shy and broken-hearted after Fanny Harville's death, but eager to find a new object for his affections.

When we come to Chapter 14, we hear two items of news about him. First, he accepted an invitation to Uppercross, then suddenly and with an embarrassed manner changed his mind. Charles interprets this as love and shyness about Anne, but his guess does not fit what we know of Benwick. He has not shown any shyness about Anne – indeed he has rather put himself forward. Second, he refuses an invitation to accompany Captain Wentworth to Plymouth. Charles again misinterprets, and contradicts himself in the process (if Benwick is 'disposed to ride over to Kellynch' all the way from Lyme, how can he be too shy to come to Uppercross, only three miles away?).

In short, these speculations about Benwick are not to be taken seriously. The entire portrait of this melancholy enthusiast for sentimental verse prepares for the comic transformation of Louisa into 'a person of literary taste, and sentimental reflection' (p. 178), one of the funniest outcomes of the crucial bang on the head.

Yet Anne does allow Benwick to occupy her mind. When she is alone and indulging her reflections, her mind turns to him. Indeed, she could not 'return from any stroll of solitary indulgence' without wondering about him. The final part of our extract adopts an ironic, teasing tone which again highlights the insignificance of Benwick in Anne's life: he (with sententious inversion) 'came not'; Either he was 'less disposed' than Charles 'imagined', or 'he was too shy'. At the end of a week, Lady Russell gives up thinking about him. This extract, then, ridicules the speculation about Benwick in two ways: first, Charles is a bad advocate, being unperceptive and illogical. Second, Jane Austen treats Benwick with indulgent, teasing comedy. Yet Anne fills her mind with wondering about him. Why? Clearly, her anxiety about Wentworth disturbs and pains her; and she is frightened of allowing her hopes to rise. Yet, in her helpless dependent position, separated from the Lyme scene, she must think and pass the time – particularly the time when she is alone. So, her mind fills with Benwick, a convenient, non-threatening substitute for the speculations about Captain Wentworth that she dare not encourage.

This is a thoroughly believable description of the state of Anne's inner feelings. What is remarkable is the subtle economy and unobtrusiveness of Jane Austen's narrative. In the case of this extract, we have drawn our conclusions by connecting several strands of Anne's experience over four chapters, and by noticing subtle effects of style (such as the alteration to sentence structure between the third and fourth sentences; the extra *frisson* of anxiety conveyed by 'hazarded'; or the teasing tone of the final sentence). All that has actually happened is that Anne's thoughts have smoothly turned from Wentworth to Benwick, and it is only the complex, fully integrated magic of Jane Austen's technique that enables us – even as we read the passage for the first time – to feel that we understand the heroine: we are led to 'sense' the complex, almost subconscious process of her mind, as we read.

It is typical of Jane Austen that her characterisation is lightly touched in, in this way: she is reticent about complexities in her heroines' psychology, and leaves us to make use of the whole narrative context as well as constant subtle shifts of style. So, she creates natural psychological effects, and only openly delves beneath her character's conscious experience very rarely. We often 'sense' the character long before we 'understand'.

Reticence about character is, of course, an aid to irony of outcome. In Chapter 14 of *Persuasion*, for example, Jane Austen buries her clues about Benwick quietly, behind the deafening quarrels of Charles and Mary, bickering about Benwick and his motives. Most readers do not realise until much later in the novel, that their news was revealing: he twice refused tempting invitations, preferring to stay with Louisa. Such subtle ironic effects exploit the deceptive surface of reality, and the difficulty of perceiving truth.

We drew conclusions about a central 'duality' in the world of Jane Austen's novels, from studying Elizabeth and Emma. We suggested that both heroines are confronted by the issue of marriage, in the form of an unresolved conflict between romance and materialism. In both cases, we can build a more detailed sense of this fundamental dilemma from a general knowledge of the novels. In *Pride and Prejudice*, Darcy and Wickham present, respectively, upright respectable principle with social solidity, and charming but shallow attractions covering a lack of principles. In *Emma*, Mr Knightley and Frank Churchill present a similar contrast; while in our extract the qualities of sensible caution and materialism are identified with masculinity, and those of strong passion and emotional sensitivity sufficient to overthrow caution, are ascribed to the 'feminine' character. So, the dilemma of **romance vs. materialism** is part of a wider debate in the novels, which encompasses many aspects of character and behaviour, and presents in broad terms two opposed approaches to the pursuit of goodness and happiness.

Can we develop our understanding of these crucial themes further, after studying the characters of Fanny Price (*Mansfield Park*) and Anne Elliot (*Persuasion*)?

Our extract from *Mansfield Park* led us to appreciate Fanny's terror of a lively, charming but dangerous new influence – the fashionable new ways of London which are represented by the Crawfords. She resolutely defends values of principle and moral rectitude, and fights the beguiling attractions of fashion with every means in her power. The extract we studied reveals the hard selfishness of her triumph: her delight when the opposing army stabs itself, and the battle is won. In these ways the extract, and Fanny's character, illuminate the theme of conflict between the new self-indulgence, and the old values of virtue and principle.

In *Persuasion*, our extract focused on Anne's fear of hoping too much. Captain Wentworth has valued decisive courage above other qualities. We can think of Louisa's thoughtless, headstrong pursuit of sensation as similar to the careless dash of the Crawfords' life; while Anne hopes that Wentworth will learn to value flexibility and compromise. She feels that she is beginning to win the argument, that he must now begin to value 'a persuadable temper'. Again, the conflict is between considerate thoughtfulness and care on the one side; and a thoughtless, headstrong attitude to life on the other.

Central dualities of meaning are indicated by Jane Austen's exploration of these conflicts. We must beware of drawing conclusions too firmly, however. Anne Elliot may wish Wentworth to distinguish between obstinacy and courage, as we observed; but she deeply regrets her caution of eight years ago: she wishes she had taken a risk. The major conflicts in Jane Austen's works are *dualities*, then: attitudes that clash constantly, but cannot be resolved. There are truth and right, absurdity and error, on both sides.

## Conclusions

1.  Jane Austen's characterisation is present in the narrative in continuously observed detail. We can use the techniques developed in Chapter 1 to analyse characters. In particular, look for changes in the style of language, the 'voice' of the narrative and its point of view. Characters are also often portrayed through their distinctive style of speech. This can be analysed in the same way as a narrative passage, looking for what it reveals about the character's cast of mind.

2.  Jane Austen's characters are structured to form an integrated group, so each person we meet illuminates the others. We noticed that Harriet's presence in *Emma* provokes revelation of the heroine's character. In particular, notice how **subordinate characters illuminate the heroine**, and look for **parallel characters** or foils (for example, in *Emma*, Jane Fairfax acts as a foil to highlight the characteristics of Emma herself; in *Mansfield Park* Edmund Bertram and Henry Crawford are set in structural contrast to each other).

3.  **Social events** are structured so that characters are narrowly observed from several different points of view, by others; while they in their turn are also observed. Dialogues before, during and after each social event offer alternative interpretations of behaviour. The reader sifts and analyses these in order to arrive at an assessment.

4.  Studying extracts has enabled us to make more complex deductions about the **psychological dimension** of character. We have found that characters suppress their

own thoughts (Elizabeth) and their own feelings (Emma, Fanny Price); we can detect when the character substitutes an artificial feeling, or a false explanation, for a deeper feeling they do not realise themselves (Elizabeth, Emma). Characters live vicariously through others or project others into their own circumstances (Emma); and rationalisations attempt to explain away something deeper (Elizabeth's conclusion that 'vanity' was her folly, not love). Additionally, we have encountered surprising changes or gaps in memory or logic (Elizabeth's reordered memories of Darcy and Wickham in *Pride and Prejudice*; Anne's acceptance of the illogical case for Benwick's attachment in *Persuasion*).

The densely argued rationalisation of speeches and behaviour, and the intensity of speculation within the narrow society Jane Austen depicts, provoke the reader to explore omissions, illogic and contradictions. These reveal unstated undercurrents, which we have called a 'subtext' because it is something we 'read' metaphorically, between the lines of the text. It is the very presence of so much detail and reasoning, that draws our attention to omissions and absences of logic so strongly.

## Methods of Analysis

Three particular approaches have proved fruitful in our analyses of extracts in this chapter:

- First, notice words which convey stronger emotion than is justified by the event, or emotion that is inappropriate to the circumstances. For example, we noticed that Emma felt 'dread' at the thought of Harriet encountering Mr Martin while she was out; we noticed that Fanny sought 'instant annihilation' before knowing the true horror of Maria's elopement, and was 'exquisitely happy' afterwards. When you come across a word which stands out as charged with excessive emotion, think about where the emotion comes from and what it stands for. This will often lead you to conclude that the character's feelings are hidden in some way – they are suppressed, or redirected, or they belong somewhere else.

- Second, use deductive reasoning to analyse the character's thoughts, emotions and actions. Identify their self-contradictions, and incongruous elements and gaps in the way they explain things to themselves. It is helpful to create a bare summary of the character's situation. In the case of Elizabeth in *Pride and Prejudice*, for example, our summary threw up a startling question: why does she change her mind? It is also helpful to look back at what the reader already knows, and compare this to the interpretation you are studying. For example, we rejected Charles's theory that Benwick was too shy to come to Kellynch, because we remembered that Benwick was the opposite of shy when they were at Lyme.

- Third, always be critically aware when the subject-matter changes. It is worth questioning each shift in the narrative focus, particularly when the narratorial viewpoint is that of the heroine. In *Persuasion*, for example, we noticed how Benwick takes the place of Wentworth in Anne Elliot's thoughts, and this led us to understand the defensive process in her mind; while in *Emma* we noticed how Emma transfers negative feelings from inside (herself) to outside (Harriet). Jane Austen's novels are crafted in exquisite detail. The author motivates each subtle shift or move of her narrative. So, there is always a reason why a new subject is begun or an existing subject curtailed, in the character's mind.

## Suggested Work

Choose a passage from the novel(s) you are studying, in which a discussion takes place involving the heroine and the hero. Analyse their discussion and the narrative closely, looking for its psychological 'subtext'. Use the methods suggested above, and in particular, think about their choices of subject or opinion, and any unexpected or inappropriate responses. Here are suggested passages to study, one from each novel:

- In *Pride and Prejudice*, look at pp. 77–80, when Elizabeth and Darcy dance together at Netherfield. Begin at 'When the dancing recommenced, however ...' and go as far as the end of their dance, at '... procured her pardon, and directed all his anger against another'.
- In *Emma*, study pp. 120–5, when Emma and Mr Knightley discuss Frank Churchill's failure to visit his father. Begin at 'She was the first to announce it to Mr Knightley ... ' and continue to the end of the chapter.
- In *Mansfield Park*, look at pp. 212–15, when Fanny visits Mary Crawford and is given a necklace to wear at the ball. Begin at 'Thursday was the day of the ball ...' and read to the end of the chapter (this extract does not involve the hero, Edmund; but makes a fascinating study when Fanny's thoughts and opinions are set against her actions; and when we think about the subject-matter).
- In *Persuasion*, try pp. 109–11, when Anne overhears Captain Wentworth and Louisa discussing the importance of determination. Begin at 'Anne, really tired herself, was glad to sit down ...' and read as far as '... which must give her extreme agitation'.

# 3

# Structure in Jane Austen's Novels

The 'structure' of a text is present in anything the author does to give a 'shape' to the reader's experience as they read. This is where we begin, by thinking about the text in a particular way, concentrating on the question of its 'shape', and how it is all fitted together. So, studying 'structure' means studying the way the author fits 'parts' of the text together, aiming to find out why she fits them together in that particular way.

A novel is made out of various different things – events, characters, themes and words. These 'parts' are like units, or building-bricks, and the novel is a structure built from them.

If we have fifty bricks, and we place them one on top of another, we end up with a very tall, thin 'structure'. If, on the other hand, we place them all next to each other, we end up with a very low, wide 'structure'. They are the same bricks, but the resulting structure is completely different. So, we focus on **how the author fits the parts together**, because this tells us what sort of building she intended to build, what sort of novel she intended to form.

Here is an example of 'structure' in characters, themes and setting in *Mansfield Park*. Reminding ourselves of these will make clear how the structures in a novel can be recognised and written about.

1. **Characters**. In *Mansfield Park* we can think of the main characters as falling into two groups: Sir Thomas, Edmund and Fanny stand for traditional principles; the

Crawfords, Maria, Julia, Tom and Yates, on the other hand, stand for a careless and fashionable, young generation's approach to life.

2. **Themes**. *Mansfield Park* explores two views of or attitudes to life. First, there is a traditional attitude which places a high value on moral principles, caution and balanced judgment. Second, there is a self-indulgent attitude, which is excited by new experiences, enjoys pleasures, and places a high value on effects – of shocking, unconventional ideas, of impressive performances, and of appearance. These two attitudes are 'built' into the novel.

   The idea that the characters can be thought of as belonging to two 'groups' is related to these themes. Sir Thomas, Edmund and Fanny all respect the conservative values, and think highly of moral principle. In the story as a whole, they seem to be natural allies, just as the other 'group' of the Crawfords, Maria, Julia, Tom and Yates, are allies in seeking lively diversion during the theatricals.

3. **Setting**. In *Mansfield Park*, the two groups of characters seem to represent the two themes, the old and the new. Places reinforce the same idea. So, Mansfield Park itself stands for the orderly virtues Sir Thomas believes in. In contrast to this, London is depicted as a dangerous place where people pursue pleasure, excitement and vanity.

We have described three elements in the structure of *Mansfield Park*. Notice that this comes from a particular way of thinking about the novel. We placed the characters in groups, Sir Thomas, Edmund and Fanny together. This is an *overall* judgment. Keep a distance from the text, and think about the whole novel: in the whole novel, is it generally true to say that Fanny, Edmund and Sir Thomas are, in the end, broadly on the same 'side'? Yes, it is. This distant surveying of the text as a whole is a vital stage in recognising 'structure', because it enables us to pass over distracting details and make an overall judgment.

For example, we know that Fanny has a bitter conflict with Sir Thomas, who is tyrannical when forcing her to accept Henry Crawford. If we only thought about that part of the story, we would not realise that Fanny and Sir Thomas belong in a 'group of characters' together. In the novel as a whole, on the other hand, she shares most of his beliefs; and ultimately he values her as a like-minded person. The more we think about it, the clearer this becomes. Sir Thomas does not come into conflict with Fanny because they disagree about moral principles, about life in general. They come into conflict because Sir Thomas does not recognise *Henry Crawford's disagreement* about moral principles. So Sir Thomas is temporarily on the wrong side, by mistake. Their conflict does not alter our *overall* judgment: they are essentially on the same side, even when in conflict.

Anything that adds a 'shape' to the way we read, can be recognised as a 'part' of the novel, by thinking in this overall way. In this chapter, we will demonstrate a number of approaches and techniques which help us to recognise, define and discuss significant 'parts' and relate these to the author's intentions.

## A Social Event

Think about *Pride and Prejudice* as a whole. What does the plot consist of? The plot consists of a series of social events: there are visits, dinners, walks and balls. Groups of characters meet, and the story moves on, during these social events. The plot is made up of many social events, so one of them is like a brick that builds the plot: one social event is a 'part' of the 'structure' of the plot. To study structure, therefore, we can examine how one social event fits into the novel as a whole.

Some social events are smaller, involving only two or three characters, and others are bigger. Now think of the whole plot, still keeping a distance from the text. Is there a big social event? Is there a social occasion that stands out, because it is a turning-point, a significant 'unit' in the string of occasions that is the plot? Yes: the Netherfield ball is big, because nearly all the characters are there. Is the Netherfield ball a 'turning-point', then? Yes. It seems to bring the first stage of the novel to an end. Several characters go away straight after the ball, so it is the last time the large group of characters we have come to know are all together in one place. The Netherfield ball is clearly an important 'part' of the plot, so we will look at the way it contributes to the novel's 'shape'.

The ball at Netherfield happens in Chapter 18 of *Pride and Prejudice*. First, how is it fitted into the novel? This question focuses our attention on before and after: how the narrative prepares for the ball, and how it is treated in retrospect.

The Netherfield ball is the major social event of the first phase of the novel. The author has prepared for it with some care. It is first mentioned on p. 12, when the fact that Mr Bingley 'talked of giving one [a ball] himself at Netherfield' is one item in a list of his amiable qualities ('he was lively and unreserved, danced every dance ...' and so on). On p. 40, Lydia has the 'assurance' to remind him of his promise, and Bingley graciously offers that – once Jane is well – Lydia can even name the day of the ball. On p. 49 Miss Bingley thinks her brother is not 'really serious' in planning a ball, and warns him that Darcy hates dancing. Bingley says that the ball 'is quite a settled thing'. Finally, on p. 74, 'Mr Bingley and his sisters came to give their personal invitation for the long-expected ball at Netherfield, which was fixed for the following Tuesday.'

What do these details tell us? First, Jane Austen prepares the event carefully. References to the ball are evenly spaced during the first seventy pages, and it becomes steadily more likely. Second, Jane Austen uses these preparations to bring out the pleasantness of Mr Bingley. He gives a gracious response to Lydia's nagging, and dismisses his sister's – and implicitly Darcy's – objections, with good humour. Structurally, this helps us to understand that the novelist has created a relationship between character and events: the ball – an event in the story – is an expression of the benevolence we find in Bingley – a character. The author has joined these two aspects of the novel together.

What expectations are raised about the ball? All of the female Bennets find the prospect 'extremely agreeable' (p. 74), and the author reports their hopes in order of age, except for Mary, whose pompous remarks are kept to the end. Mr Collins also gives his opinion. By the time the ball is imminent, many expectations have been revealed. Mr Collins, Elizabeth, Jane and Mr Bingley all wish to further their courtships. Mrs Bennet hopes that Jane and Mr Collins will further their courtships. Additionally, Elizabeth looks forward to confirming that Wickham is right in his quarrel with Darcy. So there is an expectation that a great deal will happen at the Netherfield ball, and the reader is on tenterhooks to discover the outcome. What will the ball do? Bingley might propose. Elizabeth might snub Mr Collins. Wickham and Darcy might quarrel openly. The reader knows that Darcy is increasingly bewitched by Elizabeth: will he express his feelings at the ball?

We can also think about the grouping of characters. The largest gathering that has happened in the novel so far, was the Meryton assembly in Chapter 3, when all except Mr Bennet were present. Since then, Mr Collins and Wickham have arrived in the neighbourhood. Now everybody (including Mr Bennet) will be in company together. In the sense that it brings the whole neighbourhood together, then, the ball is an important prospect.

The actual event is a matter of complex irony. Notice that most of our excitement beforehand centres on what the event will *reveal*. We expect that feelings and hopes which have remained implicit up to then, will be revealed on a major social occasion. The irony is that this happens, but not in the way we expect. Nothing is revealed *to* the Bennets, but a great deal is revealed *by* them. So, Wickham does not turn up; Bingley, Jane and Mr Collins do nothing to further courtship; and Darcy does not betray his guilt. All of these expectations are disappointed. Instead, we receive a shock: Mrs Bennet, Lydia, Mary and Mr Bennet all display their stupidity or coarseness. Elizabeth notices this at the time, thinking that her family could not have been more embarrassing had they 'made an agreement to expose themselves as much as they could during the evening' (pp. 85–6).

We can say, then, that the 'structure' of this event comments on expectations. It does so by disappointing the characters' hopes (for example, the absence of Wickham scotches Elizabeth's plan for 'the conquest of all that remained unsubdued of his heart' [p. 76]); and by surprising us with revelations we did not expect.

Why did we not expect the Bennets to make fools of themselves? After all, we are familiar with Mrs Bennet's, Lydia's and Mary's stupidities, and Mr Bennet's contemptuous insults to his family, before the ball takes place. We feel that we *should have known* what would happen at the ball. The answer is that we were not thinking about those elements of the novel. Jane Austen carefully channelled our expectations, focusing our attention on to the fascination of the love stories, and the mysterious hatred between Darcy and Wickham. We were preoccupied, just as Elizabeth was, so we did not see ahead clearly. The analysis above shows how carefully Jane Austen prepared this effect for the reader. We conclude, then, that the plotted structure of the Netherfield ball shows how short-sighted people's expectations are: reality is complex and unpredictable, and an individual's viewpoint is necessarily narrow.

Now we can turn our attention to what happens after the ball. The first sentence of Chapter 19 announces a change: the relationships we have been following are about to be cut off short: 'The next day opened a new scene at

Longbourn' (p. 88). This effect of a sudden rupture in the plot is confirmed by what follows. Mr Collins proposes to Lizzie and she rejects him; Bingley, and the next day the rest of the Netherfield group, leave for London; and Mr Collins becomes engaged to Charlotte. These events occur in quick succession.

The immediate aftermath of the ball, then, suggests that it was unimportant after all – the Bennets unexpectedly exposed themselves to ridicule, but *nothing happened*. Jane Austen delays this information until Chapters 35 and 36, when Darcy's letter describes 'the evening of the dance at Netherfield' (p. 162), and Elizabeth recalls 'the circumstances ... at the Netherfield ball' (p. 171), agreeing with Darcy's view of them. In fact, the ball was a crucial event because it provoked Darcy to interfere and put a halt to Bingley's courtship. In conclusion, then, Jane Austen seems to have plotted the aftermath of the Netherfield ball to emphasise how difficult it is to recognise an important change when it occurs, without the benefit of hindsight.

Let us summarise. We expect great things from the ball. Nothing seems to happen. Later, we realise that vital events did happen at the ball. We can call this manipulation of the reader's expectations an 'ironic structure'. What is its purpose? It seems that we are twice taken in by an author who holds a longer view than ourselves. It can be helpful to list the reader's thoughts at different points in the story, to make clear how the author manipulates us:

1.  We expect something important to happen at the ball.
2.  Nothing important happens at the ball.
3.  Something very important did happen at the ball, but it was not what we expected.

The 'shape' or **structure** of this ironic technique, where Jane Austen plays a double-bluff on the reader, is repeatedly found in *Pride and Prejudice*. For example, the first sentence of the novel is:

It is a truth universally acknowledged, that a single man in possession of a good fortune must be in want of a wife.

(*Pride and Prejudice*, p. 5)

This 'truth' sounds ridiculous. The author is clearly being ironic, mocking the silly ideas of neighbourhood gossips who are obsessed by courtship and marriage, like Mrs Bennet. The reader is encouraged to feel superior to such simple-minded people. The end of the novel, on the other hand, undermines our feeling of superiority. The gossips may be silly, but on this occasion they were proved right. Mr Bingley, the 'single man in possession of a good fortune' was 'in want of a wife', and he marries Jane Bennet. Such structural ironies bring the reader down to earth, reminding us that being clever is not everything.

The Netherfield ball, then, is a unit which fits into the novel *Pride and Prejudice*. We have studied how Jane Austen joins it to before and how she joins it to after. We have found that both of the 'joins' are deceptive. Studying **structure** can lead us to conclusions, just as a quotation can. So, from looking at the Netherfield ball, we can deduce these philosophical statements: *truth is often simpler than we expect; but it is always different from what we expect, and often hidden from us at the time.*

## A Dialogue

We often talk about things in a story, or in a character, being 'on the surface', 'superficial', or 'underneath', 'hidden'. These words all suggest the idea that a story is built up in levels. It is like an object where we can see the top of it, but there are more levels beneath the 'surface'. This is a natural way to think about a text: we thought about characters in this way extensively, in Chapter 2. Different levels or layers in the story are different 'parts' which the author has fitted together to make the 'whole' story. Now we are studying structure, so we want to find out how the 'parts' fit together.

The levels or 'layers' in a story are different from parts of the plot, however. They are part of the novel's texture: they are there all the time. When we chose to study a social event in *Pride and Prejudice*, we had to think about the whole plot: we were thinking horizontally, because the plot is made of events which happen in a line, one after the other. We, as it were, thought along the line, looking for a big event. The 'layers' in the text, on the other hand, are there above and beneath each other, all the time. So, to think about them, we adjust our minds to think vertically: we look at any 'moment' in the horizontal story, and look up and down, analysing it into its constituent parts. We will look at a 'moment' from *Emma* in this way.

In Chapter 23, Emma meets Frank Churchill for the first time. He praises his stepmother, Mrs Weston, and Emma replies:

> 'You cannot see too much perfection in Mrs Weston, for my feelings,' said Emma; 'were you to guess her to be eighteen, I should listen with pleasure; but *she* would be ready to quarrel with you for using such words. Don't let her imagine that you have spoken of her as a pretty young woman.'
>
> 'I hope I should know better,' he replied; 'no, depend upon it, (with a gallant bow,) that in addressing Mrs Weston I should understand whom I might praise without any danger of being throught extravagant in my terms.'
>
> Emma wondered whether the same suspicion of what might be expected from their knowing each other, which had taken strong possession of her mind, had ever crossed his; and whether his compliments were to be considered as marks of acquiescence, or proofs of defiance. She must see more of him to understand his ways; at present she only felt they were agreeable.
>
> She had no doubt of what Mr Weston was often thinking about. His quick eye she detected again and again glancing towards them with a happy expression; and even, when he

might have determined not to look, she was confident that he was often listening.

(*Emma*, p. 160)

This extract is typical of many found in all of the novels: the conversation is carried on harmoniously, although we are aware of a number of ironies behind what people say. We want to sort out the different levels of the characters' motives at the time of the conversation, so we can gain an understanding of the 'shape' or structure of the scene. Using the idea of 'layers', we can begin by describing the first or 'top' layer of the dialogue: what the characters say to each other.

Frank Churchill and Emma agree that Mrs Weston looks young and pretty, and both compliment her. Then, Emma invokes Mrs Weston's modest opinion of herself. This leads Frank to say that Mrs Weston has a high opinion of Emma, and to imply that he shares that high opinion of her. The conversation seems banal and mutually complimentary, on the surface.

Now we can turn to the second layer in dialogue: the unspoken, but commonly understood, implications of what the characters say. Emma does love Mrs Weston, so her statement 'You cannot see too much perfection in Mrs Weston, for my feelings', is true. However, when she goes on to suggest that he could guess her to be '*eighteen*', Emma undercuts her own statement. The implied statement here is '*We both know that you are a flatterer – the truth is different.*' Emma urges him to keep this secret from Mrs Weston and his reply shows that he enters into the deception willingly. He says 'I hope I should know better'; but turns the joke back by pointing out that he can flatter Emma to Mrs Weston with impunity. Frank's compliment is double-edged, of course. The idea of him exaggerating his praise of Emma in order to please Mrs Weston is not gallant to Emma.

The top two layers of this dialogue – what they say, and the implications they both understand – suggests the conclusion that, whatever the characters say, they are doing something else. In this case, Emma and Frank Churchill appear to be discussing Mrs Weston (surface layer). Really, however, they are agreeing to be pleasantly insincere with each other (unspoken implication).

The third layer is what the characters are thinking about, while they talk. Emma's thoughts are given in the third paragraph. She is preoccupied by 'what might be expected from their knowing each other' (that is, that they will fall in love and marry), and is aware of Mr Weston 'often thinking about' the same thing. Frank is also aware of his father's expectations; but he is thinking about using these expectations to cover his real relationship with Jane Fairfax. Both of the characters, then, are thinking about something different from the subject of their conversation; and their thoughts are different from each other's.

The fourth layer is less definite, and consists of the deeper, possibly hidden emotions occurring within the character at the time of the conversation. It arises from what we know about the character from our overall understanding of the book. For example, Emma detects that Frank is insincere, yet she is persistently pleased by what he says. Why? We know that she wishes to like him for two reasons: to please the Westons, and to spite Mr Knightley (she has argued with him about Frank). These factors influence Emma's feelings during their conversation, so they are part of the fourth layer.

We also know that Emma avoids the issues of love and marriage. She realises that Frank is insincere, so flirting with him will be safe – it will not lead to anything serious. Unconsciously, then, this feeling may influence Emma in his favour. Also unconsciously, Emma loves Mr Knightley. She may sense that flirting with Frank will provoke Mr Knightley's jealousy (Mr Knightley is certainly jealous of Frank, and Emma does provoke him elsewhere, so this is a reasonable deduction). This gives her a further unconscious motive to approve of Frank.

Frank Churchill is engaged in deliberate deception. His motives are to hide his attachment to Jane Fairfax. However, there is an implication that he enjoys manipulating and tricking others, which is put into words by Miss Fairfax herself in Chapter 54 when she is astonished that Frank can 'court' the memory of their misery (p. 393). So, both Emma and Frank seem to be motivated by feelings that are, again, different from the thoughts described in what we have called 'layer three' above.

Analysing the brief exchange between Emma and Frank Churchill, then, has enabled us to identify four separate 'layers' which exist in the story during their dialogue. The **first** or top layer consists of **what they say**. The **second** layer, unspoken beneath their words, is **the implication of what they say**. The **third** layer, separate from what they say, consists of **their thoughts and preoccupations during the conversation**; and we add the **fourth** layer by thinking about our overall understanding of the character, bringing in **feelings we know about** from other parts of the book, **which affect them at the time of the conversation**.

A noticeable characteristic of these 'layers' is that they bear so little relation to each other. In the case of Emma and Frank, we can summarise what we have found: *the* **first** *layer is a conversation about Mrs Weston; but the* **second** *layer shows that they are* **really** *discussing flattery and truth. The* **third** *layer shows that they are both* **really** *playing up to Mr Weston's expectations of them (and in Frank's case adding extra disguise to his duplicity), which is what is* **really** *on their minds. However, the* **fourth** *layer suggests that they are both deeply satisfied by their dialogue: Frank because practising deception excites him, and Emma because she is both provoking and avoiding her unconscious love for Mr Knightley; so they are* **really** *satisfying their deepest needs.*

Notice that each layer redefines what is happening between the characters, suggesting that as we delve more deeply, there is always something more, and something different, in process. In other words, the 'layers' of the conversation are joined together by irony.

However, the whole **structure** of interlocking layers we have found provokes a further conclusion: that this conversation, where the characters agree, is in fact filled with discord, misunderstanding and conflict to an extraordinary degree. The top two layers – what they say, and their tacit implications – are shared between them; but these are undercut by the third and fourth layers which emphasise the gulf between them, their isolation from each other.

So Jane Austen constructs the situation upon a series of ironic discrepancies between speech, thought and feeling. This emphasises the brittle superficiality of social harmony, exploring some of the author's major themes – the distinction between appearance and reality, the difficulty of perceiving reality, and the gap between language and reality.

One of the most interesting effects of Jane Austen's method, is the emphasis it places upon omission. The world Jane Austen creates in her novels is elaborately fitted together from many 'parts', such as the layers we have described in Frank's and Emma's conversation, so the novel's world has structure or 'shape'. Therefore, when part of the expected shape is left blank, our attention is alerted and we seek to fill the empty space. A clear example of this effect occurs in *Pride and Prejudice*. Elizabeth displays critical alertness in her discussions of character with Mr Darcy in Chapters 10 and 11. This quality of her character is not present in her conversation with Wickham in Chapter 16. The *absence* of Elizabeth's critical insight, in Chapter 16, is noticed by the reader.

The method we have used in analysing this relatively unimportant conversation from *Emma*, can be applied to most of the verbal exchanges in Jane Austen's novels.

## Structure in Themes

Our third study of structure focuses on *Mansfield Park*. This time we are thinking of major themes as 'parts' which are built into the novel. To begin with, we think about the whole novel to identify major themes. Then we turn to part of the text, examining how these themes or 'parts' of the novel are fitted into the narrative. We will study the themes of the old (conservative authority) and the new (lively self-indulgence and vanity) in a passage from Chapter 17 – at the height of the amateur theatricals at Mansfield:

'I rather wonder Julia is not in love with Henry,' was her [*Mrs Grant's*] observation to Mary.

'I dare say she is,' replied Mary, coldly. 'I imagine both sisters are.'

'Both! no, no, that must not be. Do not give him a hint of it. Think of Mr Rushworth!'

'You had better tell Miss Bertram to think of Mr Rushworth. It may do *her* some good. I often think of Mr Rushworth's property and independence, and wish them in other hands – but I never think of *him*. A man might represent the county with such an estate; a man might escape a profession and represent the county.'

'I dare say he *will* be in Parliament soon. When Sir Thomas comes, I dare say he will be in for some borough, but there has been nobody to put him in the way of doing any thing yet.'

'Sir Thomas is to achieve many mighty things when he comes home,' said Mary, after a pause. 'Do you remember Hawkins Browne's address to Tobacco, in imitation of Pope? – "Blest leaf, whose aromatic gales dispense to Templars modesty, to Parsons sense." I will parody them. Blest Knight! whose dictatorial looks dispense, to Children affluence, to Rushworth sense. Will not that do, Mrs Grant? Every thing seems to depend upon Sir Thomas's return.'

'You will find his consequence very just and reasonable when you see him in his family, I assure you. I do not think we do so well without him. He has a fine dignified manner, which suits the head of such a house, and keeps every body in their place. Lady Bertram seems more of a cypher now than when he is at home; and nobody else can keep Mrs Norris in order. But, Mary, do not fancy that Maria Bertram cares for Henry. I am sure *Julia* does not, or she would not have flirted as she did last night with Mr Yates; and though he and Maria are very good friends, I think she likes Sotherton too well to be inconstant.'

'I would not give much for Mr Rushworth's chance, if Henry stepped in before the articles were signed.'

'If you have such a suspicion, something must be done; and as soon as the play is all over, we will talk to him seriously, and make him know his own mind; and if he means nothing, we will send him off, though he is Henry, for a time.'

Julia *did* suffer, however, though Mrs Grant discerned it not, and though it escaped the notice of many of her own family likewise. She had loved, she did love still, and she had all the suffering which a warm temper and a high spirit were likely to endure under the disappointment of a dear, though irrational hope, with a strong sense of ill-usage. Her heart was sore and angry, and she was capable only of angry consolations. The sister with whom she was used to be on easy terms, was now become her greatest enemy; they were alienated from each other, and Julia was not superior to the hope of some distressing end to the attentions which were still carrying on there, some punishment to Maria for conduct so shameful towards herself, as well as towards Mr Rushworth. With no material fault of temper, or difference of opinion, to prevent their being very good friends while their interests were the same, the sisters, under such a trial as this, had not affection or principle enough to make them merciful or just, to give them honour or compassion. Maria felt her triumph, and pursued her purpose careless of Julia; and Julia could never see Maria distinguished by Henry Crawford, without trusting that it would create jealousy, and bring a public disturbance at last.

Fanny saw and pitied much of this in Julia; but there was no outward fellowship between them. Julia made no communication, and Fanny took no liberties. They were two solitary sufferers, or connected only by Fanny's consciousness.

(*Mansfield Park*, pp. 133–5)

The broad conflict between old and new, between moral principles and selfish gratification, which is exemplified throughout the novel is a dominant theme of this chapter. It opens with Tom's and Maria's triumph because Edmund has abandoned 'moral elevation', giving in to the 'force of selfish inclinations' (both p. 131). The self-absorption of most of the characters is shown also. Henry Crawford 'had not cared enough' to persevere in charming Julia, and was shortly 'too busy with his play' to pay attention. Mrs Grant was displeased by their quarrel, but 'as it was not a matter which really involved her happiness' she soon became equally involved in the play (both p. 133). As the chapter proceeds, the characters retreat further and further from each other into their selfish concerns, and the impression of isolated individuals, wrapped up in their private pleasures or sufferings, grows.

How does our extract develop these themes? We can divide it into three parts. The first concerns Mr Rushworth, and emphasises his vacuity. As Mary says, 'I often think of Mr Rushworth's property and independence, and wish them in other hands – but I never think of *him*.' She and Mrs Grant then discuss the public role Mr Rushworth might play: the position that should go with owning a large estate. The second part focuses on Sir Thomas, including Mary's observations on his importance, and Mrs Grant's description of his 'consequence'. Finally, Jane Austen returns to the question of Julia's and Maria's mutual jealousy.

The discussion of Mr Rushworth distinguishes between property and character, and Mary ridicules the system that would put him in Parliament: even the 'mighty' Sir Thomas cannot give him 'sense'. She implies that there is something wrong in a system that relies on Sir Thomas alone to perform improbable miracles. Countering this, Mrs Grant asserts that Sir Thomas is a fitting head of family. His position is 'just and reasonable', and he 'keeps every body in their place'. His influence defines the existence of those who are under his patronage: for example, Lady Bertram's existence seems to have more meaning when he is present, but in his absence she is a 'cypher'. So, we are given an ambiguous picture of authority: it is either an artificial position, occupied by a fool (Mr Rushworth); or a solid influence which orders the world and directs the lives of those under its authority (Sir Thomas).

The discussion of Julia and Maria that follows raises the idea of nature, and what nurture adds to it. The two sisters have been generously gifted by nature – there is 'no material fault of temper, or difference of opinion' between them, so they should be 'very good friends'. However, they lack sufficient 'affection or principle' to withstand the conflict of jealousy, and this brings discord and a breach between them.

So, the theme is built into this chapter in the form of a contrast between two emblematic characters – Mr Rushworth and Sir Thomas – and the resulting discussion of wider responsibilities and influence. Elsewhere in the chapter, Mansfield society falls apart into selfishness. The placing of a discussion of authority within a context of petty squabbles suggests that the disintegration of relationships in Mansfield itself, is part of a wider social malaise. In English society, where a man of authority can give purpose and consequence to weaker characters (as Sir Thomas does for Lady Bertram), it is also possible for a vacuous fool (Mr Rushworth) to represent 'the county'. In the absence of proper authority, people will become preoccupied with selfish pursuits, and social cohesion will break down. We deduce that society depends upon affection, which leads people to care enough about each other; and moral principle, which guides people to follow 'right' behaviour. Fanny's role as observer of this fissured and creaking social system, riven by conflict and unable to encompass change, is emphasised at the end of the extract. When social order breaks down, individuals suffer alone, and their common lot is 'connected only by Fanny's consciousness'.

It is clear that major themes are thoroughly integrated into the text in this chapter, then. The structure Jane Austen uses is one where minor individual events are related to greater matters. So, the theatricals are emblematic of the artificiality of appearances: people misrepresent themselves in order to pursue self-interest. The Mansfield party at this point lacks any authority, just as the country will lack authority if a corrupt Parliamentary system elects Mr Rushworth, and is ruled by property rather than sense, financial rather than true worth. The result of social breakdown will be discord, and isolated suffering.

Reading Chapter 17 of *Mansfield Park*, we have noticed a connection between events in the novel – which only concern the small circle of characters – and events on a national scale. This is a 'shape' or structure within the novel because the narrative is arranged so as to provoke parallel ideas on a larger scale, when, during the breaking-up of personal relationships at Mansfield, the author inserts a discussion of influence and Parliamentary position. Its effect can be likened to ripples from a stone thrown into a pool. A minor event in Mansfield Park is the stone, which immediately affects the immediate locality. So, in this chapter, Edmund's capitulation affects the mood of the other characters. However, our thoughts move out from this centre, like ripples, passing over Sir Thomas, Mr Rushworth, public influence, property, to society as a whole.

## Linguistic Structure

In Jane Austen's novels there is something we can call a 'verbal structure', consisting of words and phrases which recur, either repeated in a different context, or in different mouths, or slightly modified. This structure in the language of the text is what we will focus on, taking a speech from *Persuasion* as our starting-point. Anne Elliot is discussing constancy in men and women with Captain Harville:

'We certainly do not forget you, so soon as you forget us. It is, perhaps, our fate rather than our merit. We cannot help ourselves. We live at home, quiet, confined, and our feelings prey upon us. You are forced on exertion. You have always a profession, pursuits, business of some sort or other, to take you back into the world immediately, and continual occupation and change soon weaken impressions.'

(*Persuasion*, p. 236)

This time we want to study 'parts' or 'units' in the language, so we begin by selecting words and phrases that seem to carry particular importance. In this passage the word 'forget' is important – Anne uses it twice. We will focus on 'forget', then, including its other forms. We now have to look elsewhere to see whether we can establish definite links between the language Anne uses here, and language used elsewhere.

'Forget' is our first focus. Anne is replying to Captain Harville's exclamation that his sister would not have 'forgotten' Benwick so soon. This is the immediate context in which Anne talks of men who 'forget' and women who cannot. Soon afterwards, Captain Wentworth returns having 'forgotten' his gloves (p. 239) which is ironically a sign that he has remembered his love. He tells Anne five pages later, 'he had meant to forget her, and believed it to be done' but had been 'constant unconsciously' (p. 244). Earlier in the novel, forgetting and recollection are referred to several times. One example is Anne's thought that Wentworth's look, just after Louisa's accident, 'could never be forgotten by her' (p. 132), clearly because she believes him to be in love with Louisa. Later in the novel we learn that Anne misinterpreted his look. Wentworth had suddenly understood the 'perfect excellence' of Anne, while he felt bound to the inferior Louisa. So, Anne will remember his look, but ironically, for different reasons from those she imagined at the time. 'Forget' and its other forms, then, is a word that appears repeatedly in the novel.

Returning to the speech we started with, Anne said that 'we certainly do not forget you [men]'. Connecting this with her vivid memory of Wentworth's look after the accident, complicates her statement: women may remember men, but still not understand them. This effect is very subtle. It works on a half-conscious level, as if we hear an echo of the earlier 'forgotten' when Anne uses the word 'forget' twice. The second time she uses 'forget' is in saying that men 'forget' women. This idea is quickly elaborated by Wentworth's forgetting: his gloves, and also trying to forget Anne. Her statement about men is therefore also complicated by the reappearance of the word. Perhaps men do not 'forget' women so soon, but manage to put things out of their minds more easily because their lives are more full of 'exertion' and 'occupation'.

The links between words we have analysed here create a very subtle effect. Some 'verbal structure' in Jane Austen's novels is much more noticeable. In *Pride and Prejudice*, for example, the word 'gentleman' appears at crucial moments: Elizabeth says that Darcy, when he first proposed, was not 'gentlemanlike'; Darcy quotes her 'gentlemanlike' back to her, after they are engaged; and Elizabeth uses it in refuting Lady Catherine de Bourgh's snobbery: 'He is a gentleman; I am a gentleman's daughter.' The repeated use of 'gentleman' develops the word's meaning and significance: it eventually stands for all the good qualities Darcy has learned from his experiences.

## The Analysis of Plot

We have looked at 'parts' of the language of the text, which recur. The same happens with 'parts' of the plot, and analysing parallel scenes in the plot of a novel provides rewarding insights.

First, we need to define the 'part' of the story we want to study. This 'part' may be a social event, a conversation, a chapter, or even just a single paragraph describing the heroine's state of mind. Whatever it is, we can choose and define a 'part' of the novel simply on the basis that it seems to be a 'unit' which contributes to the way the book is built. If we use our common sense to define this 'part' of the structure in the first place, we are likely to find comparable 'parts' elsewhere in the text.

When we have selected a part of the novel to focus on, we describe what it does, or what kind of a part it is. It is still of vital importance to think analytically, however: there is a danger that this kind of analysis will degenerate into merely retelling the story. Our aim is the opposite of this – we aim to highlight the bare skeleton of the book, ignoring the covering of everyday events and minor details in the story. To illustrate the approach to use, we will look at Chapter 47 of *Emma*.

What kind of a unit is this chapter? Now we want to make clear, short statements that describe the chapter. We should formulate statements which say what the chapter is, and avoid telling the story of what happens in it. Here are two such statements:

1.  It is a conversation between Emma and Harriet, about Harriet's romantic hopes.
2.  A character [Emma] has to comfort and cushion another [Harriet] in the face of bad news [Frank Churchill and Jane Fairfax are engaged].

These two statements, then, describe the kind of unit Chapter 47 is. Now turn them into questions asking about comparable units in the rest of the text. The first statement turns into: are there any other conversations between Emma and Harriet concerning Harriet's romantic hopes? Yes, there are several, and we can list them:

● Chapter 4: Emma disparages Mr Martin
● Chapter 7: Emma writes Harriet's reply to his proposal
● Chapter 9: Emma interprets Mr Elton's charade for Harriet

- Chapter 17: Emma tells Harriet about Mr Elton
- Chapter 21: They discuss Harriet's chance meeting with the Martins
- Chapter 31: Emma advises Harriet to think less about Mr Elton
- Chapter 40: Harriet tells Emma that she loves someone else

The final scene of this kind is Chapter 47. Now, can we draw any conclusions from this list, about the way the novel's plot works? Two points stand out. First, that there is a series of such scenes, and they occur fairly regularly. For example, Harriet's chance meeting with the Martins, and the Eltons' marriage, provide occasions for scenes between Emma and Harriet even during the middle section of the novel, when Harriet has no active romantic plans, and when Emma is less concerned with Harriet's love-life. So, discussions of romance between the two girls are a recurrent part of the book's structure, and Jane Austen maintains their regularity throughout.

Second, the initiative passes from Emma to Harriet. So, Emma initiates their discussions in Chapters 4, 7, 9 and 17; in Chapters 21 and 31, Harriet initiates the scene, but her demand is in the form of distress to which Emma responds. In Chapters 40 and 47, however, Harriet starts the scenes herself, with an announcement. So, we can see that this series of scenes demonstrates the steady transfer of energy in the relationship from Emma to Harriet.

Our second statement about Chapter 47 turns into the question: are there other scenes where a character has to comfort another in the face of bad news?

We do not have to look far for comparable scenes. Emma herself thinks it 'almost ridiculous, that she should have the very same distressing and delicate office to perform by Harriet, which Mrs Weston had just gone through by herself' (p. 332). The Westons are anxious about their news, believing Emma to be in love with Frank. Now, Emma is anxious, believing Harriet to be in love with Frank. In Chapter 49, Mr

Knightley is anxious, believing Emma to be in love with Frank; and in a parody of these scenes in Chapter 54, Mr Knightley makes heavy weather of revealing Harriet's engagement to Mr Martin, believing that Emma will take it badly. So, we see that the revelation of bad news and comforting the upset, make a repeated motif at this point in the plot.

The motif is handled in a variety of different styles. In Chapter 46, the accent is upon Emma's alarm; and Jane Austen uses the opportunity to give Emma some of the most powerful lines she speaks in the novel, prophetically heralding her emotional self-discovery in the following chapter: 'Which of them is it? I charge you by all that is sacred – not to attempt concealment' (p. 324). Harriet's scene is completely different: she happily blurts out the news herself, creating a comic bathos just as Emma decides there is 'no chance' of her taking the news well (p. 332); unexpectedly, it is Emma who waits 'in great terror' (p. 333) as Harriet reveals her love for Mr Knightley. The final two revelations gently satirise Mr Knightley, and they are daring strokes by Jane Austen. We will look at the last one first. Here we find that even the perfect gentleman Mr Knightley can enjoy giving bad news, when it proves that he was right all along: Emma accuses him of 'trying not to smile' and he is described 'composing his features' before delivering the dreaded news about Harriet's engagement to Robert Martin (both p. 385). However, when Mr Knightley has to comfort Emma, supposing her to be heartbroken, he is sincere and deeply moved; yet there is the slightest hint of absurdity in the scene, heightened by his dramatic actions and clichéd turn of phrase:

> she found her arm drawn within his, and pressed against his heart, and heard him thus saying, in a tone of great sensibility, speaking low, 'Time, my dearest Emma, time will heal the wound...'
>
> (*Emma*, p. 349)

It is only in the context of our knowledge – that he is completely wrong – that the melodrama of this writing becomes amusing. It is a measure of Jane Austen's exact control of her material, however, that she can succeed in making fun of her hero at this crucial moment.

Chapter 47 is therefore one of a series of scenes where people prepare to cushion and comfort others in the face of upsetting news. The author varies the styles and outcomes of these scenes, but we can see a clear link between them, because they have one point in common: none of the people who are supposed to need comforting, are at all upset about the item of news revealed. These scenes, then, comically highlight the misunderstandings and deceptions – deliberate and accidental – that have complicated the plot of *Emma*.

Analysing the plot, then, involves purposeful thinking about its shape, and the connections between units the novel is built from. Notice that the end of an investigation into plot structure, can often bring detailed textual analysis, and focus on selected quotations; but the process does not begin close to the text – it begins by observing the text from a distance, seeing the quite sizeable 'units' which, when put together, make up the 'whole' novel.

## Conclusions

1.  Jane Austen 'shaped' the patterns and parallels within her novels, in great detail. Therefore, you can look at almost any 'part' of the novel you are studying, and analyse its **structural** place and function. In this chapter, we have focused on structure in social events (*Pride and Prejudice*), dialogue (*Emma*), themes (*Mansfield Park*) and language (*Persuasion*). We have also taken a part of *Emma*, and thought about its relation to other parts of the novel, analysing structure in the plot.

2.  The effect of this intricate shaping of each novel is to create a self-illuminating whole. Each 'unit' in the novel – whether a conversation, a chapter, or merely a reflective paragraph – throws light on, and is illuminated by, several other parts of the text.

3.  We have remarked the importance of omission in Jane Austen: the fullness of the novel's structures means that we can define gaps precisely: they are elements we expect, but which are absent from the narrative for the time being. Our example of this effect concerned the uncharacteristic lack of critical perception in Elizabeth Bennet when she heard Wickham's story (*PP*, Chapter 16).

4.  Points we have noticed in this chapter, added to conclusions from our first two chapters, begin to reveal central preoccupations common to all four novels. Jane Austen's **central themes** are beginning to become clear. It is now time to attempt a description of them.

### The serious/lively (vain) duality

This is still difficult to describe. The Netherfield ball in *Pride and Prejudice* shows the thoughtless behaviour of the Bennets in contrast to Darcy's quiet, critical eye. In *Emma*, Mr Knightley's sincerity and seriousness contrast with Emma's lively but irresponsible behaviour. In *Mansfield Park* the duality is well-defined, the theatrical party's short-term pleasures, as well as Mr Rushworth's vacuity, being strongly contrasted with Sir Thomas's solidity and Fanny's sympathy. In *Persuasion*, our extract in Chapter 1 contrasts the vanity of Sir Walter with the 'good principles and instruction' Lady Elliot and Lady Russell provide. Jane Austen seems to be constantly concerned with two approaches to life; her novels depict both the importance of serious, principled thought guiding behaviour, and the tempting attractions of a livelier, more careless form of behaviour whose aims are less principled and more short term.

## The duality of appearances and truth

There is a major concern with obtaining insight into the 'truth' of people and events in everything we have studied. Our analysis of characters and ironic structure shows that Jane Austen depicts a complex, even bewildering appearance, which needs to be minutely observed and thoughtfully analysed before any insight is obtained.

## A whole duality

A duality simply means an idea or group of ideas that is two-sided. It can often appear in the form of conflict, contrast or paradox. Thinking about the two dualities we have tentatively described above, suggests that they fit together to make a single concern in Jane Austen's novels: there seem to be two major forces at work. First, a serious and moral sense of right, which can be pompous, cruel and unjust; and in opposition to this, the excitement and cleverness of irony, amusement and manipulation, as well as vanity, stupidity and deception.

## Stability and change

Jane Austen is clearly concerned about the permanence of conservative values, and her novels explore the question of change, the adaptability of solid principles to new circumstances. This issue will be looked at in greater detail in Chapter 6.

## Methods of Analysis

1.  Focus on social events – whether merely meetings between two characters, or full-blown social occasions – and analyse (a) how Jane Austen prepares for them, and (b) the expectations characters have before the event. Then analyse the event itself, the outcome. Compare expectations with what actually happens. Often, social events overturn expectations or change the point of view. They emphasise that reality cannot be predicted, and is not understood at the time.

2.  Study conversational scenes. Identify the four 'layers' in characters' communication:

    i.   What the characters say
    ii.  What their conversation implies
    iii. What they are thinking about
    iv.  Other elements of character which affect their behaviour in the scene.

    Then define the ironies that exist between these different layers, and draw conclusions about characters and Jane Austen's intentions from understanding these ironies.

3.  Think about the major themes of the novel you are studying, then look for what is relevant to the themes, in an extract chosen for study. Trivial events in the novel are linked to wider discussions, broadening the themes. We likened this effect to the spreading circles of ripples from a small stone thrown into a pool.

4.  Pick out significant linguistic features in a passage. Look for other places in the text where the same linguistic features occur, to discover how Jane Austen uses echoes of language in different contexts to develop the significance of key words.

5.  When analysing the plot, summarise what kind of a 'unit' you have to focus on, then turn your definition into questions: are there other units of the same kind elsewhere in the novel? Finding other comparable

'units' will enable you to reach conclusions about the structural role, in the novel as a whole, of the part you are studying.

## Suggested Work

Choose any social event or gathering, and analyse it in the manner demonstrated in this chapter. For example, it would be rewarding to study the visit to Pemberley in Chapter 45 of *Pride and Prejudice*; the party to Box Hill in Chapter 43 of *Emma*; the party to Sotherton in Chapters 9 and 10 of *Mansfield Park*; or the concert in Bath, Chapter 20 of *Persuasion*.

You can begin by comparing expectations and what actually happens, as we did with the Netherfield ball from *Pride and Prejudice*. However, you can also gain practice at the other forms of analysis we have shown in this chapter: simply **choose an extract of dialogue** from the social event you are working on, and analyse its ironic layers as shown in our *Emma* extract. **Choose a major theme**, and analyse the way it is expounded in the narrative, as we did with *Mansfield Park*. **Pick out significant words and phrases**, those that seem to you to 'resonate' because they recur in the text, and research other places where they appear.

# 4

# Society

This chapter is about the society depicted in Jane Austen's novels. Our aim is to understand how the author presents the relation between the individual and society, and any general truths or conclusions about society itself, that the novels convey.

Jane Austen's novels are a special case in respect of the society they present. They focus almost exclusively on a narrow stratum of the upper-middle class in rural English settings, and their entire narrative interest is in the 'neighbourhood', made up of a few families of this class, and one or two professional people such as clergymen or naval officers, who visited each other on a regular basis. The style of social life is that of the end of the eighteenth century rather than the different forms of behaviour and social interaction that began to become the norm during the nineteenth century.

The narrowness of Jane Austen's subject is easy to demonstrate. In *Emma*, Miss Woodhouse makes charitable visits to the poor, taking Harriet Smith with her. On p. 75 we hear that 'they were now approaching the cottage'. The author tells us that Emma was 'very compassionate', gave relief 'with as much intelligence as good-will', and that this visit concerned 'sickness and poverty together'. At the end of the visit, Emma leaves the cottage 'with such an impression of the scene' that she remarks: 'I feel now as if I could think of nothing but these poor creatures all the rest of the day; and yet, who can say how soon it may all vanish from my mind?' Emma then twice says that the impression will stay with her; and stops for a last look at the 'outward

94

wretchedness of the place' which helps her to recall 'the still greater within'. However, within three lines 'Mr Elton was immediately in sight' and within another half-page Emma is thinking of charity as a breeding-ground of love between Harriet and the clergyman: 'to meet in a charitable scheme; this will bring a great increase of love on each side' (p. 76).

This episode dips its toe delicately into the dirty lives of the neighbourhood poor, but we notice two points: the author's viewpoint does not enter the cottage, so no description of a poorer way of life is allowed into the novel. Secondly, Emma's mind only briefly considers the poor family. The preoccupation with courtship, marriage and the social activities of her own class, that is her normal state of mind, is very quickly re-established. Jane Austen laughs at Emma's temporary social conscience; but it is a firm rule that the novels do not attempt to depict any other way of life outside that of the class to which Jane Austen herself belonged.

It can be argued that Fanny's visit to her family in Portsmouth, in *Mansfield Park*, is an exception to this rule. Certainly, the Prices' home is the poorest household Jane Austen describes in any of her novels. On the other hand, Mr Price is a naval officer and Mrs Price was a Miss Ward with seven thousand pounds. Their life is disorganised, and money is short, but they are – or have been – members of the 'visitable' class.

At the other end of the social scale are large landowners, or members of the minor aristocracy. Sir Thomas Bertram in *Mansfield Park*, Lady Catherine de Bourgh in *Pride and Prejudice*, and Sir Walter Elliot in *Persuasion*, are all from the baronet level. Mr Darcy and Mr Knightley are both large landowners from long-established families. However, we should remember that these are not the 'great' aristocracy, the 'upper' class of the nation: they are simply the longer-established of the upper-middle class; the country *gentry*, not the *nobility*.

Jane Austen famously described the narrowness of her subject-matter in a letter to her nephew Edward, in 1816:

> the little bit (two Inches wide) of Ivory on which I work with so fine a Brush, as produces little effect after much labour.[1]

We should therefore think of Jane Austen's aim in her novels, as similar to that of a painter of miniatures. She is conscious of the smallness of her subject, but works in close detail in order to produce a faithful representation. Clearly, this implies also that the artist in Jane Austen was satisfied by working in this way – that she saw a good artistic reason for concentrating so acutely on the faithful representation of such a small subject. Perhaps she felt that general truths are revealed just as clearly as a result of a narrow but deep exploration, as they are from any wider-ranging survey. We thought about this question in the last chapter: a trivial event in *Mansfield Park* (Edmund's decision to act) gives rise to implications about government and the structure of English society as a whole. We used the image of a stone thrown into a pool, with the ripples spreading outwards as the widening implications of significance from a trivial event.

*     *     *

We begin our analysis of the miniature world Jane Austen describes, with an extract from *Pride and Prejudice*. In Chapter 56 Lady Catherine de Bourgh arrives at Longbourn. She demands a walk in the garden with Elizabeth, and during the walk, demands a promise from Elizabeth that she will not attempt to marry Mr Darcy. Elizabeth refuses, and her ladyship is 'highly incensed':

> 'Obstinate, headstrong girl! I am ashamed of you! Is this your gratitude for my attentions to you last spring? Is nothing due to me on that score?

'Let us sit down. You are to understand, Miss Bennet, that I came here with the determined resolution of carrying my purpose; nor will I be dissuaded from it. I have not been used to submit to any person's whims. I have not been in the habit of brooking disappointment.'

'*That* will make your ladyship's situation at present more pitiable; but it will have no effect on *me*.'

'I will not be interrupted! Hear me in silence. My daughter and my nephew are formed for each other. They are descended, on the maternal side, from the same noble line; and, on the fathers', from respectable, honourable, and ancient, though untitled families. Their fortune on both sides is splendid. They are destined for each other by the voice of every member of their respective houses; and what is to divide them? The upstart pretensions of a young woman without family, connections, or fortune. Is this to be endured? But it must not, shall not be! If you were sensible of your own good, you would not wish to quit the sphere in which you have been brought up.'

'In marrying your nephew I should not consider myself as quitting that sphere. He is a gentleman; I am a gentleman's daughter: so far we are equal.'

'True. You *are* a gentleman's daughter. But who was your mother? Who are your uncles and aunts? Do not imagine me ignorant of their condition.'

'Whatever my connections may be,' said Elizabeth, 'if your nephew does not object to them, they can be nothing to *you*.'

'Tell me, once for all, are you engaged to him?'

Though Elizabeth would not, for the mere purpose of obliging Lady Catherine, have answered this question, she could not but say, after a moment's deliberation, 'I am not.'

Lady Catherine seemed pleased.

'And will you promise me never to enter into such an engagement?'

'I will make no promise of the kind.'

'Miss Bennet, I am shocked and astonished. I expected to find a more reasonable young woman. But do not deceive yourself into a belief that I will ever recede. I shall not go away till you have given me the assurance I require.'

'And I certainly *never* shall give it. I am not to be intimi-
dated into anything so wholly unreasonable. Your ladyship
wants Mr Darcy to marry your daughter; but would my giving
you the wished-for promise make *their* marriage at all more
probable? Supposing him to be attached to me, would *my*
refusing to accept his hand make him wish to bestow it on his
cousin? Allow me to say, Lady Catherine, that the arguments
with which you have supported this extraordinary application
have been as frivolous as the application was ill-judged. You
have widely mistaken my character, if you think I can be
worked on by such persuasions as these. How far your
nephew might approve of your interference in *his* affairs I
cannot tell; but you have certainly no right to concern yourself in mine. I must beg, therefore, to be importuned no
farther on the subject.'

'Not so hasty, if you please. I have by no means done. To all
the objections I have already urged, I have still another to add.
I am no stranger to the particulars of your youngest sister's
infamous elopement. I know it all; that the young man's marrying her was a patched-up business, at the expense of your
father and uncle. And is *such* a girl to be my nephew's sister?
Is *her* husband, who is the son of his late father's steward, to
be his brother? Heaven and earth – of what are you thinking?
Are the shades of Pemberley to be thus polluted?'

'You can *now* have nothing farther to say,' she resentfully
answered. 'You have insulted me in every possible method. I
must beg to return to the house.'

And she rose as she spoke. Lady Catherine rose also, and
they turned back. Her ladyship was highly incensed.

'You have no regard, then, for the honour and credit of my
nephew! Unfeeling, selfish girl! Do you not consider that a
connection with you must disgrace him in the eyes of everybody?'

'Lady Catherine, I have nothing further to say. You know my
sentiments.'

'You are, then, resolved to have him?'

'I have said no such thing. I am only resolved to act in that
manner which will, in my own opinion, constitute my happiness, without reference to *you*, or to any person so wholly
unconnected with me.'

'It is well. You refuse, then, to oblige me. You refuse to obey the claims of duty, honour, and gratitude. You are determined to ruin him in the opinion of all his friends, and make him the contempt of the world.'

'Neither duty, nor honour, nor gratitude,' replied Elizabeth, 'has any possible claim on me in the present instance. No principle of either would be violated by my marriage with Mr Darcy. And with regard to the resentment of his family or the indignation of the world, if the former *were* excited by his marrying me, it would not give me one moment's concern – and the world in general would have too much sense to join in the scorn.'

(Pride and Prejudice, pp. 286–8)

What is there in this extract, about society? Clearly this is an argument between a bigoted, snobbish woman and a more rational and liberal-minded girl. However, to fully understand the issues of class raised in this extract, we should analyse the attitudes expressed. We can begin by listing the arguments Lady Catherine puts forward and collecting the outstanding words and phrases which express her feelings under each head of her argument. This is like making a résumé of her views:

1.  I showed you attentions last spring, and you owe it to me to do as I wish in return. In putting this argument forward, Lady Catherine uses *gratitude*, *due to me*, and *score*. She returns to this theme at the end, using *to oblige me* and *obey the claims of ... gratitude*.
2.  I insist on having my own way. I always have my own way. In asserting this, Lady Catherine uses *determined resolution* and *carrying my purpose*; *not ... used to submit to any person's whims*. *I have not been in the habit of brooking disappointment*. Lady Catherine then says *I will not be interrupted*, and that *it [Elizabeth marrying Darcy] must not, shall not be*! Later, she promises never to *recede*, saying *I shall not go away till you have given me the assurance I require*.

3.   Darcy and Miss de Bourgh are destined for each other. Here, Lady Catherine brings in *formed*, *descended*, *noble*, *respectable*, *honourable*, *and ancient*, *splendid*, *destined*, and also *sphere*, when referring to the different social world inhabited by Elizabeth.

4.   Elizabeth's life as Darcy's wife would be miserable. Lady Catherine connects this argument to others, that his family and the world will disapprove of Elizabeth. However, this argument seems to be part of Lady Catherine's ideas of *honour* and *duty*, mentioned near to the end of the extract.

5.   Elizabeth's family is socially beneath Darcy's. Here, Lady Catherine uses *upstart pretensions*, *without family*, *connections*, *or fortune*, and *their condition*.

6.   Elizabeth's sister eloped with and is now married to Wickham, the son of Darcy's steward. Lady Catherine's diction goes to town in advancing this argument. *Infamous, a patched-up business, **such** a girl*, and *are the shades of Pemberley to be thus polluted*?

7.   By marrying Darcy, Elizabeth will ruin him. Darcy, Lady Catherine says, will lose *honour* and *credit*, it will *disgrace him in the eyes of everybody*, *ruin him* in the opinion of his *friends* [that is, his relations], he will be *the contempt of the world*.

This is a long catalogue of snobbery and its attendant insults, of course; and Elizabeth is clinically accurate in puncturing the unreasoning class prejudice Lady Catherine puts forward. However, we need to look at what the arguments are. Certain clear points emerge.

First, Lady Catherine appeals to a system that has endured unchanged for a long time. This system seems to be a fixed constant in Lady Catherine's mind. So, she uses the words 'destined' and 'formed' when referring to Darcy and her daughter, as well as 'noble' and 'ancient' for their families. The suggestion is that her fixed idea of social heirarchy has become a belief in destiny. The superstitious overtones of this belief are reinforced by her reference to 'the shades of Pemberley'. Lady Catherine's use of the word 'sphere' is also interesting in this respect. It describes a complete, self-sufficient whole, so that Elizabeth's 'sphere' need not interact with any other separate 'sphere'. The word has an additional overtone of religious belief (think, for example, of the 'heavenly spheres' or the 'spheres' of Dante's *Paradiso*) and recalls medieval beliefs that the feudal order was God-given, that the 'spheres' in their appointed places make 'harmony' – a beautiful, heavenly music. More prosaically, Lady Catherine claims precedent for having her own way – she is in the habit of succeeding and cannot understand the possibility of being defied.

Second, Lady Catherine appeals to Elizabeth's 'gratitude'. It seems that in her mind, meeting another person is an 'attention' and confers an obligation. This suggests that Lady Catherine's fixed idea of her station in society interferes in her relationships with others. However, she also broadens this part of her argument to include ideas of 'honour' and 'duty'. 'Honour' in particular is mentioned twice. So, not only does Lady Catherine believe in an ancient social hierarchy; she also conceives that 'honour' is preserved by preserving one's place, and that hierarchy is held together as a complete system by definable 'duty' owed to those above by those beneath. Thus, relationships between human beings are fixed, conditioned by the social structure in which Lady Catherine believes. Hence her particular point about Elizabeth's lack of 'gratitude'. The connection with 'honour' also explains one of the oddest words Lady Catherine uses. When Elizabeth begins to defy her, she claims to feel 'ashamed'. We can now understand that shame, disgrace and a deep discomfort is associated with any threat to her rigid belief system, almost as if it is an unspeakable sin that 'dishonours' the doer, Lady Catherine herself, and the whole of society.

Finally, money sits uneasily in the middle of Lady Catherine's social concept. Darcy's and Miss de Bourgh's

fortunes are 'splendid', while Elizabeth is 'without...
fortune'. Thus far, money seems to appear as the natural
adjunct of those with 'family' and 'connections'. However,
her disgust at the sordidness of money – that Lydia's
marriage was 'at the expense of your father and uncle' –
complicates her attitude. It seems that, in Lady Catherine's
mind, as long as money joins money it is 'splendid'; but any
hint of commercial activity, or the *use* of money, disgusts her.
Notice that Jane Austen is precise in defining this hypocrisy:
the connection occurs to us, but not to Lady Catherine. The
idea that she might depend on money to preserve her position, is too sordid for her ideas of social class.

Lady Catherine de Bourgh is a grotesque – an exaggerated, caricatured figure; and her snobbery is therefore an
extreme, satirised view. However, Elizabeth's opposing view
is serious. Here are Elizabeth's arguments, again in list form:

1.  You have no relationship with me, and therefore no
    rights over me. In making this point, Elizabeth is
    emphatic, using *no effect, nothing to you ... no right to
    concern yourself in [my affairs], you, or to any person
    so wholly unconnected with me*. Elizabeth rejects her
    supposed social obligation to Lady Catherine, saying
    *Neither duty, nor honour, nor gratitude ... has any
    possible claim on me*, and that Darcy's family's resent-
    ment *would not give me one moment's concern*.
2.  I am Mr Darcy's social equal. Elizabeth uses *gentleman*
    and *gentleman's daughter* to assert this.
3.  I will seek my own happiness.
4.  People in general will not be horrified if I marry Mr
    Darcy. Elizabeth thinks that the *world in general would
    have too much sense* to be outraged by the marriage.
5.  Much of Elizabeth's part in the dialogue is rebuttal of
    Lady Catherine. Here, she uses the following terms:
    *pitiable, unreasonable, extraordinary, frivolous, ill-
    judged, mistaken, insulted*. These terms mix her
    personal outrage at Lady Catherine's bullying, insulting

attack, and her final argument: that Lady Catherine's
ideas are illogical. In putting this at the forefront of her
views, Elizabeth points out Lady Catherine's intellectual
inferiority. For that reason, despite her social superiority, she is 'pitiable'. So, Elizabeth's view comes close to
reversing Lady Catherine's view of society. Elizabeth
suggests that people with good reasoning powers are
superior to others; and she believes that the world in
general agrees with her (see 4, above).

There are two crucial points in Elizabeth's view of society,
which are radically modern for her time. First, she broadens
and softens Lady Catherine's rigid ideas of social distinction.
Elizabeth implicitly acknowledges that there could be such a
disparity of education and manners as to make marriage
impossible between two people. So, she erects a benchmark
expressed by the word 'gentleman'. Her argument seems to
be that belonging to a 'gentleman's' family provides her with
a sufficient background and education. In this way, she
regards all of a broad sector of society to be 'equal'.

Second, and more challengingly, Elizabeth repeatedly
emphasises her own and Darcy's rights, as individuals, to
make free decisions for themselves. She states that she will
decide what 'will, in my own opinion, constitute my happiness'; and she points out that Darcy will marry a woman to
whom he is 'attached', not who Lady Catherine wants him to
marry. This argument goes to the heart of the question about
society. Remember that Lady Catherine's idea of society
entails fixed relationships between social ranks, not
between individual human beings. Elizabeth stands in opposition to this, and argues the more modern and 'democratic'
view of individual freedom of choice.

These two characters, then, have utterly contradictory
beliefs. Jane Austen has shown, in the course of this argument, that their minds work in different ways, making their
thoughts and assumptions comprehensively incompatible.
Their opposition is total. Lady Catherine is firmly convinced

that Darcy would become 'the contempt of the world'; that is to say, that everybody shares her belief in a rigid social system. Elizabeth contradicts this. She asserts that 'the world in general would have too much sense to join in the scorn', believing that practical good sense will rule society's opinions.

We now understand the conflict between Elizabeth and Lady Catherine in some detail. We have listed their arguments, and then looked at the language they use in connection with particular ideas. This method has helped us to organise the material and reach some subtle insights (for example, the superstitious overtones in Lady Catherine's language about social order). However, these two views of society are extreme: looking elsewhere in the text will bring forward ironies, and complicate our idea of the theme of society. We do not have space to pursue such a large subject through the whole text in this chapter, but a selection of points will quickly show how Elizabeth's forthright view is complicated, and toned down, when we take account of the whole novel.

First, there are Elizabeth's conversations with Mrs Gardiner concerning Wickham. Elizabeth has to acknowledge that a 'gentleman' and 'gentleman's daughter' need money as well, in order to live in comfort. So, despite his education and manners, Wickham is not 'equal' enough to marry her. This makes Elizabeth unhappy, but she says 'if he becomes really attached to me – I believe it will be better that he should not. I see the imprudence of it' (p. 122).

Additionally, there is an exploration of Elizabeth's feelings in response to Pemberley. She learns about Darcy's character from his house ('she saw, with admiration of his taste, that it was neither gaudy nor uselessly fine' [p. 202] and Georgiana's room makes her comment 'He is certainly a good brother' [p. 204]). Her feelings about this process are perplexing: she felt that to be mistress of Pemberley 'might be something!' (p. 201), and the house creates a 'gentle sensation' towards Darcy (p. 205). Elizabeth is sufficiently conscious of Pemberley's influence on her feelings, to joke about it months later, telling Jane that her love for Darcy started 'from my first seeing his beautiful grounds at Pemberley' (p. 301). She also justifies the effect to herself more reasonably, thinking of Darcy's responsibilities as master of an estate: 'As a brother, a landlord, a master, she considered how many people's happiness were in his guardianship!' (p. 205). Pemberley becomes, in fact, a potent conservative symbol that Elizabeth must learn and come to terms with, because it represents society as it is, and as it will be for the foreseeable future. Pemberley is a powerful monument to the landlord's influence, taste and judgment.

These two points are selected from many which bring us more complex insights into the social structures presented in the novel. It appears that Elizabeth began the novel with a straightforward emphasis on love and mutual understanding (she expresses this to Charlotte in Chapter 6), centred on an individual's feelings; and her initial ideas do not acknowledge the constraint of a social system, the power of either money or society's mores. During the course of the novel, Elizabeth collides with parts of the social system, and her insight becomes a more complicated balancing act, full of awkward compromises. So, for example, Elizabeth realises that Darcy occupies an important social position, and this influences her opinion of him (see p. 205). She also reaches a compromise between romance and economic reality, seeing that 'handsome young men must have something to live on as well as the plain' (p. 126).

Other parts of the novel show further complexities in Elizabeth's opinions. Lady Catherine is insulting towards Elizabeth's mother and her family, and Elizabeth is outraged. Yet in another part of the book we find her deploring her Aunt Phillips' 'vulgarity', ashamed of her mother's vulgarity, and ashamed of the coarseness of her younger sisters' behaviour. The point here is not that Elizabeth agrees with Lady Catherine – who includes the Gardiners in her insult – but that Elizabeth recognises social qualities as 'coarse' and 'vulgar', or 'refined' and 'superior'. That is, her concept of social hierarchy favours those blessed by nature and education, who have become refined. It is a cruel truth of *Pride and Prejudice*, that Mary Bennet could never occupy the social position Elizabeth attains, however hard she tries. To put it very bluntly, she doesn't have the brains, she doesn't have the looks, and she can't sing and play well enough. Society, then, allows some upward mobility; but this may depend on natural advantages, or luck, and should not be confused with modern ideas of equality.

*          *          *

We now turn to *Emma*. The Highbury neighbourhood attends a ball being given at the Crown Inn:

> The ball proceeded pleasantly. The anxious cares, the incessant attentions of Mrs Weston, were not thrown away. Every body seemed happy; and the praise of being a delightful ball, which is seldom bestowed till after a ball has ceased to be, was repeatedly given in the very beginning of the existence of this. Of very important, very recordable events, it was not more productive than such meetings usually are. There was one, however, which Emma thought something of. – The two last dances before supper were begun, and Harriet had no partner; – the only young lady sitting down; – and so equal had been hitherto the number of dancers, that how there could be any one disengaged was the wonder! – But Emma's wonder lessened soon afterwards, on seeing Mr Elton sauntering about. He would not ask Harriet to dance if it were possible to be avoided: she was sure he would not – and she was expecting him every moment to escape into the card-room.
>
> Escape, however, was not his plan. He came to the part of the room where the sitters-by were collected, spoke to some, and walked about in front of them, as if to show his liberty, and his resolution of maintaining it. He did not omit being sometimes directly before Miss Smith, or speaking to those who were close to her. – Emma saw it. She was not yet dancing, she was working her way up from the bottom, and

had therefore leisure to look around, and by only turning her head a little she saw it all. When she was half way up the set, the whole group were exactly behind her, and she would no longer allow her eyes to watch; but Mr Elton was so near, that she heard every syllable of a dialogue which just then took place between him and Mrs Weston; and she perceived that his wife, who was standing immediately above her, was not only listening also, but even encouraging him by significant glances. – The kind-hearted, gentle Mrs Weston had left her seat to join him and say, 'Do not you dance, Mr Elton?' to which his prompt reply was, 'Most readily, Mrs Weston, if you will dance with me.'

'Me! – oh! no – I would get you a better partner than myself. I am no dancer.'

'If Mrs Gilbert wishes to dance,' said he, 'I shall have great pleasure, I am sure – for, though beginning to feel myself rather an old married man, and that my dancing days are over, it would give me very great pleasure at any time to stand up with an old friend like Mrs Gilbert.'

'Mrs Gilbert does not mean to dance, but there is a young lady disengaged whom I should be very glad to see dancing – Miss Smith.'

'Miss Smith – oh! – I had not observed. – You are extremely obliging – and if I were not an old married man. – But my dancing days are over, Mrs Weston. You will excuse me. Any thing else I should be most happy to do, at your command – but my dancing days are over.'

Mrs Weston said no more; and Emma could imagine with what surprise and mortification she must be returning to her seat. This was Mr Elton! the amiable, obliging, gentle Mr Elton. – She looked round for a moment; he had joined Mr Knightley at a little distance, and was arranging himself for settled conversation, while smiles of high glee passed between him and his wife.

She would not look again. Her heart was in a glow, and she feared her face might be as hot.

In another moment a happier sight caught her; – Mr Knightley leading Harriet to the set! – Never had she been more surprised, seldom more delighted, than at that instant. She was all pleasure and gratitude, both for Harriet and

herself, and longed to be thanking him; and though too
distant for speech, her countenance said much, as soon as she
could catch his eye again.

His dancing proved to be just what she had believed it,
extremely good; and Harriet would have seemed almost too
lucky, if it had not been for the cruel state of things before,
and for the very complete enjoyment and very high sense of
the distinction which her happy features announced. It was
not thrown away on her, she bounded higher than ever,
flew farther down the middle, and was in a continual course
of smiles.

Mr Elton had retreated to the card-room, looking (Emma
trusted) very foolish. She did not think he was quite so hard-
ened as his wife, though growing very like her – *she* spoke
some of her feelings, by observing audibly to her partner,

'Knightley has taken pity on poor little Miss Smith! – Very
good-natured, I declare.'

(*Emma*, pp. 270–1)

This extract centres its attention on the ceremonial behaviour of the 'neighbourhood' at a ball. Mr Elton breaks the
code when he snubs Miss Smith; Mr Knightley restores the
proper balance. Let us look first at the 'code', the formal
ritual of behaviour to which each person present is expected
to conform. We already know, from our analysis of the
Netherfield ball in *Pride and Prejudice* (see Chapter 3) that
much goes on beneath the surface, at social gatherings. So
we can think of this ceremonial code of conduct as a
'surface' which must be preserved.

First, we realise that the ceremony is complicated and
there is considerable worry about arrangements both before
and during the event. Mrs Weston gives 'anxious cares' and
'incessant attentions' so that everyone 'seemed' happy and
the ball was pronounced 'delightful'. We are, by now, sensitive enough to Jane Austen's style to notice the careful
superficiality of 'seemed happy', and the conventional
compliment 'delightful'. These contrast with 'anxious' and
'incessant' cares about the arrangements, leading us to

conclude that Mrs Weston has invested real effort and emotion into producing a shallow, artificial outcome. In this society, harmony is – as we know – only on the surface; but for some reason it is deeply important to create and maintain that surface harmony.

The surface soon shows a flaw: Harriet has no partner. Emma finds this extraordinary, since the numbers of men and women dancing are carefully balanced to avoid such a distressing event. The careful predictability of the ball arrangements are emphasised. Harriet is a 'young lady sitting down', which defines her as a female awaiting a partner. This event poses a question, but the answer is equally easy to find: 'Mr Elton sauntering about'. Notice that Mr Elton has no fixed place: he belongs in partnership with a female, not with the 'sitters-by' nor with the 'standers-by' who are mentioned on the preceding page, 'the husbands, and fathers, and whist-players ... the bulky forms and stooping shoulders of the elderly men' (p. 269). So, Mr Elton's 'sauntering about' is a contradiction of the system, where a man is expected to belong to one group or another, and to behave accordingly. On the preceding page, Jane Austen described Mr Knightley as having 'placed himself' and 'classing himself' with the old men. Emma's first expectation is that Mr Elton will now 'place himself' and 'class himself' in order to avoid dancing with Harriet. Emma expects, then, that Mr Elton will manipulate the ritual they all understand. He will 'escape into the card-room'. This would change him from a dancing male into a card-playing male. Harriet would still be snubbed, but Mr Elton would have – to an extent – worked within the social system.

The next paragraph highlights how destructive Mr Elton's aberrant behaviour is, by emphasising the contrast between his movements and the formal positioning of everybody else. Mr Elton does not class himself with the card-players – he openly defies the system. After 'sauntering', he actually approaches the 'sitters-by' and he 'walked about in front of them, as if to show his liberty'. The emphasis on formal positioning quickly returns. Emma is in place, and is able to observe the scene without moving out of her place and 'by only turning her head a little'. When her position changes, however, she does not turn her head further but stays within the norm, 'she would not allow her eyes to watch'. Mrs Elton is also in place, 'standing immediately above her'.

In this context, Mr Elton's conversation prompts further conclusions about the surface code. In refusing to do what Mrs Weston asks, and rudely snubbing Harriet, he uses the following phrases: 'Most readily'; 'I shall have great pleasure'; 'it would give me very great pleasure'; 'You are extremely obliging'; 'excuse me'; 'most happy'; 'at your command'. These phrases can be classed with the adjective 'delightful' we noticed earlier – they are part of the expected language of a ballroom, and a stream of them must be part of each person's speech. However, Mr Elton's meaning is the opposite of polite, so the emptiness of his courtesies becomes ghastly.

We have discovered several elements of the expected 'code', then. We know that people are classed in groups, and the system demands that they behave according to the laws governing their group. Now, how does the system respond to Mr Elton's rebellion?

First, Mrs Weston approaches him, and asks him to conform. However, his reply issues a further challenge: in order to bring him into line, she would have to break the code herself and tell him, to his face, to stop misbehaving. In other words, he challenges her to say what she means, outright. Mrs Weston, then, is unable to defend the system against his determined opposition. Ironically, she is disabled by the very code she is anxious to uphold. So she 'said no more' even though Emma is certain that she feels 'surprise and mortification'. This encounter is a crisis in the conflict between Mr Elton and the system, and it is significant that Emma now becomes anxious about breaking the code herself, even if only temporarily. She feels so strongly that she moves out of the order – 'she looked round for a moment' – and the connection between strong feeling and outward appearance becomes an issue. Emma's 'heart' glows, and she fears losing control over her appearance because 'her face might be as hot'.

The second response to Mr Elton's challenge comes from Mr Knightley. He rectifies the situation, leading Harriet to the dance. Jane Austen again uses the formal placing of people into classified groups, as well as a military term, to show that the 'code' has won the battle. Mr Elton eventually goes where Emma first thought he would, 'into the card-room', and his defeat is expressed by the use of 'retreated'. Furthermore, the joys of living securely within the system are amusingly portrayed by Harriet's ecstatic bounding and flying in 'a continual course of smiles'.

In this passage, society's superficial ceremony comes under direct threat. It is unable to defend itself at first, since its shallow artificiality is also its weakness. Only Knightley can take effective action, and he powerfully supports the system.

Now, we turn to the rebellion. How does Jane Austen present the force that is in conflict with this social code? The rudeness and pettiness of Mr and Mrs Elton's behaviour are apparent in this scene; but it is worth bearing in mind their motive, as Emma and Mr Knightley see it two pages later. Mr Knightley comments that the Eltons 'aimed at wounding more than Harriet' and that they are Emma's 'enemies'; and she replies that the Eltons 'cannot forgive me' for having matched Harriet and Mr Elton. Mr Knightley's comment continues the military metaphor, and expresses a judgment about Highbury society by referring to Emma as 'more than Harriet'. Effectively, he says that this was a serious attack by 'enemies'. Their motives are resentment and revenge, but what stands out is that they 'cannot forgive'. Jane Austen pointedly contrasts them with Knightley, whose criticism of Emma's mistake is tempered by 'a smile of indulgence'.

Returning to our extract, we notice that the battle is pursued with gusto. The Eltons communicate with 'significant glances' and when they believe themselves victorious, 'smiles of high glee' pass between them. The final victory of the system confers equal pleasure. Harriet is in 'very complete enjoyment' with 'a high sense of the distinction'; and Emma is 'delighted', being 'all pleasure and gratitude'. She communicates with Knightley by looks, also: 'her countenance said much'.

This commentary on the incident of Mr Elton's rudeness highlights some details of the social 'code' of the time. However, by putting these details together, we can begin to answer more important questions about society. Here are some statements which suggest further ideas:

- Mrs Weston puts genuine effort into creating a superficial harmony
- People are given prescribed positions and behaviour, and self-expression is severely limited
- Mr Knightley acts as a pillar, upholding this structure
- The Eltons' motives are unchristian, in that they 'cannot forgive'

In this list, we are struck by the seriousness of Mrs Weston's and Mr Knightley's commitment: what is so important about the ritual 'code' of a ballroom? Why does this shallow ceremony engage their inner feelings, and those of Emma? The answer Jane Austen seems to imply is that social harmony represents a mutual Christian 'indulgence', a form of compromise between conflicting individuals where faults are not punished, but are tolerated or forgiven. Therefore, the polite 'code' of behaviour protects the weak, who might be hurt in its absence. In this instance, Harriet has been exposed to 'the cruel state of things' by Mr Elton. Her happiness, as well as the system, is rescued by Knightley. This is why the smooth 'surface' of society is worth preserving, and helps us to understand the importance of Jane Austen's theme of social harmony.

Before we move on to look at *Mansfield Park*, it is worth comparing the Mr Elton incident with another incident in *Emma*. In Chapter 43, at Box Hill, Emma makes an unkind joke at Miss Bates's expense. In other words, Emma herself breaks the code, and causes pain to a vulnerable member of the social group. Mr Knightley's rebuke after this event further underlines the serious theme of social harmony:

> Were she your equal in situation – but, Emma, consider how far this is from being the case. She is poor; she has sunk from the comforts she was born to; and, if she live to old age, must probably sink more. Her situation should secure your compassion.
>
> (*Emma*, p. 309)

This reminds us of Harriet's situation when snubbed by Mr Elton; and Knightley's words make clear the connection between social harmony and a Christian attitude to others, particularly with the strength of his final word, 'compassion'. Jane Austen clearly suggests that the polite forms of behaviour she satirises with such sharp amusement, are nonetheless important.

\*    \*    \*

In Chapter 21 of *Mansfield Park*, Fanny and Edmund discuss their family circle now that Sir Thomas has returned from the West Indies. Edmund thinks that Dr and Mrs Grant would enliven their evenings at Mansfield. Fanny replies:

> 'Do you think so?' said Fanny. 'In my opinion, my uncle would not like *any* addition. I think he values the very quiet-ness you speak of, and that the repose of his own family-circle is all he wants. And it does not appear to me that we are more serious than we used to be; I mean before my uncle went abroad. As well as I can recollect, it was always much the

same. There was never much laughing in his presence; or, if there is any difference, it is not more I think than such an absence has a tendency to produce at first. There must be a sort of shyness. But I cannot recollect that our evenings formerly were ever merry, except when my uncle was in town. No young people's are, I suppose, when those they look up to are at home.'

'I believe you are right, Fanny,' was his reply, after a short consideration. 'I believe our evenings are rather returned to what they were, than assuming a new character. The novelty was in their being lively. – Yet, how strong the impression that only a few weeks will give! I have been feeling as if we had never lived so before.'

'I suppose I am graver than other people,' said Fanny. 'The evenings do not appear long to me. I love to hear my uncle talk of the West Indies. I could listen to him for an hour together. It entertains *me* more than many other things have done – but then I am unlike other people I dare say.'

'Why should you dare say *that*? (smiling) – Do you want to be told that you are only unlike other people in being more wise and discreet? But when did you or any body ever get a compliment from me, Fanny? Go to my father if you want to be complimented. He will satisfy you. Ask your uncle what he thinks, and you will hear compliments enough; and though they may be chiefly on your person, you must put up with it, and trust to his seeing as much beauty of mind in time.'

Such language was so new to Fanny that it quite embarrassed her.

'Your uncle thinks you very pretty, dear Fanny – and that is the long and the short of the matter. Any body but myself would have made something more of it, and any body but you would resent that you had not been thought very pretty before; but the truth is, that your uncle never did admire you until now – and now he does. Your complexion is so improved! – and you have gained so much countenance! – and your figure – Nay, Fanny, do not turn away about it – it is but an uncle. If you cannot bear an uncle's admiration, what is to become of you? You must really begin to harden yourself to the idea of being worth looking at. – You must try not to mind growing up into a pretty woman.'

'Oh! don't talk so, don't talk so,' cried Fanny, distressed by more feelings than he was aware of; but seeing that she was distressed, he had done with the subject, and only added more seriously, 'Your uncle is disposed to be pleased with you in every respect; and I only wish you would talk to him more. – You are one of those who are too silent in the evening circle.'

'But I do talk to him more than I used. I am sure I do. Did not you hear me ask him about the slave-trade last night?'

'I did – and was in hopes the question would be followed up by others. It would have pleased your uncle to be inquired of further.'

'And I longed to do it – but there was such a dead silence! And while my cousins were sitting by without speaking a word, or seeming at all interested in the subject, I did not like – I thought it would appear as if I wanted to set myself off at their expense, by shewing a curiosity and pleasure in his information which he must wish his own daughters to feel.'

'Miss Crawford was very right in what she said of you the other day – that you seemed almost as fearful of notice and praise as other women were of neglect. We were talking of you at the parsonage, and those were her words. She has great discernment. I know nobody who distinguishes characters better. – For so young a woman it is remarkable! She certainly understands *you* better than you are understood by the greater part of those who have known you so long; and with regard to some others, I can perceive, from occasional lively hints, the unguarded expressions of the moment, that she could define *many* as accurately, did not delicacy forbid it. I wonder what she thinks of my father! She must admire him as a fine-looking man, with most gentlemanlike, digni-fied, consistent manners; but perhaps having seen him so seldom, his reserve may be a little repulsive. Could they be much together I feel sure of their liking each other. He would enjoy her liveliness – and she has talents to value his powers. I wish they met more frequently! – I hope she does not suppose there is any dislike on his side.'

'She must know herself too secure of the regard of all the rest of you,' said Fanny with half a sigh, 'to have any such apprehension. And Sir Thomas's wishing just at first to be only with his family is so very natural, that she can argue nothing from that. After a little while I dare say we shall be meeting again in the same sort of way, allowing for the difference of the time of year.'

'This is the first October that she has passed in the country since her infancy. I do not call Tunbridge or Cheltenham the country; and November is a still more serious month, and I can see that Mrs Grant is very anxious for her not finding Mansfield dull as winter comes on.'

(Mansfield Park, pp. 164–6)

This brief mention of the slave-trade and the West Indies marks a boundary to the world and viewpoint of Jane Austen's novels. What is the relevance of the whole passage, to ideas about society?

First, Fanny and Edmund discuss two different ways of life: a quiet and regular life, confined to the family circle, which Fanny likes; and a more varied and lively way of life with frequent visitors, including the mention of town amusements, which Edmund seems to hanker after. Second, the figure of Sir Thomas seems to be at the centre of their conversation, influencing both of them in many ways. Third, there are gender issues in Edmund's manner of talking about female vanity and Fanny's appearance. Finally, there is the question of the West Indies and the slave trade. We can take these four topics in order, and look at the extract more closely in relation to each.

First, examine the two ways of life Fanny and Edmund discuss. How is the quiet life Fanny enjoys conveyed in this passage? Fanny says that Sir Thomas 'values' it and it is 'all he wants'. She identifies her own feelings as singular: 'I am graver than other people' and 'I am unlike other people'; but the evenings 'do not appear long' to her, she says 'I love to hear' Sir Thomas talking and 'It entertains me.' When Fanny argues that family life is the same as it used to be, she comments on the atmosphere as 'serious', 'never much laughing' and evenings that are never 'merry'. The words 'quietness' and 'repose' take on a more specific meaning later in the passage, when Edmund comments that Fanny is one of those who are 'too silent' and Fanny mentions 'such a dead silence' with others 'sitting by without speaking a word, or seeming at all interested'. Edmund, meanwhile, suggests that this life is even more 'serious' and 'dull' in autumn and winter. Finally, Fanny finds Sir Thomas's wish to be only with his family 'natural', and believes that young people's amusements are always suppressed 'when those they look up to' are present.

The extract, then, builds up a powerful impression of a quiet and limited life without amusement or humour. Fanny finds this 'natural' and serious conversation 'entertains' her. However, our collection of details gives rise to two observations. First, this way of life is described ambiguously. Is it quiet and satisfying, or unnaturally silent and oppressive? Even Fanny betrays this ambiguity when describing the silence that greeted her question about the slave-trade. So, we are left in doubt whether there are any positive values ('natural' and 'repose' in which the young 'look up to' the old), or whether Mansfield family life is rotten, the younger generation oppressed and unnatural in Sir Thomas's presence, their watchful silence nothing but a cynical competition for his approval, utterly insincere. This ambiguity therefore applies also to the idea of authority: is it based on respect and consent, or fear, self-interest and economic power? Second, this quiet country life is deeply affected by the seasons. Shorter, darker days and weather that keep people indoors, exacerbate the limitations of Mansfield family life.

Edmund conveys a strong impression of the social life he has recently experienced for the first time, and this way of life is clearly connected with the character of Miss Crawford. Edmund found 'novelty' in a 'lively' life which made a 'strong ... impression', so much so that 'I have been feeling as if we had never lived so before'. Edmund repeats 'lively' and 'liveliness' in describing Miss Crawford, and mentions

'Tunbridge or Cheltenham', which are fashionable towns, as places where life would suit her. On the other hand, his language suggests that this liveliness entails some risk – involving 'hints' and 'unguarded expressions of the moment' which are almost what 'delicacy' would 'forbid'. Edmund's wishes are simply for more people, more often, with more conversation. He wishes Fanny 'would talk to him [Sir Thomas] more' and hoped that her question 'would be followed up by others'. He says of his father and Miss Crawford 'I wish they met more frequently!' and seems excited by defining people 'accurately' and discussing them with 'discernment'.

Edmund's excitement is clear enough. Notice, however, that this 'lively' way of life is also presented ambiguously. There would seem to be positive values in 'novelty', 'talents', 'discernment' and 'liveliness' which can be enjoyed. Yet there is danger, and 'delicacy' will 'forbid' some of this enjoyable liveliness from being expressed.

The figure of Sir Thomas is crucial. We have already noticed that his authority is ambiguous – either the result of respect, or of oppression and economic power. Notice also that both Fanny and Edmund attribute feelings and ideas to Sir Thomas. Fanny says that he 'values' a quiet life; Edmund says that 'it would have pleased your uncle to be inquired of further', to which Fanny agrees because 'he must wish his own daughters to feel' curiosity and pleasure in his information. Edmund thinks his father 'would enjoy' Miss Crawford's liveliness and would like her. Amusingly, the only part of the extract which reports Sir Thomas's definite opinion, tells us that he thinks Fanny 'very pretty'. He has commented favourably on her 'complexion', 'countenance' and 'figure'. Ambiguously again, Edmund describes Sir Thomas's external manners, using some positive words – 'gentlemanlike, dignified, consistent' – and calls him 'fine-looking', before saying that his 'reserve' might appear 'repulsive'. 'Repulsive' is a surprisingly strong word for Edmund to use. It describes a strong negative emotion, much worse than mere quietness.

We conclude that there is a crucial ambiguity here, again. Sir Thomas is either a thoughtful man who 'values' quietness and serious conversation, of which he would like to have more; or he is a silent, unperceptive man with a repulsive manner, who talks shallowly about Fanny's looks and ignores the quality of her mind. The division is between what the young people attribute to Sir Thomas, and the only evidence about him that appears in the extract. Our uncertainty is increased when we notice that both Fanny and Edmund imagine him to be like themselves. Edmund is sure he would like Mary Crawford and enjoy her 'liveliness'; Fanny imagines that Sir Thomas 'values' the life that 'entertains' her. Both of them, then, want him to be like themselves, but what he is actually like remains enigmatic.

Edmund's – and by extension Sir Thomas's – stereotyping of women, is very apparent in this extract. Edmund embarrasses Fanny ('Nay, Fanny, do not turn away about it') by teasingly complimenting her looks, saying she is 'worth looking at'. He patronisingly finds Mary Crawford's intelligence 'remarkable' for 'so young a woman', but accepts her view that most women seek 'notice and praise' and fear 'neglect'. Edmund might seem to be less chauvinistic when he mentions Fanny's 'beauty of mind'; but even here he leads on to a stereotype. The purpose of her intelligence is to flatter ('please') Sir Thomas by asking him for information. Here, the roles of men and women are again rigidly defined: 'information' is given by men, and received by women, a system Fanny also accepts. This extract is partly a critical analysis of the patriarchal family, then: it trenchantly observes the secondary position of women, and the absurdly mysterious, god-like figure of the father.

The fourth and final topic we noticed in this extract, is the mention of a wider world in the background – the information that Sir Thomas talks about 'the West Indies', and that Fanny asked him a question about 'the slave-trade'. There are several interesting suggestions in this delicate mention of a world beyond the scope of the novel. First, Fanny accepts that the outside world is man's domain, and accepts her female role by taking 'pleasure' in 'information' about it, given to her by a man. We may wonder what 'pleasure' she could get from information about the slave-trade. Second, the wider world is specified in only eight words in this extract, and we are told very little about Sir Thomas's business in Antigua, anywhere else in the novel. Why, then, does Jane Austen refer to it at all? The author could have taken Sir Thomas away for other reasons, and Fanny could have asked about other subjects. Why Antigua and why the slave-trade? To understand Jane Austen's purpose, we have to understand what readers of her own time knew about plantations in the West Indies.

The slave-trade was a much-debated issue throughout Jane Austen's life. The Anti-Slavery Committee was established in London in 1787, and efforts to abolish the trade were repeatedly put to Parliament throughout the 1790s. The law in Britain was finally changed in 1808, but the slave-trade carried on for several decades, with the covert involvement of many British traders; and the owners of slaves were awarded heavy compensation when existing British-owned slaves were emancipated in 1833. Clearly, at the time Jane Austen writes about, slavery was a contentious political issue, in the process of rapid and often violent change. Similarly, many well-off English families owned land in the West Indies. However, at the time Jane Austen writes about, economic changes (particularly the collapse in the price of sugar) had severely reduced the profits from these plantations. The reference to Antigua is therefore also a reference to rapid and disturbing economic change. Jane Austen's readers would immediately recognise Sir Thomas's difficulties, connecting them to current stories of economic insecurity and huge financial losses; and current arguments over the moral issue of slavery.

Jane Austen has chosen particularly disturbing, and morally ambiguous, references to the outside world. Her reticence is equally noticeable: in particular, she does not reveal Sir Thomas's practice or his attitude in the matter of slaves. These references, then, leave us with two important questions: first, is Sir Thomas moral outside his family, or immoral? Second, how far does Sir Thomas rely on income from Antigua, in order to maintain Mansfield Park, and his family's genteel way of life?

We receive no answer to the first of these questions; but a partial answer to the second. The Bertrams do depend on the income from Antigua. Tom's extravagances very quickly force Sir Thomas to economise in his plans for Edmund, and the visit to Antigua is described as a 'necessity ... in a pecuniary light' which forces him to 'the effort of quitting the rest of his family' (p. 28). These references, then, carry disturbing hints that the Bertrams' way of life is under threat, that the world is changing and the economic base of the landed gentry is far from secure. They also imply that there is something artificial about the whole structure of family house and estate. The Bertrams cannot live in their accustomed style on the proceeds of the estate – there is a hidden, hardly mentioned subsidy from the other side of the world, on which the whole edifice of Mansfield Park rests or falls.

It seems, then, that everything we have learned about society from this extract increases the ambiguity of Jane Austen's theme. We are left with a very complex situation that the author's hints do not resolve. The reader is forced to pose unanswerable questions: is Sir Thomas's effort to preserve the old way of life right, or wrong? Is he preserving something of value, or a hypocritical, narrow-minded edifice that is already declined past its time? Is he perceptive and intelligent, or myopically stupid? Is 'liveliness' dangerous, or natural?

One of the most important questions about society raised in this extract is a consequence of Edmund's musings about Mary Crawford and his father. He believes that they would like each other, but says 'I wonder what she thinks of my father!'. The reader is used to Edmund's self-deceptions about Mary Crawford, so we are sceptical whether Sir

Thomas, representative of the old order, and Mary Crawford, representative of the new, can have a good relationship. Jane Austen's irony leaves us with another vital question about society: is any accommodation possible between these opposed generations and attitudes to life? Or are they set, irreversibly, on conflicting courses?

*          *          *

We now turn to an extract from *Persuasion*. In Chapter 21, Anne Elliot is listening to Mrs Smith's account of Mr Elliot's character:

'I have been doubting and considering as to what I ought to tell you. There were many things to be taken into the account. One hates to be officious, to be giving bad impressions, making mischief. Even the smooth surface of family-union seems worth preserving, though there may be nothing durable beneath. However, I have determined; I think I am right; I think you ought to be made acquainted with Mr Elliot's real character. Though I fully believe that, at present, you have not the smallest intention of accepting him, there is no saying what may happen. You might, some time or other, be differently affected towards him. Hear the truth, therefore, now, while you are unprejudiced. Mr Elliot is a man without heart or conscience; a designing, wary, cold-blooded being, who thinks only of himself; who, for his own interest or ease, would be guilty of any cruelty, or any treachery, that could be perpetrated without risk of his general character. He has no feeling for others. Those whom he has been the chief cause of leading into ruin, he can neglect and desert without the smallest compunction. He is totally beyond the reach of any sentiment of justice or compassion. Oh! he is black at heart, hollow and black!'

Anne's astonished air, and exclamation of wonder, made her pause, and in a calmer manner she added,

'My expressions startle you. You must allow for an injured, angry woman. But I will try to command myself. I will not abuse him. I will only tell you what I have found him. Facts shall speak. He was the intimate friend of my dear husband, who trusted and loved him, and thought him as good as himself. The intimacy had been formed before our marriage. I found them most intimate friends; and I, too, became excessively pleased with Mr Elliot, and entertained the highest opinion of him. At nineteen, you know, one does not think very seriously, but Mr Elliot appeared to me quite as good as others, and much more agreeable than most others, and we were almost always together. We were principally in town, living in very good style. He was then the inferior in circumstances, he was then the poor one; he had chambers in the Temple, and it was as much as he could do to support the appearance of a gentleman. He had always a home with us whenever he chose it; he was always welcome; he was like a brother. My poor Charles, who had the finest, most generous spirit in the world, would have divided his last farthing with him; and I know that his purse was open to him; I know that he often assisted him.'

'This must have been about that very period of Mr Elliot's life,' said Anne, 'which has always excited my particular curiosity. It must have been about the same time that he became known to my father and sister. I never knew him myself, I only heard of him, but there was a something in his conduct then with regard to my father and sister, and afterwards in the circumstance of his marriage, which I never could quite reconcile with present times. It seemed to announce a different sort of man.'

'I know it all, I know it all,' cried Mrs Smith. 'He had been introduced to Sir Walter and your sister before I was acquainted with him, but I heard him speak of them for ever. I know he was invited and encouraged, and I know he did not choose to go. I can satisfy you, perhaps, on points which you would little expect; and as to his marriage, I knew all about it at the time. I was privy to all the fors and againsts, I was the friend to whom he confided his hopes and plans, and though I did not know his wife previously, (her inferior situation in society, indeed, rendered that impossible) yet I knew her all her life afterwards, or, at least, till within the last two years of her life, and can answer any question you wish to put.'

'Nay,' said Anne, 'I have no particular enquiry to make about her. I have always understood they were not a happy couple. But I should like to know why, at that time of his life, he should slight my father's acquaintance as he did. My father was certainly disposed to take very kind and proper notice of him. Why did Mr Elliot draw back?'

'Mr Elliot,' replied Mrs Smith, 'at that period of his life, had one object in view – to make his fortune, and by a rather quicker process than the law. He was determined to make it by marriage. He was determined, at least, not to mar it by an imprudent marriage; and I know it was his belief, (whether justly or not, of course I cannot decide) that your father and sister, in their civilities and invitations, were designing a match between the heir and the young lady; and it was impossible that such a match should have answered his ideas of wealth and independence. That was his motive for drawing back, I can assure you. He told me the whole story. He had no concealments with me.'

(Persuasion, pp. 205–7)

Before beginning to look at this extract in detail, it will be helpful to summarise the understanding of 'society' that we have pieced together so far. In *Pride and Prejudice* we met an old-fashioned, hierarchical view of society that was so devoid of value or reason as to be absurd (Lady Catherine de Bourgh) and a new individualism, strongly advanced in Elizabeth's views. In *Emma*, we found a ceremonial 'code' by which society operates, powerfully justified in moral terms by Jane Austen, but also satirised for its artificiality. In *Mansfield Park*, there is a problematic conflict between an old order and way of life, and a younger generation given over to new attitudes, seeking pleasure and entertainment.

Can we find a single concern in common between these three instances of Jane Austen's 'society' theme? There is something about a fixed and established social system, in all three of them; yet if we attempt to rank them together, we have to class the ridiculed caricature of Lady Catherine de Bourgh, with Jane Austen's evident approval of Mr Knightley, and to do so is absurd. We can also say that two of the societies we have studied – those in *Pride and Prejudice* and *Mansfield Park* – are depicted as in the process of radical change, in conflict between an old and a new order. This is not true of society in *Emma*, however. Perhaps we need to look at society in a different way, to find a common element in Jane Austen's presentation of this theme.

We can suggest that the crucial element in all the social forms we have looked at – the one thing that determines its value or perniciousness – is the relationship between sincerity and manners. Where the social form or system is divorced from sincere emotions, then the system is laughable, mischievous, oppressive or unjustifiable. On the other hand, when society is an expression of sincere emotion, moral principle and 'social' or tolerant attitudes, it has value. Manners are then important adjuncts to the individual's life, part of a positive theme of social harmony. So, we can analyse society in Jane Austen's novels by looking at the relationship between social structures and forms, on the one hand, and a set of personal values – including sincerity, and Christian emotions such as compassion and forgiveness – on the other.

This idea is tentative. Any attempt to find a single explanation for the multiplied instances in Jane Austen's novels must be tentative. However, the unchristian selfishness of Lady Catherine de Bourgh and the Eltons, and the problems of morality and cynicism, of sincerity and dishonesty, raised in *Mansfield Park*, support the suggestion that the values underlying social forms, are Jane Austen's primary concern.

Even on first reading, our extract from *Persuasion* adds strength to this argument. Various social issues are raised in the conversation between Anne and Mrs Smith. For example, they discuss the relative value of money and rank. However, the insistent theme is Mr Elliot's lack of humane or Christian feeling, and the consequent opinion that he is dangerous and destructive.

Mrs Smith's startling condemnation of Mr Elliot is entirely in these terms. Evil is described as 'designing, wary, cold-blooded being, who thinks only of himself', 'guilty of ... cruelty ... treachery', 'no feeling', 'ruin ... neglect ... desert' and 'black at heart, hollow and black!' The emphasis is on his absence of feeling, and the majority of this condemnation focuses on the social issue – that is, Mr Elliot's relations with others. These are guided by self-interest, not mutual interest, so he is accused of 'cruelty', 'treachery', 'neglect', and can 'desert' anyone. Mrs Smith's diatribe also provides a list of social virtues, that Mr Elliot lacks: 'heart or conscience', 'feeling for others', 'sentiment of justice or compassion'.

In contrast to Mr Elliot's selfishness, Mrs Smith cites her 'poor Charles, who had the finest, most generous spirit in the world' and would have 'divided his last farthing'. Clearly, Mr Elliot is accused of being an enemy of society because society operates on an assumption of generosity, or at least giving and taking. Mr Elliot only takes, and misuses society in order to do so. His hypocrisy is emphasised by Mrs Smith's repeated use of 'intimate friend' and 'friend', and her comment that he would do anything possible 'without risk of his general character'.

This analysis reminds us of the conclusions we came to from *Emma*: people have a responsibility to others, and the social forms protect the weak. Mr Elliot's lack of 'compassion' reminds us of Mr Knightley's rebuke to Emma – that she should feel 'compassion' for Miss Bates. The *Emma* extract is recalled in another way. Remember that Mrs Weston devoted 'anxious cares' to arrangements for the ball. Mrs Smith also sees an intrinsic value in social harmony, which is worth preserving even if it is artificial. She says that 'Even the smooth surface of family-union seems worth preserving, though there may be nothing durable beneath.'

We understand the social assumptions behind Mrs Smith's speech, then. She believes in the value of society, and believes that the unfettered pursuit of self-interest is inimical to it just as the possession of 'heart or conscience' is necessary to it. However, if we ask whether this version of 'society' is the only one in *Persuasion*, we quickly meet complications. One example occurs on the next page, when Mrs Smith herself admits that self-interest was the dominant value of the 'society' she and Mr Elliot lived in. She remarks that marrying solely for money is 'too common'; and 'I saw nothing reprehensible in what Mr Elliot was doing. "To do the best for himself," passed as a duty' (p. 208).

## Conclusions

1.  Society, in Jane Austen's novels, is often presented as hierarchical, and its behaviour is described as ceremonious or codified. Jane Austen often satirises ceremonies and forms, but also suggests that these 'codes' have an intrinsic value: they represent moral values of tolerance and compassion.

2.  Landed men occupy an important position. They are presented as trustees, holding influence which they can use well or badly (see, for example, Sir Thomas Bertram and Mr Rushworth discussed in Chapter 3 above), and holding the happiness of others in their power (see Mr Darcy's importance, in *Pride and Prejudice*).

3.  A wider world, the outside world beyond the 'neighbourhood', is seen as the province of the man. Information about this wider world is channelled to the woman through the man, but she is unlikely to gain any experience of it herself (the notable exception to this principle is Mrs Croft in *Persuasion*).

4.  Jane Austen is deeply concerned about how society copes with change. In several parts of the four novels, a conflict between conservative stability and a new, young individualism is explored. Jane Austen presents us with different 'portraits' of this struggle. For example, Elizabeth Bennet's individualism is well-reasoned and responsible in *Pride and Prejudice*. Mr Elliot's individualism is selfish and destructive in *Persuasion*. This conflict is at its most ambiguous and problematic in *Mansfield Park*, where it

is also set within a context of wider social and economic changes, and a generational conflict.

5.   Our exploration of 'society' in the four extracts studied in this chapter, has thrown up questions that are relevant to the novels:

  (a)   how important is the connection between sincerity and manners, and hence the inevitable gap between truth and appearance in social interactions?

  (b)   what is the right basis of society, quality of a person or social position? Stability or openness to the new?

6.   We may have noticed that there is an uneasy relationship between money and financial self-interest, which is not condemned when pursued in moderation; and the overt morality of a principled tolerance and consideration for others. We are entitled to ask whether financial inequality is encouraged by this essentially charitable system. In other words, do the rich protect themselves by their goodness to others? However, we must be wary of importing twentieth-century ideas into novels written at the start of the nineteenth century. Our conclusion should reflect Jane Austen's stated aim in painting her 'little bit (two Inches wide) of Ivory on which I work with so fine a Brush'. She reflects the narrow band of society that is her subject, in close detail and faithfully. This provokes numerous moral questions; but Jane Austen is an ironical observer, not a writer with a radical or social agenda. Her novels ultimately convey unresolved dualities: they do not join one 'side' or the other.

## Methods of Analysis

We have used techniques demonstrated in previous chapters, as appropriate. However, in approaching the text with a specific interest in society, we have found it helpful to begin by taking an 'overview'. This involves:

- asking the question: what is there in this extract that is relevant to the theme of 'society'?
- describing the content of the extract in brief summary form, in order to help us to think clearly about it, and relate it to the theme of society.

This way of starting the analysis gives us an idea of what to focus on within the text, so that our analysis can develop purposefully. Once you have this clear idea, you can approach the material in the usual way, looking closely at features of the writing.

## Suggested Work

It will be helpful to look at the caricatured or irritating character in the novel(s) you are studying, a person who occupies an inferior but partly tolerated position. Here are four suggested extracts to study:

- In *Pride and Prejudice*, look at the presentation of a social theme in Mr Collins's proposal, on pp. 88–92.
- In *Emma*, look at Miss Bates's speeches on the subjects of Frank and the spectacles, and Mr Knightley and the apples, on pp. 196–8.
- In *Mansfield Park*, analyse the discussion between Mrs Norris and Sir Thomas Bertram after his return from Antigua, which takes place on pp. 157–9.
- In *Persuasion*, study Mary Musgrove's discussion with Anne Elliot, on the subject of who should look after her sick child, which takes place on pp. 81–3.

---

[1] *Jane Austen's Letters*, ed. Chapman, R.W., London 1932, p. 469.

# 5

# The Place of Women

The limited scope of this chapter must be stressed at the start. 'The place of women' in the world of Jane Austen's novels is an enormous subject, and the aim of this chapter is restricted to finding some definite pointers in the four extracts selected for study. These pointers are then related to the heroine's circumstances in a brief extension discussion, in each case. However, these discussions cannot do more than suggest ideas that the student should develop independently by studying other parts of the text.

We will start without further preamble. Our first extract, from *Pride and Prejudice*, is drawn from Chapter 8. While Jane Bennet is ill at Netherfield, Elizabeth stays there to nurse her. In the evening, Miss Bingley begins to talk of Darcy's sister Georgiana:

> 'How I long to see her again! I never met with anybody who delighted me so much. Such a countenance, such manners! and so extremely accomplished for her age! Her performance on the pianoforte is exquisite.'
>
> 'It is amazing to me,' said Bingley, 'how young ladies can have patience to be so very accomplished as they all are.'
>
> 'All young ladies accomplished! My dear Charles, what do you mean?'
>
> 'Yes, all of them, I think. They all paint tables, cover screens, and net purses. I scarcely know anyone who cannot do all this, and I am sure I never heard a young lady spoken of for the first time, without being informed that she was very accomplished.'
>
> 'Your list of the common extent of accomplishments,' said Darcy, 'has too much truth. The word is applied to many a woman who deserves it no otherwise than by netting a purse

or covering a screen. But I am very far from agreeing with you in your estimation of ladies in general. I cannot boast of knowing more than half-a-dozen, in the whole range of my acquaintance, that are really accomplished.'

'Nor I, I am sure,' said Miss Bingley.

'Then,' observed Elizabeth, 'you must comprehend a great deal in your idea of an accomplished woman.'

'Yes, I do comprehend a great deal in it.'

'Oh! certainly,' cried his faithful assistant, 'no one can be really esteemed accomplished who does not greatly surpass what is usually met with. A woman must have a thorough knowledge of music, singing, drawing, dancing, and the modern languages, to deserve the word; and besides all this, she must possess a ceertain something in her air and manner of walking, the tone of her voice, her address and expressions, or the word will be but half-deserved.'

'All this she must possess,' added Darcy, 'and to all this she must yet add something more substantial, in the improvement of her mind by extensive reading.'

'I am no longer surprised at your knowing *only* six accomplished women. I rather wonder now at your knowing *any*.'

'Are you so severe upon your own sex as to doubt the possibility of all this?'

'*I* never saw such a woman. *I* never saw such capacity, and taste, and application, and elegance, as you describe united.'

Mrs Hurst and Miss Bingley both cried out against the injustice of her implied doubt, and were both protesting that they knew many women who answered this description, when Mr Hurst called them to order, with bitter complaints of their inattention to what was going forward. As all conversation was thereby at an end, Elizabeth soon afterwards left the room.

'Eliza Bennet,' said Miss Bingley, when the door was closed on her, 'is one of those young ladies who seek to recommend themselves to the other sex by undervaluing their own; and with many men, I dare say, it succeeds. But, in my opinion, it is a paltry device, a very mean art.'

'Undoubtedly,' replied Darcy, to whom this remark was chiefly addressed, 'there is meanness in *all* the arts which ladies sometimes condescend to employ for captivation. Whatever bears affinity to cunning is despicable.'

Miss Bingley was not so entirely satisfied with this reply as to continue the subject.

*(Pride and Prejudice*, pp. 35–6)

It is immediately clear that the characters are discussing the place and function of 'young ladies': the subject of their discussion is the subject of our inquiry in this chapter, so we can begin by assembling the relevant information directly from the extract. However, as this is a conversation, and the characters also seem to have unspoken views, feelings and intentions, we will adopt an approach first used in Chapter 3, looking at four distinct 'layers' in the conversation.

The surface layer of this conversation is what the characters say. The extract includes two lists of the 'accomplishments' of 'young ladies'. Mr Bingley begins, mentioning 'paint tables, cover screens, and net purses'. Miss Bingley and Mr Darcy then compile a more demanding list which includes 'a thorough knowledge of music, singing, drawing, dancing, and the modern languages'; 'a certain something in her air and manner of walking, the tone of her voice, her address and expressions' (Miss Bingley); and 'something more substantial, in the improvement of her mind by extensive reading' (Mr Darcy). Elizabeth then rephrases the second list as 'such capacity, and taste, and application, and elegance'. The theoretical part of their discussion, then, analyses the word 'accomplished' according to lists of 'accomplishments'.

What we can call the practical part of the conversation revolves around how many 'young ladies' they know who are 'accomplished'. In this connection, they discuss Miss Darcy, then the first list, then the second list. Miss Bingley says that Miss Darcy is 'so extremely accomplished for her age' with reference to her 'countenance', 'manners', 'performance on the pianoforte' and perhaps her height. This view is not contradicted by anybody. Miss Bingley suggests that Miss Darcy 'delighted me' by being so accomplished.

Bingley says that 'all' young ladies are accomplished, with reference to the first list. Nobody contradicts, but Darcy redefines the subject as '*really* accomplished', meaning the second list. He knows only 'half-a-dozen' who are accomplished according to list 2. Miss Bingley also knows only six such young ladies. Elizabeth does not know any. Miss Bingley and Mrs Hurst then say that they know 'many women' who answer this description.

There is also discussion of Elizabeth. Darcy says that doubting the possibility of any woman being accomplished is being 'severe upon your own sex'. Miss Bingley says that Elizabeth criticises women in order to recommend herself to men. Mr Darcy and Miss Bingley then agree about the 'meanness' of 'arts' – feminine cunning – when they are used for 'captivation' of a man. Darcy calls 'cunning ... despicable'.

The above summary shows that these characters cover a great deal of ground in a short conversation. It is also noticeable that, despite a variety of different views, there is only one stated disagreement: Elizabeth disagrees with Darcy and Bingley's sisters. She thinks no woman fits their definition. However, the main outcome from what the characters say is a strong impression of unreality which is clear in three ways. First, Miss Bingley's flattery of Miss Darcy is unrealistically overstated. The words 'delighted' and 'exquisite', and the exclamations she uses ('such countenance!') betray the artificiality of her tone. Second, Mr Bingley's idea that 'all' young ladies are accomplished is unrealistically uncritical. He bases his opinion on hearsay ('I never heard a young lady spoken of ... etc.'). We do not know whether Mr Bingley is being deliberately satirical here, but clearly his statement bears no relation to reality. Finally, Miss Bingley and Mr Darcy compile list 2, which is unrealistically demanding. The absurdity of their list is betrayed both by the qualifying words they use, which make assessment impossible ('*greatly* surpass', '*thorough* knowledge', 'a *certain* something', '*more* substantial' and '*extensive* reading') and by Miss Bingley's self-contradiction about the number of such women she knows: she agrees to 'half-a-dozen', then says accomplishment must greatly surpass 'what is usually met with', and finally claims to know 'many women' who are accomplished. Additionally, list 2 seems to include different kinds of quality in an uncritical mish-mash. So, physical 'feminine' qualities such as the 'certain something in her air and manner of walking' are lumped together with learned information ('thorough knowledge of the modern languages') and 'knowledge' also seems to cover achievement or skill ('singing, drawing, dancing'). Finally, there is something gratuitously absurd in Mr Darcy, on top of Miss Bingley's list, wanting something 'more substantial'. What is 'more substantial' than excellence in four arts and several languages? Even when analysed by their own internal features, then, the views expressed by the Netherfield party – including Mr Darcy – are rubbish.

Why is this? We understand Jane Austen putting absurdities into Miss Bingley's mouth – but why does she do this for Darcy as well? The answer seems to be twofold. First, there is the weakness of the list, the heavy dependence on qualifying words. We could rephrase Miss Bingley's list as 'a bit of music, singing, drawing, dancing, and a smattering of French and German'. Perhaps Darcy is aware of the shallowness of female education, even in 'feminine' subjects, so he is provoked into adding his idea of 'extensive reading'. Second, however, Miss Bingley lists 'feminine' subjects (the arts, modern languages). The fact that Darcy wants something 'more substantial' implies that he regards 'feminine' subjects as insubstantial, or not really serious. His 'more substantial' refers, in part, to the education a man would receive in those days, and assumes that a man's education was somehow more solid and weighty than a woman's. Darcy's remark is therefore interestingly contradictory: he accepts male/female educational stereotypes, but looks for some 'masculine' qualities in his ideal woman.

The second layer of conversation is the more or less deliberate implication of what a character says. These implications are quite easy to analyse since we know these characters well. Miss Bingley speaks to please Mr Darcy.

Throughout the novel, we are never sure how ironically Mr Bingley makes artless remarks: does he satirise his own naïvety? Lizzie's intervention implies the criticism that they are talking unrealistically. In particular, her summary of 'capacity ... taste ... application, and elegance' highlights the different personal qualities they have lumped together without distinguishing between natural advantage, education and talent. Mr Darcy implies a critical judgment of the shallowness of feminine education; then, at the end of our extract, he implies a rebuke to Miss Bingley for using her 'feminine' cunning in order to 'captivate' him, to which he adds the insult 'despicable'. From these implications, we gain a slightly different impression of the whole conversation. Characters are competing and seeking to demonstrate their greater intelligence (Miss Bingley, Mr Darcy); or asserting the values of common sense (Mr Bingley, Elizabeth).

We are not told what these characters are thinking about at the time of this conversation, although evidence from other parts of the book allows us to guess that Miss Bingley and Darcy are both thinking about Elizabeth. So, we can move on to the fourth layer of the conversation: what does our deeper knowledge of these characters contribute, that may be relevant to the scene?

Elizabeth, at this stage of the book, believes herself to dislike Mr Darcy; yet her conversations with him at Netherfield while Jane is ill, at the ball while dancing, and at Rosings, all have a quality of interest in his opinions and readiness to argue, that betray how important he is to her. In this conversation, her examination of his views ('You must comprehend a great deal in your idea of an accomplished woman') and her disagreement, emphatically expressed ('I rather wonder now at your knowing *any*'), remind us of what Elizabeth says near the end of the novel, that 'you were disgusted with the women who were always speaking and looking and thinking for *your* approbation alone. I roused and interested you, because I was so unlike *them*' (p. 306).

Darcy's character is the most interesting in relation to gender stereotypes. We have already remarked that he accepts the conventional narrow definition of 'feminine'; yet he deplores the cynical use of the 'feminine' stereotype to weaken a man's defences, which he says is 'despicable'. In the battle of the sexes, Darcy is immune to the conventional, stereotypical attack, then. On the other hand, this extract reveals that he is looking for female companionship. His comment that he looks for 'something more substantial' in the form of intellectual equality, shows that Elizabeth did more than merely provoke Darcy's interest. She met a need he already had, a need for a relationship of greater reality and equality than conventional masculine and feminine roles could provide for him.

Much of this extract seems, on the surface, to explore the stereotype of femininity. The conversation treats women as objects, with marketable qualities, and therefore contributes to the theme of commerce between the sexes that is so prominent in Jane Austen's tales of courtship and marriage. Yet the author does go beyond these fixed roles, and hints at the possibility of a less fixed and more equal relationship between the sexes. The irony is that Darcy is still intellectually a chauvinist. He does not question the rigid gender definitions of his time. Instead, he adds to them, 'topping up' the list of accomplishments to suit his own deeper and more human need. We can imagine Jane Austen's amusement: Darcy's positive and human quality expresses itself as a ridiculous male arrogance – he speaks as if any woman who aspires to *him* (the uncriticised male) must be extraordinarily perfect, impossibly accomplished.

Jane Austen's characters are imprisoned within a rigid, materialist system of courtship and marriage. The importance of this system to her heroines cannot be exaggerated: it is the single most crucial issue in their lives, and will literally make or break them. Several minor characters exemplify this point powerfully. For example, Jane Fairfax and Miss Bates in *Emma*, Maria Rushworth in *Mansfield Park* and

Charlotte Collins in *Pride and Prejudice* all convey the
horror of unmarried, or disgraced, life for a woman of the
time. The marriage system was the only means by which Jane
Austen's heroines could make a comfortable and respectable
life for themselves; yet it is presented to them as an incompatible contradiction between romantic qualities (love, intellectual equality, warmth of mutual feelings) and economic
imperatives (equality of class and fortune, sufficient money,
equality of education and 'accomplishments', and so on). In
our first extract we have seen what a powerful grip gender
roles and the buying and selling of 'femininity' has upon the
characters. Jane Austen shows acute awareness of this. She
portrays both Darcy and Elizabeth as unconventional in their
attitudes, yet not able to issue any fundamental challenge to
the system. Whatever they achieve in their relationship, *must*
be achieved within the limits of what society will recognise
and accept. Luckily for them, the disparity of fortune and
class between them is not *too* great. It is useful to look back
at Chapter 4 above, and reread the argument between Lady
Catherine de Bourgh and Elizabeth, from this point of view.

\*       \*       \*

We now turn to *Emma*. Emma Woodhouse is the only
heroine who is financially independent and openly rejects
marriage. Our extract comes from Chapter 10. Harriet is
surprised that Miss Woodhouse does not wish to marry:

> 'I do so wonder, Miss Woodhouse, that you should not be
> married, or going to be married! so charming as you are!' –
> Emma laughed, and replied,
> 'My being charming, Harriet, is not quite enough to induce
> me to marry; I must find other people charming – one other
> person at least. And I am not only, not going to be married, at
> present, but have very little intention of ever marrying at all.'
> 'Ah! so you say; but I cannot believe it.'
> 'I must see somebody very superior to any one I have seen
> yet, to be tempted; Mr Elton, you know, (recollecting herself,)

is out of the question: and I do *not* wish to see any such person. I would rather not be tempted. I cannot really change for the better. If I were to marry, I must expect to repent it.'

'Dear me! – it is so odd to hear a woman talk so!' –

'I have none of the usual inducements of women to marry. Were I to fall in love, indeed, it would be a different thing! but I never have been in love; it is not my way, or my nature; and I do not think I ever shall. And, without love, I am sure I should be a fool to change such a situation as mine. Fortune I do not want; employment I do not want; consequence I do not want: I believe few married women are half as much mistress of their husband's house, as I am of Hartfield; and never, never could I expect to be so truly beloved and important; so always first and always right in any man's eyes as I am in my father's.'

'But then, to be an old maid at last, like Miss Bates!'

'That is as formidable an image as you could present, Harriet; and if I thought I should ever be like Miss Bates! so silly – so satisfied – so smiling – so prosing – so undistinguishing and unfastidious – and so apt to tell every thing relative to every body about me, I would marry to-morrow. But between *us*, I am convinced there never can be any likeness, except in being unmarried.'

'But still, you will be an old maid! and that's so dreadful!'

'Never mind, Harriet, I shall not be a poor old maid; and it is poverty only which makes celibacy contemptible to a generous public! A single woman, with a very narrow income, must be a ridiculous, disagreeable old maid! the proper sport of boys and girls; but a single woman, of good fortune, is always respectable, and may be as sensible and pleasant as anybody else. And the distinction is not quite so much against the candour and common sense of the world as appears at first; for a very narrow income has a tendency to contract the mind, and sour the temper. Those who can barely live, and who live perforce in a very small, and generally very inferior, society, may well be illiberal and cross. This does not apply, however, to Miss Bates; she is only too good natured and too silly to suit me; but, in general, she is very much to the taste of everybody, though single and though poor. Poverty certainly has not contracted her mind: I really believe, if she had only a shilling in the world, she would be very likely to give away sixpence of it; and nobody is afraid of her: that is a great charm.'

'Dear me! but what shall you do? how shall you employ yourself when you grow old?'

'If I know myself, Harriet, mine is an active, busy mind, with a great many independent resources; and I do not perceive why I should be more in want of employment at forty or fifty than one-and-twenty. Woman's usual occupations of eye and hand and mind will be as open to me then, as they are now; or with no important variation. If I draw less, I shall read more; if I give up music, I shall take to carpet-work. And as for objects of interest, objects for the affections, which is, in truth, the great point of inferiority, the want of which is really the great evil to be avoided in *not* marrying, I shall be very well off, with all the children of a sister I love so much, to care about. There will be enough of them, in all probability, to supply every sort of sensation that declining life can need. There will be enough for every hope and every fear; and though my attachment to none can equal that of a parent, it suits my ideas of comfort better than what is warmer and blinder. My nephews and nieces! – I shall often have a niece with me.'

(Emma, pp. 73–4)

We can begin by looking at Harriet's contribution to this dialogue, as she represents the conventional view. Harriet expresses three attitudes in turn. First, she finds Emma's decision not to marry so astonishing as to be unbelievable (it makes her 'wonder', 'I cannot believe it' and 'it is so odd to hear a woman talk so!'). Second, she is horrified at the idea of an 'old maid' which is 'so dreadful'. Finally, she asks a practical question: 'how shall you employ yourself when you grow old?' Harriet's disbelief and astonishment are a testament to the unchallenged hegemony of the conventional view. Her naïve remark that it is 'odd to hear a woman talk so' also reveals that men enjoyed an intellectual freedom denied to women: a man might have unorthodox thoughts, but not a woman. Accepted social attitudes also govern her use of 'old maid' as a pejorative or pitying description. Equally, her third question – what will you do with your life? – expresses the conviction that marriage, child-bearing and housekeeping are the purpose of a woman's life. Any other purpose for female existence is unimaginable. While the rest of Harriet's exclamations simply parrot common prejudice, this question does finally present a clear challenge to Emma. If she does not define her life in terms of marriage, how does she define it?

At the start of the conversation, a modern reader is likely to applaud Emma. Her early speeches have a quality of fresh thought, taking a detached view of social conventions, that is refreshing., Emma's diction is clipped and forthright in these speeches, also. She torpedoes Harriet's illogic precisely: 'My being charming, Harriet, is not quite enough to induce me to marry', at the same time exposing Harriet's assumption that women passively agree to marry: if they are 'charming' enough to be asked, they say yes. Emma continues, reaching concise conclusions and formulating clear premises, in uncharacteristically short sentences such as 'If I were to marry, I must expect to repent it'; and 'I have none of the usual inducements to women to marry'. Emma's argument is that women marry for 'fortune', 'employment' or 'consequence', or to be 'beloved', all of which she has. She has therefore no reason to marry.

A modern reader finds this argument refreshing and exciting, as we already remarked; and we readily laugh at Harriet's simple-minded conventions. However, there is already an irony because Emma's argument is cynical. We commented above that the 'courtship and marriage' theme in Jane Austen's novels explores the incompatibility between human and material values. Emma attempts to deal with both sides of the issue. First, she analyses material imperatives and finds – rightly – that she has no need to marry. When she attempts to deal with human needs, however, her cynical attitude renders her argument absurd. She says that she is already 'so always first and always right' in her father's eyes, that she has no need of another man's admiration. Emma believes, then, that being 'beloved' means never being criticised. Since her ideal lover is modelled on the wittering, brainless Mr Woodhouse, no wonder she (with Jane Austen's emphatic italics) does '*not* wish' to meet a 'very superior' man!

This same cynicism informs Emma's next long answer. She argues that a *poor* old maid is contemptible in the eyes of the world, but a *rich* old maid is not. This, she says, is because poverty 'has a tendency to contract the mind' and makes people bad-tempered. Having advanced this argument, Emma then discusses Miss Bates. The structure of the final two sentences of her speech, from 'This does not apply, however, to Miss Bates', is in marked contrast to the logical tone with which she began the argument. The first of these sentences has four main sections, with two interjections as well ('however' and 'in general'). The conjunctions which relate these four clauses to each other, and the sentence to the one before, are 'however', 'only', 'but' and 'though'. These can be simplified into 'but ... but ... but ... but', a structure of confusion, unable to reach a conclusion. The final sentence of this speech is also in four parts. This time, the four parts can be analysed as *statement, illustration, illustration, statement*. The dislocation in this sentence occurs when the illustration of the first statement ends ('... give away sixpence of it') and Emma changes the subject. Now ('and nobody is afraid of her') she is illustrating a statement she has not yet made, with the effect that for a moment we do not know what she is talking about.

Earlier in the extract, Emma's list of Miss Bates's shortcomings has the same uncontrolled quality: six descriptions linked by dashes. Emma's diction, then, deteriorates when she talks about Miss Bates. The irony is that, while she denies the possibility of becoming like her, Emma's own speech mirrors the directionless clumsiness of Miss Bates's ramblings. We therefore wonder how safe Emma really is from becoming like Miss Bates.

Far more seriously, Emma's initial logic has deserted her. Notice, for example, that at the start of this speech she opines 'A single woman, with a very narrow income, must be a ridiculous, disagreeable old maid!' At the end, she argues that the old maid they are discussing is neither ridiculous nor disagreeable. Her theory is also flawed: the idea that poverty narrows the mind and can 'sour the temper' may sound plausible for a moment, but we soon ask whether it could be the other way around, that a 'narrow' or uneducated mind causes poverty, instead? At all events, Emma clearly enjoys being rich; and finds the poor 'narrow' in mind and 'disagreeable'. She seems eager to project her own narrowness on to others. Most horrifying to the modern reader, Emma regards a 'poor old maid' as 'the proper sport of boys and girls'.

Finally, we turn to Harriet's one real question, and Emma's answer. What will you do with yourself? Harriet asks. Typically, Emma begins with practical materialism – how to pass the time; then she deals with the 'human' side of the question, how she will occupy her heart. On the material question, she replies that she will be busy with 'Woman's usual occupations', and mentions drawing, music and carpet-work. With regard to her 'affections', she will find enough, but not too much, to care for in Isabella's children. Emma says that she does not want a mother's affections, which are 'warmer and blinder'; instead, she will opt for a cooler set of relationships which 'suit my ideas of comfort better'.

This analysis develops the conclusion we reached from studying our *Pride and Prejudice* extract above, that Jane Austen analyses the stereotypes of her time thoroughly. Her characters are variously dimly or clearly aware that they are constricted by being defined by a strict gender stereotype, but although they may twist and turn in the rigid gender role straitjacket, they are unable to formulate a practical alternative, unable to mount a fundamental challenge to the evils of the patriarchal system. So, Emma is acutely aware of the futility of the marriage market; and she analyses 'fortune', 'employment' and 'consequence' with trenchant disdain. But when asked what she will do, Emma cannot imagine other than 'Woman's usual occupations', and she mentions three of the items on Mr and Miss Bingley's lists of accomplishments. Jane Austen, then, explores the difficulties and dilemmas of women caught within the gender game; but always conveys the sheer power of indoctrination as well, which prevents Emma from conceiving an alternative purpose in life.

The extract we have studied presents a strong argument against what we have called the 'system', then; but this argument is not completed. Instead, we understand and sympathise with Emma's ultimate failure to redefine her role: we become vividly aware of the overwhelming power of the assumptions she questions.

Emma's arguments in this extract are also undercut by ironies that surround her own needs and her own character. We will mention a few of these. First, she and Harriet discuss 'employment'. This is heavily ironic since Emma's main 'employment' at this stage of the novel is matchmaking on Harriet's behalf. We are comically reminded of this irony by her sudden recollection that she must flatter Mr Elton to Harriet; and we remember that she dreaded long evenings alone with her father and eagerly sought this new activity (see the first three chapters of *Emma*). Second, Emma claims 'I never have been in love' and that she must meet 'somebody very superior to any one I have seen yet' before she is tempted. Ironically, in Chapter 47, she discovers that she has always loved Mr Knightley. There 'had never been a time' when Mr Knightley's regard was not 'infinitely the most dear'; but she had been 'ignorant of her own heart' (all from p. 339). So, the confident rationalism of Emma's attack on marriage is undercut by self-evasions and self-deceptions. A young girl, being unaware and frightened of her own feelings, engages in surrogate courtship using Harriet (see Chapter 2); this is what a psychologist would

call 'displacement' activity, satisfying her own unacknowl-
edged needs through another. The same girl is terrified of
intimacy, and justifies her avoidance of relationships by
attacking the institution of marriage, calling isolation
'comfort'. Having used Harriet to provide her with the vicarious thrill of courtship, she then plans to use Isabella to
provide her with vicarious motherhood.

Emma's psychology does display all of these twists and
turns: the points raised in the preceding paragraph can all be
argued from evidence in the text. However, we should also
look at the issue of gender roles the other way around. Jane
Austen introduces us to heroines who are under an enormous, all-pervading social pressure to define themselves in
terms of 'femininity', so that they will find a husband and
marry. Elizabeth Bennet reacts by rebelling against materialism: she adopts romantic ideas, and undergoes a bitter,
painful and lengthy education at the hands of life before she
is lucky enough to satisfy both personal and financial needs
in the person of Darcy. Emma's reaction seems to be one of
fear. Her opinions and behaviour through most of the novel
show a young woman attempting to deny the power of social
imperatives. At the same time she denies her own natural
feelings, only discovering her own heart nine chapters from
the end of the novel. Both of the heroines we have discussed
so far, then, have their natural development warped, and
have to struggle through bitter experience in order to understand themselves, largely as a pernicious consequence of the
pitiless gender role they are born and brought up to.

\*     \*     \*

Our extract from *Mansfield Park* shows the cruelty of male
power, enforcing the gender role. Sir Thomas Bertram hears
that Fanny will reject Henry Crawford's proposal:

> 'I do not catch your meaning,' said Sir Thomas, sitting
> down again. – 'Out of your power to return his good opinion!

what is all this? I know he spoke to you yesterday, and (as far as I understand), received as much encouragement to proceed as a well-judging young woman could permit herself to give. I was very much pleased with what I collected to have been your behaviour on the occasion; it shewed a discretion highly to be commended. But now, when he has made his overtures so properly, and honourably – what are your scruples *now*?'

'You are mistaken, Sir,' cried Fanny, forced by the anxiety of the moment even to tell her uncle that he was wrong – 'You are quite mistaken. How could Mr Crawford say such a thing? I gave him no encouragement yesterday – On the contrary, I told him – I cannot recollect my exact words – but I am sure I told him that I would not listen to him, that it was very unpleasant to me in every respect, and that I begged him never to talk to me in that manner again. – I am sure I said as much as that and more; and I should have said still more, – if I had been quite certain of his meaning any thing seriously, but I did not like to be – I could not bear to be – imputing more than might be intended. I thought it might all pass for nothing with *him*.'

She could say no more; her breath was almost gone.

'Am I to understand,' said Sir Thomas, after a few moments' silence, 'that you mean to *refuse* Mr Crawford?'

'Yes, sir.'

'Refuse him?'

'Yes, sir.'

'Refuse Mr Crawford! Upon what plea? For what reason?'

'I – I cannot like him, Sir, well enough to marry him.'

'This is very strange!' said Sir Thomas, in a voice of calm displeasure. 'There is something in this which my comprehension does not reach. Here is a young man wishing to pay his addresses to you, with every thing to recommend him; not merely situation in life, fortune, and character, but with more than common agreeableness, with address and conversation pleasing to every body. And he is not an acquaintance of to-day, you have now known him some time. His sister, moreover, is your intimate friend, and he has been doing *that* for your brother, which I should suppose would have been almost sufficient recommendation to you, had there been no other. It is very uncertain when my interest might have got William on. He has done it already.'

'Yes,' said Fanny, in a faint voice, and looking down with fresh shame; and she did feel almost ashamed of herself, after such a picture as her uncle had drawn, for not liking Mr Crawford.

'You must have been aware,' continued Sir Thomas presently, 'you must have been some time aware of a particularity in Mr Crawford's manners to you. This cannot have taken you by surprise. You must have observed his attentions; and though you always received them very properly (I have no accusation to make on that head), I never perceived them to be unpleasant to you. I am half inclined to think, Fanny, that you do not quite know your own feelings.'

'Oh yes, Sir! indeed I do. His attentions were always – what I did not like.'

Sir Thomas looked at her with deeper surprise. 'This is beyond me,' said he. 'This requires explanation. Young as you are, and having seen scarcely any one, it is hardly possible that your affections – '

He paused and eyed her fixedly. He saw her lips formed into a *no*, though the sound was inarticulate, but her face was like scarlet. That, however, in so modest a girl might be very compatible with innocence; and choosing at least to appear satisfied, he quickly added, 'No, no, I know *that* is quite out of the question – quite impossible. Well, there is nothing more to be said.'

(*Mansfield Park*, pp. 260–1)

There is no question about what is happening in this extract. Sir Thomas represents male authority, and his words and actions speak for the male-dominated system which arranges a woman's life for her. Fanny represents female resistance, setting up her individual feelings and her judgment in opposition to the power Sir Thomas wields. In the words 'calm displeasure', Jane Austen expresses Sir Thomas's male confidence in his rightness and power, and his annoyance when a woman attempts to oppose him. In 'She could say no more; her breath was almost gone', Jane Austen conveys the appalling pressure exerted on the female victim of this process. This much is plain, but our aim in studying the extract is to reach more detailed understanding of the system; and to gain as much insight as we can into the author's purpose, drawing conclusions from the way in which this scene is written.

First, we can look at the contrast between Sir Thomas's and Fanny's styles of speech. Here is a sentence from Fanny:

> I gave him no encouragement yesterday – On the contrary, I told him – I cannot recollect my exact words – but I am sure I told him that I would not listen to him, that it was very unpleasant to me in every respect, and that I begged him never to talk to me in that manner again.

The structure and punctuation of this sentence convey the weakness of Fanny's position. She begins with a statement ('I gave him no encouragement yesterday') but then breaks off at a dash. Here, she seems ready to oppose Mr Crawford's version of events ('On the contrary I told him'), but this momentary impression of assertion is broken. Fanny stops at a dash again, and apologises because she cannot remember her 'exact words', then, after another break and a dash, makes do with the gist of what she said ('but I am sure I told him'). Finally, Fanny comes out with what she said to Mr Crawford in three quick clauses. It is as if there is an almost insurmountable block against her speaking, and each time she tries she comes up against a barrier; then, finally, she breaks through and rushes out her three statements. In this sentence, Fanny contradicts the men and expresses her version of events. However, the rhythm of her speech reveals that she feels insecure, and that it demands an enormous effort for her to speak against Sir Thomas. Jane Austen is precise, however, in conveying Fanny's insecurity. Her doubts are 'I cannot recollect my exact words'. Fanny is not insecure about the truth; but she is insecure about whether she will be believed. Fanny feels that she will need concrete evidence to support her case.

Sir Thomas's way of talking contrasts with this. In the middle of the extract, when he is confronted by Fanny's opposition, we might expect similar signs of anxiety in his speech. Here is one of his sentences:

> Here is a young man wishing to pay his addresses to you, with every thing to recommend him; not merely situation in life, fortune, and character, but with more than common agreeableness, with address and conversation pleasing to every body.

Sir Thomas is sure of himself and sure of the whole world around him. The structure of this sentence shows his belief that he has taken everything into account. The first statement summarises Mr Crawford ('with every thing to recommend him'). The semicolon introduces Sir Thomas's explanation of 'every thing'. In the second part of the sentence, he lists 'situation in life, fortune, and character' (the material considerations); then he lists 'agreeableness,... address and conversation' (the personal considerations). As far as Sir Thomas is concerned, this is a complete list of all the qualities Fanny should consider. His satisfaction with his own system of thought is conveyed in the tone of certainty and finality he reaches in the final four words 'pleasing to every body'. The same certainty that life can be listed and categorised, that life is a closed system, is expressed by Sir Thomas's final words in this extract: 'Well, there is nothing more to be said.' He is certain of his mind, then. On the one occasion when he leaves a sentence open, it is in fact a direct question to Fanny, and he emphasises this when 'he paused and eyed her fixedly'.

Jane Austen increases the contrast, heightening the impression of Fanny's powerlessness, in her descriptions of the two characters. Sir Thomas 'said' (several times), 'continued' and 'added'. In contrast, Fanny 'cried', 'could say no more; her breath was almost gone', 'said ... in a faint voice', and 'her lips formed into a *no*, though the sound was inarticulate'. Notice that Fanny's ability to speak is progressively suppressed, while Sir Thomas continues to speak with ease. Physical details confirm the contrast: Sir Thomas was 'sitting down again', 'looked at her' and 'eyed her fixedly'. He speaks without hurrying, 'after a few moments' silence', 'in a voice of calm displeasure', 'presently', and 'he paused'. The only time he rushes is when he assures himself that she is not already in love, when he 'quickly added'. However, Jane Austen makes it clear that he is quick at this point because he wishes to close off a doubt. Fanny, by contrast, is seen 'looking down with fresh shame', and 'her face was like scarlet'.

Sir Thomas's power over the truth is emphasised by the comment 'choosing at least to appear satisfied'. Not only is Sir Thomas sure of his thoughts: he can also choose what to think, and impose that thought on Fanny. Jane Austen develops this idea repeatedly: Sir Thomas has a well-organised understanding of people and life, and he is thoughtful and conscientious according to his system of beliefs. We have already noticed that he feels able to list Mr Crawford's attributes, and is in no doubt that he has thoroughly defined the man. However, Sir Thomas's system of thought is a closed system. He *only* considers those things he already expects to consider, and he is therefore unable to deal with the variety or unpredictability of life. In this extract, we hear Sir Thomas say 'I do not catch your meaning', 'what is all this?', 'This is very strange!', 'There is something in this which my comprehension does not reach', and 'This is beyond me ... This requires explanation.' Jane Austen has chosen her man carefully: Sir Thomas is not a tyrant, but an earnest and honest man. When he says 'There is something in this which my comprehension does not reach', he is telling the truth.

From this characterisation we gain insight into the limited nature of a male belief system. As a man in authority, Sir Thomas has been used to making decisions for himself and others based on a closed system of thought. When confronted with something new, or challenging, or something that cannot be explained by his system, he is at a loss.

Hence his repeated expressions of bafflement, and his astonished repetition of Fanny's astonishing answer: 'Refuse him?'

In his astonishment, Sir Thomas turns to supports that he
understands, and uses these as levers to force the situation back
into a shape he can recognise. In other words, he tries, using
every means he knows, to make Fanny change her answer.

First, he affects not to understand her ('I do not catch
your meaning'). Then, he attempts to redefine what she says
so that it means the opposite. He begins this by flattering
her, saying that he was 'very much pleased' with her 'discretion' which was 'highly to be commended'. The conclusion
of this effort by Sir Thomas is the suggestion that, because
her refusal does not make sense to him, 'I am half inclined
to think, Fanny, that you do not quite know your own feelings.' Along the way, Sir Thomas has added obligation to the
pressure he applies. He mentions that Mr Crawford 'has
been doing *that* for your brother, which I should suppose
would have been almost sufficient recommendation to you,
had there been no other'. The effect of this strategy is
powerful. Fanny feels 'fresh shame' and 'did feel almost
ashamed of herself ... for not liking Mr Crawford'.

Second, Sir Thomas turns to his understanding of
women. He cannot understand that a woman would refuse
an offer that he analyses as a 'good' offer put forward 'so
properly, and honourably'. The only reason he can imagine
for such a refusal, is if she already loves somebody else.
This is why he asks her 'it is hardly possible that your affections – '. Sir Thomas's attempts to overcome Fanny's resistance, then, lead us to two conclusions. That he is prepared
to use any pressure and any cruelty to force her to comply
with his decision; and that there is no room in his mind for
any independent opinion from her. Indeed, his very question about her heart paradoxically shows that he cannot
conceive of a woman *not* dependent on a man. We have
seen that Sir Thomas will tell her she means the opposite
of what she says, will 'choose' what to believe, and cannot
conceive of her heart not being occupied by a man.

The pressure on Fanny, then, is to *be* what Sir Thomas believes a woman to be; and she is not allowed to be herself. It is interesting to think about this conclusion in relation to other contexts in the novel, also. A brief look elsewhere reveals several occasions when Fanny is similarly treated. In Chapter 33, for example, Henry Crawford does not believe that she will not love him. He might be saying, as Sir Thomas did, that she does not know her own feelings. More particularly he declares that he loves her 'for her gentleness, and her goodness' (p. 270). In the next chapter he says that she is 'infinitely my superior in merit' and has 'some touches of the angel' in her that he will 'worship' (p. 284). When Edmund pressures her, he tells her that she will 'make him [Crawford] every thing' because he has unsteady principles, but she is 'firm as a rock in her own principles' (p. 291) with 'a gentleness of character' (p.290). When Fanny argues the case for a woman's freedom of choice, Edmund does not hear her. He reinterprets her statements as meaning that the 'novelty' of Crawford's proposal put her off, and concludes from this that Crawford should 'persevere' (p. 293). Finally, when Edmund's heart turns from Mary to Fanny, Jane Austen wryly emphasises that he approaches proposing to Fanny in a typically male manner. Edmund tries 'to persuade her that her warm and sisterly regard for him would be foundation enough for wedded love' (p.387).

These examples have one element in common: they are all examples of men who try to force Fanny to *be* the person they imagine her to be. The final example is perhaps the most poignant. Even when he proposes, Edmund attributes a 'sisterly' feeling to her, the emotion he has wrongly imagined her to feel for him since they were children. The irony is that she has never been – and still is not – the Fanny he imagines. But on this occasion, what he offers for all the wrong reasons and with a typical masculine failure to comprehend either himself or her, she wishes to accept. The novel as a whole, then, explores Fanny's experience as a female victim of male power and gender stereotypes. Men are blind to her feelings, deaf to what she says, and project several imagined characters upon her, that they have dreamed up themselves.

We have noticed before that Jane Austen often uses her irony to tease us for being too clever. Remember our comment on the opening sentence of *Pride and Prejudice*: we are invited to think ourselves cleverer than the common opinion; yet, as it turns out, Mr Bingley *is* 'in want of a wife'. So Jane Austen reminds us of the comic laws of nature, and is amused by their predictable simplicity. Irrespective of social expectations or personal opinions, young people do tend to fall in love. This effect of an ironic 'double-bluff' occurs in *Pride and Prejudice*, as we have noticed. It is also present in *Emma*: the ironic background to Emma's determination not to marry, is that she is in love already. In the case of Fanny, we have analysed a devastating satire on blinkered male tyranny. Ironically, however, Sir Thomas's guess was right: Fanny's affections are already engaged, and she is protected from Crawford's advances because she is already in love with another man. Male power deprives Fanny of the right to her own feelings, then. But what would her own feelings have been, had she been free to express them? Only the same, natural feelings other young girls have; and Jane Austen implies that it is natural that this should be so.

\*     \*     \*

Our next extract, from Chapter 4 of *Persuasion*, explains the considerations that led Anne Elliot to break her engagement to Captain Wentworth, seven years before the start of the novel:

> Anne Elliot, with all her claims of birth, beauty, and mind, to throw herself away at nineteen; involve herself at nineteen in an engagement with a young man, who had nothing but himself to recommend him, and no hopes of attaining affluence, but in the chances of a most uncertain profession, and

no connexions to secure even his farther rise in that profession; would be, indeed, a throwing away, which she grieved to think of! Anne Elliot, so young; known to so few, to be snatched off by a stranger without alliance or fortune; or rather sunk by him into a state of most wearing, anxious, youth-killing dependance! It must not be, if by any fair interference of friendship, any representations from one who had almost a mother's love, and mother's rights, it would be prevented.

Captain Wentworth had no fortune. He had been lucky in his profession, but spending freely, what had come freely, had realized nothing. But, he was confident that he would soon be rich; – full of life and ardour, he knew that he should soon have a ship, and soon be on a station that would lead to every thing he wanted. He had always been lucky; he knew he should be so still. – Such confidence, powerful in its own warmth, and bewitching in the wit which often expressed it, must have been enough for Anne; but Lady Russell saw it very differently. – His sanguine temper, and fearlessness of mind, operated very differently on her. She saw in it but an aggravation of the evil. It only added a dangerous character to himself. He was brilliant, he was headstrong. – Lady Russell had little taste for wit; and of any thing approaching imprudence a horror. She deprecated the connexion in every light.

Such opposition, as these feelings produced, was more than Anne could combat. Young and gentle as she was, it might yet have been possible to withstand her father's ill-will, though unsoftened by one kind word or look on the part of her sister; – but Lady Russell, who she had always loved and relied on, could not, with such steadiness of opinion, and such tenderness of manner, be continually advising her in vain. She was persuaded to believe the engagement a wrong thing – indiscreet, improper, hardly capable of success, and not deserving it. But it was not merely selfish caution, under which she acted, in putting an end to it. Had she not imagined herself consulting his good, even more than her own, she could hardly have given him up. – The belief of being prudent, and self-denying principally for *his* advantage, was her chief consolation, under the misery of a parting – a final parting; and every consolation was required, for she had to encounter all the additional pain of opinions, on his side, totally unconvinced and unbending, and of his feeling himself ill-used by so forced a relinquishment. – He had left the country in consequence.

A few months had seen the beginning and the end of their acquaintance; but, not with a few months ended Anne's share of suffering from it. Her attachment and regrets had, for a long time, clouded every enjoyment of youth; and an early loss of bloom and spirits had been their lasting effect.

*(Persuasion*, pp. 55–7)

This extract falls into sections, so we can begin by noting what they are. The first paragraph adopts Lady Russell's point of view, and expresses her hostility towards Anne's engagement. The second presents Captain Wentworth's optimism, but the final five sentences swing back to express Lady Russell's objections to his character. The third paragraph explains the pressures Anne was under, and narrates her breaking the engagement and the final quarrel with Wentworth. Finally, Jane Austen takes a distanced view of the brevity of the whole affair, bringing the reader back to the present, seven years after these events.

Jane Austen's narrative is not static, then, but dynamic: her viewpoint shifts from Lady Russell to Captain Wentworth and back to Lady Russell. She writes both sides powerfully. So, when describing Lady Russell's views, she says 'It must not be'; while Captain Wentworth 'had always been lucky; he knew he should be so still'. The shift between the first paragraph (Lady Russell) and the second (Captain Wentworth) is stark, conveying their total opposition. Halfway through the second paragraph, however, the viewpoint passes through Anne. The sentence begins with Captain Wentworth ('Such confidence') and exerts its pressure on Anne ('must have been enough for Anne') before passing to the opposite view.

The last two paragraphs of the extract show Anne in an increasingly subjected role. 'Combat', 'withstand', 'relied on', 'persuaded', 'self-denying', 'misery', 'encounter ... additional pain' and 'suffering'. So, as these arguments and events unfold, Anne is increasingly presented as a battleground for which the other two fight. Now, what are these two views that battle it out through Anne?

Lady Russell's opinion is founded on two ideas. The first is a calculation of sexual value. In her view Anne Elliot has value because of her 'birth, beauty, and mind' while Captain Wentworth has no value – he is 'a young man, who had nothing but himself'. Lady Russell thinks about their inequality in terms of price and the values of the marketplace, so she calls the alliance 'a throwing away', a phrase Jane Austen inserts twice into this paragraph, underlining the commercial foundation of these ideas. Lady Russell's second idea is her hostile assessment of Captain Wentworth's character. She reacts to his enthusiasm and optimism in relentlessly negative terms. They are an 'evil', and he is 'dangerous', 'headstrong', with 'imprudence' which makes her feel 'horror'. In the middle of this oppressive list of risks, Jane Austen places the one word 'brilliant'. This word also provokes Lady Russell ('[she] had little taste for wit'), but for the reader it conveys the ambivalence of the whole conundrum. We know, from reading the novel, that Captain Wentworth's optimism turned out to be justified: he did make a fortune quickly. On the other hand, he acknowledges (see p. 90) that his career was very chancy, and on one occasion at least he was very nearly lost at sea. How, then, should we attempt to predict the future? By presenting these two powerful views so starkly opposed, and by highlighting Anne's suffering as they use their domination of her to fight over her, Jane Austen reveals how open any true understanding of life's potential must be; and how futile is the attempt to rationalise such decisions as Anne faced at the age of nineteen. The truth is, that had she married Wentworth then, Anne would have had to accept the 'chances of a most uncertain profession': nobody, not Wentworth himself or Lady Russell, could predict what would happen.

The main thrust of Jane Austen's criticisms in this extract are against Lady Russell's view, then. As we have seen, she relies on lists of qualities ('claims of birth, beauty, and mind'; and 'dangerous ... headstrong ... imprudence') in order to assess the situation and reach an understanding of life. This thought process reminds us of Miss Bingley's motley list of different qualities jumbled together in *Pride and Prejudice* (notice that Anne has claims of 'birth' and 'beauty'!); and Sir Thomas Bertram's definition of Mr Crawford as the ideal young man, which is also based on a list (see the *Mansfield Park* extract above). The dominance of such lists over Lady Russell's mind is further emphasised when Anne is 'persuaded': the engagement is 'indiscreet, improper, hardly capable of success, and not deserving it'. Notice that Jane Austen expects us to reach our own conclusions: she lists four objections, three of which are not relevant to the situation, but expects the reader to actively compare the terms with the reality, and reach this judgment. The engagement is not 'improper' or 'indiscreet' (Anne and Captain Wentworth have done nothing immoral), and there is no reason why their mutual love is 'not deserving [success]'. Lady Russell simply adds more objections, indiscriminately, to her one real one: that the future is uncertain.

There is another bitterly ironic touch in this extract, where the author plainly expects us to make a direct comparison and draw our own conclusions. Lady Russell feels that the marriage would place Anne in 'a state of most wearing, anxious, youth-killing dependance'. The author does not comment on this directly, but in the final paragraph we hear that Anne's regrets 'clouded every enjoyment of youth; and an early loss of bloom and spirits had been their lasting effect'. The irony is precise: Lady Russell, with her tabulated, cautious assessment of life, has achieved precisely the evil she tried to avoid.

What is Jane Austen's interest in these developments? Our reading of the whole novel does not allow us to reach partisan conclusions. At the end of the book, Anne herself concludes that Lady Russell did 'err in her advice' and says that she would never 'give such advice'. On the other hand, she believes that she was 'perfectly right in being guided' by Lady Russell at that time. Wentworth's success is simply the outcome – it is what happened – but we are reminded several times that his career could have gone terribly wrong. It seems, then, that Jane Austen presents life as full of surprise and variety. Reality is open-ended, and it is this openness she contrasts with the several portraits of closed, limited thought systems that we have found in this chapter.

Our interest in this chapter, then, has been to analyse the closed thought system about women, and particularly about courtship and marriage, which comes broadly under the heading of 'gender stereotyping'. As we would expect from Jane Austen, our extracts have found the theme treated in a variety of manners and contexts. So, Miss Bingley and Mr Darcy, with their list of 'accomplishments', are absurd; Emma, with her argument against marriage, is ironically self-deceived, and although she struggles half-way out from gender conditioning, she fails to formulate an alternative; Sir Thomas Bertram's closed mind is oppressive and cruel; and finally, Lady Russell's attempt to reduce and rationalise life causes bitter suffering.

## Conclusions

Jane Austen, then, analyses sexual stereotypes and prejudices in detail, and continuously, in her novels. However, she goes further than merely to deplore the prevailing attitude towards women. Here are some summary conclusions that can be drawn from the studies we have carried out in this chapter.

1.  Jane Austen takes the disadvantaged position of women, both as wives and in upbringing and courtship, as a major theme in all of the novels. Gender stereotyp-

ing, and the marriage choice in particular, are the overwhelming issues confronting all four of the heroines. In
each case, Jane Austen presents this theme as a problem
the heroine is initially unable to cope with.

2.  Male and female power and helplessness are fully
    analysed and explored in the novels. Manipulation in
    'gender games' is constantly shown in action.

3.  A single romantic partnership, as equal as is attainable
    within that society, is the desired aim of the heroines;
    and is celebrated by the author, but with a delicate
    implication of cynical laughter. Each heroine has to
    come to terms with the unchallengeable power of
    social conventions, and reconcile this with her own
    natural feelings.

4.  Jane Austen broadens the theme from specific satire of
    gender conventions, to a more general critique of atti-
    tudes towards life. The closed mind, with a limited
    thought system, typically causes suffering and does
    harm, or reaches absurd conclusions. In contrast to this,
    life is presented as ironically surprising, unpredictable
    and open. This means that life contains exciting and
    limitless possibilities.

5.  In (4) above, we mention life with 'limitless possibili-
    ties'. Jane Austen, however, also conveys the enor-
    mous power of social conditioning and convention;
    and her heroines recognise – sooner or later – that
    they will have to reach their solutions as individuals,
    within the bounds of convention, not by means of
    rebellion. Ultimately, then, the novels present a
    compromise of outcome.

6.  Conflict between gender role and personal identity is a
    serious problem in the psychology of each of the hero-
    ines. For example, Emma Woodhouse does not under-
    stand her own feelings for a long time, partly because
    she reactively denies and avoids the marriage pressure;
    and Fanny Price's personal identity is constantly misrep-
    resented by men, even at the end of the novel.

7. We discussed dualities between appearance and truth, and between conservative and radical forces, in the conclusion of Chapter 3 above. We suggested, tentatively, that these form a central 'theme' in Jane Austen's novels. In this chapter, we have found further points to add to our concept of **central dualities**. First, there are two related views of women and their role in marriage: on the one hand, that they are objects of decoration and entertainment; and on the other hand, that men and women seek an intellectual and behavioural equal with whom to 'share' life.

8. The second duality we have found in this chapter, is that between closed and open thought systems. Closed thought systems (for example, those of Sir Thomas Bertram in *Mansfield Park* and Lady Russell in *Persuasion*) are often related to conservative forces and the principle of stability, as opposed to an open attitude to life and reality, which faces more towards change, and the unexpected outcomes of an ironic life.

## Methods of Analysis

- We have used analytical techniques demonstrated in previous chapters, as appropriate. However, as when we analysed **structure**, or **society**, in this chapter we have approached each extract with a particular question in mind. We have focused on the question of gender: *how does the fact that this character is female, affect her words/actions/thoughts/emotions at this moment; and how does her gender affect (alter, limit) the behaviour of others towards her?*

- So, it is helpful to begin analysing with a specific question in your mind. We have now shown the usefulness of this approach in three successive chapters. Naturally, it would be possible (but difficult in Jane Austen's work!) to choose an extract where there is hardly anything to say about the place of women and men, or what we have called 'gender issues'. Then we would have to accept the lack of an answer to the specific question. So, use common sense and your general knowledge of the text, when deciding which questions to bring to the fore in relation to a particular passage.

- Normally, however, you are likely to find that several different questions can bring enriched understanding, all applied to the same passage. For example, the argument between Sir Thomas Bertram and Fanny Price, from *Mansfield Park*, analysed in this chapter, would yield rich material if we were to study it from the points of view of either thematic **structure** or the **structure of conversation, society** or **character**.

- As you become more confident and experienced at detailed textual study, then, you will become used to keeping several questions about the text in your mind. This is a great help, as you will then quickly identify the important or outstanding concerns within an episode.

### Suggested Work

Jane Austen's analysis of gender issues pervades the novels so fully, that your best course will be to study further passages from this point of view. Here is one suggestion from each of the four novels we focus on. There are, of course, innumerable others, but these will get you started and provide good practice.

- In *Pride and Prejudice*, look at Mr Collins's letter to Mr Bennet on p. 240. Mr Collins's attitude to marriage is an absurd combination of hard materialism and improbable romantic cliché, and makes a fascinating study. This may spur you to think about romantic cliché in the novel as a whole, and to look at Mrs Bennet's and Lydia Bennet's approaches to love and marriage.

- In *Emma*, look at pp. 246–8, from 'Oh! my dear, we cannot begin too early ...' to '... that nothing really unexceptionable may pass us.' In this passage, Mrs Elton and Jane Fairfax discuss Jane's future career as a governess.

- In *Mansfield Park*, look at Fanny's comments and thoughts about her mother when she visits Portsmouth. Begin on p. 323 from 'Her disappointment in her mother ...' and go as far as p. 324, '... how they would have managed without her.' This extract shows a side of female duty and life not often seen in Jane Austen's novels, although sometimes alluded to: housekeeping and the orderly running of the home. The ironic context of this passage – in that Fanny is used to the orderliness brought by wealth – and its place in promoting Mr Crawford's near success with Fanny when he visits Portsmouth, provide avenues of further thought and investigation.

- In *Persuasion*, study the narrative of Anne soothing Captain Benwick's broken heart on pp. 121–2, from 'While Captain Wentworth and Harville led the talk . . .' to the end of the chapter. Here, you may find Benwick's display of 'female' characteristics, and his seeking out female company, an interesting and amusing topic to investigate more widely in the text.

# 6

# The Theme of Change and the Change of Theme

## The Theme of Change

There is a theme of change in each of the four novels we are studying. However, the idea of change takes a different form in each text. In the extract from *Pride and Prejudice* we examined in Chapter 4, we noticed that the conflict between Elizabeth and Lady Catherine de Bourgh hinges on two different perceptions of society, a more reactionary view in conflict with the 'modern' view articulated by Elizabeth; whereas in *Emma*, the heroine's progress leads her towards a deeper appreciation of Mr Knightley's serious principles, and her traditional role of patronage in society. Emma moves away from her initial light-hearted attitude, which values amusement and entertainment more highly. In this chapter we begin by taking a short extract from each of the novels, to discuss the form a theme of change takes in that particular text. Later in the chapter, we search more widely and freely through the novels, seeking to understand Jane Austen's underlying concept of change and how this develops between her early and later works.

In *Pride and Prejudice*, Elizabeth Bennet rapturously accepts her aunt and uncle's invitation to join them in a tour of Derbyshire and the Lake District:

> what delight! what felicity! You give me fresh life and vigour. Adieu to disappointment and spleen. What are men to rocks and mountains? Oh! what hours of transport we shall

spend! And when we *do* return, it shall not be like other travellers, without being able to give one accurate idea of anything. We *will* know where we have gone – we *will* recollect what we have seen. Lakes, mountains, and rivers shall not be jumbled together in our imaginations; nor when we attempt to describe any particular scene, will we begin quarrelling about its relative situation. Let our first effusions be less insupportable than those of the generality of travellers.

(*Pride and Prejudice*, p. 129)

Elizabeth's exclamation 'what are men to rocks and mountains?' is partly tongue-in-cheek, as she has just been talking with Mrs Gardiner about Wickham's desertion. Most of this speech, however, expresses her feelings. She uses powerful language: the tour will be 'delight' and 'felicity', bringing her 'fresh life and vigour' and 'hours of transport'. This language contrasts with the single contemptuous monosyllable 'men', and emotions that are clearly of lesser strength and importance, 'disappointment' and the angry self-pity of 'spleen'. The contrast is striking: Elizabeth has been involved in the affairs of Longbourn and Meryton, and the irritation of this life has built up into the petulant, nihilistic mood in which she said to Mrs Gardiner 'I am sick of them all [young men]' and 'Stupid men are the only ones worth knowing, after all' (p. 129). Suddenly, she expresses eagerness and hope, wishing to find something more worthwhile than 'disappointment' and 'spleen'. Her enthusiasm is striking, suffusing the end of this cynical chapter with a sudden idealistic glow. As we have seen, there is a strong contrast between significant experience ('delight', 'felicity'), which Elizabeth desires, and small, self-absorbed emotions ('disappointment', 'spleen') from which she longs to escape.

The second half of Elizabeth's speech expresses her resolve to observe accurately and rationally. Her determination is emphasised by the twice italicised '*will*': 'we *will* know' and 'we *will* recollect'. Elizabeth insists on having an 'accurate idea' of their experiences: she is determined to 'know' and 'recollect'; and she must understand things in their 'relative situation' without having them 'jumbled together' in the mind. In this, she sees herself in contrast to 'other travellers' and 'the generality of travellers', who are 'insupportable'. Here, then, Elizabeth yearns for some experience of real significance; and is determined to use the powers of her mind to reach and communicate the truth about it.

This extract relates to the theme of change in *Pride and Prejudice*, as it expresses a longing for something of real, intrinsic value, and the vigorously rationalist approach to reality Elizabeth adopts. During her argument with Lady Catherine de Bourgh, for example, Elizabeth points out the illogic of Lady Catherine's prejudices with merciless accuracy, saying 'would *my* refusing to accept his hand make him wish to bestow it on his cousin?' (p. 287), and as we remarked in Chapter 4, Lady Catherine's reference to 'the shades of Pemberley' aptly shows the superstitious nature of her ideas. We can suggest, then, that Elizabeth's rationality is a strong weapon against the absurdity and triviality of the life we find her living at the start of the novel.

Several other aspects of the novel seem to follow a parallel pattern of change. Darcy, for example, points out that his 'good principles' were not put into practice until he was 'humbled' by Elizabeth. Until she rejected him, he was too insubstantial a person and his 'pretensions to please a woman worthy of being pleased' were 'insufficient' (p. 297). The crucial word here is 'worthy'. In this word, Jane Austen again makes the distinction between those others, the 'generality of travellers', whose experiences and recollections are jumbled and inferior, and someone 'worthy' who – she implies – has significance and intrinsic value. Elizabeth seems to refer to the same quality of real value, when she thinks that Darcy's 'judgment, information, and knowledge of the world' would give her benefit of 'importance' (p. 252).

Just as Darcy moves from being a spoiled man whose principles, although sound, are not founded in experience to becoming a man of active generosity, so Elizabeth moves from approving the superficial qualities of Wickham to appreciating the 'greater importance' of Darcy. Pemberley itself brings forward this point, and Elizabeth's response to touring the house is littered with contrasts between real and superficial values. Mrs Reynolds' testimony is of 'no trifling nature' but is 'valuable'; Darcy's taste is not 'gaudy or uselessly fine' and has less of 'splendour' and more 'real elegance' than Lady Catherine's. Her thoughts emphasise the importance of Darcy: 'how much of good or evil must be done by him!'.

The theme of change in *Pride and Prejudice*, then, seems to be expressed as a vigorous movement towards discovering real values that will stand up to rational scrutiny; and the discarding of false, superficial values, the trivia and absurdities so abundant in Longbourn and Meryton at the start of the novel.

It is important that this is a movement involving change, not merely the discovery of more important values. Jane Austen reminds us of this on the final page of the novel. The Gardiners have proved to be Elizabeth's most valuable relatives, showing warmth, loyalty and rational good sense. They provide vital help to the two eldest Bennet girls, giving Jane a home in London during the winter, and taking Elizabeth with them on their holiday. In the new rational world, where superficial old hierarchies give way to real values of merit and reason, they have earned their place. So, with an explicit reference to the absurdity of Lady Catherine's views, Jane Austen rewards them with regular visits to Pemberley: 'at Pemberley, in spite of that pollution which its woods had received, not merely from the presence of such a mistress [Elizabeth], but the visits of her uncle and aunt from the city' (p. 312). In the first half of the novel, we remember, Darcy commented that having an uncle in trade was a serious disadvantage to the Bennet girls: '… it must very materially lessen their chance of marrying men of any consideration in the world' (p. 33), he said. Things have, indeed, changed.

\*          \*          \*

In *Emma*, the theme of change is largely integrated into the education and maturing of the heroine: she needs to learn the difference between insincere and self-regarding sensations, and sincere emotion. The overwhelming change in the novel occurs as Emma's vain pursuit of match making for others, gives way to her genuine and necessary pursuit of happiness in marriage, for herself. However, in the course of the novel, some other, wider changes take place that hint at longer-term adjustments in the social fabric of the times. The theme can be compared to that in *Pride and Prejudice*, yet it is muted. In *Emma*, everything is undercut by the author's irony. For example, when Emma – first lady of the district – is prevailed upon to dine with the Coles for the first time ever, this is a significant social milestone in the development of Highbury. Miss Wodehouse, of the landed class, acknowledges the family of a working professional as part of her social milieu. We are reminded of Darcy's early opinion of the Gardiners (he disapproves of them because Mr Gardiner earns his living), and the dramatic change in his attitudes during *Pride and Prejudice*. In the case of *Emma*, however, Jane Austen lessens our impression of movement by emphasising continued social distinctions. Emma wondered whether she would regret accepting the invitation, but did not regret it because: 'She was received with a cordial respect which could not but please, and given all the consequence she could wish for' (p. 177).

Occasionally, a deeper theme of change surfaces, however, as in the following passage which considers the import of Mrs Churchill's death:

> Even Mr Weston shook his head, and looked solemn, and said, 'Ah! poor woman, who would have thought it!' and

> resolved, that his mourning should be as handsome as possible; and his wife sat sighing and moralising over her broad hems with a commiseration and good sense, true and steady. How it would affect Frank, was among the earliest thoughts of both. It was also a very early speculation with Emma. The character of Mrs Churchill, the grief of her husband – her mind glanced over them both with awe and compassion – and then rested with lightened feelings on how Frank might be affected by the event, how benefited, how freed. She saw in a moment all the possible good.
>
>                                            (*Emma*, p. 319)

This passage begins by remarking that Mr Weston looked 'solemn'. Before this, the news of Mrs Churchill's death has thrown 'every thing else into the back-ground' (pp. 318–19) and Jane Austen, in mock-sonorous tone, has written 'The great Mrs Churchill was no more' before more soberly commenting that 'It was felt as such things must be felt' (both p. 319). In the passsage, Emma also feels 'awe and compassion' on hearing the news. These elements give the finality of death its due, and suggest that the event has a grand aspect which touches everybody, whether they knew and liked the dead woman, or not. A counter-movement in contrast to 'awe' is also present, however. Mr Weston thinks about his 'handsome' mourning; Mrs Weston sits 'sighing and moralising over her broad hems' – a bizarre combination of the large theme, death, with small everyday pursuits. This is echoed by Emma's mind which 'glanced' over death but quickly 'settled' on the future. Very soon, the words 'lightened', 'benefited' and 'freed' and the emphasis on sudden speed – 'the earliest thoughts', 'very early speculation', 'she saw in a moment' – bring a feeling of imminent liberation and change.

    In the context of the novel, Mrs Churchill wields unchallenged reactionary power. Frank Churchill and Jane Fairfax cannot contemplate marrying, as long as she is alive. Set against this irrational, hierarchical snobbery, are the valuable qualities of sincerity, ability and firm principles embodied in

Jane Fairfax. The situation therefore mirrors the conflict between Elizabeth and Lady Catherine de Bourgh, in *Pride and Prejudice*. Mrs Churchill's death removes a powerful oppressive influence which has prevented the forces of modernisation and reform from giving new energy to society. Jane Austen's treatment of the event, in the passage we have looked at, pays due respect to its significance, and expresses its liberating effect.

*          *          *

In *Mansfield Park* the struggle between generations is at its fiercest. We have already met the pervasive conflicts of *Mansfield Park*, when studying extracts in previous chapters; and we have suggested that there is really a single, all-embracing conflict between two forces, which manifests itself as bitter opposition between London and the country, between an older and a younger generation, and shows up in the form of disputes on almost every subject, such as improvements, the clergy, marriage, theatricals and acting, and finally family morality. The following brief extract concerns the custom of family prayers. Fanny, Edmund, Miss Crawford and others are in the chapel at Sotherton. Mrs Rushworth is speaking:

> 'It is a handsome chapel, and was formerly in constant use both morning and evening. Prayers were always read in it by the domestic chaplain, within the memory of many. But the late Mr Rushworth left it off.'
>
> 'Every generation has its improvements,' said Miss Crawford, with a smile, to Edmund.
>
> Mrs Rushworth was gone to repeat her lesson to Mr Crawford; and Edmund, Fanny and Miss Crawford remained in a cluster together.
>
> 'It is a pity,' cried Fanny, 'that the custom should have been discontinued. It was a valuable part of former times. There is something in a chapel and chaplain so much in character with a great house, with one's ideas of what such a household

should be! A whole family assembling regularly for the purpose of prayer is fine!'

'Very fine, indeed!' said Miss Crawford, laughing. 'It must do the heads of the family a great deal of good to force all the poor housemaids and footmen to leave business and pleasure, and say their prayers here twice a day, while they are inventing excuses themselves for staying away.'

(*Mansfield Park*, p. 73)

The two views are opposed. Fanny sees family prayers as a 'valuable' custom 'in character' with a 'great' house. In her mind, she has an 'idea of what such a household should be' and regards it as being 'fine'. We notice that part of her vision of a well-regulated life is a 'whole family assembling', in other words the orderliness and harmony we have remarked before about Sir Thomas's rule at Mansfield Park. Miss Crawford, on the other hand, argues on behalf of individuals who do not share the interests of a harmonious group. She sees unwilling servants taken away from their work or leisure by 'force'; and a master and mistress who prefer to pursue individual goals, so they invent 'excuses' to avoid communal prayers. Later in the argument, Miss Crawford suggests 'leave people to their own devices' and 'Every body likes to go their own way.' She objects to 'obligation', 'formality', 'restraint'. In her view, communal prayers inspire everybody with 'unwilling feelings'.

This passage, then, presents us with a direct argument between an old custom involving communal duties, and a modern attitude where personal wishes, the individual's right to freedom from duty to the group, are of supreme importance. Jane Austen ironically undercuts each of these views. Fanny puts forward an 'idea' of what 'should be'. But we know the cruelty and hollowness of Mansfield Park's 'harmony': with Sir Thomas absent, the family has begun to break down into a set of individuals pursuing personal gratification and in conflict with each other. At the same time, Mrs Norris's power and her persecution of Fanny both show that there is something terribly wrong with the Bertram family. Therefore, Fanny's 'ideas of what such a household should be' are a fantasy: she is talking about the kind of family the Bertrams pretend to be, not about what *is*.

Miss Crawford's argument is undercut by her cynicism. She assumes the master and mistress to be selfish and lazy, just as she assumes uncooperative servants. This view poses as realism, in opposition to Fanny's idealism; but what it amounts to is an indictment of humanity: everybody is selfish, nobody will do anything for the good of the group. Miss Crawford is describing humanity in her own image, then, and her cynicism ironically cuts against herself. When, on the next page, she wonders whether the chaplain was an attractive man, irony puts her in the spotlight again: Miss Crawford is, unwittingly, falling in love with a clergyman.

There can be no doubt that this argument is about change. Fanny, for example, calls family prayers a 'part of former times'; and Miss Crawford imagines those from the past seeing the freedoms of modern life with 'joy and envy'. So, there is a battle between the old order of family and social responsibilities, and a new order built upon individual desires. The brief discussion of family prayers is related to another argument about conservation and change, by Miss Crawford's pun on 'improvements'.

In *Mansfield Park*, then, the theme of change takes the form of multiple conflicts: many skirmishes and battles are fought on many battlegrounds, between different groups and individuals in the novel. The outcome – as we will see later in this chapter – is a theme shot through with ambiguity, a complex and partly tragic view of stasis and change, where no solution is found.

\*          \*          \*

*Persuasion* brings significant historical changes into the novel. With the exception of brief mentions of Antigua in *Mansfield Park*, this is the only one of the four novels where a historical or economic backdrop is more than sketchily alluded to. The novel begins with the peace, the end of the protracted Napoleonic Wars. The opening chapters are dominated by economic change: the value of an agricultural estate was diminishing, and we hear considerable detail of Sir Walter Elliot's financial difficulties. At the same time, naval commanders are a new class of rich, successful men, and the vigour and virtues of naval officers figure prominently throughout *Persuasion*. In Chapter 3, Sir Walter Elliot criticises the worn-out looks of those who have been to sea. Mrs Clay makes the following observation:

> is not it the same with many other professions, perhaps most others? Soldiers, in active service, are not at all better off: and even in the quieter professions, there is a toil and a labour of the mind, if not of the body, which seldom leaves a man's looks to the natural effect of time. The lawyer plods, quite care-worn; the physician is up at all hours, and travelling in all weather; and even the clergyman – ' she stopt a moment to consider what might do for the clergyman; – 'and even the clergyman, you know, is obliged to go into infected rooms, and expose his health and looks to all the injury of a poisonous atmosphere. In fact, as I have long been convinced, though every profession is necessary and honourable in its turn, it is only the lot of those who are not obliged to follow any, who can live in a regular way, in the country, choosing their own hours, following their own pursuits, and living on their own property, without the torment of trying for more; it is only *their* lot, I say, to hold the blessings of health and a good appearance to the utmost: I know no other set of men but what lose something of their personableness when they cease to be quite young.'
>
> (*Persuasion*, p. 50)

The vision of life put forward in this speech is one where every activity, every movement, involves physical wear. Our enemies are 'toil and labour of the mind', 'all weathers', and the 'poisonous atmosphere' of 'infected rooms', not to mention the hardships of military service. All of these things bring about a regrettable change, ruining one's good looks. The only escape from change is to live without any activity and without needs, according to Mrs Clay. Only those who are 'not obliged to follow' any profession can live 'without the torment of trying for more' and be wonderfully preserved from the ravages of time.

The speech is a flattering compliment to Sir Walter, of course: it is part of Mrs Clay's scheme to worm her way into his favour so he will marry her. However, in the context of the novel it does articulate a more widespread view. For example, in Chapter 1 Jane Austen observes that Elizabeth Elliot is still as handsome at twenty-nine as she was at sixteen, and comments that Sir Walter can therefore be excused or thought 'only half a fool' (p. 38) for imagining that he and his daughter have not aged in thirteen years. Sir Walter reads the Baronetage to 'drive [his debts] from his thoughts' (p. 40). So, the hope that change can be avoided by inactivity, or hidden from by burying your head in contemplating an obsolete aristocracy, is one that is shared between Sir Walter and Elizabeth. We should note that this view also influenced Lady Russell, to a lesser extent, when she originally persuaded Anne to break her engagement to Frederick Wentworth. So, in *Persuasion*, there is a theme of resistance to change which is presented as an absurdity (Sir Walter; Mrs Clay's compliment), and as all-too-plausible caution (Lady Russell's prejudice and persuasions). The vigorous energy and practical activity of the naval characters are in marked contrast to this, and their frank sincerity is portrayed as refreshing: 'Admiral Croft's manners were not quite of the tone to suit Lady Russell, but they delighted Anne. His goodness of heart and simplicity of character were irresistible' (p. 142).

When we attempt to summarise the 'theme of change' we have found in each of the novels, we find some points of resemblance between them; but Jane Austen treats different aspects in different novels. The theme is far from being a single overarching idea throughout her work.

One common element seems to be criticism of reactionary attitudes. There are strong similarities between the defeat of Lady Catherine de Bourgh's rampant snobbery, in *Pride and Prejudice*, and the liberation consequent upon Mrs Churchill's death, in *Emma*. The caricature of absurd narcissism that is Sir Walter Elliot in *Persuasion*, and the hollow authority of Sir Thomas Bertram in *Mansfield Park*, are two further representatives of a futile and impotent past. The rigid system of social rank and snobbery, then, is shown to be obsolete because it does not reflect the real world. We remember Elizabeth Bennet saying to Lady Catherine that the world will have 'too much sense' to condemn her marriage to Darcy.

The idea that 'sense' will be the ultimate judge of forms and events brings us to another motif that is consistent in the novels. Jane Austen tests traditional values against life experience and analyses them rationally. In three cases, we are shown situations where the morality and principles are sound, but they have become powerless because they are not connected to any real lived experience. In other words, even positive moral values are seen to decline and become artificial when they are not accompanied by genuine emotional experience. In *Pride and Prejudice*, Darcy explains: 'As a child, I was taught what was *right*; but I was not taught to correct my temper. I was given good principles, but left to follow them in pride and conceit' (*PP*, p. 297). In *Mansfield Park*, Sir Thomas Bertram regrets having made the same educational error with his children:

> He feared that principle, active principle, had been wanting, that they had never been properly taught to govern their inclinations and tempers, by that sense of duty which can alone suffice. They had been instructed theoretically in their religion, but never required to bring it into daily practice.
>
> (*Mansfield Park*, p. 382)

In both of these novels, Jane Austen draws a clear distinction between theory and practice. Even where the theory is sound, the character will not learn and benefit unless through practical experience, particularly an experience of suffering or self-denial. So, Darcy is grateful to Elizabeth for rejecting him when he first proposed: 'You taught me a lesson, hard indeed at first, but most advantageous. By you I was properly humbled' (*PP*, p. 297); and in *Mansfield Park*, Sir Thomas thinks the superior virtue of Fanny derives from 'the advantages of early hardship and discipline' (*MP*, p. 389). In *Emma*, the heroine is benevolent and has good principles; but she wastes her time in pursuit of triviality and in self-deception, until she is suddenly confronted by the threat of unhappiness: 'Till now that she was threatened with its loss, Emma had never known how much of her happiness depended on being *first* with Mr Knightley, first in interest and affection' (*Emma*, p. 341). Hardship, grief, suffering: these, then, are the experiences that form character. They turn principles – which are nothing in themselves – into what Sir Thomas Bertram calls 'active principle', that is, good ideas put into practice in daily life.

It follows from this, that a stagnant society has a tendency to decline into an artificial, futile structure. Each generation is increasingly in need of the invigoration and rejuvenation of ideas which comes with practical experience of life; and without such a correction, society will become morally debased or irrelevant. There can be no better argument for the importance of a theme of change, in Jane Austen's novels.

On the other hand, the themes we have discussed do differ when it comes to the kind of change that is shown, and the author's apparent attitude towards it. For example, the individualist philosophy of Elizabeth Bennet in *Pride and Prejudice*, expressed in her forthright statement 'I am only resolved to act in that manner which will, in my own opinion, constitute my happiness' (*PP*, p. 288) clearly has the author's blessing; while Miss Crawford's espousal of individualism, in *Mansfield Park*, is opposed by Fanny's concept of duty to a family and social group. Also, Miss Crawford's lively manners, which Edmund finds so refreshing that he had been 'feeling as if we had never lived so before' (*MP*, p. 165), eventually reveal a shallow and self-indulgent character; while the manners of the naval characters in *Persuasion* are genuinely refreshing and sincere.

This observation brings us on to the question of Jane Austen's development: do her ideas themselves progress and change during the course of these four novels? The remainder of this chapter explores this question by looking at the different heroes and villains we meet.

## The Change of Theme

George Wickham in *Pride and Prejudice*, Frank Churchill in *Emma* and Henry Crawford in *Mansfield Park*, are all deceptive and ultimately unsatisfactory young men, in their different ways.

Wickham is introduced as 'of most gentlemanlike appearance', and the effect of his looks is universal: 'All were struck with the stranger's air' (*PP*, p. 62). Jane Austen's description of him insistently returns to these two themes: his fine appearance, and the powerful attraction he exerts upon others. So, he 'wanted only regimentals to make him completely charming', and 'His appearance was greatly in his favour; he had all the best part of beauty, a fine countenance, a good figure, and very pleasing address.' Lydia and Kitty immediately feel that he is superior to the other officers, who, in comparison, are suddenly 'stupid, disagreeable fellows' (p. 64); and Jane Austen confirms his striking superiority more soberly: 'The officers of the ... shire were in general a very creditable, gentlemanlike set, and the best of them were of the present party; but Mr Wickham was as far beyond them all in person, countenance, air, and walk ...' (*PP*, p. 65). Wickham, then, is introduced with a list of qualities that are highly praised, and he stands out among the other men as having a marked superiority in these qualities. We notice that the author confines her praise to Wickham's appearance and manners, however: it is his 'beauty', 'countenance', 'air' and suchlike that attract her praise, while she tells us nothing of his mind or his morals.

Wickham's effect upon those around him is also repeatedly emphasised. Lydia and Kitty are bowled over by him; and on seeing him for the second time, 'Elizabeth felt that she had neither been seeing him before, nor thinking of him since, with the smallest degree of unreasonable admiration' (*PP*, p. 65). His charm is generally effective: 'Mr Wickham was the happy man towards whom almost every female eye was turned' (*PP*, p. 66). Elizabeth is particularly susceptible to this charm, and when they talk she dismisses her surprise at the story he tells about Darcy, under the influence of his charm and his looks. So, for example, 'Elizabeth honoured him for such feelings, and thought him handsomer than ever as he expressed them', and she thinks of saying to him 'A young man, too, like *you*, whose very countenance may vouch for your being amiable' (both from *PP*, p. 69). In short, Wickham's charm is so powerful that it puts Elizabeth's critical faculties to sleep; and Jane Austen shows that this happens entirely as a result of his external qualities, his handsomeness and his 'countenance'. Elizabeth goes away from this meeting with 'her head full of him' (*PP*, p. 72). Mrs Gardiner is a level-headed character, so, noticing the attachment between Wickham and her niece, she warns Elizabeth to take care. Even she, however, is under the influence of Wickham's pervasive charm. We hear that she adapts her own memory to suit Wickham's slanders ('she ... was confident at last that she recollected having heard Mr Fitzwilliam Darcy formerly spoken of as a very proud, ill-natured boy' – p. 121); and she calls Wickham 'a most interesting young man', adding that Elizabeth 'could not do better' if only he had financial independence.

Wickham's outstanding qualities, then, are his good looks, and his persuasive, charming manners which affect all who meet him. His manners put critical and reasoning faculties to sleep, and influence even level-headed characters to become prejudiced in his favour.

Frank Churchill, in *Emma*, is introduced in very similar terms. Where Wickham created public interest by the power of his looks and charm, Frank Churchill is already a centre of attention before he arrives. Otherwise, our first meeting with him seems to employ the same range of words and phrases:

> The Frank Churchill so long talked of, so high in interest, was actually before her – he was presented to her, and she did not think too much had been said in his praise; he was a *very* good looking young man; height, air, address, all were unexceptionable, and his countenance had a great deal of the spirit and liveliness of his father's; he looked quick and sensible. She felt immediately that she should like him; and there was a well-bred ease of manner, and a readiness to talk ...
>
> (*Emma*, p. 158)

His looks are so attractive that Emma does not think 'too much had been said in his praise', just as Elizabeth felt that she had not thought of Wickham with 'unreasonable admiration'. The same emphasis on 'good looking', 'air', 'address' and 'countenance' applies to Frank Churchill, as to Wickham. The words 'ease' and 'readiness' describe the way both of these young men enter into conversation.

Frank Churchill also shares with George Wickham the ability to use his charm so that other people's critical faculties are lulled: people are persuaded to believe him even when he says improbable things. For example, when he is charming Mrs Weston by expressing his great love for Hartfield, the question of why he has never visited before 'passed suspiciously through Emma's brain'. However, she persuades herself to give him the benefit of the doubt: 'if it were a falsehood, it was a pleasant one, and pleasantly handled. His manner had no air of study or exaggeration. He did really look and speak as if in a state of no common enjoyment' (*Emma*, p. 159). So, Frank's charm is such that the 'pleasant'-ness of what he says, coupled with his manner – his ability to 'look and speak as if' he is sincere – overwhelms the doubts Emma's critical intelligence would otherwise maintain. We notice that he makes an effort to please everybody, also, including people whose foibles might make them difficult to satisfy. So, he 'admired Hartfield sufficiently for Mr Woodhouse's ear' (*Emma*, p. 163). We are again reminded of Wickham when we hear that Frank Churchill's personality has added enormously to Highbury society, so that when he leaves, Emma 'foresaw so great a loss to their little society from his absence' (*Emma*, p. 216). His fortnight's visit has been so 'happy' that it stands out in Emma's memory in contrast to the 'common course' of days (*Emma*, p. 216), just as Wickham's appearance stood out in contrast to the inferior appearance of the other officers.

These two characters have manners and charms that are very similar indeed, then; and we have found that Jane Austen uses strikingly similar language in her descriptions of them. Henry Crawford, in *Mansfield Park*, is not remarkably handsome, as Wickham and Frank Churchill are; but his manners and charm are powerful in the same way. So, despite his lack of conventional good looks, Mr Crawford is introduced with the same vocabulary we have found in the other two novels. He had 'air and countenance' and his manners were 'lively and pleasant' (*MP*, p. 36) so that in three meetings his charm influences the Miss Bertrams in his favour, despite their original low opinion of his looks: 'he had so much countenance, and his teeth were so good, and he was so well made, that one soon forgot he was plain' (*MP*, p. 38). Mrs Grant is equally lulled by his charm, and 'immediately' gave his character credit for 'everything else' (*MP*, p. 36).

The power of Henry's charm is turned upon the heroine – Fanny Price – much later in the novel; and although Fanny herself is virtually proof against it, Jane Austen acknowledges its strength when she observes that Crawford courted

Fanny with 'all that talent, manner, attention, and flattery can do' and says that Fanny 'could [not] have escaped heart-whole from the courtship (though the courtship only of a fortnight) of such a man as Crawford' had she not been already in love with Edmund (*MP*, p. 193). Indeed, Crawford's charm does begin to work upon Fanny when he visits her in Portsmouth. Here, his agreeable manners are in contrast to the meagre disorder and coarse behaviour of her family; and when he leaves, Fanny feels that 'It was parting with somebody of the nature of a friend' and thinks of 'The wonderful improvement which she still fancied in Mr Crawford' which made him 'astonishingly more gentle, and regardful of others, than formerly'. We remember Mrs Grant's assumption that Henry's manners must stand for good character; and Emma's assumption that Frank Churchill's 'look' of sincerity is the real thing. In *Mansfield Park*, even supercritical Fanny Price adopts this uncritical pattern of thought: Henry's improvement appears in 'little things', and she thinks 'must it not be so in great?' In persuading herself that Crawford is sincere, Fanny's thoughts give rise to one of Jane Austen's most subtle juxtapositions: two words which encapsulate the effect of a frank and lively manner perfectly, yet carry more than a hint of self-contradiction. His sincerity is what 'really seemed' (all quotations from *MP*, p. 342).

All three of these male characters, then, possess the gifts of a magnetic charm and ease of manners. They are characterised as lively, humorous and interesting company, and they please everybody. Yet Wickham is an unprincipled liar and philanderer; Frank Churchill is insincere and deceptive, enjoying his deceptions even in retrospect; and Henry Crawford's character is ruled by 'the freaks of a cold-blooded vanity' (*MP*, p. 385), which bring ruin upon himself and Maria Rushworth. Jane Austen appears to be sending us a very clear message through these three characterisations: distrust charm, magnetism, good looks, and easy agreeable manners. Men with these qualities are worthless and dangerous.

The novels provide a consistent contrast to these three figures, in the persons of Fitzwilliam Darcy in *Pride and Prejudice*, Mr Knightley in *Emma*, and Edmund Bertram in *Mansfield Park*.

Darcy is introduced as 'fine, tall' with 'handsome features, noble mien'. This physical appearance is distinct from Wickham as the word 'handsome' denotes something stronger, less soft than Wickham's 'beauty' or Frank Churchill's 'good looking'. The words 'fine' and 'noble' suggest a more statuesque, remote and superior bearing than that of the charmers. Sure enough, Darcy's manners also contrast with Wickham's. Where Wickham is instantly popular, Darcy's manners give a 'disgust' because people think him 'proud' and 'above being pleased'. He is said to have a 'forbidding, disagreeable countenance'(all from *PP*, p. 12). It is interesting to note that people forget that Darcy is handsome just as they forget that Mr Crawford is *not*, and both changes of opinion are wrought by manners. Darcy's reserved manner has softened a great deal before the end of the novel, but Elizabeth still believes him to be too stiff. When thinking of their marriage, she imagines herself helping him: 'by her ease and liveliness, his mind might have been softened, his manners improved' (*PP*, p. 252). Even at the end, there is an authority in Darcy's manner that makes him an intimidating figure to others. Mr Bennet jokingly comments, 'I have given him my consent. He is the kind of man, indeed, to whom I should never dare refuse anything which he condescended to ask' (*PP*, p. 303).

Mr Knightley is a blunt and decisive man. His manners are a pattern of perfect propriety, and delicate consideration of others. His conversation is funnier and more energetic than Darcy's, but we find that in any general conversation his contributions are invariably shorter and less frequent than those of others, and several scenes in the novel show him silent, observing the talkative antics of those around him (for example, in Chapter 41, Knightley says nothing while Emma and Frank Churchill play puzzles with a set of letters). He has, then, blunter and less elaborate manners than other characters. His speech is often short, and he can be withdrawn and taciturn. People sense his superiority, and look up to him with a degree of awe. Emma, for example, 'had a sort of habitual respect for his judgment in general, which made her dislike having it so loudly against her; and to have him sitting just opposite to her in angry state, was very disagreeable' (*Emma*, p. 57); and even the impervious Mrs Elton senses his authoritative manner: 'Under that peculiar sort of dry, blunt manner, I know you have the warmest heart', she observes (*Emma*, p. 294). Ironically, Mrs Elton is right about both his manner and his heart, which are qualities he shares with Mr Darcy. Even when she realises her love for Knightley, Emma thinks of him as 'infinitely the superior' (*Emma*, p. 339); and when he is on the point of proposing, his manner is still so formidable that Emma thinks in terms of being 'entitled to his clemency' (*Emma*, p. 350).

In *Mansfield Park* we meet Edmund Bertram. The contrast between his quiet manners and those of the livelier, more gregarious Tom Bertram, is repeatedly underlined. When Miss Crawford begins to feel attracted towards Edmund, she is unable to understand her own feelings: '... he began to be agreeable to her. She felt it to be so, though she had not foreseen and could hardly understand it; for he was not pleasant by any common rule, he talked no nonsense, he paid no compliments, his opinions were unbending, his attentions tranquil and simple. There was a charm, perhaps, in his sincerity, his steadiness, his integrity ...' (*MP*, p. 56).

These three characters, then, have a quality of manners in common. Of course, it is not true to say that they are the same as each other. Darcy, for example, has positively forbidding manners which repel some other people, while Knightley is liked and respected in Highbury; and Edmund reveals a naïvety, rationalising his selfishness to Fanny when he is besotted with Miss Crawford, of which neither Knightley nor Darcy is guilty. Nonetheless, these three men share quieter manners which are in contrast to the liveliness, flattery and 'readiness' to talk shown by Wickham, Frank Churchill and Henry Crawford.

We already observed that the charm and sociability of the men with 'lively' manners is deceptive. The truth about these men is that they are not to be trusted: they lack sound moral principles, and their wickedness varies from Wickham's and Henry Crawford's seductions to the less vicious moral levity of Frank Churchill. The main point is that Jane Austen's conclusion, and her advice, seems to be consistent. Powerful personal charm and flattering manners are signs of a careless heart and mind; while sober manners which, at first sight, seem more forbidding, are more likely to token a man of sound principle and a deeper, warmer heart. Put crudely, this means that you should trust quiet men, but not talkative ones.

Jane Austen's last novel, *Persuasion*, presents us with the opposite outcome. Let us continue our analysis of heroes and villains.

Captain Wentworth was 'a remarkably fine young man, with a great deal of intelligence, spirit and brilliancy' (*Persuasion*, p. 55). He is still outstandingly good-looking seven years later, when Anne observes that the passage of time had added 'a more glowing, manly, open look, in no respect lessening his personal advantages' (*Persuasion*, p. 86). Like Wickham and Frank Churchill, Captain Wentworth has the power of pleasing the people he meets, and his effect on the two Miss Musgroves reminds us of Henry Crawford's effect on Maria and Julia Bertram, or Wickham's on Lydia and Kitty: '... how perfectly delighted they were with him, how much handsomer, how infinitely more agreeable they thought him than any individual among their male acquaintance'. Throughout his first visit to Uppercross, the Miss Musgroves say, 'he had looked and said every thing with such exquisite grace, that they could assure them all, their heads were both turned by him' (both from *Persuasion*, p. 80). These descriptions emphasise energetic and open manners, and the powerful effects of charm together with outstanding good looks. 'Brilliancy' and 'glowing' make Wentworth seem to shine; and he surpasses all the other local gentlemen just as Wickham was 'superior' to the other officers. Wentworth does and says everything with 'exquisite grace', and we later find that 'his disposition led him, to talk' (*Persuasion*, p. 88). He shares, then, many of the qualities of a George Wickham or a Frank Churchill, being apparently open and gregarious, possessing a magnetic social charm, and being both talkative and instantly popular.

Mr Elliot contrasts with Wentworth. Anne observes his manners closely and concludes 'That he was a sensible man, an agreeable man, – that he talked well, professed good opinions, seemed to judge properly and as a man of princi-ple . . . He certainly knew what was right' and was 'rational, discreet, polished' and 'cautious' (all from *Persuasion*, pp. 172–3).

Faced with the contrast between these two men, then, a reader of Jane Austen's works might expect that the unre-strained, impetuous character of Captain Wentworth will end in wickedness: Anne would do better to trust the careful manners of Mr Elliot, with his respect for propriety. *Persuasion* is not like the other novels, however. In this book, the idea of 'openness' is of paramount importance. Anne worries that Mr Elliot is 'not open', and explains her impression further by saying that he is too much in control of himself: 'There was never any burst of feeling, any warmth of indignation or delight', so that 'she could not be satisfied that she really knew his character' (all from *Persuasion*, pp. 172–3).

So far, then, we have simply seen that the outward char-acteristics, the manners, of heroes and villains seem to have been turned the other way around. In this novel, the hero has manners comparable to those of the three earlier villains; and the villain has manners more like those of the three previous heroes. We could conclude from this the simple wisdom that it is difficult to judge a man from his outward appearance: any appearance, any style of behaviour, may be deceptive; and only more intimate knowledge of a man's character will reveal the truth about him. However, in *Persuasion* Anne Elliot seems to go further, stating a preference for 'open' manners. She finds Mr Elliot's self-control 'a decided imperfection', and continues:

> She prized the frank, the open-hearted, the eager character beyond all others. Warmth and enthusiasm did captivate her still. She felt that she could so much more depend upon the sincerity of those who sometimes looked or said a careless or a hasty thing, than of those whose presence of mind never varied, whose tongue never slipped.
>
> (*Persuasion*, p. 173)

The outcome of the novel shows that Anne's instinct was correct. Mr Elliot is eventually described by Mrs Smith as 'black at heart, hollow and black!' (*Persuasion*, p. 206), and he carried on an affair with Mrs Clay while he was courting Anne. The author, then, has finally written a novel in which the modern, lively man who is impulsive and unreasonably optimistic, is valued; while the man of caution and propriety turns out to be a hypocrite. Anne's statement, that self-control is an 'imperfection' and that she can forgive careless or hasty behaviour for its sincerity, adds depth of meaning to this reversal in the structure of characters. As always, the author uses a structure in which the comparison of men to each other, and contrasts between them, provoke us to consider their differing qualities and explore our reasons for valuing one above another. In *Persuasion*, it appears that the author's own assessment of men, their manners and the character those manners expose or cover, has undergone some change. The prudent advice we deduce from *Pride and Prejudice*, *Emma* and *Mansfield Park* has its place in this final novel: it is the prudence Anne submitted to seven years before when she broke off the engagement to Captain Wentworth. The adviser was Lady Russell, and the echoing question in *Persuasion* concerns that advice. Jane Austen sets out the change of views Lady Russell has to confront at the end of the novel, with a lucid emphasis on the word 'manners':

> She must learn to feel that she had been mistaken with regard to both; that she had been unfairly influenced by appearances in each; that because Captain Wentworth's manners had not suited her own ideas, she had been too quick in suspecting them to indicate a character of dangerous impetuosity; and that because Mr Elliot's manners had precisely pleased her in their propriety and correctness, their general politeness and suavity, she had been too quick in receiving them as the certain result of the most correct opinions and well regulated mind. There was nothing less for Lady Russell to do, than to admit that she had been pretty completely wrong, and to take up a new set of opinions and hopes.
>
> (*Persuasion*, p. 251)

We could possibly read this passage as an admission of error by Jane Austen herself, so thoroughly has she reversed the qualities of her heroes and villains. It is plausible to see Lady Russell as a gentle satire of Austen's own earlier novels and the distrust of popular and dashing men they express. The idea of an affectionate self-satire is strengthened by the deprecating humour with which the author admits that 'there is a quickness of perception in some, a nicety in the discernment of character, a natural penetration', and that 'Lady Russell had been less gifted in this part of understanding' (*Persuasion*, p. 251). We can imagine Jane Austen writing these lines with a wry smile about her own change of mind.

*Persuasion* has a strong and complicated theme of time. The events of the novel itself are emotionally joined to a short period of time seven years before, a time when Anne

Elliot and Captain Wentworth expressed their feelings openly and truly: a time which is still the underlying pattern for the present reality. Captain Wentworth insists, in Chapter 23, that he has 'loved none but her [Anne]'; but he is forced to explain 'that he had been constant unconsciously, nay unintentionally'. He mentions being 'angry' and 'unjust', and meaning 'to forget her' (*Persuasion*, p. 244). So time – the passage of those seven years of separation – has obscured the basic reality of his feelings. His love has been hidden, buried beneath his resentment, during all of that time. The revival of Anne's beauty is also remarked on by several characters. Mr Elliot admires her in passing, at Lyme, and Sir Walter comments that she is 'less thin in her person, in her cheeks; her skin, her complexion, greatly improved – clearer, fresher', then asks what cosmetic she has been using (*Persuasion*, p. 158). The sense that a past 'golden age' is returning, then, is woven into several aspects of the novel, further elaborating the theme of time.

Finally, we should notice that the underlying truth about Mr Elliot was also apparent seven years ago: he was openly contemptuous of his relations, and entered into a loveless marriage for money. Again, the underlying pattern of truth in this novel lies seven years away in the past, and it is the refreshing, clarifying influence of that past which is alone powerful enough to resolve the complicated issues of the present. So, Anne's renewed bloom and Wentworth's re-discovery of his love, and Mrs Smith's connecting narrative, draw a resolving strength from the past to bring about the happy denouement. Jane Austen emphasises the importance of this process several times. For example, when Mr Elliot admires Anne at Lyme, Wentworth gives a look which says: 'even I, at this moment, see something like Anne Elliot again' (*Persuasion*, p. 125); and later, when they are declared lovers for the second time, he declares that 'to my eye you could never alter' (*Persuasion*, p. 245).

Time has a curious effect in *Persuasion*, then: the past was a time of openness and truth, which returns to redeem the present. The present is a time of oppression, error, hypocrisy and absurdity, which needs to be redeemed by the past. The connection between the present and the past is interpreted in contrasting ways. First, there is a rational response to the chance which brings Anne and Captain Wentworth into each other's company again: Anne thinks it 'absurd' to feel or expect anything. 'What might not eight years do? Events of every description, changes, alienations, removals, – all, all must be comprised in it; and oblivion of the past – how natural, how certain too!' (*Persuasion*, p. 85). Captain Wentworth comments on the coincidence which brings them their second chance at happiness: Anne was 'thrown in his way' (*Persuasion*, p. 244); and Anne finds his apparent indifference 'of sobering tendency' because it helps her to control the 'folly' of her hopes when they meet again. Rationally, then, seven or eight years are a long time, and a great deal of change will have taken place. Their meeting again is mere chance: no expectations can be built upon it.

On the other hand, Jane Austen presents us with a suggestion that there is something extraordinary about their second courtship. Anne knows that her feelings are 'absurd'; yet, paradoxically, her feelings provide a different, subjective perspective on time: 'to retentive feelings eight years may be little more than nothing' (*Persuasion*, p. 85). Jane Austen is typically ambivalent in the tone she uses to describe this theme. So, she treats romantic idealism with indulgent amusement in Chapter 21: 'Prettier musings of high-wrought love and eternal constancy, could never have passed along the streets of Bath, than Anne was sporting with from Camden Place to Westgate Buildings. It was almost enough to spread purification and perfume all the way' (*Persuasion*, p. 200). The alliteration of 'purification and perfume', and the contrast between 'high-wrought ... eternal', and prosaic 'Westgate Buildings' as well as the belittling 'Prettier', highlight the author's amusement; yet the suggestion contained in this description is rather astonishing. Elsewhere, Bath is a 'dim view' of 'extensive buildings, smoking in rain' full of 'dash ... heavy rumble ... bawling ... ceaseless clink' (*Persuasion*, p. 149). Jane Austen's amusement suggests the paradox and absurdity that a subjective emotion might be strong enough to purify and 'perfume' this aggravating chaos.

Later, the same theme of renewal and redemption is treated more seriously. The hour of conversation between Anne and Captain Wentworth, after his proposal in Chapter 23, is described in terms which suggest more than a return to their original feelings:

> There they returned again into the past, more exquisitely happy, perhaps, in their re-union, than when it had been first projected; more tender, more tried, more fixed in a knowledge of each other's character, truth, and attachment; more equal to act, more justified in acting.
>
> (*Persuasion*, p. 243)

In *Persuasion*, then, the theme of time has overtones of irrational absurdity: the workings of chance bring the past to refresh the present, and Jane Austen hints at a further transformation of life, something like a miracle.

The beguiling fantasy of *Persuasion*, of course, is that Anne Elliot and Frederick Wentworth have an opportunity to relive their lives, to correct their mistakes. Coincidence enables them to return to a point in their lives where they went wrong, and to take up the thread of their emotions and happiness from there. This factor in the plot elaborates the effect of the change we have noticed in Jane Austen's attitudes: prudence was the wrong course, and *Persuasion* puts forward optimistic trust in the sincerity of an open character, and in the future, as the alternative view. Lady Russell has to admit that she was wrong, in terms which suggest that Jane Austen is also disavowing something of her earlier writings. It is a thorough change of mind (Lady Russell had been 'pretty completely wrong' – p. 251). When and how did Jane

Austen change her assessment of manners so radically? The answer seems to lie in the unsatisfactory, unresolved conflicts of *Mansfield Park*.

We do not have the space here to analyse the complex conflicts of *Mansfield Park*, or to weigh up the many ironies and inconsistencies of its flawed world. In this chapter, we have to be satisfied with outlining a view as briefly as possible.

In earlier chapters, we have noticed that *Mansfield Park* seems to be built around a single, central conflict between two kinds of world and two kinds of attitude to life. On one side is an older, traditional approach to living and morality that is exemplified by the ideal of Mansfield Park itself, a settled life in the country, and the supposed authority of Sir Thomas. On the other side are the excitements of entertainment, vanity and town, where morality is apparently relative, and admiration is given to that which is new and fashionable, whether it is sound or unsound. The Crawfords are proponents of the new attitudes of town, while Edmund and Fanny represent traditional country life and virtues. Most of the novel turns on the attempts of these two 'sides' to bridge the gulf between them, to come together. Edmund and Miss Crawford are fascinated and attracted by each other and seek to overcome their differences. Henry becomes fascinated by Fanny, and seeks to overcome his difference from her. All of these attempts fail, and at the end of the novel the traditional 'world' of Mansfield, in the persons of Edmund and Fanny, abandons any attempt to look beyond itself and turns inward: they find comfort and satisfaction in each other. Mary and Henry Crawford are left to their fate in the conflicting 'fashionable' world, a fate that is defined by their failure to reach the moral standards demanded by Mansfield Park.

This generalised view of the novel suggests that it is merely a fable with a moral, in which Fanny's faultless virtue triumphs and gains the prize of Edmund in the end. However, *Mansfield Park* is much more than this. We will look at two aspects of the ending, which show that the novel's final effect remains complex.

First, Jane Austen tells us that the ending was not inevitable. She is explicit about Henry Crawford: his vanity went on 'a little too long', and the repeated 'could he have ... could he have ... would he have ... would he have persevered' create a regretful tone about his failure to remain true. The crucial decision was trivial: 'Had he done as he intended, and as he knew he ought, by going down to Everingham ... But he was pressed to stay for Mrs Fraser's party.' And this decision – to reject a single invitation to a party – 'might have been deciding his own happy destiny'. Elsewhere in the same discussion, the author makes unequivocal statements about what might have been: 'there would have been every probability of success and felicity for him'; 'there can be no doubt that more [affection from Fanny] would have been obtained'; and 'Fanny must have been his reward – and a reward very voluntarily bestowed – within a reasonable period from Edmund's marrying Mary' (all quotations are from *Mansfield Park*, p. 385).

These authorial comments are untypical: Jane Austen has no need to speculate about an alternative outcome: she could have allowed Henry to disappear into unregretted iniquity as she does with Wickham at the end of *Pride and Prejudice*. However, she chooses to state that the novel could have ended differently. A double marriage between these two conflicting worlds was possible; and Jane Austen goes even further than this, for she asserts that Fanny would have bestowed her hand 'very voluntarily' on Crawford, who would thus find 'felicity' and ensure his 'happy' destiny. So, not only could the novel end differently, but also, a different ending would have led to happiness.

By writing these paragraphs, Jane Austen throws open the entire denouement of the plot and forces us to think and feel differently about the ending. We notice that she writes of Henry's failure in a tone of regret, and her explanation ('ruined by early independence and bad domestic example') tends to pity him and deflect blame, rather than censure him. A regretful tone also fills Edmund's account of his final meeting with Miss Crawford: 'For where, Fanny, shall we find a woman whom nature had so richly endowed? – Spoilt, spoilt! – ' (*MP*, p. 375). The only conclusion we can fairly draw, is that the Crawfords did have fine qualities and fine potential, and that it is sad that they were, eventually, too spoilt by the world to preserve their own value.

Jane Austen's treatment of the 'villains', then, is ambivalent. What about her treatment of the 'good'? Here again we find ambivalence. The opening paragraph of Chapter 48, the final chapter, announces Jane Austen's tone:

> Let other pens dwell on guilt and misery. I quit such odious subjects as soon as I can, impatient to restore every body, not greatly in fault themselves, to tolerable comfort, and to have done with all the rest.
>
> (*Mansfield Park*, p. 380)

This is funny. The self-consciously ironic word 'odious' characterises a cheerful, optimistic author; and her impatience to get away from misery is amusing. This irony may deflect our attention from the care with which Jane Austen chooses her words: Fanny, Edmund and Sir Thomas are the characters referred to as 'not greatly in fault themselves'; yet with all her cheerful desire to bring about a happy ending, the author only promises to bring them a measure of contentment: 'tolerable comfort'.

This opening prepares us for a light-hearted conclusion, and we are not disappointed. Jane Austen treats Edmund as a subject for comedy, not sympathy: his transparently self-absorbed antics make us laugh, as 'After wandering about and sitting under trees with Fanny all the summer evenings, he had so well talked his mind into submission, as to be very tolerably cheerful again' (*MP*, p. 381). His courtship of Fanny is treated with similarly arch amusement. Jane Austen refuses to tell us how long Edmund took to be consoled. She asks us to work out for ourselves how difficult it is to effect 'the cure of unconquerable passions, and the transfer of unchanging attachments' (*MP*, p. 387), and later makes fun of his sham humility with 'She was of course only too good for him; but as nobody minds having what is too good for them, he was very steadily earnest in the pursuits' (*MP*, p. 388). The passage which details the young couple's happiness ends with a reflection on how Sir Thomas's attitude has changed since Fanny first arrived at Mansfield. What he feared then and rejoices in now makes such a contrast 'as time is for ever producing between the plans and decisions of mortals, for their own instruction, and their neighbour's entertainment' (*MP*, p. 389).

This levity in the author's tone raises the question of whether Fanny and Edmund are *too* predictable in the final chapter. The author treats their happiness as genuine, but in these passages she belittles them, and suggests that they are no longer interesting because they will not surprise us again. However, in the final two paragraphs of the novel, there are two more serious ironies, which cast a deeper doubt over the author's feelings.

First, Jane Austen refers to an event which is 'to complete the picture of good', and this is 'the death of Dr Grant' (*MP*, p. 390). In such a sensitive author, we must assume that the sheer callousness of this is deliberate: it is a reflection on the attitude of Fanny and Edmund, who are only too pleased to acquire the living of Mansfield because 'they had been married long enough to begin to want an increase of income' (remember that the commonest way of obtaining increased income, in Jane Austen's world, was over somebody's dead body). Second, the final paragraph asserts that the parsonage became 'as thoroughly perfect in her [Fanny's] eyes, as every thing else, within the view and patronage of Mansfield Park, had long been' (*MP*, p. 390). We must remember that Jane Austen is unerringly accurate in her choice of words. She could have written that Mansfield Park was 'dear' to Fanny – which would have been reasonable – but she does not. Instead, she writes that it had long been 'perfect' in her eyes – which implies a monumentally uncritical prejudice in its favour.

These final ironies have serious implications. If we take them into account, we have to conclude that Fanny and Edmund become callous, and limited in their outlook, after their marriage. There is at least a suggestion here that the 'happy' ending is not a matter for celebration. It allows the victorious side of the conflict – Mansfield Park – to become unhealthily narrow, isolated from outside comparison, self-satisfied and inhumane. The inclusion of the word 'patronage' in the final sentence also jars, with its reminder of the authority Sir Thomas has wielded so clumsily from the start.

The points raised at the end of *Mansfield Park* suggest a cynical reading of the novel. It is important to remember that this discussion is only a brief outline: the ending of the novel is a more complex balance than this, and criticism of Mansfield is not the only strand. For example, Jane Austen promised to bring the deserving to contentment; but she spends a proportion of the final chapter consigning the wicked to misery (not only Maria and Mrs Norris, but also Henry and Mary Crawford, suffer for the rest of their lives). However, the elements of cynicism and regret are there, and should not be ignored when assessing the novel as a whole. Our particular interest in them is in relation to the altered opinions about characters that Jane Austen expresses in *Persuasion*. We noticed that *Persuasion* brings a change of attitude, that there is an element of self-confession when she writes that Lady Russell had been 'pretty completely wrong' in the past; and we asked, when and how did this change of attitude take place?

We cannot answer such a question, since we are attempting to read back into Jane Austen's personal development, from studying her novels. It is only possible to say that the very issues on which she seems to change her opinions, are in a state of turmoil in *Mansfield Park*. The question of a new, lively and exciting life in conflict with older and more solid principles, remains an unsettled complexity, and leaves behind it unresolved feelings of contempt and regret, at the end of that novel. *Emma*, written after *Mansfield Park*, does not condemn its villain: the ending forgives and indulges Frank Churchill, and expects him to thrive under Jane's direction. Therefore, it is arguable that in *Mansfield Park* we find Jane Austen questioning her own assumptions, exploring the issues, and reflecting the difficulty of reaching a comic synthesis of views that were in an unsettled state.

## Conclusions

We began this chapter by discussing the theme of change, noticing that it manifests itself in various ways at different moments in the novels. Looking for a common element behind each example, we suggested that change is consistently related to a duality the novels explore: a duality which we can find various ways to describe. Here is a list of antitheses which help to expound the central 'duality':

- reactionary or conservative/modern
- closed/open
- stagnation/change
- hierarchy (social rigidity)/equality
- prudence/impetuosity
- principles/appearance and reputation

It would be possible to continue this list to include many more concepts, arranged into antithetical pairs. Notice that the words in the list are all concepts and issues that have been raised by studying the novels in this and previous chapters.

We then discussed the heroes and villains from the four novels, and this revealed a common pattern of characterisation in the three earlier novels, followed by an inverted pattern in *Persuasion*. Finally, the ending of *Mansfield Park* suggests that Jane Austen's attitudes are in a state of flux and unsettled exploration, in that novel.

In conclusion, then, we can say that Jane Austen explores the 'theme of change' in all four novels, and presents this theme as numerous manifestations of a pervasive choice, a duality or conflict that is central to her way of representing the world. Settled or one-sided conclusions are not found, however; but different ways of balancing or synthesising the contradictions of life inform the different novels. Further, the four novels show that exploring this duality led Jane Austen to develop and present a significantly altered outlook in her final novel *Persuasion*.

However, any conclusions we reach regarding 'change' and Jane Austen's attitudes towards this theme, have to be qualified. For example, one of the dualities in the list above is 'Hierarchy (social rigidity)/ equality'. Obviously, the word 'equality' only stands for a very limited equality. It means 'equality' within the narrow social class that is her subject – what Elizabeth Bennet means when she says of herself and Darcy 'He is a gentleman; I am a gentleman's daughter: so far we are equal.' Therefore, we should think of 'change' in Jane Austen as more like a change of direction, or of emphasis, and eschew thoughts of radical or revolutionary reform.

# 7

# Irony, and the Author

## The Difficulty of Finding the Author

In the last chapter, we found ourselves discussing what we called a 'change of opinion' or 'change of attitude' in Jane Austen. Discussing 'Jane Austen's attitudes' is only a convenient pretence, of course. It is a convenient shorthand for getting at the meaning and effect of the texts.

The novels are creative works of literature, they are not 'Jane Austen's view'. So we cannot say that the novels present 'views' or 'attitudes' at all. We can only say 'this is the kind of world this novel presents' and 'this is the kind of world that novel presents'. This point becomes clear if we look back to one of the conclusions from the last chapter.

In *Mansfield Park*, the gulf between two conflicting groups, the Crawfords and the Bertrams, is sadly impossible to bridge, and they break apart at the end of the novel. This is a tragic state of affairs. Why cannot the liveliness of the Crawfords and the steadiness of the Bertrams join together to produce a richer world?

The answer is in what happens. Henry Crawford indulges his vanity once too often, elopes with Maria Rushworth, and there is a final rupture with the Bertrams. Then, who made this happen? The answer is obvious: Jane Austen. Couldn't she have made the two worlds unite at the end of the novel? Yes, she could have done this. Henry Crawford could have been a stronger character who resisted temptation. So there was nothing 'inevitable' about the way *Mansfield Park* turned out: it was up to Jane Austen.

What if she had imagined a man who combined Crawford's charm and quick intelligence, with Edmund's sound warmth of heart? In other words, what if Frederick Wentworth had been in *Mansfield Park*, instead of *Persuasion*? In that case *Mansfield Park* would have been a different book with a different ending. So, what is the difference between *Mansfield Park* and *Persuasion*? Well, Jane Austen put a weaker man in one, and a stronger, better man in the other.

So, what we have found is – strictly speaking – not a 'change of attitude in Jane Austen' at all. It is merely her decision to imagine different men. This reasoning is patently obvious, of course, but it is also patently pointless. We only come back to the conundrum which underlines how careful we have to be when discussing the author's intentions. The author can do what she likes, but what she likes to do tells us something about why she does it.

When the author tells us that Fanny and Henry could have been happy, then, she is being disingenuous: yes, we could answer, but it was up to you. The discussion at the end of *Mansfield Park* is therefore a very cheeky double-bluff Jane Austen plays on the reader, testing how far she can go with the pretence that the people and events of her story are real, and playing with our relationship to her fiction. Is she simply relishing the author's power, boasting of what she could have done? Does she herself regret the ending she has written (this idea leads only to infinite paradox)? Among these ironies, we cannot find the author.

This difficulty of finding the author is particularly acute with Jane Austen, because she writes ironically. Whatever the words mean on the page, we repeatedly find that they imply other, different meanings. Remember our analysis of the structure of dialogue, finding four layers of meaning in a simple conversation; or our study of the opening sentence of *Pride and Prejudice*, which invites us to feel superior, then laughs at our folly because the outcome of the novel supports it. Jane Austen weaves a careful web of alternative ironic meanings around her own views; and she usually includes enough contradictory implications to prevent us from reaching a single conclusion about whatever aspect of the work we are concerned with. Each time we think we have found her 'real' statement, we realise that it is undermined by the implication of something else. In the end, we cannot know what the author 'really' thinks.

### Irony

What is irony? We have used the word repeatedly, but it will be useful at this point to define what we mean. Here is the definition I give in *How to Begin Studying English Literature*:[1]

> **Irony** exists where there are two or more related meanings or attitudes to be understood from what is written in the text. These two meanings could seem to contradict each other; yet the text not only suggests both meanings, but also suggests that they both have some validity. Irony is the relationship between these different meanings and attitudes in a work of literature.

So, irony occurs when there are two or more different meanings in the text on the page. For example, when Mr Bennet says to his wife 'I have a high respect for your nerves. They are my old friends' (*Pride and Prejudice*, p. 6), the words mean that he approves of and has affection for her nerves. We have no difficulty in understanding what he means, however, which is different: he means that she has complained about her nerves incessantly ever since their marriage, and he finds the mention of her 'nerves' intensely irritating, or ridiculous. This is a straightforward example of irony, because there are clearly two meanings in the text, as we read.

However, the definition also mentions 'two or more ... attitudes'. In this chapter we will analyse some more complex examples of irony, showing how to define, and develop our thinking about, the different attitudes they present. Our first example comes from the final sentence of *Mansfield Park*:

> the parsonage there... soon grew as dear to her heart, and as thoroughly perfect in her eyes, as every thing else, within the view and patronage of Mansfield Park had long been.
>
> (*Mansfield Park*, p. 390)

Begin by defining the different meanings or attitudes presented in the text. Here, the attitude Fanny has towards Mansfield Park is entirely positive, and the word 'perfect' shows that she does not criticise the house or its occupants at all. The meaning of the language, then, is that Fanny has long believed Mansfield Park to be 'thoroughly perfect'. However, if we think about the novel we have read, this attitude does not strike us as true, even for Fanny. We understand a different attitude, critical of Sir Thomas's children, Mrs Norris and Sir Thomas himself when he was putting pressure on Fanny to marry Henry Crawford. Fanny has also frequently disagreed with Edmund.

So, the novel forces us to be sceptical about Fanny's attitude in the final sentence, and to think of a different attitude ourselves. The irony is between these two attitudes.

The effect of irony is that it provokes us to think about the different meanings and attitudes we find. So, the final sentence of *Mansfield Park* provokes thoughts and questions: has Fanny forgotten all her sufferings at Mansfield Park? Does Fanny now believe Sir Thomas's oppressive, male authority to be 'perfect'? Has Fanny become short-sighted, narrow-minded, now she has the man she always wanted?

These thoughts are the first stage – they are straightforward questions about Fanny's character, which come into our minds because of our surprise at the difference between her attitude and ours. Now think about these questions in relation to the text as a whole. How do these doubts about Fanny relate to the whole story of *Mansfield Park*? How do these doubts affect our understanding of the themes, or the author's aims? Further, wider questions occur to us. Here are three of them:

1.  Does happiness always tend to narrow one's outlook? This is an interesting question, since the author, and Sir Thomas Bertram, have put forward the theory that a valuable character is only formed by having 'the advantages of early hardship and discipline' (*MP*, p. 389). We could think about this question in relation to the rest of the novel, asking: is it true to say that people only come to their senses when they suffer? When people are not suffering, do they always become complacent and narrow?

2.  Reading that Mansfield is 'perfect' surprised us, because we remembered the faults of Maria, Julia, Tom and Edmund; the cruelty of Mrs Norris, and the oppression and mistakes of Sir Thomas himself. The text mentions everything 'within the view and patronage' of Mansfield, so we should include the Crawfords and Grants in our list of faults. Where are these faults now? Maria and Mrs Norris have been exiled to 'another country – remote and private' (*MP*, p. 383); Julia lives elsewhere with her husband; Tom is more responsible since he hurt his head; Edmund is no longer a worry, since he loves the right woman, not the wrong one; and Sir Thomas, having been proved wrong, now places a high value on Fanny. Additionally, Mary and Henry Crawford have been exiled, and Dr Grant has died. In short, the world of Mansfield Park has now been re-modelled entirely to suit Fanny's desires, but this has entailed excluding several people.

    This line of thought leads us to the theme of conflict between old, conservative values and new, lively ones, that we have discussed several times in previous chapters. Does Jane Austen imply that the final breach between these two worlds leaves the world of Mansfield Park limited and complacent? Is this the reason why she gives Fanny such a complacent attitude in the final sentence?

3. What do we mean by 'perfect'? If something is 'perfect', it is complete and never needs to change. When we think of 'perfection', do we also mean static, limited, unchanging?

These thoughts remind us of the question of decline in Mansfield Park and the Bertram family. In the first chapters of the novel, there is a strong sense of decay in the house, because the young generation lacks the firm principles of Sir Thomas, and his authority – like so much else in the house – has become hollow, artificial. Is Mansfield Park about to enter another static phase of narrowing and decay, becoming increasingly artificial and isolated, during the remainder of Fanny's and Edmund's lives? In other words, does the author imply that 'perfect' is a reactionary, negative idea, because life always needs to change?

The simple irony of Fanny's uncritical attitude, in the final sentence of the novel, has given rise to far-reaching questions, which touch on the novel's themes and the author's philosophy. On the other hand, although they seem to go a long way, these questions are all reasonable. They are based on thinking about the final sentence, and relating it to the novel as a whole. Our analysis began by defining the different meanings or attitudes in the text; then we listed the questions that are raised by thinking about the difference.

\*     \*     \*

Here is an example from *Emma*, which we will analyse in the same way. In Chapter 45, Emma goes to visit Jane Fairfax at Miss Bates's, but Miss Bates comes to the door, saying that

Jane is too ill to see anybody, although she has seen Mrs Elton, Mrs Cole and Mrs Perry earlier in the day. The author gives us Emma's reaction:

> Emma did not want to be classed with the Mrs Eltons, the Mrs Perrys, and the Mrs Coles, who would force themselves anywhere.
>
> (*Emma*, p. 321)

We begin by defining the meaning. The meaning of the words is that Emma wishes to be different from three inferior women, so she decides not to insist on seeing Jane. However, we are surprised at this assertion, for two reasons which come from the same chapter. First, Emma has been humbled, and is determined to be tolerant of others. Emma has learned the lesson of Mr Knightley's rebuke after her cruel remark about Miss Bates at Box Hill; so her revived snobbery and contempt in 'Emma did not want to be classed with ...' surprise us. Second, Emma sent a note to Jane, and the answer effectively told her not to come. But 'In spite of the answer ... she ordered the carriage' (p. 321). In fact, Emma has already 'forced' herself on the Bates's, so her idea that she will not 'force' herself on them now, does not seem to make sense.

Clearly, there are two attitudes in this part of the text. First, there are the words, which give Emma's thoughts; second, there is our surprise, which makes us disbelieve Emma's motives and question what is really happening. These two attitudes give rise to some questions about Emma: has she changed, or is she still the same snob she was before Box Hill? Why does she want to see Jane: is it to make Jane feel better, or to make herself feel better (in other words, is it an unselfish or a selfish act)?

These questions about the character are the first stage of thinking about irony. As in the case of our *Mansfield Park* example, they provoke further, wider questions about the novel as a whole. Here are two:

1.  How can we define right action? In this case, Emma
    understands Jane's reluctance to see her, but still thinks
    that she should 'force' herself on Jane so that she can
    make amends for mistreating her in the past. She has
    genuine friendly feelings towards Jane now. Sometimes,
    then, it may be *right* to ignore a rejection, because what
    you are doing is definitely benevolent. There is a differ-
    ence between this and the busybody interference of Mrs
    Elton, who has no delicacy of feeling and does things
    'for' Jane insensitively, things that Jane would *really*
    rather she didn't do. Mrs Elton's interference is *wrong*.
    So, the irony highlights how difficult it is to tell right
    from wrong, in a real-life situation.
2.  Is Emma like the Mrs Eltons, Mrs Coles and Mrs Perrys,
    or is she different? Thinking about this question makes
    us think about the novel as a whole. Emma has been
    compared with and contrasted to these other women –
    especially Mrs Elton – repeatedly. The irony we are
    looking at now, provokes us to think about this complex
    question again. How does the present situation relate to
    that wider question?

In the passage we are studying, Emma has actually been
insulted. Beneath the politenesses, the truth is that Jane was
'in' to the other three women, but 'out' to Emma. Emma's
decision not to 'be classed with' them, then, is probably a
compensating reaction. She feels the snub, and thinks
herself superior in order to make herself feel better.

What, then, does the author think? Clearly, Emma is a far
better person than she was before Box Hill: we know that she
has taken Mr Knightley's rebuke to heart. On the other hand,
she reacts to a snub with a snobbish thought, which suggests
that she still needs to feel superior. Here, then, Emma does
the right thing; but does she do it for the right motives? Does
Jane Austen think we can ever know what is right, and avoid
selfish motives; or does she imply, cynically, that people are
always driven by their selfish needs, at least partly?

Notice that thinking about irony has again taken us a long way; and that there is no single answer to the questions we have reached. There is no rule which helps us to tell right from wrong actions: what people do is either good or bad, depending on the circumstances at that moment. It is a matter of sensitivity, and each decision is a matter of judgment. Emma *is* a 'better person' than before; but she *is* partly motivated by a need to feel superior. People are complicated, always a mixture of blindness and understanding, good and bad motives.

Analysing irony, then, confirms that Jane Austen does not tell us a single view: she gives us several different views, which often seem contradictory; and she makes us think about them without resolving them.

*        *        *

Our next example comes from *Persuasion*. After Louisa's accident, Anne Elliot watches Captain Wentworth:

> The tone, the look, with which 'Thank God!' was uttered by Captain Wentworth, Anne was sure could never be forgotten by her; nor the sight of them afterwards, as he sat near a table, leaning over it with folded arms, and face concealed, as if over-powered by the various feelings of his soul, and trying by prayer and reflection to calm them.
>
> (*Persuasion*, p. 132)

This is a case of different 'meanings' in the sense of the difference between what the two characters understand. Anne interprets Wentworth's actions as a sign of strong love for Louisa. When we read this passage for the first time, Anne's supposition seems reasonable; although we have noticed that Wentworth is more aware of Anne since another man admired her. Much later in the novel (in Chapter 23) Wentworth reveals that this interpretation was wrong: his behaviour was a sign of strong love for Anne, not Louisa. In fact, he had realised that he did not love Louisa at all – he loved Anne. There are two understandings of this passage, then: one is Anne's interpretation at the time, and the other is revealed much later.

The irony provokes questions about Anne: why does she misinterpret his feelings? Is it because she is frightened of allowing herself to hope? Following our method, we then ask what wider questions are raised by this irony? We will look at two:

1.    Can people ever know what others feel? This question provokes us to think about the theme of deceptive appearances, the complexity of reality, which is a major element in the whole text. Appearances are so deceptive that we cannot decode reality: we cannot look at outward signs and discover the truth, because the signs always suggest more than one possible truth. Here, the two possible truths are that Wentworth loves Louisa and that Wentworth loves Anne. His outward behaviour would be the same in either case.
2.    What are the conventions of the novel *Persuasion*? It is clearly a romantic novel, Anne and Wentworth are obviously hero and heroine, so they are bound to marry in the end. So, the reader is engaged in a game where both reader and author know the rules: reading a romantic novel. In this passage, the author plays with the rules by reviving Wentworth's love, as expected, but disguising it as something else.

The effect of this teasing by the author is to bring us down to earth: the story turns out to be simpler, and more predictable, than we thought at the time. The hero was falling in love with the heroine, just as we expected. We should have known. The irony reminds us that life is often simpler than we think: there are simple laws of nature (like the simple laws of romantic fiction), but things are apparently so complicated that we are distracted from the underlying triteness. Sometimes we are so clever that clichés take us by surprise.

So, what is a 'fiction'? Is there a simple 'fiction' behind life? These questions are where we arrive from thinking about Anne's misinterpretation of Wentworth's behaviour.

\*          \*          \*

The examples of irony we have studied so far have been about elements in the text: in *Mansfield Park*, Fanny's attitude to Mansfield; in *Emma*, a character's reaction to an event; in *Persuasion*, the ambiguity of a character's behaviour. We now turn to an example, from *Pride and Prejudice*, where the irony involves us directly with the author's opinion.

In Chapter 46, Elizabeth receives the letter which informs her of Lydia's elopement. Darcy arrives, and in her distress Elizabeth tells him the news. He looks serious, and quickly leaves. Elizabeth believes that she has lost him, and this prompts her, for the first time, to realise that she could love him. Jane Austen then intervenes with a discussion of love:

> If gratitude and esteem are good foundations of affection, Elizabeth's change of sentiment will be neither improbable nor faulty. But if otherwise – if the regard springing from such sources is unreasonable or unnatural, in comparison of what is so often described as arising on a first interview with its object, and even before two words have been exchanged, – nothing can be said in her defence, except that she had given somewhat of a trial to the latter method in her partiality for Wickham, and that its ill success might, perhaps, authorise her to seek the other less interesting mode of attachment. Be that as it may, she saw him go with regret...
>
> (*Pride and Prejudice*, pp. 226–7)

The passage begins 'If ...'. In the course of her intervention Jane Austen describes two different ways of falling in love. Love may be based on 'gratitude and esteem', or love may arise 'on a first interview with its object, and even before two words have been exchanged'. We realise that the author is poking fun at the romantic cliché of 'love at first sight'; the ridiculousness of falling in love 'even before two words have been exchanged' brings her tone near to sarcasm. We could conclude, then, that Jane Austen is laughing at popular romantic clichés, and pointing out that in the real world – like that of Elizabeth Bennet – people fall in love more slowly, and their emotions grow stronger as they begin to know the other person more thoroughly and intimately.

Jane Austen challenges us, the readers: silly romantic readers are the targets of her irony. If we believe in love at first sight, she says, we will either blame the author (Elizabeth is 'improbable') or the character (Elizabeth is 'faulty'), at this point. The remainder of the passage drips irony. Elizabeth's love grew in a 'less interesting' way than if she had fallen for Darcy the first time they met; 'nothing can be said in her defence', which conjures the absurdity of Elizabeth in the dock, prosecuted by gushy romantics. These elements of the passage all support the idea that Jane Austen is satirising conventional romantic clichés. There seem to be two attitudes to love in this passage, then: the gushy romantic attitude of 'love at first sight'; and the more realistic attitude the author seems to take.

However, if we relate this passage to its context – the rest of the novel – the issue becomes more complex. First, Jane Austen does believe in 'love at first sight', since Elizabeth fell in love with Wickham this way (or so the author tells us). So the operative phrase becomes 'good foundations'. It is not a question of how quickly you fall in love, but rather one of what your feeling is based on. Remember, Bingley and Jane fell in love on their first evening together.

Second, did Elizabeth fall in love with Wickham at first sight? If we check Chapters 15 and 16, we find there is no mention of Elizabeth's feelings when they first meet in the street, but she observes Wickham's frosty encounter with Darcy. At their second meeting she admires his appearance and manners, yet 'what she chiefly wished to hear ... [was] the history of his acquaintance with Mr Darcy' (*PP*, p. 66). She leaves, unable to think of anything but 'Mr Wickham, and of what he had told her' (about Darcy) (*PP*, p. 72); and in looking forward to the Netherfield ball, she 'thought with pleasure of dancing a great deal with Mr Wickham, and of seeing a confirmation of everything in Mr Darcy's look and behaviour'(*PP*, p. 74). Throughout Elizabeth's infatuation with Wickham, in fact, she is thinking about Darcy just as much as about Wickham. So it seems that her prejudice against Darcy had a great deal to do with her 'falling in love' with Wickham.

Third, is 'gratitude and esteem' a good summary of her feelings now? These words refer to a passage from Chapter 44, when Elizabeth finds that beyond 'respect and esteem ... there was a motive within her of goodwill which could not be overlooked. It was gratitude.' On the other hand, there is something more than 'gratitude and esteem' at work. She decides that these are part of her feeling for Darcy, but at the same time, the evening 'was not long enough to determine her feelings' and she lay awake 'endeavouring to make them out' (both from *PP*, p. 216).

The choice Jane Austen offers between gradual and instant love, then, seems to be a false reflection of what happens to Elizabeth in the novel. Further details from other parts of the text only serve to make the situation even more complicated. For example, Elizabeth says to Mrs Gardiner, in Chapter 26, 'At present I am not in love with Mr Wickham; no, I certainly am not' (*PP*, p. 122); and writes to her aunt, after Wickham's desertion of her, 'There can be no love in all this' because she feels no 'material pain' (*PP*, p. 126), or ill will towards her rival. When they meet and discuss Wickham, Elizabeth makes a petulant speech and Mrs Gardiner rallies her by saying 'Take care, Lizzy; that speech savours strongly of disappointment.' However, Elizabeth's angry speech is not about Wickham at all: it is about Darcy and Bingley. She said: 'I have a very poor opinion of young men who live in Derbyshire; and their intimate friends who live in Hertfordshire are not much better' (all from *PP*, p. 129). Finally, when Elizabeth reads Darcy's letter, and realises how wrong she has been about both young men, she briefly comments, 'Had I been in love, I could not have been more wretchedly blind' before concluding that 'vanity, not love, has been my folly' (both from *PP*, p. 171). This is a delicate hint from the author: it is tempting to suggest that Elizabeth has in fact been in love with Darcy, not Wickham, throughout the first half of the book. We cannot go as far as this, because there is not enough evidence. However, we can say that Darcy is the one who has been constantly on Elizabeth's mind, even while she persuades herself that she hates him.

We have noticed (see Chapter 3 above) that Jane Austen uses certain key words in her novels, placing these important terms at crucial moments to create a 'verbal structure' which subtly suggests that the reader should compare passages distant from each other. Here, we notice that gradual love is called 'less interesting' in the passage we are studying. In Chapter 26 Elizabeth writes to Mrs Gardiner, that she would be 'more interesting' if she were heartbroken about Wickham (*PP*, p. 126). 'Interesting' creates an echo in the reader's mind: Elizabeth and Jane Austen are equally aware of romantic cliché, and both laugh at popular ideas of romance using the same ironic term.

We began with Jane Austen's intervention in Chapter 46, and we have tried to pin down the author's views on love. How can we summarise all that we have found? With irony as complicated as this, it is again helpful to use our method. First try to define the meanings, then relate them to the context of the whole text. Here is an attempt at sorting out the ironies of the passage we are looking at:

1.   (Define the meanings or attitudes present in the text)
     Two attitudes appear:
     (a)   Jane Austen suggests that 'gratitude and esteem' are better grounds for love than love at first sight.
     (b)   Silly romantics who believe in love at first sight, will blame the author or the character.

2. (The attitudes broken down and compared with the context)

 (a) 'gratitude and esteem' – Elizabeth feels this, but it is only part of love, which is not defined.

 (b) 'love at first sight: Wickham' – This did not happen. Darcy was always as much in her mind as Wickham, and she concludes that she has not been in love.

 (c) 'love at first sight: Darcy' – Elizabeth may have been in love with Darcy for longer than she knows herself (hint on p. 171). Darcy has preoccupied her feelings since their first meeting.

 (d) 'silly readers' – in the light of (a), (b) and (c) above, it is foolish to either believe in or dismiss the power of sudden, irrational attractions.

3. (Conclusions)

 (a) Each apparent statement is implicitly contradicted. For example Elizabeth fell in love with Wickham at first sight (no); Elizabeth did not fall in love with Darcy at first sight (perhaps she did).

 (b) The emphasis of the text changes after comparison with the wider context. For example Elizabeth had given 'somewhat of a trial' to falling in love at first sight, now suggests that her romance with Wickham was always artificial: she was artificially trying out romance to see what it felt like!

 (c) Jane Austen invites us to adopt a more 'sophisticated' view of love (we laugh at simple romantic clichés); but the more we think about the novel, the more she undermines us: there is *some truth* in the simple romantic view.

 (d) However, there is no *final truth* in either view. Reality is a complex experience, and the rational 'choice' between gradual and instant love, seemingly offered in Jane Austen's intervention, is artificial.

## Conclusions

1. The investigations of irony in this chapter have all led to questions. Ultimately, these ironies present us with contradictions which we are not able to resolve. Jane Austen teases us, inviting us to laugh with her, and laughing at us in her turn. In this way she is an 'invisible' author. We cannot discover Jane Austen's opinion, because she gives us several contradictory opinions to choose from, all of which are partly right and partly wrong when compared with the text.

2. The novels are full of characters persistently and vainly attempting to use observation, rational analysis and interpretation in order to understand reality. They are never more than partly successful. Elizabeth Bennet and Emma Woodhouse – although both very clever young women – are spectacularly wrong about reality. Notice that Jane Austen's ironic treatment of the reader often provokes us to make mistakes, as well.

3. People always do and always will struggle to use their intellects, trying to understand life. The intellect will always, in the end, have to give up: life is too complicated, and emotions too irrational, to be understood in simple, rational terms. We should feel the same humility about language. The words we use – labels we give to qualities and feelings, motives and things – never represent the thing, life, itself. Jane Austen's ironies, in which characters and author continually search for language to describe an essentially ironic reality, highlight the inevitable gap between language and actual experience: there are no final answers.

## Methods of Analysis

1. Reading Jane Austen's text, we are usually aware that there are two or more meanings or attitudes present as

we read. Choose any extract which makes you understand two or more meanings or attitudes, and analyse
its irony. Use the following method:

(a) define the different meanings or attitudes that are
    present in the text (but remember that a second
    meaning may only become clear later, as in our
    example from *Persuasion*);

(b) note the immediate questions that are raised by the
    irony (about character or situation, for example, at
    that point in the narrative);

(c) think about wider questions which are provoked by
    the irony, by relating it to your knowledge of the
    whole text, and to understanding Jane Austen's
    aims and views. Such wider questions are likely to
    go a long way. It is worth making a list of them,
    with a brief discussion of each question you think
    about.

2.  Remember that Jane Austen is a complex and teasing
    author. You are more likely to find unanswerable ques-
    tions than answers. However, studying irony signifi-
    cantly adds to the richness of our understanding and
    appreciation of the text.

## Suggested Work

Jane Austen's writing is always ironic to some extent – even
if this only means that she does not tell us the characters'
thoughts at the time. So, you could choose any sentences
from the text, at random, and practise analysing irony.

Here are four suggestions, one from each of the four
novels, which will be rewarding to practise on:

● From *Pride and Prejudice*, look at the irony of the first
  sentence of the last chapter: 'Happy for all her maternal
  feelings was the day on which Mrs Bennet got rid of her
  two most deserving daughters' (*PP*, p. 310).

- From *Emma*, look at Emma's comparison between Frank Churchill's evasive answer, and Jane Fairfax's reserve, in Chapter 24: 'Upon my word! you answer as discreetly as she could do herself. But her account of every thing leaves so much to be guessed, she is so very reserved, so very unwilling to give the least information about any body, that I really think you may say what you like of your acquaintance with her' (*Emma*, p. 166).

- From *Mansfield Park*, look at this extract from Edmund's letter to Fanny, in Chapter 44. He is discussing his hopes of marrying Miss Crawford: 'I have no jealousy of any individual. It is the influence of the fashionable world altogether that I am jealous of. It is the habits of wealth that I fear' (*MP*, p. 348).

- From *Persuasion*, look at the irony of Captain Benwick receiving Anne's advice, in Chapter 11: 'Captain Benwick listened attentively, and seemed grateful for the interest implied; and though with a shake of the head, and sighs which declared his little faith in the efficacy of any books on grief like his, noted down the names of those she recommended, and promised to procure and read them' (*Persuasion*, p. 122).

---

[1] By Nicholas Marsh (2nd edn, Macmillan, 1995). Readers may find it helpful to read the discussion of irony, and the examples I give in Chapter 5 of that work. There is no space for such an extended discussion of irony in the present chapter.

# Conclusions to Part 1

1. The conclusions to each individual chapter in Part 1 I have tended to move forward on two fronts. First, they have built on the initial insight that **Jane Austen's novels are densely and carefully crafted**, and this makes the text extraordinarily rich in meaning and implications. Second, we have found growing evidence that the many concepts, forces and elements in the novels coalesce into a 'shape' in which they all participate, and that this takes the form of what we call **duality**. 'Duality' is a two-sided way of arranging thoughts, and in Jane Austen we have found, in very generalised terms, a system of **reactionary or conservative** and **progressive or renewing** impulses. Characters find their places and make their compromises, solving the problems of their lives, within the framework of these two background forces.

2. These two developing understandings of Jane Austen's novels seem to pull our critical conclusions in different directions. According to the dense complexity, and insoluble ironies of the texts, we are urged to limit our conclusions and be careful: we must qualify all our perceptions because Jane Austen is so careful to moderate her fable, balancing all influences and revealing insight in carefully measured quantities. We must work in close detail, paying attention to the effects of individual words, or the modulation of tone of voice or attitude, between two short phrases. If our conclusions go too far in any one direction, Jane Austen will laugh at us. On the other hand, the idea that there is a framework 'duality' (which is often conflict) in the world of these

novels, is a large, sweeping idea. This tempts us to use grand terms like 'change' and 'progress', and generalise about the overall aims of these novels, thinking of them as wholes.

3.   The solution is to recognise that the larger framework is there in the background; but also remember that it is never simplified. It is always made up of many different strands. Whenever a character's life is affected by what we call 'duality', they have to reach a detailed, practical compromise with the terms of their existence. For example, Elizabeth Bennet in *Pride and Prejudice* is affected by the material imperative of marrying for money. That is part of the existing, traditional social system she is born into. On the other hand, she is drawn by her romantic nature to seek a mutual and equal relationship with a man. Her life, then, is touched by the traditional system (marriage for material reasons) and a more progressive, individual aspiration (marriage for love). This sounds – and is – quite simple: our sweeping, large ideas put conflicting pressures on Elizabeth. The 'duality' we have been analysing, presents her with a dilemma. However, her solution is far from simple. Details of the compromise she eventually reaches include her recognition that even handsome men must have enough to live on, and her reinvigoration of the spoilt, rigid character of Darcy, the landed gentleman. In fact, Elizabeth has to change herself towards the traditional, and at the same time change the traditional (Darcy) to accommodate herself. So, we must remember to **combine a sense of the larger ideas and forces** in Jane Austen's world, with a **constant, rigorous attention to details**.

4.   In Chapter 6, we examined the idea of change. There is a theme of 'change' which runs through all four of the novels in different forms. *Mansfield Park* presents the most polarised version of two opposed sides, and explores conflict. The other novels have a more 'comic' emphasis.

Although there is conflict, their emphasis suggests that a compromise synthesis is always possible. However, we found that the novels show a **consistent exploration of duality and conflict in the world**, and focus on **how this conflict affects the individual heroine**.

5.    Finally, we have found a **change of emphasis** in the last novel, *Persuasion*, where it appears that **Jane Austen's and the reader's sympathies gravitate towards the new individual and romantic energy** more than in the other three novels.

6.    This final **emphasis in favour of the frank, enthusiastic character** involves **throwing off some of the caution** of the previous novels. Anne prefers the frank character even though it may sometimes make mistakes.

# PART 2

# THE CONTEXT
# AND
# THE CRITICS

# 8

# Jane Austen's Life and Work

## Jane Austen's Life

We know the external facts of Jane Austen's life in some detail. We know where she lived, when she moved, where she visited and when, and we know the minutest details of her income as well as a number of her possessions and expenses. So, for example, we know how much blood the doctor took from her brother Henry when he was ill; and the tiny, perfectly stitched bag Jane made for her friend Martha Lloyd, at the age of seventeen, still exists. Facts about Jane Austen and her numerous relations are plentiful, then. However, we know next to nothing about Jane Austen's emotional experiences. The story of her life therefore gives a curious impression: the more we read of external details, the more ignorant we feel about her personality and character. It is as if the void in the middle becomes clearer, the more we concentrate on everything else. We know what she did, and what she thought about the people she met; but we know nothing about her feelings.

Biographers react to this frustration in different ways. After Jane Austen's death, her sister Cassandra burnt and censored her personal papers. Cassandra presumably destroyed many early drafts of the novels; and she went through Jane's letters, burning all those which expressed feelings she considered private, and taking out expressions of private emotion from others. So, although we can still read a large number of letters written by Jane Austen, they do not reveal her personal life. Biographers like Jane Aiken Hodge[1] express annoyance: 'Cassandra's hand was a heavy one. We can only respect, and regret it.' Having vented their feelings, they then describe a Jane Austen who *must have felt* certain emotions at certain crises in her life. So Jane Aiken Hodge speculates about Jane's feelings when Cassandra became engaged. Having wondered whether Jane was also in love with Cassandra's fiancé ('it does seem a possibility not to be ignored'), she concludes 'It must have been very lonely, all of a sudden, in the shared bedroom at Steventon' (*op. cit.* p. 43). It is on the basis of this kind of imaginative empathy that the biographer creates what she calls Jane Austen's 'double life'. We prefer to study the complex experiences of life created in the novels, however, and in this chapter we will content ourselves with a simple summary of where and how the author lived.

Jane Austen was born in 1775. Her father was a country clergyman and the family lived in the rectory at Steventon in Hampshire. Jane had five elder brothers, an older sister and a younger brother. The eldest brother, James (b. 1765), became a clergyman like his father; the second son, George (b. 1766) was mentally defective and was sent away to live out of sight of the family; the third son was Edward (b. 1768) who was later adopted by childless rich relations and took their surname, Knight. His generosity became a mainstay for the female Austens after the death of the reverend George Austen, and he provided them with Chawton Cottage, where Jane lived from 1809 until the end of her life. The fourth brother, Henry (b. 1771) tried careers as a soldier and banker before becoming a clergyman. Henry was closely concerned with the publication of Jane's novels, and she stayed with him in London quite frequently, seeming to enjoy this brother's company. Cassandra Austen (b. 1773) was Jane's closest companion and confidante. She never married, and survived her younger sister, living until 1845. A fifth brother, Francis (b. 1774), and Jane's younger brother Charles (b. 1779) both went into the Navy, and both ended their lives with the rank of Admiral.

When Jane was twenty-five years old, her father decided to retire and move the family to Bath. His eldest son James was to take over as rector of Steventon. In May 1801 Jane and her mother went to search for a house in Bath, and stayed with their relations the Leigh Perrots. The family moved in to 4 Sydney Place during June, and during the same summer they went to Sidmouth for a seaside holiday. It appears that Jane met a young gentleman at Sidmouth, and the patchy accounts we have suggest that they fell in love. Cassandra expected that the man would make it his business to visit the Austens again, and propose to Jane. However, they never met again: during the autumn Jane received news that the young man had died unexpectedly. In November of the following year Jane and Cassandra were staying with their brother James at Steventon, and the twenty-one-year-old son of the Bigg-Withers family, old friends of the Austens, proposed to Jane and was accepted. However, the next morning Jane had changed her mind. She broke off the engagement and she and her sister hurried away back to Bath.

In January 1805 Jane's father died, after a short illness. This left Jane, Cassandra and the widowed Mrs Austen in straitened circumstances; but James, Henry, Edward and Francis each contributed some income and the women were left, if not as well off as during the Reverend Austen's life, at least comfortable. In 1806, they moved to Southampton, sharing a house Francis and his wife had taken while he waited for a new posting from the Navy. They lived at Southampton for three years. Jane and Cassandra both went on long visits to their brother Edward's house Godmersham, in Kent, during 1808. During Cassandra's visit, Edward's wife died, after bearing their eleventh child. Perhaps because of the help and comfort Cassandra provided him during this upsetting time, Edward decided to do something towards settling his mother and sisters more permanently. He offered them a choice of two houses – one near Godmersham in Kent, and the other

a house called Chawton Cottage on the Chawton estate
Edward had also inherited from his rich adoptive parents, the
Knights. Chawton was close to the family's original home at
Steventon, where the James Austen family lived, and Mrs
Austen decided to move there. Jane, her mother and sister
moved in 1809, and stayed at Chawton Cottage in Hampshire
for the rest of Jane's life.

The years between 1809 and 1817, when Jane Austen died,
were full of incident in the form of the steady stream of births,
marriages and deaths occurring in the numerous Austen
family, and regular visits of several weeks at a time both to and
from relations. These years also saw the writing of *Mansfield
Park*, *Emma* and *Persuasion*, and the publication of the
novels, beginning with *Sense and Sensibility* in October
1811. The Chawton years seem to have been markedly stable
for Jane Austen; they are characterised by her increasing
success as a novelist, and satisfaction in her writing.

Towards the end of 1815, or early in 1816, Jane Austen
began to feel ill. She suffered from inexplicable weakness
and fatigue, and pains in her back. The physicians of her
time did not understand the cause of her malady, but we
now know that she was suffering from a condition called
Addison's disease, for which there was then no cure. At first,
and for some time, the illness did not show itself continuously, and only occasionally interfered with her life. The
symptoms appeared more frequently as time went on,
however, and it seems to have been a steadily worsening
condition throughout 1816 and the first part of 1817. In May
of that year, Jane Austen's physician noticed new symptoms
he did not understand, and advised her to move to
Winchester where a Doctor Lyford, a specialist, would be
able to attend her. Jane and Cassandra therefore took lodg-
ings at a house in College Street, Winchester, and lived there
while Jane's illness continued to worsen, until, on 18th July
1817, she died peacefully.

This has been a bare account of Jane Austen's life. I have
omitted numerous events – the marriages of brothers,

Francis's and Charles's voyages and returns to England; the births of numerous nephews and nieces (several of these became favourite friends of their Aunt Jane, who seems to have been a warm and entertaining adult who attracted their affection and confidences); the worrying lawsuits of Mr and Mrs Leigh Perrot and Jane's brother Edward Knight, and the bankruptcy of her brother Henry, which caused his second career change out of banking and into holy orders; and, of course, the unceasing round of visits to and from her many relatives. So, although Jane Austen's life may seem rather uneventful and humdrum in this bare account, it is important to remember that it was also a life of ceaseless activity and social involvement, and it contained several moves between different settings: the quiet Hampshire village of Steventon; the bustle of society in Bath, 'all vapour, shadow, smoke and confusion';[2] Southampton, city, seaport and Naval centre; and finally another quiet country village in Hampshire.

There were three clear stages in Jane Austen's life. She spent her first twenty-five years growing up in a noisy, bright family who enjoyed charades and amateur theatricals. She began to write comic parodies very early, and entertained her family with them. During her teens Jane Austen took part in the usual round of balls and social events at neighbouring houses and at the public Assembly Rooms in Basingstoke. She seems to have been full of fun and laughter, and to have enjoyed herself a great deal.

Following the family's move to Bath, a new phase seems to have begun. Mrs Austen was ill, and Cassandra and Jane nursed her; then Mr Austen died and they were subject to anxieties and financial rearrangements as well as several moves, so that the next few years, including the Southampton period, remained unsettled. The amusement and laughter of Jane's youth are less apparent during these years.

Finally, the three remaining women of the family settled at Chawton Cottage. Life there seems to have been settled, and largely without financial worries, but productive and happy.

The cottage was not always quiet, however, as nieces and nephews frequently stayed with their aunts and grandmother. Also, during this period, Jane regularly stayed with Henry in London, seeing about the publication of her novels.

Jane Austen was born in the year of the American War of Independence. She lived through the French Revolution, the Terror, and the Napoleonic Wars – that long struggle between Britain and France which continued for most of her life. Of her two brothers in the Navy, Charles was on the American station during the Anglo-American War of 1812–14, and Francis counted himself unlucky to have just missed – by chance – the Battle of Trafalgar in 1805. Her cousin Eliza Hancock, later wife to her brother Henry, married a French aristocrat who was guillotined in the Terror. At the same time, the Industrial Revolution was going at full speed, changing the face of English towns and changing both the occupations of people and the economic balance of power between agriculture, trade and industry. Jane Austen lived through all these upheavals. She seems to have been well informed on international events. Her novels, however, reflect these momentous changes only as a distant background behind the day-to-day social concerns of the country gentry, their wives and daughters. This narrowness and limitation in the novels have attracted a great deal of critical discussion. It seems to be the result of Jane Austen's conscious decision to limit herself to what she knew intimately, and not the result of any abnormally narrow understanding or lack of interest in the outside world.

## Jane Austen as Novelist

Jane Austen wrote six finished novels. Here is Cassandra Austen's note on the dates when they were written:

> *First Impressions* begun in October 1796. Finished in August 1797. Published afterwards, with alterations and contractions under the title of *Pride and Prejudice*.

> *Sense and Sensibility* begun November 1797. I am sure that something of this same story and characters had been written earlier and called *Elinor and Marianne*.
>
> *Mansfield Park* begun sometime about February 1811 – Finished soon after June 1813.
>
> *Emma* begun January 21st, 1814, finished March 29th, 1815.
>
> *Persuasion* begun August 8th, 1815, finished August 6th, 1816.
>
> *Northanger Abbey* was written about the years 1798 and 1799.

The novels were written in a different order from the order of their publication. *Sense and Sensibility* came first, published at Jane Austen's expense with a commission to Thomas Egerton, the publisher, in October 1811. Egerton then bought the copyright of *Pride and Prejudice*, which was published in January 1813, but *Mansfield Park*, which came out in May 1814, was again published on commission at the author's expense. Jane Austen then changed her publisher, taking those novels for which she owned the copyright, and the newly finished *Emma*, to John Murray. *Emma* came out in December 1815, and John Murray also put out further editions of *Sense and Sensibility* and *Mansfield Park*. The other two novels – *Northanger Abbey* and *Persuasion* – were published together after Jane Austen's death, in 1818.

There is no special significance in this difference between the orders of writing and publication. It was natural that her most recent finished work when Jane Austen approached Egerton, should be the first to go into print (*Sense and Sensibility*) while she revised her earlier effort. The long delay in publication of *Northanger Abbey* is explained by the fact that this was the first novel Jane Austen sold. It was sold in 1803 to a publisher called Crosby & Cox, who never printed it but refused to return the manuscript to the author. Her brother Henry eventually managed to prise it loose from them sometime around the beginning of 1816. The author did carry out some revision of *Northanger Abbey* when she finally had the manuscript back in her possession, but she was simultaneously finishing *Persuasion* and already suffering from her final illness.

How did Jane Austen write? Unfortunately, we do not have early drafts, which would enable the scholars to examine the differences between her initial inspiration and her final, polished versions. However, we do know that she persistently revised and changed her novels. She wrote of *Pride and Prejudice* that 'I have lop't and crop't so successfully ... that I imagine it must be rather shorter than S. & S. altogether' (*Letters*, p. 298), and showed her unwillingness to let a novel she considered unrevised go to the publisher, when she wrote of *Northanger Abbey* 'Miss Catherine is put upon the Shelve for the present, and I do not know that she will ever come out' (*Letters*, p. 484). *Northanger Abbey* had originally been called *Susan* (the author changed the heroine's name) and was sold thirteen years before. This comment, and the evidence of rewriting, show that Jane Austen was determined to bring the old manuscript up to her more mature standards before allowing it to be read. We also know that two conclusions were written for *Persuasion*. The circumstances – we are told by James Edward Austen-Leigh (*A Memoir of Jane Austen*, 1870) – were as straightforward as the author waking up with renewed vigour the day after writing the first ending. In that day, it appears, she cancelled the first version and wrote two full chapters giving the ending we have in published editions today. The cancelled chapter is also the only manuscript of a Jane Austen draft still in existence.

The author repeatedly revised and polished her work, then. This process must have been encouraged by the family habit of reading aloud, and in particular the fact that she tried out her novels on her family and some close friends. We should not forget that Jane Austen began to write parodies and skits at the age of eleven; her first purpose in writing was to entertain her family. Later, she went to the trouble of copying out her early burlesques into neat volumes for the Austens' amusement. Clearly, Jane Austen had a lively, dramatic 'ear' for the sound of dialogue, refined and exercised by the Austens' frequent amateur dramatic productions when her father was alive and they were all together at Steventon. Jane complains, in one of her letters, that her mother could not do justice to the dialogue and characters' voices in *Pride and Prejudice*: 'Our second evening's reading to Miss Benn had not pleased me so well, but I believe something must be attributed to my mother's too rapid way of getting on: and though she perfectly understands the characters herself, she cannot speak as they ought' (*Letters*, p. 299). While her brother Henry was reading *Mansfield Park*, she reports that he 'admires H. Crawford: I mean properly, as a clever, pleasant man' (*Letters*, p. 378); and we know that both Cassandra and the Austen sisters' friend Martha Lloyd had read *First Impressions* (the first version of *Pride and Prejudice*) before 1799. This practice of putting her novels into family-and-friend circulation must have enabled Jane Austen to notice and correct any writing that offended her ear. It also clearly gave her characters a vivid life, almost a 'real' life as people off the page who were discussed, liked and disliked, by the Austens and their friends.

Several comments in the letters show that the author developed quite a personal relationship with her heroines, in particular. She remarks that Mrs Knight 'will like my Elinor' in *Sense and Sensibility* (*Letters*, p. 273); she is reported as saying that Emma Woodhouse is 'a heroine whom no one but myself will much like',[3] and writes that her niece 'may perhaps like the Heroine [Catherine Morland of *Northanger Abbey*], as she is almost too good for me' (*Letters*, p. 487). Several critics and biographers have thought that Elizabeth Bennet of *Pride and Prejudice* is the heroine who most closely resembles her author. Certainly, Jane Austen expressed strong affection for her creation: '... she [a Miss Benn] really does seem to admire Elizabeth. I must confess that I think her as delightful a creature as ever appeared in print, and how I shall be able to tolerate those who do not like *her* at least I do not know' (*Letters*, p. 297).

After moving to Chawton Cottage in 1809, Jane Austen wrote during the mornings at a little mahogany desk in the combined dining-room and hall of the house. She must, therefore, have left the drawing-room to her sister and mother, and decided to compose fiction in a sort of thoroughfare, where servants and visitors would pass her. She used a small paper format, and always had some other documents handy with which to cover her manuscript. Although happy to show the fruits of her work in the family, Jane Austen clearly did not wish to be questioned or have to discuss the progress of her book while she was in the act of writing.

Jane Austen's original inspiration was comic. She discovered and exercised her talent for writing through satires and burlesques, and from an early age her targets were hypocrisy and absurdity in the people she met or imagined, and artificial sentiment or pompous morality in the romantic novels she read. We have discussed the question of her development during her literary career, in Chapter 6 above ('The Theme of Change and the Change of Theme'). It is very difficult to reach firm conclusions about the growth of her talent or any change in her preoccupations. However, it is clear that the six novels do show a growth in the sincerity the author could allow herself to express, and in seriousness. Look, for example, at this extract from the early *Northanger Abbey*:

> No one who had ever seen Catherine Morland in her infancy would have supposed her born to be a heroine. Her situation in life, the character of her father and mother, her own person and disposition, were all equally against her. Her father was a clergyman, without being neglected or poor, and a very respectable man, though his name was Richard and he had never been handsome. He had a considerable indepen-

dence, besides two good livings; and he was not in the least addicted to locking up his daughters.

(*Northanger Abbey*, Chapter 1)

In this extract, the information about Mr Morland is given within a structure of sarcasm: Catherine could not have been a 'heroine' because her father was not 'neglected' or 'poor' and not in the habit of 'locking up his daughters'. This is the opening of the novel, in which a very pleasant girl who is besotted with the horrors of Gothic romance manages to meet and marry a clever, amusing young man. However, the author's continuous aim is to laugh at the clichés of sensational novels: the real characters, and their less melodramatic world, seem to appear as a by-product of Jane Austen's satire. Now look at the following, from the final novel *Persuasion*:

> 'All the privilege I claim for my own sex (it is not a very envi-able one, you need not covet it) is that of loving longest, when existence or when hope is gone.'
>
> She could not immediately have uttered another sentence; her heart was too full, her breath too much oppressed.
>
> 'You are a good soul,' cried Captain Harville, putting his hand on her arm quite afffectionately.
>
> (*Persuasion*, p. 238)

Anne Elliot is expressing her own deepest feelings here, as the reader knows. It is done under the guise of a general discussion where men's and women's constancy is the supposed subject; but the sincerity of her words is not undercut by any satirical irony, and Jane Austen allows her narrative to enhance the sense of strong emotion, by detail-ing Anne's physical sensations ('her breath too much oppressed') and the physical appeal of her passion which brings this intimate response from Harville: 'putting his hand on her arm quite affectionately'. Clearly, during her life as a writer, Jane Austen found herself able to depict an increasing variety and range of feelings and behaviours in her characters. The satirical stiletto is never absent from her work – look, for example, at the devastating opening sentence of *Persuasion*, describing Sir Walter Elliot – but a greater seriousness and naturalness, of feeling and behaviour, are added to the comic whole.

On the other hand, Jane Austen was vividly aware of her limitations, and consciously restricted her own subject-matter. She famously commented on her work as being like that of a miniaturist. Writing to her nephew Edward, who had shown her part of a manuscript of his own, she contrasts his style with hers: 'What should I do with your strong, manly, spirited Sketches, full of Variety and Glow? – How could I possibly join them on to the little bit (two Inches wide) of Ivory on which I work with so fine a Brush, as produces little effect after much labour?' (*Letters*, p. 469). We notice that she is conscious of Edward's writing as 'manly', and remember that in all six of her novels there is no scene without a woman present. Jane Austen may have been self-deprecating about her 'little bit' of ivory, but she was serious about not attempting any subject-matter that was outside her personal experience. So, for example, she advised her niece Anna, who was also writing a novel: 'Let the Portmans go to Ireland, but as you know nothing of the Manners there, you had better not go with them' (*Letters*, p. 395); and in writing to Anna she also defined the scope of her own work: '3 or 4 Families in a Country Village is the very thing to work on' (*Letters*, p. 401). This narrowness of subject-matter seems to have been a rule Jane Austen kept to conscientiously, but it was also something necessary as a result of her character and upbringing. She wrote 'pictures of domestic life in country villages' because she could be sure the details in these pictures would be true to life; and her sense of humour would not allow her to become expansive or over-serious in her choice of theme: 'I could no more write a romance than an epic poem. I could not sit seriously down to write a serious romance under any other motive than to save my life' (*Letters*, p. 452).

Jane Austen kept to her self-imposed limits in terms of subject-matter, then; but as she wrote, the range of human experience she depicted, within that small social scene, developed and grew.

---

[1] *The Double Life of Jane Austen*, London, 1972, p. 13.

[2] *Jane Austen's Letters*, ed. R W Chapman, 2nd. edn, London, 1952, p. 123. Further references to this work in the text are identified as *Letters*, followed by the page-number.

[3] *A Memoir of Jane Austen*, by James Edward Austen-Leigh, 1870. 2nd edn, 1871, p. 157.

# 9

# Jane Austen's Contribution to the Development of the Novel

## The Novel before Jane Austen

Jane Austen had read the novelists we now think of as the classical writers who came before herself: Defoe, Richardson and Fielding; and she knew the work of her contemporary Fanny Burney very well. It is quite easy to draw comparisons between, for example, Richardson's use of the novel in letters form and Jane Austen's use of the same in her unpublished works. We can also easily draw a line of development between Richardson's collections of letters in *Clarissa* and *Pamela*, and the development of internal narrative to analyse and introspect about experience, found in Jane Austen's more sophisticated technique, where the author's seamless movement from one point of view to another enables events to be 'viewed' and related by a character, and their thoughts given in their own recognisable diction.

Similarly, we can see that Fielding's love of burlesque, and his habit of bringing pomposity heavily down to earth, were qualities Jane Austen inherited and carried forward in the novel form. The 'Bill of Fare' with which Fielding opens *Tom Jones* promises plain 'Human Nature', and includes a sideswipe at over-elaborated fictions by promising to leave 'all the high French and Italian seasoning of affectation and vice which courts and cities afford' as a 'hash and ragoo' for the end of the novel. His first, and main, subject will be 'Human

Nature ... in that more plain and simple manner in which it is found in the country.'[1] This amused dismissal of sensational settings and plots, and Fielding's advocacy of truth to nature in its familiar, everyday form, foreshadows Jane Austen's determination to keep within the limits of her own observation of life, so that she finds '3 or 4 Families in a Country Village' the right subject-matter for her novels.

However, the most obvious target of Jane Austen's satire was the contemporary fashion for novels of romantic sentiment and horror: the industry that turned out sensational fiction of various kinds, whether 'Gothic' or otherwise inspired. These novels tended to have features in common: a grand or distant setting in place and time, and a tendency to grossly oversimplify, and exaggerate, the characters' sentiments. In Chapter 7 we noticed the elaborate ironic double-bluff Jane Austen constructs around the subject of 'love at first sight' (see *Pride and Prejudice*, pp. 226–7). The characterisation of Catherine Morland in *Northanger Abbey*, whose Gothic imaginings under the influence of Mrs Radcliffe's *Mysteries of Udolpho* lead her to entertain horrific suspicions of General Tilney, is another obvious example of Jane Austen's reaction against sensationalism.

The 'Gothic' novel of the time was typically set in a distant time or place and filled with exotic titles – princes, dukes and counts – and names – *The Castle of Otranto* (1765) and *The Mysteries of Udolpho* (1794) for example – as well as violent, horrific and often supernatural action. These novels generally evoked fear and pity for a suffering or persecuted maiden, and tended to use the sinister setting of ruins or ancient buildings. For example, in Matthew Lewis's *The Monk* (1796) the climax of the plot occurs in catacombs deep beneath an ancient cemetery. Jane Austen clearly found these stories far-fetched to the point of ridiculousness, and their style inferior.

However, in typically ironic style she was at pains to point out that real life, although apparently less lurid, could be equally malicious and cruel. So, for example, Catherine is

wrong to suspect that General Tilney murdered his wife. On
the other hand, she has correctly sensed that he is a self-
willed, proud man, capable of great meanness and cruelty.
His mistreatment of Catherine, when he throws her out of
Northanger Abbey, is monstrous.

Jane Austen, then, laughed at the excesses of inferior
novels, and found a rich vein of absurdity in the 'Gothic' and
sentimental productions of her time, as subjects for satirical
analysis. In this sense, she helped to develop the novel as a
serious genre in the tradition of both Richardson and
Fielding. However, as always with Jane Austen, if we read her
closely we find that she is not simply negative in her satire.
She used bathos to great comic effect, but was not anti-
romantic or destructive of what was worthwhile in the literary trends of her own time. We must remember that
Elizabeth Bennet is enthusiastic about seeing the Lake
District. She exclaims 'what delight!' at the prospect of
seeing 'rocks and mountains', anticipating 'hours of transport'. Then, however, she determines that her head will
remain clear: 'Lakes, mountains, and rivers shall not be
jumbled together in our imaginations', but 'we *will* know
where we have gone – we *will* recollect what we have seen'
(*Pride and Prejudice*, pp. 121–2). Jane Austen insists on
rational, accurate enthusiasm. She does not decry strength
of feeling itself, only confusion and the irrational.

## Integrating Aspects of the Novel

### Characterisation

At the conclusion of *Tom Jones*, the heroine Sophia very
properly suffers from a conflict between her love of Tom,
and her distrust of him because he has been with other
women while declaring his love for her. She expresses this
problem in deliberate terms: 'if I can be prevailed on by your
repentance to pardon you, I will at least insist on the

strongest proof of its sincerity' because 'A human mind may be imposed on; nor is there any infallible method to prevent it' (*Tom Jones*, p. 788). Here, Fielding has created a fine comic conflict in his character; and the way her scruples are eventually overcome joyously conveys her real eagerness to marry Tom – as well as making the reader laugh. On the other hand, Fielding's character has no level of introspection, self-deception or hidden emotion. It is all on the surface: both her attraction towards Tom, and her scruples, are publicly shown and discussed.

We give this example to show how far Jane Austen's characterisation has developed beyond that of Fielding. Here is Elizabeth Bennet, similarly in the grip of attraction and hesitation:

> and the evening, though as it passed it seemed long, was not long enough to determine her feelings towards *one* in that mansion [Pemberley]; and she lay awake two whole hours endeavouring to make them out. She certainly did not hate him. No; hatred had vanished long ago...
>
> (*Pride and Prejudice*, p. 216)

We cannot imagine Sophia Western struggling to 'make out' complex nuances in her own feelings in this way. Elizabeth goes on to try various emotional labels on her own heart, but none of them is satisfactory. 'Hatred' has vanished; then 'dislike', 'respect' and something 'friendlier' follow, with 'esteem', 'goodwill' and finally 'gratitude'. However, Jane Austen preserves the depth and humanity of her character. Elizabeth seems to test all these labels against the actual, indefinable feeling in her heart. In the end she can only say that the feeling is 'by no means unpleasing, though it could not be exactly defined'. The fact that Elizabeth has not managed to fathom her own feelings is emphasised at the end of the paragraph, when she hears that they will visit Pemberley the next morning: 'Elizabeth was pleased; though when she asked herself the reason, she had very little to say in reply' (all from *Pride and Prejudice*, pp. 216–17).

Jane Austen has added psychological depth to her characters, then, and they confront their crises with earnest attempts at introspection which, the author is careful to show, do not plumb the full depth of their experience. Jane Austen extends this subtlety of psychological insight over time, as well. In Fielding's *Tom Jones*, Sophia's capitulation, with its joyous revelation of her love for Jones, is broadly comic. It is obvious, direct and comes straightaway, only a page after the conflict quoted above. Now turn to *Pride and Prejudice*. In Chapter 50, Elizabeth reasons that Darcy's character would most suit her own because they are 'unlike', so their marriage would be 'to the advantage of both' (*PP*, p. 252). On the other hand, in Chapter 55 and thirty pages on, she reasons that Jane and Bingley will be happy because of 'a general similarity' between them (*PP*, p. 280). Jane Austen gives us, here, a continuity of feeling and a subtle smile about the continuity of Elizabeth's attempt to interpret and rationalise her feelings: Elizabeth contradicts herself, but the simple truth is that she *feels* confident of the happiness in both matches – for whatever reason – and her reasons do not matter. This example shows how carefully the undercurrent of internal emotion, and of the character's continuous attempts to make sense of her feelings, is maintained throughout Jane Austen's text, in a way that would be unimaginable within the broader, more superficial strokes of Fielding's characterisation.

In short, Jane Austen's narrative has moved the novel significantly towards conveying the indefinable, inexplicable reality of emotional experience. Characterisation is a far subtler and more flexible narrative tool in her hands than it had been before. If we think about our own experiences, we are aware of constantly telling stories to ourselves and about ourselves, trying to explain our feelings and actions, trying to capture life in words; and we also know that we can never entirely succeed – life experience is too fluid and complex to be contained in words. Fielding's characters have clear, strong qualities: Squire Western has *zest*, Sophia *loves* Tom. They have loud, clear voices also, and their actions are full of energy. But we always recognise that they are figureheads acting out the author's drama. Their purpose is to entertain us with the clash and harmonies of their prominent characteristics. There is sympathy, anxiety and exuberance, but a well-defined limitation to the people presented in Fielding's novel, because their lives *can be* put into words. Jane Austen led fiction towards the modern novel, because her characters share our experience, which 'could not be exactly defined', when a long evening 'was not long enough to determine her feelings'; and when we ask ourselves questions and have 'very little to say in reply'.

The implications of this development cannot be exaggerated. Here is an extract from D. H. Lawrence's *The Ladybird*. Daphne is persuading herself to love her absent husband, but loses the thimble which was a gift from the disturbingly attractive Count Dionys:

> Her husband was coming, quite soon, quite soon. But she could not raise herself to joy. She had lost her thimble. It was as if Count Dionys accused her in her sleep of something, she did not quite know what.
>
> (*The Ladybird*, in 'Three Novellas', Penguin, 1981, p. 41)

Notice the label, 'joy', which Daphne's mind applies to the emotion she hopes to feel. Like Elizabeth Bennet, she tries this label on what she actually feels, but it does not fit. Also like Elizabeth, she is aware of a feeling she cannot describe: it is a guilt so vague she feels 'accused . . . in her sleep' and 'she did not quite know what'. The narrative focuses on a mundane, trivial object – a thimble. It is surprising to find Jane Austen's technique alive and flourishing in Lawrence's post-Freudian narrative; and it is particularly ironic since Lawrence himself attacked her for failing in characterisation, giving 'the sharp knowing in apartness instead of knowing in togetherness ... thoroughly unpleasant, English in the bad, mean, snobbish sense of the word'.[2] Jane Austen might have smiled to hear Lawrence mistaking her characters' intellectual efforts for an author's intellectual arrogance; but his indebtedness to her, whether he knew it or not, shows how great an addition she brought to the novelist's armoury.

## Social satire

Jane Austen's presentation of the world outside her characters is based on a satirical analysis of society. She exposes hypocrisy and absurdity, and her novels are full of grotesque 'types': the inordinately vain Sir Walter Elliot in *Persuasion*, the garrulous Miss Bates in *Emma*, the sanctimonious Mr Collins in *Pride and Prejudice*, and ponderous, humourless Sir Thomas Bertram in *Mansfield Park* are all examples of social caricature. Their outstanding features are drawn boldly, and drawn to our attention by repetition and exaggeration.

Yet Jane Austen carries her feeling of natural, real life even into these cartoon sketches of the outside world, in a way that Fielding's figures with their caricature names – Thwackum, Square, Allworthy, Slipslop and Booby – never do. Two qualities in Jane Austen's satirical grotesques take them far beyond those of Fielding. First, they all have an intimate effect on the heroine's inner current of feeling. So, in *Persuasion*, Anne 'must sigh that her father should feel no degradation in his change' (*Persuasion*, p. 152) when he proudly shows their house in Bath; and 'her spirits improved' when Sir Walter acknowledged Wentworth, even though it was 'late and reluctant and ungracious' (*Persuasion*, p. 191). Even in her happiness at the end of the novel, Anne 'felt her own inferiority keenly' because her father was too stupid to be valued by her husband (*Persuasion*, p. 253). Sir Walter, then, the buffoon who thinks only of cosmetics, is vitally connected to the sensitive undercurrent of the novel as well. Miss Bates, whose long, muddled speeches provide outrageous comedy in *Emma*, also brings the shock which wakes Emma up to herself. Emma 'felt it at her heart. How could she have been so brutal, so cruel to Miss Bates!' and she 'felt the tears running down her cheeks almost all the way home' (*Emma*, p. 310). Mr Collins's first letter, in *Pride and Prejudice*, marks him down as an 'oddity', yet his function in the novel is much more than this. When he speaks to Darcy, Elizabeth's innermost feelings are disturbed: she 'eagerly watched' and 'It vexed her to see him expose himself to such a man' (*PP*, p. 83); and his letter following Lydia's elopement is not funny. It is unchristian, as we would expect from such a hypocrite; but it is also vicious and hurtful, and vengefully increases Elizabeth's misery by harping on the damage done to her own and Jane's prospects. Finally, the cruel pressure Sir Thomas Bertram applies to Fanny, trying to bend her to his will in the matter of marrying Henry Crawford, is only one example of his presence in the sensitive inner life that is *Mansfield Park* (see Chapter 5). Jane Austen's social satire, then, is not made up of two-dimensional figures: it is thoroughly intertwined with inner emotions and moral life, with the novel's central experience.

Second, Jane Austen's burlesque characters are endowed with convincing psychology, and they are not static. The author sketches in enough for us to imagine their experience as well, so that there seems to be an inner story for each, which is not told but is naturally portrayed. Jane Austen achieves this with the lightest of touches. For example, the moment of delay before Miss Bates understands Emma's cruel remark at Box Hill, is perfectly observed. She is 'deceived by the mock ceremony of her [Emma's] manner'(*Emma*, p. 306). This detail momentarily, but powerfully, conveys the confusion felt by the slow-witted in the presence of clever irony. It is a moment out of Miss Bates's life, which enables us to imagine her constant panic in the company of cleverer people.

There are many such delicate touches. For example, when Mr Collins meets Elizabeth at breakfast on the day she leaves

Hunsford (*PP*, Chapter 38), he recites all the advantages of his situation, repeatedly boasting about Lady Catherine and Rosings. His speech is full of false humility, begging to be contradicted ('We know how little there is to tempt anyone to our humble abode', p. 177). The telling moment, however, is when his speech leads him on to a sudden stop: 'and altogether I trust it does not appear that your friend has drawn an unfortunate – But on this point it will be as well to be silent' (*PP*, p. 178). This has an extraordinary effect. Suddenly, in the moment when Mr Collins stops himself, a whole vista of his insecurities opens out before us. He felt unsure of himself for the first time in his life, when Elizabeth rejected his proposal ('he was comparatively diffident', p. 102); now we realise that his insecurity has festered within him for months, and all his boasts are compensation for this. The sudden break in his speech reveals more than this, however: somewhere within Mr Collins, there is a shadowy awareness that his wife is far from happy. The reader is thus given enough to imagine a continuous experience of life from Mr Collins's point of view. We can believe in him, living in the background of the novel with his own needs and worries, because this one moment reveals an inner self to our view. The effect is sustained throughout the novel. So, when Mr Collins finally writes that he can 'reflect, with augmented satisfaction, on a certain event of last November' (*PP*, p. 240), since Lydia's elopement has brought disgrace on the Bennets, we understand that he has finally managed to overcome that little devil of insecurity, which has plagued him ever since Elizabeth said 'no'.

### The 'whole' event

We have discussed the way in which Jane Austen weaves together, inseparably, the inner and external features of the world she presents in her novels. One way of putting this is to say that every aspect of the narrative is fully integrated into the whole. The effect of this is that an event, in one of Jane Austen's novels, is created by contributions from both within and outside the heroine's consciousness. An event is therefore a 'whole' event, and the extraordinary quality of Jane Austen is the complex fitness of things. One short discussion will make this clear.

When Elizabeth Bennet overhears Darcy's rude comment, in the third chapter of *Pride and Prejudice*, she reacts by making fun of him to her friends. This is easily understood on a straightforward level: he is rude to her, so she is rude about him. Now let us look at this event from several standpoints:

1.  *Internal*: Why does Darcy say this? There is enough evidence lightly sketched in to the chapter, to suggest that he is a shy man. He detests dancing 'unless I am particularly acquainted with my partner' (*PP*, p. 13). Elizabeth turns her hurt into humour, and revenges herself on Darcy by ridiculing him. She does this so effectively that this event underpins her prejudice until Chapter 36. We understand the inner feelings of both characters intimately, and the event makes psychological sense.

2.  *External factors*: Marriage is a problem for Elizabeth because she – like other young ladies of the time – is under pressure to reconcile the conflicting demands of prudence and romance, money and love. Elizabeth is a romantic (see her argument with Charlotte in Chapter 6), but sensible enough to be practical as well (see her reception of Mrs Gardiner's advice about Wickham, Chapter 26). Elizabeth cannot emotionally square this circle: her conclusions about Wickham (see Chapter 27) are bitter – she resents the materialism in which she is caught. In Chapter 3 she meets Darcy, a handsome, attractive man; yet his social position and his superciliousness emphasise that he is out of her reach. In short, although she is a romantic, Elizabeth is not confident enough to believe that she can marry 'above her station', at the beginning of the novel. She is bitter,

and resents the cage she is trapped in by society's rigid hierarchy. This fact fuels her resentment, and motivates her determined hatred of Darcy as well as her flirtation with Wickham. Elizabeth resents Darcy's rank and power, then; and she uses her own power in gaining revenge. The foolishness and inconstancy of Meryton society aid her here, since she is clever enough to manipulate those around her. Elizabeth forms the fickle opinion of the neighbourhood, even guiding her mother's mind, to further her revenge.

We could continue this analysis, bringing more and more aspects of the novel's construction into play to amplify this one event. For example, it is fitting that Elizabeth should have created the prejudice against Darcy which causes her problems on two later occasions: when she decides not to expose Wickham (Chapter 40), and when she has to reveal her engagement to her parents and Jane (Chapter 59). Also, this event prepares us for the sense of triumph when Elizabeth declares her belief that she is Darcy's equal (Chapter 56). In short, the event is 'fitting', and becomes more and more significant, and more and more convincingly real, as we think about it from many different points of view.

This development of narrative technique into a fully flexible and fully integrated tool for conveying a 'whole' event, may be Jane Austen's most significant contribution to the history of the novel.

## Other influences

We should remark on two further points: Jane Austen's use of a small neighbourhood as a 'microcosm' of a whole society; and her experiments with the convention of the 'courtship' fable.

We discussed Jane Austen's use of '3 or 4 Families in a Country Village' as her subject, in the last chapter. It is reasonable to draw a connection between this development in the novel genre, and some more grandiose attempts, later in the nineteenth century, to represent complete societies. The common idea between Jane Austen and later novelists was to use the world of the novel as a microcosm of society, depicting a range of different people. However, where Jane Austen limits herself to a narrow focus on a single stratum in the class system, Charles Dickens and George Eliot in particular were much more ambitious. The sense of panorama over an entire town that we find in Dickens's *Hard Times* (1854), or the depiction of London society from near the top to the bottom we find in his *Our Mutual Friend* (1864–65), can be seen as developments and expansions of Jane Austen's insight: that a carefully structured 'sample' of humanity can, in the novel, become a complete, self-sufficient world. George Eliot's great masterpiece *Middlemarch* (1871–72) also exhibits this quality.

With regard to the conventions of the 'courtship' fable, Jane Austen's six novels present innovative variations on this theme. Richardson's *Pamela* (1740–41) is a rags to riches story, where the heroine's virtue wins a rich man's hand in marriage. Jane Austen's *Northanger Abbey*, *Pride and Prejudice* and *Mansfield Park* are all developments of this fable; but Elizabeth Bennet wins her Darcy through 'impertinence'; Catherine Morland wins her Henry Tilney through naïvety; and *Mansfield Park* is a darker study of the fable in which our feelings about Fanny's virtue and perseverance are equivocal. In *Emma*, the conventional 'courtship' plot is elaborately satirised: both Emma's and Harriet's stories present conventional possibilities which come to nothing, and the outcome marries the heroine to Knightley, who has filled a paternal rather than a romantic role throughout. The marriage of Marianne Dashwood and Colonel Brandon at the end of *Sense and Sensibility* similarly disappoints the conventional plot, in which Willoughby is the romantic hero. *Persuasion* is different again, a novel of revived love, in which courtship is relegated to a distant past, and the fable concerns the reanimation of love.

Finally, we must not forget that Jane Austen's novels are those of a woman. Her contribution to the development of feminine perception, and awareness of the woman's predicament in a male-dominated society, is considerable. We should listen again to Fanny Price:

> 'I *should* have thought... that every woman must have felt the possibility of a man's not being approved, not being loved by some one of her sex, at least, let him be ever so generally agreeable. Let him have all the perfections in the world, I think it ought not to be set down as certain, that a man must be acceptable to every woman he may happen to like himself... How then was I to be – to be in love with him the moment he said he was with me? How was I to have an attachment at his service, as soon as it was asked for? His sisters should consider me as well as him... And, and – we think very differently of the nature of women, if they can imagine a woman so very soon capable of returning an affection as this seems to imply.'
>
> (*Mansfield Park*, pp. 292–3)

---

[1] Fielding, Henry, *The History of Tom Jones, A Foundling*, Collins Classics, London 1955, pp. 34–5. Further references to this edition are to *Tom Jones*, followed by the page number.
[2] Quoted in Gilbert, S. and Gubar, S., *The Madwoman in the Attic: The Woman Writer and the Nineteenth-Century Literary Imagination*, Yale 1979.

# 10

# A Sample of Critical Views

## Controversy

In the case of Jane Austen we should preface this sample from the critics with a word about the particular virulence of the argument about her. There are plenty of different interpretations of Jane Austen, of course; but there is another, more personal controversy polarising her readers into partisan affection or hatred. Jane Austen seems to arouse these extremes of feeling, and here are a few samples.

Sir Walter Scott, author of the Waverley novels, was an enthusiast. He wrote a complimentary review of *Emma* when it first appeared; and wrote in his journal about 'Miss Austen's very finely written novel of *Pride and Prejudice*. That young lady had a talent for describing the involvements, and feelings, and characters of ordinary life, which is to me the most wonderful I ever met with'; and he praised her 'exquisite touch, which renders ordinary commonplace things and characters interesting'.[1] Mark Twain, on the other hand, commented when comparing her with Poe, 'I could read his prose on salary, but not Jane's. Jane is entirely impossible. It seems a great pity that they allowed her to die a natural death';[2] and Emerson called her 'vulgar in tone, sterile in artistic invention ... Never was life so pinched and narrow ... Suicide is more respectable'.[3] Charlotte Brontë is hardly more forgiving:

> Anything like warmth or enthusiasm – anything energetic, poignant, heartfelt is utterly out of place in commending these works: all such demonstration the authoress would have met

245

with a well-bred sneer... The passions are perfectly unknown
to her; she rejects even a speaking acquaintance with that
stormy sisterhood. Even to the feelings she vouchsafes no
more than an occasional graceful but distant recognition.[4]

We mentioned D. H. Lawrence's dislike of Jane Austen in
Chapter 9; but she was defended by Henry James, and
Rudyard Kipling's celebrated story *The Janeites* (1926)
shows positive appreciation of her merits.

Generally, those who hate Jane Austen hate the etiquette
of her class, and accuse her of coldness, a lack of passion.
The extraordinary thing about these reactions, however, is
that they accuse her with so much personal vitriol – disliking
Jane Austen seems to make people very angry.

## Samples of Criticism

The violent difference of feeling between lovers and haters
of Jane Austen's novels, is relatively straightforward; but the
hundreds of varieties of approach and opinion among the
interpreters of her works are not at all simple. In this
chapter we look at three different critics' reactions to the
novels, but without any pretence that they are 'representative'. Those who are interested in the varieties of critical
theory and approach should go on to read from the suggestions in Further Reading below, and make use of further
bibliographies in the critical works themselves to pursue
their research. Such reading will reveal that there are several
very different strands of each of feminist, psychoanalytical,
socio-political, structuralist and post-structuralist criticisms,
as well as a wealth of other critics, writing about Jane
Austen, who have no single theoretical approach but borrow
their concerns and techniques eclectically.

The virtue of the three critics we discuss here, then, is
simply that they are different from each other. We begin with

Andrew H. Wright, whose *Jane Austen's Novels: A Study in Structure* was published in 1953.

Wright begins by pointing out that Jane Austen embarrasses the critics because she eludes categories, and because she arouses such dissenting feelings in her readers. He then suggests that the novels can be considered on three levels: first, as representations of country life among the upper-middle classes at the time Jane Austen lived; second, as allegories 'in which Sense, Sensibility, Pride, Prejudice' and several other virtues and defects are 'set forth in narrative form and commented on'; and finally they can be read on 'the ironic level', which leads us to consider the various aspects of the novel as symbolic, or implying something 'beyond what they embody'.[5] Wright then briefly surveys several interpretations which have emphasised social history or allegory, concluding that the first two levels of reading are unsatisfactory and incomplete:

> My argument will be that Jane Austen's novels are too complex to allow a merely didactic interpretation, too serious to be dismissed as simply light-hearted ... Indeed, it is possible to go further: it is possible to say that Jane Austen's themes are ironic.
>
> (Wright, *op. cit.*, p. 34)

Irony is a term Wright uses to describe 'a world view, as the juxtaposition, in fact, of two mutually incompatible views of life'. He explains that Jane Austen was perceptive about the contradictions in life and experience, but also emotionally involved in them. The important element in irony, and that which distinguishes it from mere contrast, is that the ironist is emotionally involved in both of the contradictory, or mutually incompatible, views of life. Austen sees both the virtues and limitations of each, and this ambivalence about things that are contradictory or irreconcilable is ironic vision.

Wright then comments on the theme of each of the novels, suggesting in what way each can be interpreted as an ironic

work. *Pride and Prejudice* puts forward a complex situation, since pride and prejudice are hard to separate and
often engender each other. Quoting Elizabeth's comment to
Mr Bingley, that 'intricate characters are the *most* amusing',
Wright explains that the novel is about 'Intricacy and
Simplicity' in the personalities of characters. There are three
couples: the simple couple whose ideas and behaviour are
conventional and naïve (Jane and Bingley); the central
couple (Elizabeth and Darcy), 'whose breadth and depth
involve them in the dangers of Prejudice and Pride'; and
another pair (Charlotte Lucas and Wickham) who 'have a
great deal of the cleverness of the two main characters' but
who, for different reasons, both abandon virtue. '*Pride and
Prejudice* is thus concerned with the contradictions of
human personality – one might say, the price of intelligence'
(Wright, *op. cit.*, p. 43).

Wright considers *Emma* in the context of the heroine's
envious remarks about Harriet's simplicity, and the value
Emma places on 'tenderness of heart'. The heroine is, in
fact, a complex character in whom there is a strong intellect
and a drive towards clarity, self-importance and a wish to run
or control things; yet at the same time there is abundant
'tenderness of heart', which is often obscured by Emma's
higher, more intellectual and manipulative qualities. Wright
says that 'the irony of *Emma* is that tenderness of heart
opposes itself to sharpness and clarity of perception'
(Wright, *op. cit.*, p. 44).

*Persuasion* is about the conflicts between parental authority and 'sanguine hopes for love'. Both qualities have merits:
'both qualities are seen to be desirable, both are defended
with warm sympathy by Jane Austen; but neither can be
achieved without some sacrifice of the other' (Wright, *op.
cit.*, p. 44).

Wright's suggestion, then, is that there is no single, firm
interpretation for a Jane Austen novel. Instead, she presents
us with contradictions, irreconcilables, qualities and experiences in which good and bad, virtues and faults, are mixed

so that our judgment never comes down to a single, simple conclusion. This, he suggests, is because her view of the world is an 'ironic' view; and he goes further to say that the depth and challenging effect of these novels lie in their 'ironic' themes. He then asks how irony appears in the writing, and this leads on to the main analytical part of Wright's study, in which he investigates the structure and style of the novels.

Jane Austen's writing is ironic because the narrative is not managed by the adoption of a single 'point of view', but on the contrary is written from a number of different angles and levels of intimacy or detachment from the characters. Wright identifies six modes in the writing, in particular:

1.  **The objective account** is written as if an omniscient author is telling her reader the truth; yet it is hardly ever that simple, and within this mode of writing, Jane Austen adopts a variety of different standpoints.
2.  **Indirect comment** occurs where a comment is added, or the author interposes some general truth or speculation, which does not belong to any of the characters. Wright cites the discussion of 'gratitude and esteem' as foundations for love, in *Pride and Prejudice* Chapter 46, and comments that the author's apparent view 'can be misleading only if the reader forgets the rest of the novel' (Wright, *op. cit.*, p. 68), then looks at the more moralising tone of authorial comment in *Mansfield Park*.
3.  **Direct comment** happens when the author intervenes, but the 'I' is usually an assumed personality and not Jane Austen herself. An example is the opening of the final chapter of *Mansfield Park*, 'Let other pens dwell on guilt and misery. I quit such odious subjects as soon as I can ... and so on.' Other critics have taken this statement at face value, but, Wright comments, 'we have learned to distrust statements which Jane Austen makes, even in her own person' (Wright, *op. cit.*, p. 75)

and goes on to point out that the final chapter deals with 'guilt and misery' quite thoroughly, and that 'Jane Austen in this very chapter more nearly approaches the boundaries of tragedy than in any other part of her work' (Wright, *op. cit.*, p. 76).

4.   The '**universally acknowledged truth**'. This heading drawn from the famous opening sentence of *Pride and Prejudice* covers Jane Austen's habit of sprinkling neat epigrams that either are or pretend to be maxims. The 'universally acknowledged truth' in *Pride and Prejudice* (that rich young men are looking for wives) appears so trite as to be ridiculous, yet contains ironic truth in the context of the novel as a whole.

5.   **The dramatic mode** is Wright's fifth category, and he draws attention to the splendid dramatic irony of, for example, Lady Catherine de Bourgh's monumental self-ignorance in her argument with Elizabeth Bennet (*PP*, Chapter 56). The author's habit of abbreviating long conversations 'which by their compression make for a greater ironic impact than would otherwise be possible' (Wright, *op. cit.*, p. 81), a technique often employed for Miss Bates's speeches in *Emma*, also belongs in this discussion of the 'dramatic mode'. Wright suggests that the reporting of dialogue off-stage, in the case of the proposal scenes in all of the novels, partly serves the purpose of compression to give the joyous effect of speed; however, he says, 'this method saves Jane Austen the inaccuracy of reporting directly what she cannot hear clearly' (Wright, *op. cit.*, p. 83).

6.   **Interior disclosures**. Wright begins with a discussion of fiction's advantages over life, where inhibitions distort or suppress the expression of character in a way the novelist can circumvent. He suggests that Jane Austen abandoned writing epistolary novels because of the limitation on interior revelation the letter format imposed, since the character can be more intimate when alone with only the author reporting their

thoughts, than with a correspondent. However, his central concern in this discussion is to emphasise the author as ironist, by showing us that Jane Austen allows her heroines' thoughts to reveal more than they know or can acknowledge about themselves: he sets himself to refute what he calls 'the autobiographical fallacy', committed by critics who identify Elinor Dashwood, Elizabeth Bennet and Anne Elliot with Jane Austen herself. 'Altogether, Jane Austen maintains some distance without which irony would be impossible' (Wright, *op. cit.*, p. 86). In the passage describing Elizabeth Bennet's thoughts and sensations as she reads Darcy's letter for a second, and finally a third, time, 'the sequence of thought here is evidently more obvious to the reader than to Elizabeth herself – from disdainful disbelief to somewhat reluctant acceptance. This is artistic objectivity' (Wright, *op. cit.*, p. 88).

Wright then examines the central triangle of characters (heroine, hero and villain) from each of the six published novels. He has shown that Jane Austen depends on 'more than a single viewpoint for the exposition of her themes', so now he examines how her characterisation focuses 'upon interrelationships between characters rather than upon a single individual' (Wright, *op. cit.*, p. 90). Here, it is worth looking at what Wright says of *Emma*, as an example of how he develops his broad insight of ironic tension between clever intellect and 'tenderness of heart', in a fuller analysis.

Emma undergoes a crisis at Box Hill when 'for the first time she feels a warm sympathy for Jane Fairfax ... Emma's "tenderness of heart", always incipient and intellectually desired, now begins to manifest itself spontaneously' (Wright, *op. cit.*, p. 154), so she exemplifies the ironic contradictions of life: 'Throughout the book we have loved her for the contradictions in her nature: they are amusing; they are deeply human' (Wright, *op. cit.*, p. 156). Wright then proceeds to analyse the union of the heroine and Mr Knightley:

Sensible, proper, kind, open, and vigorous – these are the words which come most readily to mind to describe George Knightley. But what would have happened had his advice been followed, his views been attended to? Emma would not have made a match for Mr Elton; Harriet would have married Mr Martin at once; Frank Churchill would not have been made so much of by Emma, and so forth: in short, the book could not have existed. Are we then to suppose that Emma is meant merely to exhibit the foibles of the world against a constant standard of values exemplified by Mr Knightley? Not at all: for then we should have seen him as the central figure, and the novel would have been a didactic treatise. Instead, Emma Woodhouse is the centre of attention and attraction. Cleverness, charm, subtlety, wit, receptivity – these are often in conflict with what Mr Knightley represents. But though contradictory, they are as thoroughly beloved by the author as the less exciting ingredients in Mr Knightley's philosophy.

(Wright, *op. cit.*, pp. 159–60)

This critic, then, proposes that the central subject-matter of the novels is a dualistic, or ambivalent vision of the world, where contradictory elements in character and feeling must be sifted, refined, puzzled over and finally accepted as profoundly impossible to reconcile; and that these ironic forces are embodied in multiple points of view in the narrative, and in conflicts and ironic accommodations between the characters:

Generally speaking... Jane Austen's characters are instruments of a profound vision: she laughs at man, but only because she takes him seriously; examines humanity closely, but the more she perceives the less she understands – or perhaps one had better say, the more she understands, the more is she perplexed by the contradictions which she finds.

(Wright, *op. cit.*, p. 172)

Wright's book can often seem to make over-simple judgments: for example, we may long to point out that Harriet Smith does not have 'tenderness of heart' at all: she has obsequious vapidity; and in the chapter which brings about Emma's self-awakening, Harriet reveals herself as a hard, selfish rival ('But Harriet was less humble, had fewer scruples than formerly' – *Emma* p. 340). We may wish to point this out to show that even 'tenderness of heart' is an illusion to Emma's fertile mind: it is a projection from the part of her own personality with which she feels ill at ease, and this realisation doubles the irony of her character and her relationship with Harriet. However, Wright convincingly refutes the idea that these novels are like fables with an explicit moral. He highlights their ironic complexity and the inevitable consequence of that: that the novels' central communication is ambivalent, unresolved, and so far more profound and human than had previously been widely acknowledged.

*       *       *

The second critic we look at is Leroy W. Smith. We examine the argument he puts forward in 'Jane Austen and the "Drama of Woman"' , the second chapter of his book of the same title.[6] Most of the remainder of Smith's work consists of chapters developing his theory by analysing each of the novels in turn. We will look at the conclusions he reaches on *Emma*, as an example of the direction in which his argument leads.

He begins by discussing the idea of a 'feminist' writer, and makes the point that Jane Austen lived in a 'patriarchal' society. This means that a young woman of the gentry would face a set pattern in her personal development. First, she would be under pressure to adapt herself to the wishes of men; and she would be persuaded that this adaptation is her true nature. If she did adapt, this would reduce her anxiety about being feminine, while any resistance would increase her feeling of being abnormal. She could only begin to question this oppressive system from within herself, as no external stimulus to criticising the system existed; and society would meet any dissent with social prohibition and 'an opposing social expectation' (Smith, *op. cit.*, p. 20). Finally, her further adaptation would lead her to define herself according to her attractiveness to men, not as a separate individual; and any conflict between her and the system would bring her tension, anxiety and anger.

A woman novelist born into such a society would have to pass through a struggle for self-recognition, and even then she would be confronted by a vacuum – the absence of any visible alternative to her 'feminine' role, and the absence of any 'social basis for a movement of the oppressed' (Smith, *op. cit.*, p. 20). The critic then states his central thesis:

> Austen very probably did experience constraints in developing her vision and her art... but the effects of such constraints seem not to have been acquiescence, alienation or a resort to duplicity but commitment, exploration and a positive resolution in the tradition of great art. Her novels portray the possibility of an authentic existence for a woman.
>
> (Smith, *op. cit.*, pp. 20–1)

Austen is like Mary Wollstonecraft, a more overtly 'pre-feminist' writer, in rejecting the idea that there is a 'natural feminine' way of knowing, which women are born with. In Austen's novels the emphasis is on education, and she sees education and the roles learned from society as being the crucial factors forming women into 'feminine' stereotypes. 'The cornerstone of change for both [Austen and Wollstonecraft] is the subversive idea that women are, or should be, rational beings and can be trained to think rationally' (Smith, *op. cit.*, p. 23).

Smith rejects the label 'feminist' for Jane Austen, since it implies a concept of 'rights' and deliberate political action that she probably did not have and that did not exist in her society; however, he suggests that she can be called 'pre-feminist' because she shows much of a feminist analysis of the patriarchal society around her; but she is 'engaged in a 'limited' rebellion ... her dissatisfaction does not cause an open break with her society' (quotations are from Smith, *op. cit.*, pp. 24–5).

The 'drama of woman' is defined in a quotation from Simone de Beauvoir: it 'lies in this conflict between the fundamental aspirations of every subject (ego) – who always regards the self as the essential – and the compulsions of a situation in which she is the inessential'.[7] Smith adds to this statement of the fundamental conflict, a list of 'givens' and 'limitations' in Jane Austen's case; so, for example it is 'given' that 'For her heroines the problem of self-knowledge matches in importance the problem of adjustment to the social world' (Smith, *op. cit.*, p. 26); and a 'limitation' is that 'Of the issues usually identified with feminism, she takes up education and marriage directly and, less directly, the world of work. She shows little interest in the vote, sexual morality, access to the professions, birth control or legal rights (although the entail is criticised)' (Smith, *op. cit.*, p. 27).

Smith then surveys the novels in a wide-ranging discussion of patriarchy which, unfortunately, we do not have space to follow in detail. He comments that the novels have many absent or ineffectual fathers, and abound in the evil outcomes and victims of patriarchy such as Charlotte Lucas and Lucy Steele who, respectively, have learned to deny the self, and to scheme, dissemble and compete with their own sex. The root of the problem is what Smith calls 'bipolarity', the idea that there are different male and female qualities and characteristics, and that the two are mutually exclusive. In 'bipolarity', the sexes are contrasted and separated from each other, human qualities split rigidly into male and female.

Jane Austen presents a solution in which two conditions must be met before the personality can expect to develop and live naturally, rather than as a denied or distorted self, warped by the patriarchal system. First, there must be equality 'as the basis for open communication, mutual respect and deep affection', so 'openness between individuals is essential. Where equality is absent, genuine love between men and women is impossible.' Second, the 'bipolar' concept must be replaced by a 'dualistic' concept, 'that is, the concept that 'masculine' and 'feminine' traits are present in everyone to some degree ... In the simplest terms, the dualistic concept acknowledges the possibility of rational thought in women and of sensitivity in men' (Smith, *op. cit.*, pp. 34–5).

Another way to put this is to say that patriarchy tends to divide the psyches of its victims: in men, the aggressive overdevelopment of the ego will repress their potential sensitivity and tenderness; and the denial to women of any rights of decision, rational thought or individual action suppresses what is sometimes called the 'agency' side of the psyche. Jane Austen believes that men and women can develop and 'liberate themselves towards wholeness' (Smith, *op. cit.*, p. 41), so hers is a unifying vision and profoundly optimistic, despite her appreciation of the enormous difficulties and struggles each individual faces in becoming whole. Smith suggests that Jane Austen's ideal is very much like what more recent thinkers call 'androgyny'.

Jane Austen's novels are all about marriage, and the struggles for self-knowledge and liberation from sexual stereotyping that are the stories of her novels are crowned by the creation of a marriage between two characters who have discovered themselves, and who come together with mutual respect and deep affection. Jane Austen's ideal of such a marriage shows the way forward, and her belief that individual men and women can overcome the destructive force of a patriarchal system she so trenchantly criticises. She does not show radical change in society, but in the individuals concerned, and the liberated marriage relationships they achieve, she shows the possibility of a 'true society'. In assessing her place in 'feminist' fiction, Smith argues that 'Austen faced a major social problem openly, honestly and realistically. She placed herself thereby in the forefront of the unformed movement for its solution' (Smith, *op. cit.*, p. 45).

Smith calls his seventh chapter 'Emma: The Flight from Womanhood'. Emma Woodhouse begins her career by rejecting the role a patriarchal society holds out to her. She is unusually placed since she holds apparent power over her pathetic father, and has the money that gives her freedom from dependence. The significant event in Emma's early life is the death of her mother 'too long ago for her to have more than an indistinct remembrance of her caresses' (*Emma*, p. 7), which has prevented her from growing up identifying herself with a loved mother, and instead she follows a course of 'positional' identification, where she emulates and seeks to identify with the most influential figure in her environment, seeking 'position' or status. The most influential other is Mr Knightley, and Emma therefore competes with him. This is the background to the confusion over her gender identity Emma suffers from at the start of the novel.

She is therefore led to adopt a masculine role, in which she seeks to control and command others, manipulating them to her own ends. Her problems are those of young men who are victims of patriarchy, like Henry Crawford or Tom Bertram: 'the power of having rather too much her own way, and a disposition to think a little too well of herself' (*Emma*, p. 7). Her relationship with Harriet is like that of a patriarchal father, manipulating and bending Harriet to her will, 'for her own good'; and Emma assumes and manages the task a father would normally carry out, of finding a suitable husband for this surrogate 'daughter'. Notice also that Emma does not apply herself to the traditional elements of female education: she has talent for the 'accomplishments' but does not bother with them since she is more interested in self-assertion, command and patronage, which are masculine activities.

Emma treats women as a man would, and this is particularly apparent in her treatment of Jane Fairfax and Harriet Smith. Jane Fairfax is extremely beautiful and highly accomplished, but she is in the position of dependence that makes her a victim in the patriarchal system. Emma needs to distance herself from Jane's dependent situation, and this need, added to her jealousy of the admiration Jane receives from others, leads her to over-emphasise her own superiority over Jane, and thus to treat her badly. 'If she is sure of the distance between them, she should be safe from the dangers that threaten even women like Jane' (Smith, *op. cit.*, p. 138). Emma is only able to begin sympathising with Jane after she has invented an emotional susceptibility for her in her imagined story of a love affair between Jane and Mr Dixon. Emma is reassured by this suspicion, because she believes she is not susceptible to emotions herself.

However, Emma's psychology is not merely that of a rebel female adopting the masculine role. She is also a product of her society, and she has therefore internalised patriarchal values which lead her, illogically, to compete with Mrs Elton for precedence, for example:

> In sum, Emma's flight from womanhood is self-defeating in a variety of ways: (1) it falsifies her perception of reality; (2) her identification with the behaviour of the oppressor forces her to live vicariously and restricts the growth of meaningful personal relationships; and (3) her adoption of the masculine role limits her ability to recognise and pursue her deepest personal needs and interests.
>
> (Smith, *op. cit.*, p. 139)

Emma, then, imagines herself to be in control of those around her, and manipulating them; and her most humiliating lesson, therefore, comes when she discovers that Frank Churchill has been manipulating her without her knowledge. Far from succeeding in a man's role, Emma has been the dupe of a favoured, clever son of the patriarchy; and she learns from this lesson that society still weights the advantages in favour of the man, who is able to prosecute and get away with his manipulations and deceptions with an ease, and freedom from accountability, that would never be accorded to her. Her independent wealth gave her the opportunity to reject a woman's dependent role; but society is so thoroughly set in its patriarchal pattern that she cannot successfully compete with men, despite her comparative freedom. Smith points out Emma's humiliation at Frank Churchill's hands and the anger she feels about the young man's freedom to do as he likes: 'What right had he to come among us with affection and faith engaged, and with manners so *very* disengaged? ... How could he tell what mischief he might be doing?' (*Emma*, p. 326).

Many critics agree, substantially, with the analysis of *Emma* put forward so far; but there is wide disagreement about what happens at the end of the novel. Is Mr Knightley merely a standard of behaviour for Emma to live up to, or does he also have to learn and change during the novel? Does Emma capitulate, in self-denying frustration, or is there a positive relationship at the end, which shows a forward, optimistic development in her character? Smith suggests that *Emma* is a novel with three subjects: first, self-knowledge, then the achievement of concord between the sexes by means of the breaking down of artificial social and psychological barriers. These two are mutually necessary to each other: where there is no hope of an open and equal relationship between the sexes, full self-knowledge is unlikely to be achieved. Third, '*Emma* is a novel about the responsibility of those who possess power to protect, rather than to oppress, those without it' (Smith, *op. cit.*, pp. 142–3).

Smith's thesis is that Knightley also has to learn. In the first part of the book he exhibits some stereotypical patriarchal attitudes, for example in his expectation that a Harriet Smith *must* accept a Robert Martin, and his irritation when she does not; and in his wish for Emma to be 'in love, and in some doubt of a return; it would do her good' (*Emma*, p. 36). Knightley also tends to assume his correctness without sufficient allowance for the difference of others: that is, he does not use his imagination to understand other people's experiences or lives. This is particularly apparent when he criticises Frank Churchill, and Emma argues that Knightley has 'not an idea of what is requisite in situations directly opposite to your own', urging the power of 'habits of early obedience and long observance' which prevent people from bursting forth 'at once into perfect independence' (*Emma*, p. 123). In this argument, Emma shows greater perception and understanding of others, than Mr Knightley.

. The change in Mr Knightley comes about when 'Knightley becomes aware that his love for Emma is sexual rather than familial as a result of his jealousy of Frank Churchill', so he abandons his paternalism and 'begins to look upon her as an independent and worthy fellow being' (Smith, *op. cit.*, p. 152). This is confirmed by their exchange of acknowledgements and recognition of each other during the ball at the Crown. Knightley resists giving a lecture, and his recognition of Emma's 'serious spirit' as well as his more generous opinion of Harriet Smith, cause Emma to feel 'extremely gratified' and lead to 'their first lovers' steps [dancing together]'. Subsequently, Knightley treats Emma as 'an independent adult rather than as his pupil or charge' (Smith, *op. cit.*, p. 153).

Near the end of the novel, the falsity and futility of their previous, artificial relationship are acknowledged by both. In particular, Mr Knightley's paternal role is finally analysed, and found wanting: in proposing, he apologises for his arrogance, saying 'I have blamed you, and lectured you, and you have borne it as no other woman in England would have borne it'; and he also acknowledges that the attempt to control another human being is ultimately futile: 'My interference was quite as likely to do harm as good ... I do not believe I did you any good' (*Emma*, pp. 378–9). Smith therefore concludes that, although the main emphasis in the novel is on Emma's self-realisation, there is a clear story of self-realisation in Mr Knightley's character as well, so the development is mutual:

. Emma and Knightley experience a liberating move towards wholeness. Blessed equally with energy and vitality, they have ignored, repressed or turned away from properties of their human nature which the society has stigmatised as 'feminine', especially the emotional properties associated with tenderness, giving and sacrifice. However, they finally overcome the psychological barrier of personality stereotypes and acknowledge the range of 'masculine' and 'feminine' impulses that each possesses. By uniting their formerly divided selves, they establish the basis for mutuality and reciprocity in their marriage relationship.

(Smith, *op. cit.*, p. 154)

So the analysis of *Emma* supports LeRoy Smith's initial thesis: that Jane Austen is a 'pre-feminist' writer who is an optimist. While being aware of and critical of the oppression of women in a patriarchal society, she insists on the possibility that women can break through the barriers to self-knowledge and self-development. She also believes that men do exist who are capable of reciprocal self-development, who can manage to recognise and liberate their own 'feminine' qualities, and to value a woman for herself, in an open and equal relationship.

LeRoy Smith uses a modern 'feminist' approach in an attempt to justify and give modern values to the marriage relationships which are the culmination of each of the novels. Jane Austen's understanding of the oppression of women, and her critical attitude towards male domination, in her society, are generally agreed among the critics; but many would not follow Smith to his conclusion that Austen was an optimist; or, if she was an optimist, join Smith in his further assertion that these marriages are open, free relationships, and not – at least partly – a defeat, and a compromise between the heroine and the oppressive power of her society.

\*   \*   \*

The final critic we look at in this chapter is Barbara Rasmussen.[8] Her essay explicitly takes another critic's work on Henry James as its starting-point, and is a conscious attempt to apply a specific theory of the act of reading, to the text of *Mansfield Park*. As such, her article is different from the criticism of Smith or Wright, which we have already met. Both of them suggest that we can make valid, reliable statements about the text which are true, and their task as critics is to pursue, define and explain as much of this ultimate 'truth' as they can. Rasmussen, on the other hand, writes in an experimental spirit: she consciously puts a theory together with a text, in order to see what she can find.

Rasmussen suggests that when we read, we are lured by the idea of meaning, because if we find meaning – in the sense of a definitive interpretation – this will satisfy our desire for mastery over the text. Shoshana Felman's work on Henry James[9] came to the conclusion that it is impossible to achieve final mastery in this way: there is no 'definitive' interpretation of a text, and the process by which our desire for mastery is frustrated, and reacts by distorting or forgetting elements in the text which contradict a desired interpretation, brings the reader's unconscious into active play.

There are two concepts of 'Freudian' literary criticism. First, a critic may be 'Freudian' when analysing what there is in the text (the meaning or content of the text); and this is what psychoanalytical criticism has traditionally done. Second, a reading may be 'Freudian' in the sense that it analyses how it reads, that is, the conscious and unconscious events that take place between the reader and the text:

> If the unconscious is a reader, undermining the authority of consciousness, then neither the literary critic nor the psycho-analyst can claim a position of mastery. Literature and psycho-analysis can learn from a 'dialogue' with each other.[10] Each may help the other to rethink the very question of reading, of what happens when we read fictional narratives like *Mansfield Park* – the question of the effects of narrative and how we become involved in narratives beyond the grasp of our conscious understanding.
>
> (Rasmussen, *op. cit.*, p. 126)

Rasmussen engages in, first, a summary of Felman's writing about Henry James's *Turn of the Screw*, then an explanation of linguistic theory and linguistic–psychoanalytical theory. The conclusion from this discussion is that, as we read, we consciously focus on the limited meaning of the words in the order in which they appear (this is called the 'syntagmatic' or horizontal axis of language) while we ignore or repress the other language – other words associated with the words we read, other words which are alternatives to the words we read, and so on (the 'paradigmatic' or vertical axis of language). There is a bar between conscious and unconscious reading, therefore, which is between the meaning of the words and the other meaning that is inevitably a part of language because 'when we read a book, the meaning of any word, sentence, episode will be dependent on what precedes and what follows it. Thus meaning shifts as we read on' (Rasmussen, *op. cit.*, p. 128).

Of course, the literal meaning of the words we read actually depends on the other meaning. We all know that a single word, out of context, either has a limited meaning unconnected with any story or experience (its dictionary definition), or has no separate meaning of its own. Meaning shifts and is created by language in action, not words in isolation. It is the gap between the single, literal meaning of the language, and the other meaning on which it depends, but which is not consciously read, which returns in the critics' arguments about interpretation. What this seems to mean in less accurate but simpler terms, is that there are elements in a text we read, which we take in unconsciously; and that these elements behave like the unconscious.

In our everyday lives, repressed elements from our unconscious affect our behaviour, decisions and so on, without us being aware of them. When they show themselves in our lives, they do so disguised (to take a very obvious example, our desire to purchase an object may be hidden within some trumped-up rationalisation which persuades us that the object is *useful* or *necessary*, thus making the guilty desire more acceptable to our conscious). Rasmussen's idea is that the same happens when we read a text. When we interpret the text, repressed elements from our unconscious reading affect our opinions, ideas, and so on, without us being aware of them. When these unconscious elements show themselves in our interpretation, they do so disguised.

One further point that arises in Rasmussen's theoretical discussion is significant: the psychoanalytical observation that people compulsively *repeat* and repeatedly *act out* their traumas, the unconscious frustrations and fantasies that have been repressed.

*Mansfield Park* has provoked a polarisation between critics, between those who 'see Fanny as a true heroine who, guided by Edmund, acquires a fine moral sense and the capacity to judge properly. For these critics Fanny stands for principle, duty, self-knowledge and self-restraint and gets her just reward in marriage to the man she loves. But critics on the opposing side see Fanny as a "prig-pharisee",[11] dull and self-righteous, and champion the Crawfords as lively, human and unjustly excluded from Mansfield' (Rasmussen, *op. cit.*, pp. 136–7). This debate is astonishingly similar to the debate that takes place throughout the novel. It is as if the debate between Fanny's and the Crawfords' values, which is in the novel, has simply displaced itself, and is being re-enacted or 'performed' between the critics. Rasmussen notices that key concepts from the novel, which are couched in particular terms, and which express the way one group of characters feels about the other group, are used by one group of critics to describe what is wrong with their opponents. Rasmussen quotes several critics as examples of this phenomenon, who abuse other critics in terms borrowed from either Fanny's or the Crawfords' side of the argument in the novel. She then adds:

> Moreover, it would seem that when critics outlaw as wrong a key positional term or interpretative stance in the novel, it

has an uncanny way of returning (like the repressed) in the very terms they adopt to *defeat* their opponents. Thus Reginald Farrer, who sides with Mary Crawford *against* Fanny – 'fiction holds no heroine more repulsive in her cast-iron self-righteousness' – nevertheless uses against Fanny and against Jane Austen and her critical supporters, the very argument employed against Mary Crawford in the novel. It is not Mary but Jane Austen who has been led astray by her associates. Edmund argues that Mary does not have 'a cruel nature', rather, in her response to Maria's elopement, she speaks simply 'as she had been used to hear others speak . . . Her's are faults of principle ... of ... a corrupted, vitiated mind' (*MP*, pp. 376–7). Contesting this interpretation of Mary, excluding it as a misreading, Farrer nevertheless uses precisely the argument of a good 'nature', 'vitiated' by bad associates to condemn Austen:

> *Mansfield Park* is *vitiated* throughout by a radical dishonesty, that was certainly not in its author's own nature. One can almost hear the clerical relations urging 'dear Jane' to devote her 'undoubted talent to the cause of righteousness'.
>
> (Farrer, *op. cit.*, emphasis added)

Rejected as a reading *of* Mary, the idea of a tragically 'vitiated' nature returns as a reading of her first readers (Edmund and Austen as his supporting narrator), and is used to reject *them*.
(Rasmussen, *op. cit.*, p. 138)

These critics, then, are not able to find a definitive interpretation of the novel. They are divided within themselves, and acting out the fantasies and desires for meaning which come from the unconscious, repressed element in their reading of *Mansfield Park*. This should be an encouraging insight, since it reveals to us 'the divided structure of meaning itself' (Rasmussen, *op. cit.*, p. 140), and because there is always far too much meaning in any speech or writing, for us to understand. Instead of pointlessly hoping to understand a single 'meaning' which cannot ultimately exist, we should try a 'new way of reading' and 'follow ... the endless 'flight' of meaning down the chain of signifiers [words] that constitutes *Mansfield Park*' (Rasmussen, *op. cit.*, p. 140). Rasmussen analyses the opening of the novel as an example of this 'new way of reading':

> About thirty years ago, Miss Maria Ward, of Huntingdon, with only seven thousand pounds, had the good luck to captivate Sir Thomas Bertram, of Mansfield Park... All Huntingdon exclaimed on the greatness of the match, and her uncle, the lawyer, himself, allowed her to be at least three thousand pounds short of any equitable claim to it.
>
> (*Mansfield Park*, p. 5)

'Good luck' and 'captivate' sound like repetitions from conversations among people who knew the Ward family in Huntingdonshire. The second sentence, beginning 'All Huntingdon exclaimed', which then leads to reporting the speech of Miss Ward's uncle, 'the lawyer', takes the process further. Jane Austen is, in fact, telling us the story she has heard other people tell, and the original 'signified' – the story itself, in this case Maria Ward's courtship and marriage – retreats from our attempt to reach it through the 'frame' of language which tells it.

We cannot know whether 'good luck' is to be taken literally or ironically. Was it really bad luck, or did Maria, in fact, deserve Sir Thomas? So Jane Austen is 'performing' an act of 'reading' a story others have 'performed', and this 'reproduces the split between performance and meaning' (Rasmussen, *op. cit.*, p. 142). The result is that, as we read, the language we might naturally expect to help us 'decode' the story, only serves further to 'encode' it. As we read, therefore, the experience of reading only generates more 'signs' and interpretations, in a futile attempt to 'catch up' and reach the ultimate, original fact of the story.

Mastery of meaning can never be achieved, then: it is illusory, or blind mastery – like that of Sir Thomas in the novel, whose power only exercises an absence of understanding or true authority. Yet the reader is seduced into believing in a promise of final meaning: the apparent authority of the narrative seduces us into transference. We transfer our desire for mastery of meaning, on to the text, and we read on and continue to struggle with interpretations, in the false, *transferred*, belief that the text itself will ultimately decode the meaning for us.

This insight leads Rasmussen into a discussion of transference in the story of *Mansfield Park*. She points out that Fanny Price undergoes a long series of transfers, each of which leaves part of her desires unsatisfied. So, she transfers her affections from the disappointing Mr Price, her father, to Sir Thomas; but his law-giving authority only defers satisfaction for her. Fanny herself is a sort of displaced substitute for her mother's desire – the mother who is excluded from the comforts of Mansfield and her own early life, and is not allowed to be reinstated herself. Soon after reaching Mansfield, Fanny learned 'to transfer in its favour much of her attachment to her former home' (*MP*, p. 18); and her pain at the separation from her beloved brother William is assuaged by transference of 'much' of this feeling on to Edmund. So, Fanny's love for Edmund is, unknown to her, merely a disguised form of, or a substitute for, an earlier, lost love.

Rasmussen discusses various aspects of *Mansfield Park* from the point of view of psychoanalytical perceptions about meaning and the desire for mastery, and further explores the insight that mastery of meaning is an illusion, so not only are we deceived by our desire to interpret the novel; the characters in the novel are equally deceived by their own attempts to define themselves and the 'story' they perform. Their words and their interpretations of their actions fail to decode any 'meaning' in their lives, and they act out unconscious desires, unaware, while excluding from their minds the parts of life, the 'other meanings' in the story, which they prefer to repress. One example of this has already been mentioned – that Fanny's love for Edmund is a substitute for her earlier, lost love for William. Another example occurs with Sir Thomas, at the end of the novel, when he substitutes Fanny for Maria. Fanny becomes 'the daughter that he wanted' (*MP*, p. 389), while Maria – his real daughter – is banished to 'another country – remote and private' (*MP*, p. 383). This alleviates Sir Thomas's bitter feelings about Maria, but his attempt to banish the results of his mercenary, materialist errors, and to value 'principle and good temper' instead, does not succeed. We can tell this from the commercial language of Sir Thomas's thoughts: '*prizing* more and more the *sterling* good of principle and temper, and chiefly anxious to bind by the strongest *securities* all that remained to him … [he] *realized* a great *acquisition* in the promise of Fanny for a daughter' (*MP*, p. 388). Finally, Rasmussen comments on the extraordinary way in which Fanny manages to exclude her past experiences of suffering, persecution, neglect, vice and tyranny, from her mind. We might say that suffering makes up the major part of Fanny's experiences, yet she divides herself from that 'other language' and reads her own story narrowly in the final line of the book, in which Mansfield is said to have 'long been … thoroughly perfect in her eyes' (*MP*, p. 390).

Rasmussen acknowledges that her approach is self-contradictory, since in using language to discuss the lack of final meaning in language, she can only further 'encode'. However, she concludes:

> In the dialogue between teacher and student, or between one critic and another, over a text such as *Mansfield Park*, a knowledge emerges … in language, which is never fully in possession of itself, which can never be consciously, *rationally*, mastered. It is not simply that *Mansfield Park* is constituted out of contesting discourses but that these discourses have effects, have a force as linguistic performances which will always elude our interpretative grasp.
>
> (Rasmussen, *op. cit.*, p. 153)

The different approaches these three critics take, and the different arguments they put forward and attitudes they express, need very little discussion: they stand on their own merits. Each of them provides us with some insight we might not have stumbled upon for ourselves, and each way of looking at the text itself highlights a different set of significant ideas, or qualities in the experience of reading, which may stimulate us to perceive further riches when we return to the novels.

If I were asked to select one response all three critics exhibit, one element their three arguments have in common, I would say that it is uncertainty, or ambivalence. The subject of Andrew H. Wright's argument is the 'ironic' world view which is ambivalent and can never be resolved, but creates a more profound human understanding that is intrinsically undefinable. Even the most confident of the three, LeRoy W. Smith, concedes that Jane Austen is a 'pre-feminist' writer, one in whom feminism is 'incipient'; and that her firm optimism about personal relationships between the sexes is something of a transitional, interim achievement – an optimistic harbinger of liberation in the future rather than the thing itself. Barbara Rasmussen, of course, examines the gap between language and meaning, and the futility of a quest for final meaning, as the very stuff of literature; and her comments about *Mansfield Park* introduce us to a level in reading the text that only further complicates our experience of Jane Austen's play with dualities.

---

[1] *Journal*, quoted in Andrew H. Wright, *Jane Austen's Novels: A Study in Structure*, London, 1953 (Penguin, 1962, p. 17).
[2] Quoted in Gilbert and Gubar, *The Madwoman in the Attic*. See note to Chapter 9.
[3] Quoted in Gilbert and Gubar, *op. cit.*
[4] Quoted in Wright, *op. cit.*, p. 19.
[5] Wright, *op. cit.*, p. 27.
[6] Smith, LeRoy W., *Jane Austen and the Drama of Woman*, London, 1983.
[7] De Beauvoir, Simone, *The Second Sex*, trans. and ed. H. M. Parshley, New York, 1970, p. 103.

[8] Rasmussen, Barbara, 'Discovering "A New Way of Reading": Shoshana Felman, Psychoanalysis and *Mansfield Park*', from *Mansfield Park*, ed. Nigel Wood, in the 'Theory in Practice' series, England, 1993.

[9] Felman, Shoshana, 'Turning the Screw of Interpretation', in *Literature and Psychoanalysis: the Question of Reading: Otherwise*, ed. Shoshana Felman, Yale French Studies.

[10] Felman, Shoshana, ed., *Literature and Psychoanalysis: the Question of Reading: Otherwise*, Yale French Studies.

[11] Farrer, Reginald, 'Jane Austen's *Gran Rifuto*', *Quarterly Review*, July 1917.

# Further Reading

Your first job is to study the text. There is no substitute for the work of detailed analysis: that is how you gain the close familiarity with the text, and the fully developed understanding of its content, which make the essays you write both personal and convincing. For this reason I recommend that you take it as a rule not to read any other books around or about the text you are studying, until you have finished studying it for yourself.

Once you are familiar with the text, you may wish to read around and about it. This brief chapter is only intended to set you off: there are hundreds of relevant books and we can only mention a few. However, most good editions, and critical works, have suggestions for further reading, or a bibliography of their own. Once you have begun to read beyond your text, you can use these and a good library to follow up your particular interests. This chapter is divided into Reading around the text, which lists Jane Austen's other works, and some by other contemporary writers; Biography; and Criticism, which will introduce you to the varieties of opinion among professional critics.

## Reading around the text

Jane Austen published six novels: *Pride and Prejudice*, *Mansfield Park*, *Emma* and *Persuasion* are the four we have focused on in this volume. The other two are both early works, although *Northanger Abbey* was published posthumously in 1818; while *Sense and Sensibility* (1811) was her first published work. These novels are all available in Penguin Classics. Three of Jane Austen's shorter works, *Lady Susan/The Watsons/Sanditon* are also available in Penguin Classics in a single volume together.

Among Austen's contemporaries, it is worth reading some of the novels of her time for the purposes of comparison. Jane Austen frequently satirises or refers to the more lurid settings and far-fetched plots found in novels of the 'Gothic' type. *The Mysteries of Udolpho* (1794), by Mrs Ann Radcliffe, is a good example of the genre, and is the particular novel Catherine Morland, the heroine of *Northanger Abbey,* has been reading. However, I would suggest that *The Monk* (1796) by Matthew Lewis, is one of the most gripping and powerful productions of the 'Gothic' writers; while Mary Shelley's *Frankenstein, or the Modern Prometheus* (1818), although published after Austen's death, is a classic tale worth reading for its own sake.

Jane Austen was certainly a reader of Fanny Burney's novels, which were all published during her life. These all focus on young women at the point where they enter society. You may try *Evelina* (1778), *Cecilia* (1782), *Camilla* (1796) or *The Wanderer* (1814). Sir Walter Scott was an influential literary figure of the time, and his *Waverley* and *Guy Mannering* came out in 1814 and 1815 respectively. Jane Austen admired William Cowper's poetry.

If you are particularly interested in expanding your knowledge of the period during which Jane Austen lived, a number of books are available which consider her in her historical and social context. Two examples from among these are *Jane Austen and the French Revolution*, by Warren Roberts (London, Macmillan, 1979), and *Jane Austen and Representations of Regency England* by Roger Sales (London and New York, 1994).

## Biography

When biographers research Austen's life, the main sources of information they turn to are *Jane Austen's Letters* (collected and edited by R.W. Chapman, 2nd edn, Oxford University Press, London, 1952), the vast majority of which were written to her sister Cassandra Austen and censored by her after the author's death; the *Memoir* of his aunt, by James Edward Austen-Leigh, which was published in 1870 and in an expanded second edition in 1871; and some other memoirs, not published, written by her nieces Anna Lefroy and Caroline Austen. In a major library there may be the authoritative *Jane Austen's Life and Letters*, by W. and R. A. Austen-Leigh (1913). Several biographies are available, including Jane Aiken Hodge's *The Double Life of Jane Austen* (London, 1972), Park Honan's *Jane Austen: Her Life* (London, 1987), and *Jane Austen: A Literary Life* by Jan Fergus (London, 1991).

## Criticism

The critical works sampled in Chapter 10 are: Andrew H. Wright, *Jane Austen's Novels: A Study in Structure*, London, 1953 (Penguin, 1962); LeRoy W. Smith, *Jane Austen and the Drama of Woman*, London, 1983; and Barbara Rasmussen, 'Discovering "A New Way of Reading": Shoshana Felman, Psychoanalysis and *Mansfield Park*', from *Mansfield Park*, ed. Nigel Wood, in the 'Theory in Practice' series, Open University Press, 1993.

Anthologies of critical essays and articles are a good way to sample the critics. You can then go on to read the full-length books written by those critics whose articles you have found stimulating. For the volume in which Barbara Rasmussen's article appears, *Mansfield Park* (see above), the editor Nigel Wood provides an Introduction, and other discussions of the critical approaches the contributors adopt, which are very helpful if you are entering the world of contemporary literary criticism, with its hotly debated competing theories. The New Casebooks series (general editors John Peck and Martin Coyle) published by Macmillan, collects a variety of critical articles together, and provides an introduction which discusses the critical history of the text. There are volumes on *Pride and Prejudice* and *Sense and Sensibility*, *Emma*, and *Mansfield Park* and *Persuasion*. Each of these volumes also gives usefully selected suggestions for further reading. Finally, *Jane Austen* in the Modern Critical Views series (ed. Harold Bloom, New York, 1986) contains several stimulating contributions.

The following full-length critical works may also be of interest and should be stimulating whether you agree or disagree with the writer's analysis. Barbara Hardy's *A Reading of Jane Austen* (The Athlone Press, London, 1979) is a full study of Jane Austen as a literary artist; Margaret Kirkham's *Jane Austen: Feminism and Fiction* (Harvester, Brighton, 1984) is one of the most respected studies of Austen from a feminist point of view. Susan Morgan's *In the Meantime: Character and Perception in Jane Austen's Fiction* (Chicago and London, 1980) and Tony Tanner's *Jane Austen* (London, 1986) are further suggestions.

When you are in a library, use the catalogue system resourcefully to locate further interesting critical work on Jane Austen. There are numerous books which appear to be on different subjects – the history of the novel, women writers, and so on. A large number of these contain chapters or essays about Jane Austen which may bring an illuminating angle to bear upon her writing.

# Index